Epidemic

The Elifer Chronicles Book One

Julie Boglisch

Published by Rogue Phoenix Press

ISBN: 978-1-62420-514-9

Editor: Sherry Derr-Wille

Published in The Untied States

Dedication

To my parents, who were with me every step of the way while on this incredible journey. Thank you, Mom and Dad, you both are awesome. In my eyes, you two are the best people in the world.

Chapter One

The soft chime of a clock resonated through the two-story house at a steady rhythm. A moment of silence ensued, only to be broken by the sharp clack of running footsteps as they pounded down the stairwell. Veronica Elifer tilted her head up just in time to see her son dart past the kitchen doorway. Her eyes caught brunet hair and a lithe frame as he moved toward the front door.

"Maxwell," she called after her son.

"Sorry, Ma, but I'm going to be late!" her son replied as he threw on a pair of sneakers without even untying the laces.

Veronica crossed her hands over her chest. "Be home by dinner, all right?" she demanded which got a sharp nod from her son, along with a cheeky grin. She rolled her eyes at her son's antics.

"Of course," he replied before he darted out the door.

The door swung shut.

"That boy."

She glanced at a single picture set near the sink. The glass frame glistened as she picked it up. She gripped the picture tightly.

"Felix," she whispered.

The picture showed two people who stood side by side in obvious joy. A tall man with sea-green eyes and a small goatee stood with one arm around a young woman. The woman held one hand to her bulging stomach as she leaned against the man. Both smiled broadly toward the camera.

"You know…he's growing up to be just like you," she said, as she gazed solemnly at the picture. "I can't believe they're already fourteen, almost fifteen. Time does fly, doesn't it?" She paused before she continued, a little softer.

"Has it really been four years since then? Since that incident? You saved them then, but..." She tried to rid herself of unwanted thoughts before she looked out the kitchen window. "I just hope neither of them has to go through the same things you did."

She stopped before she gazed up toward the crystal-clear sky. She felt her expression shift to one of determination and fierce defiance as she stared up, as if in a prayer to the heavens. "I can't let it happen again."

Never again.

She heard a soft knock and jerked up. She turned warily toward the doorway, gently placing the photo down. She walked over and slowly opened the door.

There was no one there. She looked around then peered toward the ground. A white letter lay on the pavement. She squatted down and picked it up. She flipped over the paper and froze as her free hand moved up to her mouth. Her eyes widened as her fingers trembled.

"Felix!"

~ * ~

Maxwell gritted his teeth in annoyance as he ran down the street. He couldn't believe he was actually going to be late for school. He was usually never late! He frowned as he berated himself for his screw-up. Oh, his twin was going to have such a riot when she saw this. He skimmed over cracked pavement and brown sidewalks. He could see pristine hedges on either side of the long street, hiding brilliant white but squat houses. Windows were flung open to the fresh autumn morning air as people milled about, watering plants, lounging outside on plastic chairs or lying on the bright and fluffy green grass. Flowers swayed in the early morning breeze.

Maxwell took in the quaint village landscape. *It's such a beautiful day out,* he thought.

Long bangs draped into his eyes on either side of his face. In slight annoyance, he brushed them behind his ear as he moved his pace to a walk. He got his breath back as he looked at the clothes he had hastily thrown on in his panic, a gray sweatshirt with blue jeans. He had a black bag draped over his shoulder which he knew from memory had his name sewn into the smallest flap.

"Maxwell."

He peered up at the sudden shout. To his right, heading toward him, was a middle-aged woman. She wore a summer dress and had a bright smile on her face.

"Hello, Maxwell, running late to school? I saw your sister a while ago. I was surprised to see you weren't with her."

"Yeah, guess she didn't want to wake me. So, what's going on?" he asked as he finally took notice of a line of people behind her.

The woman glanced back and chuckled, a sheepish expression on her face. "I'm taking a quick break. I need it, considering how busy it's been, what with winter coming in a few months and the harvest festival a little before that, everyone's doing last minute preparations, just the usual."

"Ah, I see…must be pretty hard," he replied.

"You're right, it is a real strain sometimes, but at the same time, it's quite nice. That reminds me, are you available this week? I need some help with the store and it seems like everyone else just wants to enjoy the last bits of summer," she stated with a frown.

Maxwell, hesitating for only the briefest of moments, nodded.

She beamed. "Great. I know with school having only started a few weeks ago you're still getting in the swing of things, but I'm glad you're willing to help." She glanced at the watch on her wrist. "Oh boy, I have to get back, my break is almost over. Actually, shouldn't you already be…"

Maxwell blinked in confusion before he squinted at the watch the woman held out to him. He stared uncomprehendingly, before he yelped. *Crap!* he thought as he felt his eyes widen. "I'm sorry! Thank you for reminding me. I'll see you later. I'm going to be late," he exclaimed and with a quick wave, dashed down the road.

He noticed the woman return to her post outside her home to take care of the crowd gathered there.

The town had a population of around three thousand people and most residents had their own shop right outside their home, just like that woman. Each specialized in specific things, such as carpentry, clothing or food.

It isn't really odd though, Maxwell thought, as he ran down another street. He skimmed around a corner, just in time to avoid an elderly woman heading rather briskly in the other direction.

"Sorry," he shouted toward the woman, who only held a look of bemusement.

He let his thoughts continue where they left off. Considering the town was completely surrounded by trees, trees and more trees, each tree, according to scientific calculation, was easily over ninety feet tall. They cast long shadows over the houses and roads, even in the morning sun. Many people thought it was peaceful and quaint.

Of course, there were always exceptions.

He thought of his sister right off the bat.

Maxwell passed more houses and heard people call out enthusiastically from stands and windows alike. He waved before he continued on. His breath came in shorter and shorter gasps. Unfortunately, he couldn't take another break, considering how late it was getting. He gripped his backpack tightly so it wouldn't fall off, annoyed that his home was so far away from where he needed to go.

It was only a few minutes later that he reached the heart of town. A cobblestone plaza lay in the middle, surrounded by pavement. Right in the center of the plaza was a fountain with an eagle spreading its wings wide. Water spouted out of its beak, which was pointed upward toward the sky. On one side of the plaza was a church. Its steeple soared over the plaza. Granite steps led up to double doors made of oak.

The bell rang. It chimed over the town in a sweet melody. He peered at the steeple as he waited for the final chime. The final note rang out beautifully for a moment, before silence took over. Maxwell stared solemnly toward the bell tower before he let out a resigned groan. He turned to examine the rest of the plaza. On the other side, parallel with the church, was a school. It was a small one-story-tall building that filled up half the square by itself. He could just barely see people dart in the doors. Next to it was the convenience store. It was the go-to for anything that couldn't be made by hand.

Maxwell took in the crowded streets before he spotted a familiar figure. He hurried over to the figure.

Standing by the school was a girl about the same height as Maxwell. She leaned her back against the brick wall of the school in a nonchalant, and slightly annoyed posture. Her raven-black hair curved around her face, and fell just a little past her chin on either side. The rest of her hair was pulled back sharply and tied up in a high ponytail.

She wore a blue halter top with short tan shorts. Her arms and fingers were clad in black fingerless gloves that reached comfortably to her elbows. Worn but well-used hiking boots covered her feet. Long black socks surged up to just below her knees, finishing the ensemble. She also had a backpack draped off one shoulder.

Her face expressed boredom as Maxwell stepped in front of her. His sister seemed to sense his presence. Sky blue eyes opened to acknowledge him as he leaned against the wall beside her to catch his breath.

"Took you long enough," she stated.

He felt her gaze on him before a grin crossed her face.

"I was starting to wonder whether you were going to skip. Of course, personally, I would be happy to do that."

Maxwell huffed in annoyance before he pushed off the wall. "You could have at least woken me up, Karina," he stated with a shake of his head. "School only just started and we're going to be late for the second time."

Karina raised her eyebrow.

"Don't say the first time wasn't your fault. You thought it would be funny to steal my alarm clock and replace it with a freaking spider! Who does that?"

Karina pushed off the wall. "It was only plastic."

Maxwell's shoulders drooped. "Anyway, let's get inside."

"Yeah, because you are oh so excited for math, right?"

Maxwell groaned. He never was going to live that one down, was he? "Oh, shut up," he muttered as they walked quickly down the wooden hallway to reach the first door on the right.

Of course, he didn't have to worry too much. Math, thankfully, wasn't till the end of the day, but still. They knocked and stepped in, just as Karina's name was called.

Karina waved. "Here," she shouted as she took her seat.

Maxwell groaned audibly at his sister's antics.

The room was a normal classroom with blackboards and rows of desks set up neatly in aisles. The teacher, a balding man in his thirties, glanced up with an unsurprised look. "Maxwell Elifer? Can you try to make sure you and your sister actually get here on time?"

Maxwell took his seat, but didn't comment. *I'm just lucky that we both even get to class,* he thought in annoyance as the teacher finished his roll call. *If it wasn't for the stupid alarm clock, I would have gotten here on time, along with Kari...* He mentally sighed once more and slumped in his seat.

Only to perk up as the teacher said, "Okay, class, pop quiz time."

Maxwell glanced around as a groan vibrated around the room, filled with about twenty students around his age. He dug into his bag and pulled out a pencil. He tapped it onto the desk as he waited. He could see Karina. Her eyes were closed and she was leaned back against the chair. An unenthused look sat on her face.

"Kari," Maxwell hissed under his breath, soft enough for only her to hear.

Why couldn't his sister at least try to look like she was paying attention?

Karina opened her eyes before she sent him a glare and let the chair fall back into place.

It was then that he received his quiz.

He quickly wrote down the answers and passed it forward. After another five to ten minutes, the teacher collected all the quizzes.

"All right, let's see how you did. Question one, what was the second name of The Great War and what followed?"

A kid near Karina raised his hand and spoke. "After the conclusion of the Great War, they renamed it World War I and shortly after came World War II, promptly followed by the Eternal War Era."

"Good. Now, question two, what caused the name changes to

occur?"

This time, another kid spoke up. "The name of the Great War was originally changed because it was easier to distinguish, after the second 'great war' started, which was which. The name of the time following World War II was changed because they noticed a connection between each successive war after the fact regarding certain superpowers, including the United States."

"That's correct, because of U.S. involvement in most wars post World War II, they deemed to call the entire period between that war and the Vietnam War the Eternal War Era, in order to more easily group them together. Now, final question, what was the consequence of that time?"

Maxwell raised his hand. "There was a depletion of goods, and as a result, they wanted to find more efficient ways to preserve society. As such, they created this place, so that people could learn about nature and grow in it. After the movement, the U.S. closed all borders officially and turned in on itself. It focused on recovering its own problems and, as a result, ended up booming in private businesses…" he trailed off as the teacher gestured to him proudly.

"That is correct. As a result, they didn't need this town, so now we just learn and live in peace."

Karina tched. Maxwell smirked toward his sister who had her arms crossed over her chest. He could see one leg jitter against the table.

"I hope everyone did well. Now, turn to page two hundred and fifty-four of our textbook and we'll get started on the Industrial Revolution…"

~ * ~

Maxwell sighed as he stepped out the door of the school. He saw Karina beam with joy as she ran down the steps in the direction of the forest right past the convenience store. "Come on, Max, I want to show you something. We can go home after, 'kay?"

Maxwell's eyes narrowed as he walked down the steps as well. The afternoon sun shone down over them as the school doors opened to the rush of students leaving classes. "Kari, I'm tired. Why don't we just go home and you can show me this weekend?"

"Max, come on, it won't take that long." She frowned as she faced Maxwell with sharp blue eyes, as if to dare him to argue.

His sister could be…interesting at times, but she did mean well. "Fine, what is it?" he asked as he hefted his backpack more comfortably on his shoulder.

"You'll see," she said, sounding relieved, as she went to walk away.

"Kari…it better not be something stupid, like trying to find wild animals, or racing through the trees again…didn't you almost break your ankle last time you decided to try to swing between the trees?"

Karina shrugged. A nervous grin sat on her face, which betrayed her nonchalant posture.

"Come on, Maxwell, it won't be THAT bad…please?" she begged.

Maxwell had to mentally reiterate to himself that his sister did mean well, even if she was a bit on the hyperactive side.

Karina started to usher Maxwell forward.

Great. I don't even know HOW she finds half the things she does. I always end up caught up in them…and usually not for the best. He let his thoughts trail off with a shiver. He remembered one too many times running for dear life while his sister would grin widely, even as she muttered apologies.

He could see Karina smirk and stick her tongue out playfully before she spun away. She seemed to pause before reaching an arm backward. She grabbed Maxwell's wrist and darted toward the surrounding forest. Maxwell yelped as he followed after the energetic girl. Karina was fast, much to Maxwell's consternation, as she ran down the road without a care, plunging right into the tree line. Maxwell stumbled behind her and yelped in frustration as he tripped over another root.

"Hey!" he shouted as his backpack slammed into his back.

Karina ignored him as they darted into the trees.

"Kari. Will you slow down?" Maxwell gasped out between wheezes, as he struggled to keep up with Karina's harsh pace. *Where the heck does she get all this energy?* he thought in exasperation.

"Heck no, come on, little brother, you should be able to do this much," she called back as she swerved around another tree. Maxwell barely managed to avoid it as he let a curse slip through his lips and under his breath the whole time.

"Karina, this is ridiculous! You're running way too fast. How do you have so much energy after a full day of school?" He yelped as he managed to scramble over a fallen tree limb that his sister practically jumped over. It didn't help that she gave him no warning she was jumping anyway which made him stumble over it.

He saw Karina frown as she tilted her head to look back at him. He felt her glare even as she faced toward the deep woods. "Stupid little brothers," she muttered under her breath as she leaped over another small fallen sapling.

"You're only about two minutes older than me," Maxwell replied curtly as he followed up her leap. This one he could actually make, even as his breath caught in his throat.

The two ran through the forest with rapid speed. Occasionally, they slowed to give Maxwell a break before Karina dragged him off again. The afternoon sun shone down brilliantly, as branches shifted in a light breeze. Fallen leaves coated the ground and crunched under their feet. Maxwell followed, somewhat unwillingly.

Finally, Karina slowed her pace down to a walk. Maxwell felt his lungs gasp for air as he forced himself not to lean forward and rest his hands on his knees like he wanted to. Why did his sister have to be so athletic compared to himself?

He heard wind whisper through the trees as he felt his sister's gaze on him. He tilted his head up enough from its drooped state to see her sheepish expression.

Sorry, she mouthed as he glared at her. Really? His sister was too hyperactive for her own good.

"So…um…how was your day?" she asked tentatively after he caught his breath and they moved on, thankfully much more slowly.

Maxwell put a hand to his face before he dropped it and spoke. "Just…great…I really just need a break," he muttered as his sister dropped her pace enough to walk beside him instead of in front of him. Her gaze was even, if a little confused.

"Break? From school? From the run?" she asked.

"Well, yes, that too…" he trailed off as he suddenly remembered why he woke up so late. To be more precise, why he hadn't gotten enough sleep to actually hear his alarm properly.

He noticed Karina's eyes on him and once more looked toward his sister. It only took a moment for understanding to flit across her face. "Dad…"

"It was four years ago today after all," Maxwell responded vaguely.

He felt Karina bump into his shoulder. "Come on. If we go at this pace, it'll take all day," she said, as she gently grabbed his hand once more. Maxwell nodded, grateful for the distraction as he followed after her at a faster pace that was still much slower than before.

It was only a couple minutes later, however, when he once more thought of it.

Maxwell's lips tightened into a thin line before he forced himself to relax. He looked to see his sister and cringed. The smile on her face was weak. He instantly recognized it as a fake, one only used when she didn't want to worry others.

Sorry, Kari, he thought as he noticed the grip on his wrist tighten. *You're still trying to forget as well.*

A long low sigh slipped through his lips before he found himself jerked to a halt.

He peered up to see a rocky cliff edge surrounded by trees. the rock wall seemed a lot more intimidating up close. Maxwell saw it from a distance through the trees for a while, but since his mind was preoccupied, he hadn't really thought about it. Not until it was in his face. He tilted his head up to take in the fact that a tree lay against the rock face precariously, looking ready to fall to the ground at any moment.

He saw his sister's smile widen as she let go of his wrist. He rubbed his wrist gingerly. "So, was there a reason why you dragged me out here? This is a nice rock wall and all, but that's about it."

"Geez. THIS isn't the spot. It's just on the way. Now come on. I can't wait to show Mom as well, if I can ever convince her to come with us."

Maxwell noticed his sister's eyes glimmer as she stared up at the rock face, her expression shining with the prospect. He peered down at the ground and felt his bangs fall into his face once more. He brushed his bangs back, looked up and said, "You do realize she wouldn't have the time, right? She's the only doctor and scientist in town. This morning was one of the few times she actually had off."

He saw his sister's expression falter for a moment before she seemed to steady herself. A glimmer like determination flashed through her eyes as she looked at Maxwell.

"It's worth a shot. She's been working hard ever since…" She paused before she sighed and continued, "I think it would be a good chance for her to take a break so that we can be like a family again. As you said, she rarely has time lately, so it would be nice."

Maxwell eyed his sister. He breathed in and slowly exhaled before he looked up at the rock face with a glare. He really wasn't looking forward to this. "I hope you don't expect me to climb that, because, you know, there's no way I'm going up that thing," he said.

He saw Karina shake her head as he continued to stare at the rock face. A cloud slid over the sky to dapple it in steely grey. "One day you'll be glad to have a chance. Anyway…" He finally pulled his eyes away from the treacherous, in his opinion, rock face to look at her. He noticed her eyes gleaming with an unidentifiable emotion. She flung her hands out to either side as she exclaimed toward Maxwell enthusiastically. "Don't you want to see what's beyond these trees? Beyond this place? In the past fourteen years, we have never been away from home, ever. Mom has, and so did Dad, when he was around. Don't you want to go into that world outside and see what else is out there?"

"No," Maxwell replied with a deadpan look. "I'm quite content with staying home. This town has everything we need. I don't see the point. Plus, what about Ma? We can't just leave her."

Karina closed her eyes and seemed to debate with herself for a moment before she opened them, and said, "We'll all just go together, I think that would be more fun anyway."

Maxwell stayed silent as Karina turned to face the rock face. She reached both arms forward to give them a good stretch. “We get to the top of our rock and you won’t even have to worry about it anymore. Come on, it’s easy.”

Maxwell gave her a deadpan look as he felt his eye twitch. Karina noticed his expression and huffed. “Fine, I’ll show you,” she stated.

Maxwell scrutinized her. He tilted his head up as he noticed that everything seemed a shade darker. What was once a beautifully clear late-afternoon sky was now gradually being filled with dark, foreboding clouds. He frowned as an uneasy feeling settled in his gut. His sister seemed to sense it as well. Karina looked around once before she shook her head, as if to rid it of thoughts, and stepped toward the rock face. She pushed herself up with quick and efficient movements as her hands flew up the rocks with ease.

She reached the top and dangled her legs over it to look down. “You coming?”

“No way,” he called as he tried desperately to hide the nervousness that seemed to want to slip into his voice. Heights…why heights? He blinked and glanced up once more as a low rumble sounded in the distance. “Um…how about we go back home? Ma is probably waiting for us.” Maxwell said.

Karina tilted her head up to the sky. He heard a small, noncommittal noise from her before she frowned. “It does look like it’s going to rain, doesn’t it?”

Maxwell nodded. Karina slid over the edge and began to climb down. She took slow steps even as Maxwell felt something fall onto his cheek. He jumped as a yelp came from the rock face. He turned just in time to see Karina skid down the side. His eyes widened as he stumbled forward. Karina stopped only a foot or two below where she lost her footing.

His sister leaned against the rock face, still having a way to go. Her expression was a mix between stunned and slightly scared. Her clothes were ruffled. Her knees, elbows and hands were scratched up from trying to stay close to the rock face. A light stream of blood slipped from her fingers as a tremble racked up her spine. His sister let out a shaky breath as she took stock of any injuries. Both teens stayed in silence before Maxwell cautiously called up to her.

"You okay?"

"What do you think," Karina snapped back, her voice harsh.

Maxwell cringed as Karina stared at the wall face. Was she nervous?

Maxwell saw her grip the stone more tightly before she finished her descent, jumped to the ground and brushed herself off.

Maxwell muttered a quiet, "Show off," even as he let himself smile, relieved.

She gave him an annoyed look before she coldly walked past him. "Hurry up, slowpoke. We're going to be late."

Maxwell raised an eyebrow as he followed after her. *Wasn't that my line?* he thought in bemusement.

Karina ignored him as she walked determinedly onward.

Maxwell pursed his lips. Shadows fell over the tree canopies, as the sun's rays struggled to shine through the now completely darkened sky. "It looks like a big storm," he muttered as he eyed the horizon, feeling the apprehension well up more as he watched the fast-moving clouds.

The two continued back in an awkward silence. They kept their slow pace through the trees even as Maxwell tried to bring up a conversation. Sometimes, he made comments on the impending storm silently urging her to go a little faster, other times, he talked about how lazy the math teacher was, which was making learning the subject even harder, since it was also the last class of the day. Yet other times, he would bring up their mom.

He could see his sister glance at him, conflicted between her want to stay moody, and her wish to chat with her brother.

Moodiness won out even as a low rumble sounded once more in the distance.

"Well, this is more peaceful than I thought," Maxwell said as they slipped around another tree. *The times I don't want to talk, she annoys me to no end, the times I want to talk, she's as silent as the freaking trees...* He put a hand to his face as he quietly chuckled.

He never could understand the way his sister acted most of the time, even though they were practically inseparable since birth.

The clouds steadily grew darker as they walked. In the distance, they could hear the chime of the church bell, which signaled that it was around six, even though the dark clouds made it look like it was closer to midnight.

"Well… It looks like we're going to be late again," Maxwell muttered under his breath as he glanced at his sister's back. Karina gazed ahead steadily as she kept up with a firm pace.

They made it into the village center about five minutes later. Maxwell's legs shook from exhaustion as he stumbled tiredly after Karina. His stomach growled and his throat felt dry.

He noted how dark everything was. He could see windows that were previously wide open to the sun, shut tight, only a hint of light seeping through the panes. Plastic coverings sat over some of the plants and most of the stands, prepared for the storm. The streets were empty, to the point of it being almost eerie for both teens.

With each step, they picked up their pace as they passed house after house with barely any light peeking through. Occasionally they caught a flicker, the flutter of a curtain or the gleam of a back-porch light. Shadows weaved through the dwindling sunlight and cast tables, sheds and buildings in ominous textures. Trees and branches began to sway back and forth in the wind that started to pick up around the town. A low whistle could be heard as it swept through the houses, trees and vegetation. A groaning rumble sounded a distance away. With each moment and sound, the twins' steps grew faster until they ran, full speed, down the street. There was another low rumble in the distance that grew longer and louder. Street lamps flickered disconcertingly on either side of the road.

Soft pants could be heard over the incoming storm. An uneasy pressure filled the air as the smell of salt and water wafted toward their noses. A low rumbling boom sounded once more, suddenly a lot closer, which startled them.

Karina's eyes were narrowed in concentration as they sped around the final corner. Their house stood ahead, three down on the left.

Its windows were opened with not a single light seen.

"Something's not right," Karina said as she slowed down to a cautious walk.

"You don't say," Maxwell replied, as he slowed himself down, his own thoughts in turmoil as he scrutinized the empty streets.

The storm's pressure seemed to grow, as if it begged to be let loose and break over their heads as another, longer, rumbling sound vibrated around the town. Wind blew stronger. It pulled at their hair and clothes. Maxwell breathed out. He hadn't even realized he held his breath to begin with.

Karina ignored him. She put a finger to her lips as she walked up the front steps. Her eyes seemed to zero in on the front door as she moved.

Maxwell eyed her in a mixture of annoyance and confusion as Karina purposefully held up a hand toward him before she stepped to the doorway alone. She hesitated before she thrust the door out of the way with a jarring bang.

Chapter Two

The storm broke. Bluish-white lightning streaked across the sky in jagged strokes as thunder crashed violently like a gong.

Maxwell moved past Karina and cautiously flipped the light on in the entryway. He froze, staring in shock.

Cupboards sat at an angle against the floor as the doorways hung limply. A rug was arranged haphazardly on the ground, pulled up at uneven intervals. A chair rested on its side as if it toppled over in a skirmish.

Rain began to fall in sheets, each drop visible as it plummeted toward the earth. It tumbled down diagonally as the wind howled. A mist clouded over the roofs that surrounded them and the ground. Within seconds, everything that the rain could reach was soaked, as if a demon cast a flood over the lands. The inside wasn't much better as wind and water crashed unceasingly through open windows.

The duo hurriedly ran inside, glancing around in confusion, worry and shock. Lightning flashed once more as if to emphasize the disorganization and mayhem of the room as shadows danced and coiled over the walls and ceiling.

"Who could…?"

"Have done this?" the two murmured as they walked shakily through the front room. Smudges splattered the floor and spread outward in reddish brown streaks. A sofa was toppled over and the rug was practically pulled out of its place.

The two looked at each other for a moment before they moved simultaneously.

Almost in unison the two yelled, their voices conjoining yet clear.

"Ma," Maxwell called as Karina cried, "Mom!"

No sound returned to them except for the escalating storm outside. Karina ran into the living room as Maxwell moved to the kitchen. He looked back and forth over shattered glass and toppled plates. *What happened?* he thought nervously as he regarded the chaos.

Brownish red streaks of blood were splattered over the table top. The red stain seemed to congeal onto the granite counter before it slid down the normally pristine metal sink into the basin.

Maxwell felt his face scrunch up in panic as footsteps sounded across the ceramic floor behind him. He jumped and turned to see Karina. Her face shone with worry and suppressed fear.

"Max, did you find anything?" she asked hopefully.

Maxwell glanced over his shoulder to the stained sink before he looked back at Karina. "I wish…" he responded as he tried to calm his racing heart.

He saw Karina's lips twitch down into an anxious frown. She gazed around once before she hurried out of the room.

"Let's check upstairs," she called.

Maxwell followed after her. Unease twisted in his gut as he took the steps two at a time. When he got to the top, he noticed Karina was already heading toward the right into the main bedroom. Maxwell took in the upstairs, surprised to find that it hardly looked touched.

What the…that's weird, was it a burglar? A kidnapping? What could have happened to leave the upstairs untouched? He hurried to the left toward his and Karina's rooms. In his room, an old desktop computer still sat where Max left it, its screen black from being powered down the night before. "Ma, where are you?" he whispered under his breath as his eyes roamed around the room.

Another stroke of lightning crashed outside and illuminated the space. White caught his eye as the light vanished.

He paused before he moved closer to the source of the white flash. He felt around in the dark, only able to see vague shadow. He reached forward, only to hiss as the thin edge of a piece of paper slid painfully past his finger. He pulled back his hand sharply and stared blankly. *I don't remember leaving something there this morning, maybe I was just in too much of a rush*, he thought as he used his non-throbbing hand to pick up the paper. The paper seemed to have been thrown next to an old picture.

He held his injured hand close to nurse his wounded finger. He stuck the finger in his mouth to stop the blood as he flipped the paper over. Lightning lanced through the sky once more. Familiar black handwriting was scribbled hurriedly over the simple sheet of white in broad, shaky strokes.

Flipping on the desk lamp, he read over the note before he looked toward the doorway, paper cut forgotten. *Did I really read what I thought I read?* He gripped the paper tightly, which crinkled it up in the process. "Karina," he shouted.

Within moments, she appeared in his room, her expression flustered. "Did you find Mom?" she asked as the door slammed into the wall in her rush, hope flashed across her face.

He shook his head as he held out the paper in response. He felt confused and disheartened. Was this all that his mother left? It didn't even make sense… He noticed Karina's worry but he wasn't quite sure how he wanted to respond.

He felt Karina practically rip it from his fingers before she read it out loud. "Don't look for me. Just run. Don't trus…" She slowed down as she read. She came to a halt as she stared at the paper in a mix of what looked like disbelief and outrage. Maxwell couldn't really blame her.

Her hands shook and her posture slumped. Maxwell's thoughts spiraled in confusion even as he tried to keep his face neutral. The letter was so short. What could it possibly mean?

He looked up in time to see Karina stare out the rain-splattered window. Hopeless despair crossed her face for a split second before she loosened her fist around the note. It looked like she read it once more. "Kari?"

Karina seemed to be pained. Her face conflicted, much like he remembered from a long time ago.

It's just like four years ago, Maxwell thought with an internal shiver. He squashed down the memories that threatened to come forth.

He was jerked out of his thoughts as Karina spoke. He looked up to see Karina's gaze on him. Her blue eyes shone with determination as she said, "We have to go." He noticed her fist tighten around the note as she continued, "Mom's not here, and I doubt she's anywhere in town."

Maxwell opened his mouth before he shut it and looked away. "Fine, but then…what do you suggest? We leave town completely?" Maxwell felt dismayed at the prospect. He lived here his entire life. He had no idea what it would be like to just up and leave.

He heard Karina sigh. "Pack what you need, we'll head out once you're done," she stated as she walked out the door.

Maxwell gazed after her before he groaned quietly. "I was afraid of that."

He walked over to the closet as he slid the backpack off his shoulder. Much to his chagrin, he quickly realized it was the only bag he had that he could travel with. He dumped out the books and papers, deciding that he didn't have to worry about homework any time soon.

He grabbed some clothes and stuffed them into the bottom. Rain hammered against the roof louder than before.

Maxwell shifted his eyes toward the desk. "I guess I could bring it," he said thoughtfully as he picked up a picture frame. The same frame the letter was next to. It showed a family of four. His ma smiled broadly as his dad stood next to her and wrapped a sweater-clad arm around her thin waist. His father's signature hat sat over his raven hair. In front of them was Karina and himself, aged ten. Both grinned widely as they held each other's hands, Karina putting out her hand with her fingers up in a V for victory.

Maxwell stared at the happy picture before he slipped it in between his clothes already stuffed in the bag, in hopes to keep it safe. Next to his computer was a cellphone he forgot about earlier on his mad dash out of the house. He noticed the cord of the charger curled near it and, after a moment of indecision, he grabbed the phone as well as the charger and stuffed them in his bag as deep as they could go so that they wouldn't get wet. Once he was sure he had everything, he pulled the backpack over his shoulder and headed out the door.

~ * ~

Karina went through her own room as her conversation with Maxwell flitted through her thoughts. She frowned as she thought of her twin. He seemed so forlorn. She gritted her teeth. Now was not the time.

She dropped off her school bag with relish. She dug into her closet to find her well-used hiking compression sack buried in the dark confines. She filled it with clothes, batteries, a flashlight, and climbing gear, along with whatever else she could find. She stood and hurried over to her mother's room. She wasn't sure if she would find anything, since she already looked through once, but it didn't hurt to check again. Also, she wasn't sure if her mother's Bible was there but if it was... She gazed around her mother's room before delving into a drawer and pulling out money. She stuffed the wallet full of bills into her bag. As she looked up, she saw a simple little book. Its black leather cover sat on the bedside table, hidden slightly from sight due to the desk lamp. It was well worn and the pages were ruffled, but it had obviously been taken care of.

"Mother's Bible," She carefully picked it up as her fingers traced over the well-worn cover, feeling the cool leather before she slipped it inside the sack alongside the money. She was glad, yet worried that she was able to find it. Mom never went anywhere without it. If it was still here it must mean something. Karina was loathe to leave it home because of that.

Unease twisted her gut as the need to hurry grew. She glanced over to see Maxwell race out of his room a moment after her. She took note of his backpack and frowned.

"Is that all you're using?" she asked, gesturing at it.

Maxwell shrugged sheepishly. "It's all I have."

"Give it to me." Maxwell handed the bag over curiously. She moved downstairs and into the kitchen. She opened the still remaining cupboards and riffled through them until she found what she was looking for.

Karina pulled out some plastic bags and covered his clothes within his backpack before stuffing the rest in her sack. After, she grabbed granola bars and slipped them into her compression sack before she moved to the faucet. She pulled out the water bottle that sat in the side mesh of her bag and filled it to the brim with cold water. Karina pulled out another one and filled it up as well before she slipped it into the mesh pocket on the other side of her sack.

"Karina…you might want to hurry up."

Karina paused as the unease slipped up a notch. Her stomach churned as she faced her brother. Maxwell stood near the front windows. One hand held an undamaged curtain shakily out of the way as his gaze remained fixed on the darkened street. His face was pale and a look of worry, heightened fear and recognition flashed across his features as his body tensed.

"What's wrong?"

"I see cars."

Karina glanced around before she hurried over. Her brother moved away as she took his place.

She saw something flash and stiffened as a lightning strike illuminated men dressed in dark clothing with sparkling medallions and cuffs stepping out of black cars.

A memory flashed through her mind. A scream, her brother, and a confident, but worried smile were all she remembered before she dashed away. The unease morphed into panic and anger.

Karina looked over her shoulder to see her brother hurry into the kitchen. Karina gestured to the back door. She saw him hesitate and she gave him another glare. He frowned before he thrust his sweatshirt hood over his head and grabbed his backpack. He dashed out the back door. Karina grimaced as the door slammed shut due to the harsh wind. Her heart pounded viciously against her chest as her stomach knotted in coils.

I'm not going to let those bastards mess with us again, she thought as she ripped off a raincoat, grabbed her sack and raced after her brother. Her breath came faster as she rushed out the back door and let it swing shut just as the front door slammed open.

She ran from the closed doorway toward the back gate of their fenced-in yard.

Where are you? she thought. She could hear shouts resound through the house behind her. Rain clouded her vision and slammed into her face. Within moments, she was drenched, along with anything within the rain's grasp.

Come on, Max, where did you go? she thought as she turned back to the house once more. Lights flickered on as thunder and lightning crashed above.

She looked away just in time to see her brother wave from the open back gate. She sighed in relief as she hurried over. He held his backpack close to him in a hunched over position, as if to protect it, which was why she hadn't seen him. She slipped through the wide-open gate and held it open as Maxwell quickly followed. He huddled over even more to protect himself.

Both ran onto the back street in time to see the flash of red and blue on the other side of their house. Karina saw Maxwell shiver as he gestured for her to follow him before he ran down the lane. She threw the sack on her back, with the raincoat still in hand before she hurried after him. She noted how he seemed to barely keep himself from slipping on the wet pavement as he slid over the road. Karina gazed back at their home once more. *Luckily, they didn't block the back exit, then we might not have been able to get away so easily,* she thought as she ran past the sleepy houses.

"Where will we go? There's no way we can travel in this weather," Maxwell shouted over the storm as she caught up with him.

Karina glanced at him before she looked around. Her eyes caught sight of something familiar.

"The tables…there should be a storage room we can hide in near them," she replied as she slid onto someone's lawn, glad the lights were out in the house.

She heard Maxwell follow soon after. She swiveled around as she heard the sirens in the distance. Panicking, she managed to spot a shed and, before she really thought about it, grabbed her brother's wrist and dragged him toward the shed. She darted inside.

"Thank god," she muttered as she pushed the door closed, locked it and leaned against it. Her clothes dripped down and quickly soaked the dirty wooden floor. She closed her eyes to catch her breath before she opened them and let her gaze flicker toward Maxwell. Maxwell slumped down against the wall, soaked and panting. His head was leaned back against the wall and his face was turned away. Karina frowned, but didn't comment on Maxwell's behavior.

The two waited in silence as they tried to control their quiet, yet anxious breaths. Maxwell pulled his legs in close to his chest as he held onto his backpack tightly. Karina slid the sack off her shoulders onto the ground before she scooted closer to Maxwell. She grabbed the raincoat, throwing it around the both of them, barely covering them. She listened to the outside. She could hear sirens and shouts up and down the streets. Through a window set high above, she could see lights flash and, she wasn't sure, but she thought she saw lights turn on from nearby houses. *They must have been asleep*, she thought as she heard shouts and demands that she couldn't quite decipher. She grimaced before she pulled away, letting the coat drape around Maxwell as she crawled to the window. She peeked out.

Her eyes widened as she took in the scene before her. She could see policemen in black, running up the street and banging against doors. Woman and men, bleary-eyed from sleep and anxiety from the storm, responded, only to shake their heads after, wide awake.

Banging hit the door. Karina felt her breath catch in her throat as her head whipped toward the doorway. She noticed her brother stiffen as she slipped quickly to the ground, out of sight of the window.

The two stayed silent as the door handle rattled for a moment, only for another shout to be heard. The sound disappeared as Karina held her breath before she let it out and once more peeked out through the window. A car zoomed by before silence filled the place. Men and women looked around from doorsteps before slowly moving back inside.

"Are they gone?"

Karina tilted her head back to see Maxwell peer up through his bangs, his eyes tired. Karina gazed through the window once more as people began to move back into warm homes. Cars zipped up and down the street, before they faded into the distance.

"Yeah, they're gone," Karina murmured before she slumped down and let her head rest against the wall. She ignored it as her ponytail dug into the back of her head. "We'll stay here for tonight, then move on tomorrow after the weather has cleared up, all right?" Her eyes trailed over to her brother who nodded. His head slumped into his legs as his arms pulled them closer to his chest in a tight hug.

Karina's eyes lowered sadly before she glared out toward the street. *One of these days, I'm going to get back at those bastards,* she thought before she also pulled her legs close to her chest and let her head rest against her sack, which sat on a wooden crate. *Then, Max and I won't have to worry about them…*she thought as her eyes drifted closed.

It was four years ago, but she could still remember it…all too well.

~ * ~

A ten-year old Karina bounded into the kitchen happily, as she carelessly dragged her protesting brother with her. Maxwell tugged against the hold as he yelled at Karina to let him go.

"Dad. Mom. When's dinner? Me and Max are hungry!"

"Max and I…" a voice stated as Dad walked into the kitchen with amused green eyes, his black hair framing his face nicely. "Now, Karina, you know you shouldn't bother your mother while she's cooking."

Mom moved away from the stove as she waved a spatula at Dad. "Don't go spouting nonsense." She stopped and turned to the two children that stood in the doorway side by side. "Ignore your father, you're welcome in here any time… Actually, can you two do me a favor?"

"Sure." Karina piped up as she hurried forward. She stood next to Mom who chuckled at the response.

"Can you help me bring these things into the dining room? Be careful, they're heavy."

Karina took the plate carefully and nodded before she headed toward the dining room, connected to the kitchen. She paused as she heard her brother mumble something to Dad.

"Dad. Can you tell Karina to stop pulling me everywhere?"

"Oh, don't worry about your sister, that is just her way of showing that she cares. Who knows, you may get used to it someday."

Karina felt herself perk up, happily as she moved through the doorway, only to stop. "No way! She's annoying."

"Maxwell," her mom exclaimed sharply.

Karina felt her shoulders droop before her father spoke once more. His voice was calm and encouraging, as if he knew she was there.

"Max, you shouldn't say your sister is annoying. We want this to be a happy family, so you're not allowed to insult your sister."

"But..."

"Maxwell." The voice was stern.

Karina jumped as the door opened to reveal her mom. Blue eyes gazed down at her in surprise. Karina just looked away. She caught the last bits of the conversation as her mother gently led her toward the table, away from the voices.

"One day, you'll understand, but I'll say this, cherish this time you have. You don't know when something will happen."

Karina carefully put the dish on the table and frowned. She felt slightly sick as she looked up to her mom. "Hey, Mom…why does Max seem to hate me so much?"

Her mom jumped and eyed her in something like shock. "Kari? How could you think that?"

"Well...whenever I try to get him to play, like when we were younger, he just ignores me…and he's always calling me annoying, and…" Did she want to talk about the conversation they just had? She shook her head and looked at her mom.

Her mother sighed and set down the plate before she turned to her daughter. "Don't worry, it's just a phase, and besides, he's your brother and you're his sister, it'll work out."

Karina looked away. Confusion and sadness slid over her shoulders.

"Honey? Need any help?"

Karina jumped and looked toward the doorway to see Dad with one hand on her brother's shoulder.

"Jeez, what do you think? I'm not a servant." Her mother snapped, though the smile on her face showed she wasn't too annoyed.

"Yes, my Queen."

"Felix…"

Karina watched as her dad chuckled before he went back into the kitchen. He walked back in as he carefully placed two plates onto the table rather artfully. "Jeez, you never could get a joke."

Karina and Maxwell glanced between the two parents before they looked at each other. Karina tilted her head in confusion while Maxwell shrugged.

Maxwell and Karina jumped as lightning slipped through the curtain before a crash vibrated through the house.

"Whoa. That was close," Karina heard her dad murmur as he glanced, fascinated, toward the ceiling.

"It was definitely surprising. I didn't even hear any thunder before this," the twin's mother conceded as she placed more food on the table.

"Doesn't that happen often?" Maxwell asked curiously.

Karina shifted her gaze from her brother to their father as he walked back into the kitchen with his wife. "Not really, usually there is some warning, though it can happen."

Karina saw Maxwell nod, just to jump as the doorbell rang with a loud chime, almost as sudden as the lightning strike was.

"Who could that be?" Karina heard her mom ask from the kitchen. Karina turned in time to see Maxwell spring up. A childish look was on his face as he shouted, "I'll get it!"

Karina followed close behind as her brother ran toward the door. Something didn't seem right…but she wasn't sure what.

Maxwell grabbed the door handle and opened it as a gut-wrenching feeling of worry flitted through Karina's stomach.

In the dim light from the moon that was slowly being covered by clouds, the twins could see a man in a black uniform. A medallion sat over his chest as he looked down at Maxwell.

"Hello, young man."

Maxwell gazed up at the man as he did a low bow. His black hair fell around his chiseled face as a beard bristled against his lower jaw. "I'm here to pick up your father, Felix, and, if need be, a few other things."

Maxwell took a tentative step back. His expression was spooked.

"What are you doing here? I thought the program was cancelled…"

Karina's gaze shifted to her father, whose face paled considerably. Karina noticed movement and looked back to see the man carefully move around Maxwell, who gazed between his father and the stranger in front of him.

"Papa?" Maxwell called worriedly as their father grit his teeth.

"Felix, you can't, you know what's going to happen."

"It's either me or…" their father trailed off. Karina stepped forward to join her sibling by the door. Out of the corner of her eyes, she noted Maxwell seemed worried. Rain slowly began to thrum against the ceiling and thunder crashed outside.

"I was told that if you weren't cooperative, my superiors would have no qualms about taking them."

"NO!" Felix interrupted immediately as three sets of eyes shifted toward the twins. The man gazed at the twins with a dangerous gleam before he looked back at the father.

"Do you know something we don't?" the man stated as he took a few steps back, considerably closer to the twins.

"No, I just don't want my family to get involved. You should know they have nothing to do with…that."

"True. However, it is possible they do, and we can't let that go, now can we?"

Maxwell shivered as Karina gripped his arm tightly. What were they talking about? Why did they keep looking at them? She heard her father growl softly as the man continued to move back. Karina pulled Maxwell to the side as the man stopped right in front of them.

"You understand now, we have no time to waste. The superiors want to make sure this is done in a timely fashion," the man stated. A calloused hand extended toward the twins' father, palm up in a welcoming gesture, even though the man's posture was anything but friendly.

"Max…what's happening?" Karina asked, she finally let herself break slightly. A tremble ran up her frame as she saw Maxwell shake his head, scared. She caught her father's gaze as he gave her a soft, if worried, smile.

The man pulled his hand back as he faced the twins, who stood a little out of arm's reach. The man gazed at them; his face impassive. He narrowed his eyes before he once more looked at Dad, who pulled away from Mom solemnly.

Their mother held one trembling hand extended while the other sat on her lips, her eyes teary.

"I'm coming, don't touch them," Dad stated sharply.

Karina felt a shiver run down her spine at the cold eyes that gazed at her and Maxwell. The man's lips twitched up a bit before he nodded. "All right. For now, we'll let them go. However, we will keep close tabs on them, if something…"

"It won't be. They have nothing to do with it and they won't have anything to do with it," Dad stated.

Karina watched as his gaze grew sharp and dangerous. She never saw her father like that before.

The man stayed silent for a moment. "Well then, why don't we go? Say what you want, but quickly, we're on a tight schedule."

"Where are you taking Dad?" Karina asked as she glared at the man.

She wanted to tremble from fright, but at the same time, she was angry. Who was this man? Why did he just barge in to try to take their father? She felt Maxwell shift beside her and spared him a quick glance to notice the determined look on her twin's face. She saw the man look at them before Dad moved between him and the twins. He squatted down in front of the two. He reached forward with his hand and lightly ruffled Maxwell's hair as he put his other hand on Karina's shoulder.

"Don't worry. I'll be back. Take care of your mother while I'm gone, okay?"

Karina's gaze flickered to her sibling as Maxwell looked up, green eyes teary. Maxwell reached a hand up and scrubbed his eyes before he nodded. Relief shown in Dad's eyes as he faced Karina and lightly touched her cheek. "Take care of your brother," he stated softly as he gently laid a kiss on her brow.

Karina looked up as Dad was jerked upright. The man gazed

down at the twins before he spoke. “We have a schedule to keep, get moving,” the man finished as he pushed Dad forward.

Karina watched as she pulled Maxwell close. She could feel her twin tremble as she shivered in the cold and occasional drops that blew through the doorway.

She caught her father’s gaze once more as he was pushed through the entrance. Thunder crashed and illuminated the black uniforms scattered about the road. Silver medallions gleamed brightly as the light faded.

Chapter Three

Late morning gray light shone down weakly through the window of the shed. Karina groaned as her eyes slowly opened. She stared forward in confusion as the dream drifted through her mind. She was tired of remembering it. It made her feel sick. She tilted her head against the sack as she stared at the cross-beamed ceiling, her eyes glazed with sleep. Her mother never did tell them what happened. After the incident, she just pulled them close, hugging them to herself while repeating the words, "He'll be fine, he'll come back."

It was as if she was saying it both to comfort them and to convince herself, even though the shaking of her voice and the tears were anything but comforting. After that night, their mother worked harder than ever and never seemed to want to bring it up again. No one wanted to talk about that night. As if still waiting, but knowing, as the years passed, he was never coming back.

She jerked up as a sound rang through the room. She winced as her neck screamed at the sudden movement. Her hand darted up to massage the tense muscles as she gazed around their small wooden protector. Now that she was paying attention, it just sounded like movement outside. It was morning, after all, stores would be opening now.

She groaned as she tried to push herself up. *Of all times to remember the past,* she thought as she got to her feet.

She heard a rustle and looked over in time to see Maxwell sit up blearily, obviously still partially asleep.

"Where...?" he slurred before his eyes widened and he straightened. He looked around wildly before worried green eyes met her own. Karina slid a sheepish expression on her face before she glanced out the window beside her.

"Looks like it's morning. I think the storm finally cleared up. Are you okay? Did you get any sleep?"

Maxwell scoffed before he shakily stood, letting the raincoat drop off his shoulders. He used his hand to push against the wall before he stumbled to his feet. He winced and shook his head, as if to try to get the last remnants of sleep out of his system. "Isn't that a rhetorical question?" Maxwell muttered tiredly, as Karina eyed him worriedly.

"Standard question," she responded as she blinked rapidly. She could practically feel the dark circles that sat under her eyes as she gazed out the window and onto the wet streets outside. "Anyway, it looks like we can probably leave. This shed isn't exactly the safest place, and..." Both froze before their heads snapped toward the doorway. Footsteps resounded from outside as keys rattled.

"I thought I kept it unlocked...damn..." a familiar voice stated through the doorway.

Karina watched the door and noted as Maxwell quickly shuffled out of the way, grabbing the raincoat in the process. The door opened to reveal Mr. Parkin, a friend of their history teacher, and the rather dismal sky behind. Mr. Parkin looked at the two of them for a moment before his eyes widened. "Karina, Max, what are you...?" Mr. Parkin gulped as his gaze flickered outside before it shifted back to the two of them. "The police are planning to search this place thoroughly. Please leave, quickly."

The twins raised an eyebrow as Mr. Parkin trundled away, his back tense as his hands trembled.

"What?" Karina frowned then chuckled. *Thanks for the warning,* she thought.

Maxwell grabbed his backpack, threw the raincoat to Karina and hurried out the door.

"Max." Karina slipped into the raincoat, grabbed her sack and hurried after him.

"Either way, we have to go. As you said yesterday, Ma probably isn't here, and, no matter where we go in this town, we'll be recognized.

We can't put these people in jeopardy as well."

Karina paused before her mind flashed to last night, the scared and enraged faces of the people forced out of their homes. She tightened her hands into fists as she gritted her teeth.

The duo, hoods up and respective bags gripped tightly to their backs, slipped around another building and through the trees as more sirens wailed in the distance.

Tall redwoods and pines stood proudly and swayed in the wind with ease. The twins peered back at the town before they ran and slid between the trees and out of sight of the main road.

Karina panted softly as Maxwell stumbled beside her. She saw his breath catch in his throat. They slipped between prickly bushes and tall conifers, slick with rain.

After a little while, they came to a halt. Karina glanced around, ignoring her sibling as he groaned softly. The sky was a dismal and threatening gray, as if it wasn't sure whether it wanted to continue what it started the day before, or just go on its way. She closed her eyes as she listened to her brother's uneven breaths before she hefted her sack and looked forward.

"We still have a way to go. We're too close to town and, considering where we entered the forest, it'll probably take a day or so to get there. Of course, that's sort of taking into account that we can't move as fast as yesterday with all our things," she muttered quietly as she grabbed her brother's hand.

She looked over just in time to see Maxwell stumble once more from exhaustion. She tightened her grip on his wrist to hold him steady. She used her other hand to wipe at her eyes, misty from lack of sleep.

A shiver ran up her spine from a mix of fatigue and a brisk wind that chilled her to the bone. She could only imagine what it was like for her brother who wasn't as used to being outside.

There was still a knot in her stomach. So even through the tiredness, she pressed on.

After a while, they came to a halt. Karina looked around, then pushed herself against the bark of a large pine. The branches hung low as roots rippled above the leaf-cluttered floor. She looked over her shoulder to see if they were being followed before she pushed the hood of her rain jacket to one side to see Maxwell fall against the tree. He held a trembling hand over his chest as his hair covered his face. His legs seemed to collapse underneath him as he slid down the slick bark and bent forward.

Karina kept her eyes peeled on the surroundings. Thoughts flitted through her mind. She wanted to rest but she knew they had to keep moving. Even as part of her said that, the other just wanted to curl inward and sleep. She didn't want to worry or feel afraid.

"Kari, do you think…?" Maxwell's soft voice trailed off as he buried his face into his legs.

Karina glanced over before she sat down against the tree trunk and leaned close to Maxwell.

He shivered and a part of her guessed that it was because of shame.

She might be an 'annoying sister' as he used to like to call her, but she could still tell he blamed himself for not being able to do anything all those years ago, and now for Mom's disappearance as well. Heck, she felt that way often enough, so she could somewhat understand. But still…

Karina leaned her head against Maxwell's shoulder, which made him stiffen. "Don't blame yourself for what happened. There was nothing you or I could've done now or then, it wasn't your fault at all. They may come for us, but they won't get us. Dad gave us that chance and we will take it, all right?"

Maxwell stayed silent before he nodded. Karina stared up at the gray clouds. They were just like the ones from all those years ago.

Karina shifted her body until she was against Maxwell in an odd sort of side hug, head still on his shoulder. Maxwell said nothing even as he curled into his sister's side, laying his head against hers. They leaned against each other quietly as the rain decided to once more continue, but as a gentle drip that was more soothing than punishing.

The duo stayed that way for a while longer before Karina carefully pushed herself away from the tree. Her unease was back and, ever since the incident four years ago, she learned to trust it.

"Come on, we've got to keep moving," she stated.

Maxwell nodded and stood up. Karina forced back a yawn before she eyed her brother sidelong. Maxwell's legs seemed shaky and his knuckles were white from the tight grip on his backpack. She took a deep breath of fresh air, and moved forward. The two traveled for a while longer before the queasy feeling started to fade, much to Karina's relief.

She glanced over her shoulder before she pulled the compression sack off her back. She ignored her mud-splattered clothes and wet hair as she moved the flap and pulled the string to open it before digging inside. After a little rummaging, she found what she was looking for. She pulled out two of the bars she stuffed in earlier, along with the two water bottles.

"Here," she stated as she handed one of each to Maxwell. He took them and pulled open the packet. Karina watched. She took a bite as Maxwell munched on his halfheartedly. He swallowed harshly before he took a sip of water.

Karina did the same as she forced herself to eat.

The food went down uneasily as they continued to walk through the forest, gray with the weak light that managed to pierce the clouds.

Once done, Karina slipped the water bottles back into her bag as she stuffed the now-used wrapper into her pocket.

The two walked in silence. Her hiking boots plodded through mud-covered leaves and roots. Cold wind caused them both to shiver as they pulled their damp clothes closer to try to get some warmth from them.

After a while, Karina gestured for Maxwell toward the rock face they were at the day before. It wasn't very tall, but it was slick with the recent rain. Looking up, she could see the tops of trees continuing on, vanishing beyond her vision.

Maxwell spoke for the first time since they left as he stared up at the black speckled and slick stones. "We better not be climbing that."

Karina pursed her lips in frustration as she turned from Maxwell toward the sleek stone. Actually, she conceded, it was probably really stupid to be climbing that now. It didn't have a chance to dry due to lack of sun, and because of the sudden heavy rain, she could see little trails of water running down the sides, unable to soak into the earth.

She tentatively took a step forward before she spoke. "I know you probably won't like it, but I know someplace we can go where we won't be found. At this rate, even though we're pretty far from the town compared to earlier, there is still a chance of getting caught and remember…" she frowned as her thoughts flickered back to a certain rushed note, she felt anger and frustration well up as she continued, "Mom said…"

"To run," Maxwell finished as he grimaced and peered over his shoulder. "And with those guys back there…?"

Karina agreed, yet didn't comment as she adjusted her sack so it sat comfortably. She stepped toward the rock face, gauging the distance and best routes. Some of her normal routes were weakened by the previous rain. After a quick perusal, she nodded in satisfaction. She reached one hand up to grip the first handhold. She moved slowly up the rock face, being a lot more careful than yesterday.

~ * ~

Maxwell shivered as he watched his twin climb the rocks steadily. His heart raced. Why was she so…reckless? Couldn't she find an easier way? He followed Karina's passage and sighed in relief as she finally managed to swing her legs over the side and stand up top. He frowned at the imposing climb, or at least it was to him, no matter what his sister said.

"Come on," he heard Karina shout, when suddenly, a climbing rope came over the side of the rock wall to dangle in front of him.

Maxwell caught it and gripped it tightly while he looked over his shoulder once more. His hands were frozen as he looked up at the cliff face. His body trembled as he drew in a deep breath. "Is this the only way?" he asked, almost pleadingly, though he would never admit it out loud.

"Yeah," Karina responded as she looked down at Maxwell. "Don't worry, it's not that hard, it's a really short climb."

Maxwell gulped as he held the rope tentatively. *Can I do this? I've never gone climbing before, not like this… I can hike, no problem, stand on top and look down? No problem. Climbing something so unsteady? I'm not so sure.* He pushed the thoughts out of his head. They weren't helping him get up any faster.

"If you're that scared, just wrap the rope around your waist and I'll pull you up."

Darn twin recognition, he thought as he glared up at Karina. "I'm not scared," he shouted.

His body shook as he tried to pull himself up. He paused with one foot still on the ground, unable to move it. He gritted his teeth and pulled his other foot up, just as the slick rock crumbled beneath him. Almost instinctively, he put his foot back on the ground and jumped away from the rock face.

Darn it, he thought. First the men in black and now this stupid wall. *Is there anything else you want to show me I'm afraid of?* He knew his mental outburst wouldn't be answered, but it did help a little as he let out a sigh. "I'm fine," he called up to Karina.

"You sure? I don't want to push you. You know…I…" She paused, then continued, "When I first saw this, I was scared."

Maxwell stayed silent, listening quietly as Karina chuckled. "Yeah, me, scared of something like this, can you imagine?"

Maxwell shook his head even as the tremors slowly stopped at Karina's words.

"The thing is, I knew I wanted to see what was beyond this place, so I made up my mind to climb it. It was frightening, going so high. We never have to worry about that at home, but…" She trailed off. "After we get past here, we'll be almost there. Do you think you can manage?"

Maxwell stayed silent, amused about Karina's moment of seriousness. Slowly, he moved closer to the rock face, and gently held the rope. He pulled once and closed his eyes as he tried to steady his breathing. He wrapped the rope around his waist before nodding up to his sister. Karina nodded back, then grabbed the rope.

His arms trembled as he pulled his body upward while Karina tugged on the rope. His feet pushed against the stone to force him aloft. His eyes stayed steadily on the top as Karina grunted, pulling him up carefully. It probably wasn't the right way to climb, but it worked. Plus, the rope seemed fairly sturdy, and even if he did fall, it wasn't too great of a distance.

After a few daring moments, he made it to the top. Karina sat on the ground as Maxwell practically hugged the earth.

"I'm never doing something like that again." Maxwell groaned as he tried to control his rapidly pounding heart. *Heights…darn stupid heights…*

A moment later, he sat up. He untied and handed the rope to his sister. He stared as she put the rope back into her sack. "Where did you get the rope from anyway? It seems pretty sturdy…"

"I had it packed in there just in case I ever needed it for climbing, I just never took it out," she responded as she slipped the sack back on. She stood up and patted herself down before she continued, "Come on, we still have a way to go."

Maxwell looked up to her before he pushed himself off the ground. He gazed around, then looked back. Behind him, he could see right through the middle of the trees, as if he was on equal ground as them. A soft wind blew past and he shivered. Yet he felt relieved enough to whoop for joy. Nowhere, nowhere under the cloudy sky could he see the men from before.

It looked like they were finally out of harm's way.

Karina walked slowly into the forest. Maxwell followed as they passed through the trees in silence.

Leaves rustled as the occasional twig cracked in the undergrowth from their footsteps. The wind blew calmly as water dripped to the ground.

Maxwell blinked tiredly. His stamina was basically gone and adrenaline had all but faded away. The only bit left was from the climb and he knew that wasn't going to last much longer. Maxwell yawned before he stumbled and tripped. He grabbed hold of a nearby branch, slick with sap.

"Max. You okay?"

"Ye-yeah, just tired. I'll be fine," he said to calm his sister as he pushed away.

Karina looked at Maxwell. "I don't think it's that much farther. Do you think you can travel a little longer?"

“Kari, I already told you I’m fine. I’m just a little lacking in sleep, that’s all,” Maxwell interjected, giving his twin a pointed look to enunciate his well-being. “So, where exactly are we going?”

Karina didn’t respond as she swiveled her head left and right, as if in search for something. He heard a sigh of relief from her as light finally managed to break through the clouds. “Here it is.”

Maxwell glanced up from the ground and let his eyes widen. Sunlight streamed through the clouds and made silver glisten in the light. Maxwell stared up at the object as he blinked in surprise while Karina bent down. Karina reached forward and brushed away some dirt.

“What the...?” Maxwell asked as he tilted his head back. “Why is there a fence in the middle of the forest?” he muttered, fully at a loss as his eyes followed the crisscrossing links and rusted tips. It looked like it had been there for a while. Plant life twisted around the links as once silvery pieces pierced into the sky, easily a foot or two over his head. He looked to either side and noticed the solid metal fence curve around trees as far as the eye could see. Dew glistened as light poured through the thinning clouds.

“Weird, isn’t it?” Karina asked. Maxwell nodded as he observed the intricate, though old barrier. “Here we go, I guess that last storm did a number on it, but we should be able to get through now.”

Maxwell looked at his sister once more and noticed what she meant. Between the fence and the ground, there was a small gap that must have broken away over time. The burrow was probably used by small animals, Maxwell thought. He leaned closer to the opening to take a good look at it. *It looks like Kari widened it a bit to let us both get through. How far out has she gone?* He glanced to Karina with a mix of worry, bewilderment and a hint of annoyance.

Karina avoided eye contact. She grabbed her sack and pushed it through before she sidled under the links, careful to avoid any jagged edges that might have been left. Maxwell peered down once more before he sighed and followed suit. He slipped under the gap just like Karina. Karina patted herself down as Maxwell pushed himself up. Maxwell faced the barrier. His eyes slid over the links in confusion and wonder.

“What exactly is it for?” he murmured, more to himself than to his sister.

He swiveled his head left and right. His eyes examined the links as they traveled outward to disappear into the foliage on either side. His curiosity overtook his tiredness.

"I've tried figuring that out myself, but I can never seem to find anything out," Karina said. "I found it that way while I was exploring. I think it was two years ago when Mom let me go out alone for the first time. Of course, it was easier to see at that time due to it actually being sunny out, but..." Karina shook her head. "Come on, we're almost there."

Maxwell examined Karina and shivered as a gust of wind blew against his skin. He grimaced and followed her as he hugged his arms over his chest tightly.

"We also need to get out of these clothes and dry ourselves off or else we might get sick," Karina stated. "At least, according to Mom and the rest of the teens in town." She looked at him with a cheeky grin. "I guess I've just been lucky."

Maxwell scoffed and drew even with her, their pace a lot slower than before. "Isn't there a saying somewhere that says idiots don't catch colds?" he asked.

He couldn't help it, noting in amusement as his sister flushed. Her fingers twitched in annoyance.

"You're saying that about yourself too, you know," she shot back.

Maxwell winced. Okay, he stepped right into that one, considering he never caught a cold either. Karina rolled her eyes and chuckled softly.

~ * ~

They walked for a while as the clouds fully dispersed to reveal a brilliant clear blue sky. Behind her, Karina could hear her brother's stumbling footsteps. She could tell he was only still moving because of momentum. If he fell over, he wasn't getting back up anytime soon. She knew she was reaching that limit as well. She used up even more energy than her brother, even if she was more used to it. Plus, she was tired from the catnap-like sleep earlier. She surveyed the area, trying to get her bearings. She blinked and practically fell to the ground in relief.

"Finally, we're here," she said as she pushed her trembling and exhausted legs forward. A beam of sunlight pierced through the clouds to illuminate the little clearing in front of her. "Welcome to my sanctuary," Karina stated proudly as she flung her arms out on either side, narrowly missing her stunned brother.

He scrutinized the place, taking in the calming scene with awe and surprise. There was a small stream that trickled by through one side of the clearing, surrounded by little stones, along with one that looked perfect to sleep on. Karina knew, it was quite comfortable after the long trek. Wildflowers bloomed and swayed in the breeze as dew sparkled off their petals. A light padding of leaves covered the forest floor, along with small patches of green grass. On the other side was a simple lean-to. Its wooden beams were held up with two well-placed branches. Brush and leaves coated the top as its back faced one of the many trees that surrounded the little clearing. Karina trudged over and collapsed underneath the lean-to. Her body was soaked to the bone as she shivered even in the sun. She could tell Maxwell wasn't that far behind her, his footsteps leaden and weak. Karina's eyes slipped shut before she slapped herself. "Don't fall asleep, we have to at least dry off and get into warmer clothes," she stated as she stood up once more.

She noted how her brother was laid out on his side. He collapsed like that. One arm supported his head while his legs curled into his chest. His hood was still up and his eyes were closed.

Maxwell groaned and shifted slightly in his collapsed state. "Why?" he slurred.

"Because getting sick now won't get us anywhere," she replied tiredly.

By god, she hadn't felt that tired in a long time. She was going to sleep well tonight.

"Like we've ever gotten sick in the past," she heard Maxwell mumble, before he let his head fall back into position as he curled in tighter.

Karina moved over and slapped him across the cheek. She really didn't want to, but she had to make him stay awake, at least until they got changed and warmed. She didn't want to worry about her brother getting pneumonia if she could help it. Maxwell yelped. "That doesn't mean we won't get sick, that just means we haven't. You're being an idiot, so get up," Karina said as she walked to her sack, grateful that the rain finally ended. "It's going to get colder as it gets later, so hurry up."

"You didn't have to slap me, jeez…" Maxwell muttered as the sound of shuffling reached her ears.

She mentally grimaced as she riffled through her backpack. She gathered her things and stood. "Max," Karina called, she caught Maxwell's green-eyed weary gaze before she gestured with her free hand. "You go down that way." She pointed a little to the right of where they came. The direction followed the curve of the stream. "I'll change over here." She pointed the opposite way. She saw her twin roll his eyes before he trudged off.

Karina hesitated before she looked toward the lean-to. She put her sack down before walking toward the back corner, where there was a rolled-up piece of tarp she brought along on a previous excursion. She laid it out under the lean-to then nodded. It would do, at least to keep them dry.

She picked up her sack and walked along the stream a way before she found a large tree she could go behind. The bark was slick, but the grass and foliage weren't prickly like in other places. She quickly stripped off her clothes, before she wiped down her hands, face and hair, to get rid of some of the mud that caked them. After making sure she was clean enough, she hurriedly put on a new set of clothes she stored just in case. She relished the feel of warm, dry clothing even if it was against semi-damp skin. She closed her eyes, enjoying the sun on her clothes and skin before she carefully picked up her dirty clothing. She put them into the river. After a thorough washing, she brought them back toward the campsite.

She stepped into the campsite around the same time as her brother. Maxwell was in a set of sweatpants with a t-shirt and sweatshirt. His bangs were damp, showing he also probably used the stream to clean off as well.

She looked down at her own outfit. She still had her hiking boots and fingerless gloves on. Now, though, she instead wore a long-sleeved black shirt and granite-colored hiking pants. She slipped around the wooden construction. On the other side was a simple wire line stretched tautly from tree to tree.

She took her wet, but clean, clothes, and slipped them carefully over the line so they stayed on. She heard Maxwell walk up to her, and looked back to see he had his own clothes in hand.

"Want to give me yours?" she asked as she slipped her second sock over the line before she turned to fully face her brother.

Max nodded as he handed over the clothes quietly. He walked away, ducking under the lean-to. She heard a plop and guessed her twin was getting ready to sleep on the tarp-covered ground. Hopefully, he would still be able to go to sleep.

She returned to doing the laundry and paused. "He seriously let me hang up his boxers of all things?" she muttered as she grimaced. She quickly grabbed the pair of boxers and threw them over the line before she wiped her hands down. "Jeez, of course I'm stuck doing laundry even now. Okay, yeah, I know I said I would do it, but it doesn't mean I like it and is he seriously that tired?" She finished before her mouth split into a giant yawn.

She blinked blearily and glanced toward the sun that was already starting to sink below the horizon. "Of course, he is, dummy, it's been a long two days…way too long."

She moved away from the line and looked toward her already asleep brother. She grabbed her sack and dug into it. After a moment, she pulled out two small, but warm safety blankets. She draped one over Maxwell's shoulder before she moved toward the empty part of the lean-to, right near the entrance. She looked out to the stream.

She curled into the blanket, and let her eyes droop. Sleep washed over her in a wave as it released her from the world of reality.

Chapter Four

Maxwell groaned. His body felt stiff and his head pounded against his skull. His eyes fluttered open in confusion as the sound of trickling water and quiet humming reached his ears. He opened his eyes once more as he blinked away the early morning rays of the sun glittering over the trees. A dawn sky dangled above him as he stared at it. His legs and arms throbbed as he tried to shift around on the hard earth. His legs felt as though they had been hit by hammers and his arms were just numb. His back ached and his hair felt matted into the side of his head. The plastic of the tarp felt weird against his exposed skin.

He pushed himself upward as something fell off his shoulders into his lap. He glanced down as he used one hand to rub his eyes. Confusion clouded his mind as he stared at a blue woolen blanket, the corners stained with mud and dirt.

"You're awake."

Maxwell squinted up and noticed Karina munching quietly on what looked like a chocolate nut bar. She sat on one of the stones as she trailed her feet in the water calmly. "Here," she called as she threw a bar at him.

He jerked into a sitting position and just barely managed to catch it. He gazed at it, only to feel his stomach growl loudly in hunger.

"You're probably hungry. I'm surprised we lasted so long without eating, but it probably had something to do with adrenaline and exhaustion," Karina continued as she took another voracious bite out of the gooey delight. Maxwell ripped into the package and took a bite himself.

It wasn't the best food in the world, but it definitely helped his growling betrayer of a stomach. Once he was done, he stood up and stumbled over toward the little stream.

Karina got out of the way, as he collapsed onto her seat. "It looks like we'll be resting here for a while. We're both still exhausted, and you've probably strained a muscle with all the running and climbing we did yesterday on top of everything else."

Karina winced as she pulled one leg up. Shaking it, probably to wake it up, Karina stood and walked over to her bag. She pulled out two water bottles and walked back to sit next to Maxwell who eyed her the entire time.

"How much stuff do you have in there?" he asked as he took the water bottle gratefully.

"Hm…well, the traditional traveling gear such as food, water, blankets, climbing gear, clothes, as well as some miscellaneous other things that might come in handy when in the forest. That reminds me…" She dug into her sack once more while Maxwell choked on his water.

"You can't be serious," he stated once he recovered from his coughing fit. "You grabbed all of that and carried it all?"

Karina shrugged as she finally found what she was looking for. "I do it all the time."

She paused as her eyes trailed downward. Maxwell followed her gaze. Thin strings of grass waved in the light breeze before she spoke. Maxwell eyed Karina even as she continued her staring contest with the earth. "Though I've never felt so rushed when packing before." She paused before she looked up. "Here, it's a water purifier. We'll need it considering how fast you're downing that water, and how much you've spilled."

Maxwell pursed his lips, but didn't respond as he downed more of the much-needed water. After a little while, he was done. He wiped his mouth with his sleeve. He glanced up and watched her as she slipped some of the water from the river into the water bottle, before she placed in the purifier.

It was a slow process, but after a long while, she handed it back to him. He held it in both hands gratefully. Karina nodded before she did her own. Once done, she slipped it back into its mesh compartment. She shifted the compression sack slightly before she sat down once more and stared up at the blue sky and puffy white clouds.

Trees sprang into the air like fingers that reached toward the heavens. Maxwell took another swig of water as the sun dazzled the corner of his eyes.

"You know…"

Maxwell glanced over. He frowned as he noticed her hesitation. He pulled one leg up and listened quietly as she finally managed to speak.

"This is the place I wanted to show you and Mom two days ago. Remember that time when I told you I was out with friends?"

"And I didn't believe you because no one knew where you were, including your friends?" Maxwell responded instinctively. He looked at his sister knowingly.

She shook her head before she looked back at the sky. "I'm not sure why, but I had an urge to show you this place. Maybe because you're my twin, or maybe because I thought it would be a nice place to relax and eventually show Mom…" She stopped, her smile faded into a saddened and angered expression. "I just wish I knew what happened."

Maxwell tightened his fists around the water bottle. He squeezed it slightly before he relaxed with a long breath. "We don't know, heck, we left only knowing what Mom told us and because of them…" Maxwell shuddered as Karina winced.

Karina glared toward one of the trees. "Those black uniformed men…" She leaned forward and rested her arms on her knees. "I wish we could actually forget about that and them."

Maxwell didn't think it would help to just forget like that. He looked Karina dead in the eye. "Maybe if we knew why Dad left with them, we could find out what they were doing at our house now and why that man…" He paused while Karina clenched her fist in aggravation.

Maxwell let out a long sigh. No point on continuing on with that sentence, they both knew what happened four years ago, what's the point of bringing it up again? "Anyway, that note, it was definitely Ma's handwriting and she specifically stated not to trust anyone."

"Actually, I don't think she got to finish it," Karina cut in.

Maxwell paused before he nodded. "Probably, but…how are we

supposed to interpret it?" he asked as he gazed up into his sister's eyes.

His sister broke contact first, perturbed. "I don't know…"

The two stayed silent as they listened to the quiet breeze and rustling water. A bird chirruped in the distance as it sang its own sweet melody.

Maxwell groaned before he fell backward onto the sun-dried rock. He slipped his hands behind his head and watched as the clouds flitted by slowly without a care in the world. "Well, we won't find anything here," he said as he stretched his legs out over the edge of the rock and let his feet trail into the grass. "As you said, I doubt she's still in town, especially with those men around and all…" He stopped for a moment to collect his thoughts. "She warned us to run and not look for her. Like we're going to follow that one." He snorted quietly before he continued in a more thoughtful voice. "Still... There are too many questions that we don't have answers for. What did those men want? Where did Ma go? What happened to the house? Where did they take Dad? I'm even starting to wonder what that fence was for. Was it to keep something out, or to make sure nothing escaped?" he asked before he turned his head toward Karina who closed her eyes.

"Once more, I don't know, but…"

She sat up and faced Maxwell. Her eyes glimmered in determination and a lust for adventure. He was glad to see his sister enthusiastic and her old self again. "As you said, we won't get anywhere going back, and I've always wanted to go beyond this point. For the past two years. I've been wondering about that fence. Is there something beyond these trees and forest? Are there other lands? Those things called mountains? For so long, we've lived in one place, following one set of rules. Now, we don't have to, we can see what lies beyond this point. Doesn't the idea fascinate you? To be able to see distant lands, people. Not to mention the things Mom talked about, like seas and mountains?"

Maxwell stayed silent as Karina practically glowed in anticipation. "Honestly, I just want to find Ma and be able to go home." He stood up and shakily walked toward his clothes.

"You're so boring," Karina muttered as some of her enthusiasm vanished with her sibling's remark.

"Well, sorry," he drawled as he pulled his clothes down from the hanger and let a smirk cross his face.

It was fun to tease Karina sometimes. They both did it every so often, but he knew his sister appreciated the moments of lightheartedness. He mentally chuckled as he stuffed his clothes into his bag. He grabbed the next article of clothing and froze. By god…did he actually? He looked at the boxers in his hands and felt a blush rise to his cheeks. "Uh…"

"Yeah, you had me hang them up. I'll excuse you this time, due to what happened, but I am not touching those things again," Karina said as she leaned over his shoulder.

Maxwell, to his credit, held in the yelp threatening to escape as he quickly stuffed the embarrassing article of clothing into his backpack.

He heard Karina chuckle before she once more spoke. "We have only a few granola bars, good thing Mary J packs so much into them, I never got a chance to ask her how she makes them…" She trailed off before quickly continuing with her assessment, "and three more water purifiers. We'll have to figure out what we're going to do. We can't stay here, or else we'll run out of food and clean water."

"Is there any place besides the town where we can get those things? Wouldn't it be better just to stay around here?" Maxwell asked.

He faced his sister before he looked back down to make sure his things were cleaned and packed before zipping them up.

Karina shook her head as she walked back over to the sunning stone. She dropped her sack next to her, before she tied her now drier hiking boots and socks back on. "Not sure, but what else can we do? We'll just have to go straight, and maybe we'll find Mom in that direction. If we stay here it'll get us nothing. If anything, they'll find us. We don't want that," she finished as she looked right into his eyes.

Maxwell paused, then nodded before he sat down next to her. He slipped his own, now only slightly damp, shoes and socks on as well.

Karina stretched her arms over her head toward the sky. "That reminds me, considering how much running we did yesterday, we should stretch. It might also make you feel better."

She bent forward. She reached for her toes as her legs separated at almost a ninety-degree angle. Maxwell watched as she switched sides and reached forward right between both legs.

He looked away and scooted himself back as well. He followed her lead and cringed in pain as the aches redoubled for a moment before they eased out. Tense muscles screamed as he massaged them and tried to soothe them.

After a few more extensions and a few more winces of pain, he was able to walk straight. His legs, though still a little shaky, didn't scream in protest as much as they did earlier.

"Feel better?" Karina asked as she stood up and threw the sack over her shoulders.

"A little, I guess," he said as he did the same.

They moved to the stream. Maxwell squatted down and threw some of the stream water on his face, as Karina did the same. It felt good, but now his neckline was wet and water droplets dripped down his back a little too persistently.

Karina stood. "Well, that's where we came from." She pointed toward the right. Maxwell hitched up his backpack as he let his sister with the exceptional sense of direction lead the way. "So, we should probably just keep going this way," she continued.

Maxwell shrugged as he decided he didn't care either way. He followed.

Her pace, while still comparatively fast, was a lot slower than two days ago, which Maxwell was quite grateful for. He withheld another wince as he had to lift his leg over one of the many fallen trees that seemed to litter this part of the forest.

Karina looked around the trees, she seemed confused. Maxwell raised an eyebrow as he glanced at his sister. Karina only shook her head before she continued forward slightly faster.

The sun rose confidently into the sky. When the sun was at its peak, Karina gestured for them to stop.

Maxwell was all too happy to follow her lead. He slid to the ground, leaning his head and back against the bark of a tree. He ignored the rough and sticky feeling of sap as he relaxed against the sturdy surface. Karina joined him. She crossed her legs as she pulled out some more power bars.

Maxwell groaned, but took one anyway. He nibbled at the bar. Even though he was hungry, he really was craving something else…like orange chicken or something, anything besides that dry bar that tasted like sand on his tongue. He really must have been hungry earlier to actually be able to enjoy it.

Karina seemed to want to eat her own with the same relish. "Sorry, this was all I could grab at the time," she murmured as she gulped down the last of her bar, before she took a drink of water.

Maxwell took a drink as well, glad for the leafy trees that kept out the brunt of the sun's heat.

"It's fine," Maxwell responded as he put his bottle back down. "I'm just glad we can stop for a moment." He grimaced as he stretched out his legs. "I just wish someone told me that I would be running a marathon the last two days," he said as he rotated his shoulders backward then forward, hearing a crack at one point.

Karina winced before she slipped her water bottle back into its normal spot. She zipped her bag, then stood back up. "Well, we don't know how far we're supposed to go, but it's easier to just keep going."

"Can't we just rest for a while?" Maxwell asked as he almost pleaded with his sister.

It wasn't like he was actually going to plead with her. That would be absolutely ridiculous!

Karina seemed to notice his annoyed and tired state. They had been on the move almost constantly for the past few days. He sighed in relief as she looked away and slipped the sack back onto the ground. Once more, she joined him on the hard-packed earth. "Whatever. I guess we can stay here for a little while longer."

Maxwell nodded, forcing himself not to grin widely. He stretched out his legs, rolled his sleeves up and tilted his head back to let the light breeze whispering through the trees ruffle his hair. He closed his eyes and tried to just rest.

~ * ~

Karina looked around the forest in silence. Signs she never saw before covered the area. The trees seemed almost stunted in their growth, deformed and weak, signs of decay with fallen branches and trees being much more frequent. Every so often, she came across garbage, which disturbed her greatly. "What is happening around here?" she muttered quietly before she once more glanced toward Maxwell.

His eyes were closed and his breaths were even. His head slumped sideways on his shoulder.

Karina sighed and closed her eyes. She listened to the wind whistle through the trees and the birds call high above.

After a while, she glanced back up and noticed her brother hadn't moved an inch. She stood and walked over to her slumbering brother. "Hey, wake up!"

She frowned down at him, her hands on her hips. He only grumbled and shifted slightly. She crossed her arms over her chest. *Maxwell...* She thought as she continued to stare down at him, feeling her eye twitch. Seriously, they hadn't even been traveling that long.

Well, okay, maybe they had, but still, how could he already be in such a deep sleep?

She waited another moment before she rolled her eyes and dropped her hands to her side. With a quick movement, she slapped Maxwell across his cheek.

"Would you STOP DOING THAT!" he shouted as he rubbed his sore cheek.

He leaned against his free hand and sent Karina a glare that promised retribution. Yeah… she probably deserved that look, but she didn't want her brother sleeping out here for too long. It wasn't safe, especially since neither of them knew where they were, and they had to make as much time as possible. Karina tried to give a nonchalant shrug before she grabbed his backpack.

"Come on, you shouldn't be sleeping already, at least wait till night, or we reach our next location… wherever that may be," she stated as she tried to ignore his complaints. She threw him his backpack once he finally pushed himself to his feet.

Maxwell trudged along after her, grumbling quietly under his breath.

Karina kept her head up and gaze forward, trying hard not to show her fatigue even though she was almost certain her brother could tell anyway. The sun slowly started to fall. It dipped closer to the horizon as they continued forward. Finally, as night began to grow, she decided to stop once more. Karina looked around to find that the trees were thinner than they were before. The ground was filled with foliage and fallen leaves, but there was no garbage.

"This should work for the night," she said as she plopped her backpack on the ground.

She dug into it and found both security blankets quickly. She threw one to Maxwell. He glanced around to look for a spot before he finally settled into an area that had a slight depression in the ground. He laid the blanket over himself. He once again used his arm as a pillow to get comfortable.

Karina shifted into her own chosen spot. It was right between two sets of thicker trees. While the ground was still slightly damp, she didn't mind. She pulled the safety blanket over her shoulder and shifted herself so that her arm supported her head. She closed her eyes and lay there in silence. She listened to the calming breeze and the occasional creak of wood and animals scuttling to and fro.

Finally, after what felt like hours, she fell asleep.

The next morning, as the sun rose sluggishly into the sky, Karina awoke. She yawned and sat up to stretch the kinks out of her back and arms before she glanced over to Maxwell.

He was fast asleep, curled up in a fetal position. Karina chuckled as she pulled out her supplies and slipped the blanket back into place. She searched through the bag before she furrowed her brow and came to a halt. Her fingers felt a worn leather cover.

She slipped her hand around it and went to pull it out when she heard a groan. She started and let go before she glanced up to see Maxwell holding his head. He sat up almost as sluggishly as the sun. There were shadows under his eyes and he looked exhausted.

"What time is it?" he slurred. His eyes were blurry as he looked around.

"Approximately seven or eight in the morning," Karina responded as she squinted at the sun.

It was a total guess, but whatever time it was, it was definitely still early. Maxwell groaned once more before he seemed to force himself to his feet.

"Jeez, I feel like I didn't get a wink of sleep," he said.

Karina nodded in complete understanding. "The first night after just walking is always the hardest. It'll get easier as we go," she replied, pushing herself to her feet.

Maxwell grumbled in quiet complaint. "I know that, but still, we were walking the whole day before too. Why wasn't it as bad last night?" he responded solemnly.

"Adrenaline, dear brother. That's the only reason why we were able to go for so long. If not, you probably would have crashed much sooner than this." Karina took the blanket from him. "Anyway, let's eat. Then we can get moving. Hopefully we're heading in the right direction."

She passed him a food bar and water bottle. He munched on it before he took a swig of water. Karina did the same.

Once both were a little more awake and stretched out the kinks from sleeping on the ground, they set out. The day passed slowly, to both teens' consternation.

"I wish I knew how much farther we have to go," Maxwell groused, as he readjusted his backpack once more.

Karina just shook her head.

It wasn't until a few hours later that Karina stopped and sniffed the air in confusion.

"What's wrong?" Maxwell asked as he drew even with her.

"Not sure, something smelled off for a second. It was something I only smelled occasionally when Mom had to leave and she used the car. You know, that kind of putrid old egg smell?" Karina responded as she faced Maxwell.

Maxwell gave her a confused look before he spoke. "Was it that strong? I didn't smell anything."

"Yeah, but it was only for a moment. So, let's get going." She frowned before she hurried forward.

Maxwell nodded, and they continued on in silence.

Chapter Five

Maxwell gazed around in worry as he noticed that the trees began to thin out even more. The shrubbery and conifers were shorter and almost like children to the ones they were used to. The putrid smell Karina commented on earlier wafted to his nose more often. Maxwell began to cover his mouth and nose, willing away the smell that made his eyes water. Karina was doing much the same.

"I'm not so sure we should be going this way," Maxwell said as he glanced around at the thinning trees and signs of garbage and footprints. Animal sounds grew distant, and the squirrels and birds they were used to were almost nonexistent.

"Um…" Karina responded as she continued to trudge forward despite Maxwell's comment.

Suddenly, she stopped. Maxwell pulled up next to her. Maxwell just stared as Karina's arms lay at her side, lax in shock.

Below them, spread out on either side, was a wide, murky river. It flowed southward as it slithered over the landscape.

That wasn't what caught the teens' eyes.

Beyond the massive river was a town, with random brick and metal constructions, easily three times the size of their hometown. Long, spiraling paved roads wrapped around the huge place. Buildings varied in height: some looked to be reaching the clouds while others lay squat on the ground. Random high-rise creations stood next to oval constructions and church steeples. There was no coherent pattern. A glass building stood next to all brick next to metal. It was utter chaos. Yet at the same time, it was fascinating watching the sun gleam over the tall and short buildings alike. Artificial lights glowed brightly even against the sun as cars zipped to and fro over the paved roads. Birds fluttered through the air, diving past the shining buildings.

Right at the bottom of the hill, before hitting the river, were magnificent two and three story houses, gleaming with a white rosy hue in the sun. Exquisite little gardens and pristinely cut trees decorated their front entrances and yards. Golden gates wrapped around the houses, sharp as the day they were created. Balustrades decorated the sides of balconies which led to glass doors and windows alike. Marble pillars stood on either side of grand entranceways.

They were beautiful compared to the chaos across the river.

"Wha…" was the only thing Maxwell could utter. His eyes switched frantically from place to place as he tried to take it all in.

Karina's eyes gleamed in excitement and interest. Slowly, she started to walk forward, down the steep hill. Maxwell frowned as he watched her. "Kari… Shouldn't we be careful? We don't know anything about this place. Do we even know if Ma is here?"

Karina paused and looked back at Maxwell with a roll of her eyes. "Max, this place is huge. She has to be here. Plus, I don't think we have to worry too much at this point, they're probably still checking our home. I think we'll be fine."

"I'm just saying… Better safe than sorry."

Karina dropped her gaze before she shrugged. "All right, but I still want to check this place out, I want to know what this place is. So, come on!"

At that, she started down the hill. Maxwell pursed his lips, feeling his jaw clench worriedly before he followed after Karina. He stepped carefully as he continued to gaze over their surroundings.

Maxwell tightened his grip on his backpack, feeling the weight want to pull him down. From the corner of his eyes, he could see gold glittering off what looked like elaborate chain link fences. They went all the way up to the tree line on either side of them and descended down, past the beautiful houses and paved roads, all the way to the river where he could just barely make out a bridge that contained a golden gate. He scrutinized the area before him. It was like a large cage, which did nothing to assuage his fears, but was it trying to keep something in? Or was it trying to keep something out? Just like that fence within the forest?

They reached the first golden gate. It was intimidating.

"Wow…" Karina breathed. Her eyes glimmered in amazement as she twisted around to take in everything in sight. "It's beautiful."

Maxwell nodded, admitting the sight was quite nice even as he felt a chill run up his spine. He didn't like this place for some reason. He peeked through the golden shafts of the fence into the front yard. He could see people in fancy, high-class jewelry and dresses. Right in the middle of the front yard was a fountain, similar to their own in the community, with angels reaching toward the heavens and water pouring out of trumpets and hands alike.

It was like a dream.

"What are you doing?"

Maxwell jumped and spun around. On either side were men dressed in uniforms that resembled tuxes. Their eyes were covered in sunglasses and their mouths covered in doctor masks. In their hands were guns.

Karina growled as Maxwell frowned. *How did we not notice them? Jeez, why didn't Karina listen to me? Why were they holding guns? What was up with the doctor masks?* Maxwell slowly took a step back, moving closer to Karina. *They didn't look like the men from before, or the ones who took Dad. So then, what did they want? Were they here to take us to those people?*

"I'll ask again, what are you doing here?" one of the guards repeated.

Maxwell narrowed his eyes slightly as he noticed the cold and uncaring voice. He looked at the man who spoke. Meanwhile, his sister tensed behind him.

He paused before he replied, his voice surprisingly even and polite. "We're travelers, we just came over the hill and were wondering where we were, could you tell us?"

He felt Karina's eyes on him as he tried his best to keep his voice steady. Even so, he was positive she could tell he wasn't anywhere near the calm he hoped to be conveying.

There was a moment of silence before a click resounded along the street and the guns were raised. "Your kind should know not to travel by the forest. How did you pass the guards? You shouldn't be able to get through. Tell us the truth, what are you doing here, city dwellers?"

Maxwell and Karina moved back to back as Maxwell gulped, not liking the look of those guns one bit. Couldn't they catch a break? He responded a moment later, "What? We're telling the truth. We traveled through the forest and…"

One of the men lifted his gun higher. Maxwell snapped his mouth shut as Karina reached her hand backward and gripped his wrist tightly. Maxwell paused and gripped back slightly in acknowledgement.

"Fine, come with us. We'll bring you back instead."

Maxwell stiffened as the rest of the guards raised their guns higher. The one who talked to them reached to his waist and pulled out a radio. "This is Robin 3. We got two in sector C, you copy?"

"Copy that, sending paddy wagon a.s.a.p."

"Roger." The man clicked a button and switched off the transceiver even as he continued to stare at them with that cold gaze.

Karina and Maxwell scrutinized the surrounding guards worriedly. Maxwell knew his sister was probably thinking of a way to escape, but he thought it would be pretty stupid. The group was too tightly knit together and, if they were good, they wouldn't get shot at. He was hoping that luck, what little was left, was on his and his sister's side for once.

Only a minute or two passed before a large truck curved around the corner toward the group. It was gray and had bars in the back, along with a set of double doors. The doors were thrown open to reveal two long benches on either side of the vehicle, along with a wall at the far end. The group separated and used their guns to gesture toward the vehicle.

Maxwell got the hint. He kept hold of Karina's grip and started to walk, wary and fearful. He could feel Karina tremble and wasn't sure whether it was from fear or anger. He pushed it from his mind as he stepped into the back of the vehicle. Once fully inside, the door was slammed shut.

Maxwell and Karina jumped. Maxwell spun around just as a click resounded. He scurried forward, grabbing the handle and pulling sharply, sirens wailing in his head to escape. The car jerked forward and Maxwell barely managed to avoid slamming his face into the bars. Karina stumbled as well before she staggered onto one of the seats. Her sack dragged her down onto the metal bench with a hard plop.

"Ow…" she groaned as they moved forward.

She sat up slightly and rubbed her backside as Maxwell managed to get to his own seat unharmed, staring worriedly around the small vehicle. "Jeez, what was the welcoming party for?"

She frowned and glared toward the back of the cab with its barred windows. Maxwell just shook his head, unsure. "Maxwell? Are you all right?" Karina asked, blue eyes anxious and uneasy.

Maxwell jumped. *Do I really look that worried? Probably.* "Yeah, fine," Maxwell said, trying to convey certainty, even as his thoughts churned.

Where are we going? The man said paddy wagon, but from the books I've read, paddy wagons are used to take people to jail. Is that where we're going?

"All right…" Karina trailed off, her voice anything but sure. Maxwell felt guilt swell in his chest, wanting to tell his sister, but knowing it would be stupid to have her worry even more. So, he stayed silent.

They stayed that way for a while before Maxwell stood up once more, shaking the endless worried thoughts from his head. He leaned against the wall for balance before he stepped forward to reach the double doors. He grabbed the bars, keeping himself steady as he glanced through. Within view was a paved road with large mansions on either side. He stayed there and watched as they passed stores and a bank. The road curved before turning once more. A stretch of road appeared, leading toward the hill before turning right. To one side, if he strained his head enough, he could see the large fence from before, gleaming golden in the sunlight.

They continued for a while before they slowed down again. He tightened his grip on the bars as he felt himself sway backward. They came to a stop. They were jerked forward as the car continued on a moment later. He heard his sister move and looked over to see Karina stand up. She stumbled into him, causing him to cringe, before she managed to grab the remaining bars and peer through. Maxwell let his jaw drop.

In front of their eyes was a wrought iron gate. Its intricate design made it stand out against the metal bridge. It looked like it was added after the bridge was created.

On either side was the river that swam lazily southward. It glimmered brilliantly in the sunlight.

After another moment, they stopped. Both glanced around before they quickly moved backward. Maxwell held his breath as there was a click and the doors swung open to reveal two more guards, guns drawn. Maxwell grimaced before he slowly slipped out of the truck. Everything happened so fast, he wasn't quite sure what happened. One minute, they were walking down the hill to look at the fancy houses, the next, they were being shipped around like prisoners. Seriously? What did they do wrong?

Maxwell stared apprehensively at the guns as both gunmen gestured around the vehicle. Maxwell and Karina hesitantly followed the directions, unsure what else they could do. They walked around the vehicle where Maxwell paused in shock. His mouth, he was certain it unhinged itself at that point, dropped open in awe as he stared up at the massive buildings in front of him. Cars wound through the intricate streets. They curved around buildings and sat like predators on the side of the roads. People milled about as they hurried from place to place.

"Get moving," the two guards stated, pushing their guns into the twins' backs. Maxwell winced and looked over in time to see Karina glower before stepping toward the lights illuminating the city.

They moved in unison as they hefted their bags over their shoulders. They walked down the last stretch of road over the bridge, only to stop as a rumble and a roar resounded behind them. They glanced back just in time to see the vehicle take a sharp turn before it headed back the way they came, guards nowhere in sight.

Maxwell just stared, thought process coming to a halt. "Did… Did they just let us go?"

Karina slowly nodded, a flabbergasted expression on her face. "What the hell?" she murmured under her breath, barely loud enough for Maxwell to hear.

Maxwell ignored it though as he looked at the river flowing under the bridge, frowning. "Why would they go through the effort of picking us up then? I was so certain we were heading to…" Maxwell cut himself off as he twisted his head to his sister, who was just giving the golden gates an incredulous expression.

"Well, we won't find out here…" Karina trailed off before she turned to face the town proper. "Might as well keep going. We'll look for some real food before finding information, or a place to stay, whichever comes first."

Maxwell shrugged. Karina faced the city street, took a deep breath, and walked forward.

Maxwell followed as he took in the activity. His eyes roved over the different places and people. His nerves pulled taut with everything that was happening. They looked to be near a shopping area. Stores lined the sides, some closed with metal shutters, others surrounded by people. *Weird... I've heard of cities and stuff from history class, but I didn't imagine that it would be like this.*

They continued down the street before Karina decided to turn right. Their eyes widened as they gazed down the stretch of road before them. He was surprised he hadn't damaged them from all the times he was in awe in the past few, however long it was. He was really starting to lose track of the time.

Artificial lights glowed brightly, highlighting the surroundings in their yellowing glow. The sound of the place was incredible. People were partying and talking, sometimes practically shouting to be heard.

The buildings, all metal and glass, stood as tall as some of the trees in their town. Maxwell's eyes moved frantically from place to place to take it all in. A large mixture of smells hit his nose which almost overpowered him. Sometimes sulfur, sometimes car fumes and other times, the smell of food or cooking. It was completely overwhelming to him just how many different smells invaded the space.

"I'm getting a headache," Maxwell mumbled.

Karina nodded as she once more grabbed Maxwell's wrist. Maxwell accepted his sister's wish to keep in contact. He had a feeling she was doing that so she could hold on to something that felt real in this surreal place.

"Come on, let's get something to eat and find a place to sleep," Karina said as she walked forward to where Maxwell could smell food.

All around them were people who wore the same masks they saw on the guards. Even though the place and people seemed rowdy, there was an ever-present sense of distance and wariness between each person and Maxwell felt more than one person's gaze on them as they walked down the street. It was disconcerting.

What are those masks for? he thought as he happened to catch one of the passerby's eyes. A look of fear crossed the person's face before they hurried away. Maxwell narrowed his eyes, but stayed silent as his sister busied herself with trying to find some place to eat. He would ask her about it later.

They continued down the street as they peeked into each of the shops. In all of them, they could see workers wearing long gloves and masks, their eyes wary. Maxwell scanned around a bit more as they took another turn farther down the street. More shops lined the road, but even more had metal shutters in front of their doors and windows. Maxwell held his hand to his nose and mouth. He tried to ignore the overpowering stench as they ventured through the large place. Karina crinkled up her nose in distaste.

After they walked for a while down the seemingly random streets, getting more than one cautious gaze thrown in their direction, they finally came across something that looked decent and wasn't too crowded. It was only a simple sandwich shop, but Maxwell knew they were both starved after having just eaten bars for the last few days. They meandered into the store and heard a little bell tinkle by the doorway. They jumped before they gawked up at the metal clinking softly back into position.

"Welcome, can I help you?"

Maxwell looked at the shopkeeper, noting as the man stiffened and took a feeble step back, his mouth covered with a mask. Maxwell paused before he followed Karina, who was already heading closer to the counter. On the wall was a list of sandwiches. Her face contorted into one of confusion as she perused the items.

"I don't even know what some of these are," she said so softly, Maxwell could barely hear her.

Maxwell peered at the list and conceded. The names sounded funny, there was a rather wide variety, but a lot of the names were just weird, or made his stomach churn. Seriously, who cooks dogs? What the heck is even a hot dog? Bacon? He found hamburger and felt a bit relieved. At least they had ground beef. That's something. Still, are they trying to make people sick just from the names?

Karina dug into her backpack. She pulled out a few bills, before she looked once more at the food. She sighed heavily. Maxwell joined her, looking at the money, then at the prices, along with the price of his meal, before wincing. Karina's shoulders slumped.

"I would like the BLT, please?" she asked. The man inclined his head before he squinted at Maxwell.

"I would like the hamburger with an orange juice," he stated uncertainly before he peeked at the man, who nodded.

"Please take a seat, your food will be out shortly."

They nodded and paid before they took a seat on one of the thin plastic benches. A table stood between them as Karina put down the remainder of the money.

"I can't believe how expensive it is," she said as she riffled through the bills and change.

Maxwell nodded as he regarded the menu once more. "And compared to some of the stores we passed, this was one of the cheaper ones," he said as he shifted uncomfortably in the seat. "By the way, a BLT?"

Karina's face contorted to one of disdain as she slipped the money back in her pocket. "It sounds strange, I know, but it was the cheapest thing on the menu, and one of the only things that didn't make me want to throw up with the name. I mean, what the heck is a four-alarm patty anyway? Who would want to eat an alarm, nonetheless four of them? I mean, if they said hamburger then I'd understand, but have you ever heard it be called a patty before?" She pulled herself from her thoughts as Maxwell shook his head.

"A lot of the names sound weird, I heard mom talk about stuff you could get at the convenience store, processed foods. They used to have them there when the place was built, they don't anymore." Maxwell shrugged.

Karina sighed, before she continued. "Right, still, I went with the cheapest, even if I don't know exactly what it is since we don't know how long this is going to take or where to even get more money, we can't exactly get a job around here after all."

Maxwell agreed. "All right, just make sure to get some water or something at least, or have some of my sandwich."

Karina stuck out her tongue. "You are such a worrywart."

"From what I've seen, maybe I should be."

Karina grimaced before she waved it off. "Minor details…but anyway, we need to find a place to sleep or something. I'm not sure I want to imagine how much a room might cost."

Maxwell nodded before he looked down at his clothes. He frowned and lifted his arm before letting it drop. "As long as I can get a bath, then I don't care."

Karina chuckled. "Coming from a boy, that's pretty funny."

Maxwell glared as he raised an eyebrow. Really? Was she really going to use that train of thought? "Well, sorry if I actually enjoy being clean, unlike some people."

Karina just shook her head before she looked away.

Maxwell looked down at the table, feeling over the plastic edge as he let his thoughts roam. *Of course, I would also like some idea to what is going on, but I highly doubt that's going to be answered anytime soon.* He paused, letting his fingers run in a circle, following a small crack in the plastic. *Why were we let free? What was with the suspicious looks and those masks? Why did the shopkeeper back away? Was there some kind of health hazard going around? Should we look to get one of those masks?*

He was pulled from his thoughts as the shopkeeper stepped forward with their trays of food. He put them down as he eyed Maxwell and Karina carefully. A moment later, he hastily retreated behind the counter.

Maxwell stared at the man, feeling a sense of curiosity and unease twist his stomach into knots. He shook off the feelings before he quickly picked up the food. He felt oil coat his fingers and he grimaced as he felt something drip onto his hand.

Both took a bite and swallowed, practically in the same movement. Karina's nose crinkled while Maxwell looked at the meal critically. "Interesting," he said before he took another bite and a sip of the orange juice. He practically downed the whole drink. Karina rolled her eyes before she continued to eat her sandwich.

"This doesn't taste fresh at all. Is it on the edge? Ugh," Karina mumbled quietly.

Maxwell peered at his sister, but didn't comment. What could he say? Once the two finished, they thanked the man and left.

"Even though I said that, the food wasn't terrible, but it definitely tasted different than I'm used to. It almost felt…stale…I can't quite explain it," Karina said as she glanced back at the store.

"Yeah, I think I know what you mean, it had a strange taste, unnatural. Though the orange juice was good," Maxwell said as he thought of the cold drink.

Karina gave her sibling a deadpan look as Maxwell shrugged.

They continued down the street, sticking to the sidewalk like the rest of the pedestrians they passed as the sun started to dip between the large buildings. They walked for a while before they stopped and glanced back and forth in dismay.

"Hey, isn't this where we started?" Maxwell asked. Karina regarded him with confusion. Maxwell was sure he had the same expression on his face.

"Yeah, but I have no idea how we got back here," she murmured in reply as she swiveled around and looked down the store-lined street. In the distance, they could just barely see the river sparkle in the evening sun.

Maxwell moved to the side of the street. There was a small garden on the other side of a low wall. He moved up to it and sat on it, letting his legs droop to the ground. "I'm so tired. All we've been doing is walking and walking," Maxwell groaned as he stretched his legs.

Karina regarded the street. "All right, why don't I get a map while you wait here?"

Maxwell looked around. He didn't want her to go too far, after all. He looked across the street and sighed in relief. "Looks like there's a store across the street. While you're there, can you look for one of those masks?" He gestured toward the people.

Karina peered around and nodded. She carefully crossed the street, along with the other flustered and busy pedestrians. No one even gave her a second glance this time around, which Maxwell was grateful for. Maxwell leaned back and closed his eyes, trying to block out the noise and scents as he let his mind rest.

Chapter Six

Karina walked across the street with the crowd before stepping into the shop Maxwell spotted. She looked around before she headed toward the counter. "Um… excuse me. Do you have a map?"

The person behind the counter tilted his head up before he looked down. "Maps are in the back. Twelve ninety-nine apiece."

"Okay, thank you." Karina frowned as she slipped to the back and pulled out one of the maps. She opened it, surprised as it continued to expand. Once she got it fully opened, she blinked and regarded the pages before her. She needed to find an area that they might be able to sleep in… a park, maybe? Some sort of housing? She wasn't sure. After that, they would figure out how to find their mother. She had to be here, it wasn't that long ago when she was taken, how far could she have even gone? Karina tilted the map to one side, another, then flipped it over in hopes that the squiggly lines and random names would make more sense.

It didn't help.

She sighed and folded the map back up before she put it away and peered at another.

Five maps later and she was positive she was even more lost than when she entered the city. Her mind reeled at all the different roads and names.

She looked around the store. Maxwell said they should get some masks, but she couldn't find them. She walked up to the teller once more and received an annoyed grunt in response.

"If you're looking for a mask, we're all out, just like everyone else. Now if you're not going to buy anything, scram."

Karina glared, but didn't argue. "Jeez, the jerk. Though those maps weren't exactly helpful…talk about confusing," she said as she walked out of the store empty-handed. She crossed to Maxwell who looked to be falling asleep on the stone wall. "Max? Max. Come on. Let's go."

Maxwell groaned before he hopped down. "Did the princess find our salvation?"

"Really, Max?"

"I'm tired, what did you expect?" He paused then looked at Karina with a frown. "What about…"

"None, from the sounds of it, they're kind of running low."

Maxwell pursed his lips. "All right, no point in staying here, let's go."

Karina held a bemused smirk as she walked with Maxwell down another roadway, different from before.

This time, the buildings resembled homes. Large brick developments stood on either side. Some people aired out clothes, using open windows before they pulled them back in and shut the windows tightly. Other's meandered down the street, hands over their mouths or laden with bags.

"Jeez, is it just me or is everyone really defensive around here?" Maxwell frowned as he looked at the locked doorways.

Karina peered at her sibling before she observed the area around her. "I agree with you. This place is weird."

About halfway down, they noticed the other pedestrians and citizens looking at them oddly, similar to the looks they got when they first entered the city. People in masks stared at them from windows and doorways alike. Some shifted to avoid them altogether.

"We probably should have looked harder for one of those masks," Maxwell said as he moved closer to Karina.

Karina frowned as she shuffled closer to Maxwell.

They took another turn farther down the street. It led to more housing developments. The wind and evening sun sent a glow over the almost ghost-like area.

A shiver ran down Karina's spine. She heard a harsh cough and gargling sound. Karina glanced over to see a young child. A little hand covered her mouth as she coughed harshly. An older woman crouched next to her, hugging her tightly as tears rolled down her cheeks.

Neither female was wearing a mask.

For some reason, Karina's gut twisted at the sight, and she could feel her sibling tremble as well.

"What is happening around here?" Karina asked as she noticed more and more people without masks.

Their faces were curved downward in despair. Some had shallow cheeks while others had swollen eyes and pockmarked faces. Some seemed to walk down the street in a daze or with a drunken step.

People sat or stood on either side of the street as Karina and Maxwell passed. Accusing and hungry looks sat on their faces. They seemed to watch them avidly as Karina tightened her grip on Maxwell's hand. Maxwell's own grip tightened as well.

"I don't like this place," Karina whispered as she kept her eyes peeled on either side, her sense of fear overcoming her sense of adventure.

"Not arguing," Maxwell responded quietly as they began to pick up the pace. They took another turn, hoping to get away from the hungry and accusing eyes.

Maxwell paused and looked at the street before he continued forward at a clipped and fast pace, moving ahead of Karina. The sun decided to give up its struggle to light the world for the day. It disappeared over the horizon. Karina stayed close to her brother, gazing around with a wary eye. She was all too happy to have somebody that she knew nearby, so she was fine with watching his back as they moved.

The streets had definitely seen better days. They were littered with bottles, waste and trash. A few people were huddled into the alcoves of the obviously abandoned buildings. Their clothes were ragged and their faces were pockmarked and painful to even look at. Their skin was thin, as if they hadn't eaten for a while. The eyes were accusing before, but now just looked like rabid animals spotting their prey.

Maxwell and Karina gulped before they raced down the street. Karina had no idea why they decided to press forward like they did, when it was obvious they were in the completely wrong place. She would have to figure it out later. She ignored the hungry eyes and pressed close to Maxwell.

Up ahead, she spotted a set of factories. Smoke poured from smoke stacks, clouding the already dark sky.

Maxwell looked over his shoulder. Karina gave a small nod as she too turned her head to gaze down the lane.

Stars slowly began to appear in the night sky, but their usually bright light was obscured by the buildings and smoke rising steadily into the air. The moon shone down weakly as one of the few things that seemed to illuminate the despondent part of town.

"It's been a while. Looking for someone?"

They jumped as the voice filtered down from ahead of them, the sound, distant. Maxwell and Karina looked around hastily. For some reason, Karina expected someone to appear out of nowhere to talk to them, even though rationally, she knew that wouldn't happen.

Her sense of curiosity plagued her though. So, she walked forward, this time, pulling Maxwell along. She heard muttering and gulped as they stepped close to a man in rags, his face twisted up into something grotesque as he observed them. She hurried past, hearing a quiet murmur of feast.

She felt her brother tremble. When she got closer to the factory, and away from the people muttering such odd and disconcerting things, she noticed a road going in either direction around the location. She stopped right before the intersection and peered back at her sibling, who was giving her a wary, incredulous look. She scrutinized the streets leading in both directions.

"Lex. It's such a shame, really. Why do you insist on keeping with this charade?"

They glanced down the road to the right. Partway down, near what looked like a gated entrance, were two people.

Karina moved backward, pushing Maxwell behind her. She heard a quiet protest, but ignored it as she pressed them out of sight of the two.

"Let's just leave."

Karina looked back at Maxwell. "We can't just run, we have to at least find out what's happening, and anyway, where else can we go?"

Maxwell pursed his lips, his face clearly saying, 'Anywhere but here.'

Karina felt inclined to agree. Even so, she peered back down the lane. The one closer to her had blond hair pulled back in a loose ponytail. The second had on some sort of cap and his hands were stuffed into a pair of faded and ripped jeans.

She saw the blond shake his head before turning on his heels. "I don't even know why I bother. Just remember. No matter what…"

"Antonio, leave it."

From a distance, it appeared that Antonio scoffed at the comment, waving it away nonchalantly. "Fine, you're never any fun right after anyway. It's a shame, really, all those kids…" Antonio trailed off before walking away.

Karina and Maxwell quickly moved back, practically holding up the wall as the blond moved by to the left-hand street. Once he passed into the distance, the two teens let out a sigh of relief, then looked at each other.

"So…where do we go?" Maxwell asked as he glanced over his shoulder down the dark street.

Karina followed his gaze, noting how there were more people milling about and more than one eye glancing their way. "I really don't want to go back that way."

Karina nodded quickly. She heard footsteps and saw Maxwell stiffen.

"You two…"

Karina froze before she slowly turned her head. Standing behind her with a masked expression was Lex. His eyes were narrowed, the only indication of his irritation. "What are you two doing here."

Karina whipped around, stepping in front of Maxwell before glaring up at Lex. "None of your business."

Lex just looked at her.

Now that they had a closer look at the man, Karina had to admit that she was a little surprised. His hair was a shade lighter than hers. It was deep black with long strands gracing his face and neck. His eyes, which were slightly sunken in from what might have been fatigue, were a light shade of grayish green and he had a small goatee on his chin. His cheeks were slightly sunken in as well. From what, Karina couldn't tell. He looked relatively clean and, Karina found herself admitting, good-looking.

He wore a warm vest, zipped up three quarters of the way, and a long-sleeved, but ragged button-down shirt. His jeans were also faded and ripped, but his boots looked highly durable, usable and not that old.

She saw him swipe a hand through his hair before dropping his hand to his side, the other hand on his hip as he leaned on that same foot. "You two are idiots."

Karina bristled in indignation. *This bastard is freaking rude!* "What do you mean by that, you bastard? You just met us." Karina snapped.

Her brother frowned, fist tightening on his backpack. She heard a sigh and glared at Lex.

"I meant what I said," Lex said nonchalantly, obviously uncaring of what they thought of him. He stared back at them with an indifferent gaze. "What am I supposed to think contrary to that? I see two young teens without masks or parents. They obviously don't know where they are and yet still don't ask for help or call for the police, for that matter…anyone would say you're being stupid," he finished rather bluntly.

Karina crossed her arms over her chest in anger as Maxwell pursed his lips.

Lex let out a quiet groan before he straightened. "Fine, since it's obvious you are completely oblivious to what's around you…" At that, he peered past them.

Karina turned and almost recoiled at all the eyes. She heard Maxwell yelp next to her. "I'll give you a hint. Stay here and deal with them, or follow me. You look like you're dead on your feet, so decide."

Karina glowered. Those weren't options. She huffed and grabbed Maxwell's arm. "Neither, we can find our way ourselves."

"Suit yourself." Lex shook his head and began to walk away.

"Wait."

Karina glanced at her brother. She noticed him watching Lex, his expression unreadable. He gently pulled his arm from Karina before turning fully to face him.

"Why?" Maxwell asked, voice level.

"Hm?"

"Why do you want to help us?"

A flicker of surprise flashed onto Lex's face before it disappeared. "You're just kids, this area isn't for you. Believe whatever you want, I'm just giving you suggestions. You can even go after Antonio."

Karina was thinking about it when she noticed Maxwell narrow his eyes. "No…"

"No?" Lex asked, as he leaned on one foot. Karina peered between them before looking back at the street. She didn't want to agree with the earlier assessment, but she knew she was exhausted, just like Maxwell, and their options weren't looking too grand.

"We'll come with you," Maxwell said. Karina's gaze snapped to Maxwell.

Lex hesitated. "All right, then keep up."

Karina peered at her sibling. *What was he thinking?* Maxwell gently grabbed her hand before pulling them forward. She heard low murmuring and peered back once more to see disgruntled and angry expressions on the faces of the men and women hidden in the alcoves. The lights flickered and she shivered.

After a while, Lex turned to the left into a large abandoned building. It seemed like it once was a parking garage, but the inside was hollowed out and, for the first time since entering the city, they could see actual plant life, even if it was only amongst the ruins.

They followed Lex up a set of rugged and makeshift steps before he reached the second floor.

Once inside, they walked down the rows of cracked pavement and sidewalk into what looked like a guard room. The inside was rearranged and completely dismantled to create more room.

On the ground was a makeshift bed with clothes off to one side. A newspaper sat curled up near the head of the bed.

Lex walked forward before he slipped onto the bed. Once

comfortable, he gestured to both teens.

Karina suppressed a shiver as wind blew through the old building. She saw her brother hesitate. Indecision was clear on his face before it disappeared. He stepped inside and she followed tentatively after, closing the door behind her to keep away some of the chill.

Lex gazed at them before he released another exasperated sigh as Maxwell slowly sat down, with Karina right behind. Lex leaned against the wall of the booth.

"See…this is what I mean…"

That statement caught both teens off guard. Karina raised her eyebrows in consternation as Maxwell paused. He eyed the closed door before he gazed at Lex, who seemed to have noticed the action if the amusement on his face was any indication.

"What? Didn't you tell us to follow you?" Karina asked as she crossed her legs and put her hands on her knees.

Well, he hadn't, really, but at this point, she wasn't going to back track. They made their decision. She just hoped her brother made the right one.

Maxwell held his backpack in his arms with his legs stretched out in front of him. His gaze stayed fixed on Lex as he shifted closer to the doorway.

"This is going to take a while…" Lex muttered before he leaned back on the bed and put his hands behind his head. "Why don't you tell me what you're doing around here, then I'll explain why I called you two idiots, deal?"

Karina huffed. Maxwell and Karina peered at each other. Maxwell closed his eyes. Karina watched him quietly. Lex just gazed at them; expression closed.

"First off…how did you know we were there? You could have just kept going, ignored us entirely. We would have only needed to deal with the people on the road."

Lex looked at Maxwell. "So, you aren't a complete idiot…well, I'll just say, you two reminded me of a friend of mine, and we'll leave it at that. As for why I knew you were there?" He paused before he leaned back and stared at the ceiling. "You pick up a few things. It's lucky that

Antonio didn't notice this time. Then again…"

This time, Karina saw the grimace and pain that flashed on his face. Did Maxwell see something like that earlier? She couldn't quite recall. It disappeared before he continued, "Enough about that, what were you doing in that area?"

Maxwell began slowly, hesitating as he said, "We were lost. We just recently got to this place and we were trying to find a place to stay. As you can probably guess, we're not from here…" He paused before he hugged the backpack tighter.

Lex sat in silence. "I see…"

Both teens waited uncomfortably. "The name's Lex, by the way. It's a pleasure to meet you two."

Karina felt herself relax as Maxwell let out a sigh. His own tense posture disappeared and she was glad.

"What are your names? I told you mine," Lex stated evenly as he glanced between the two.

He leaned backward against the side of the guardroom as he laid one arm over a slightly bent leg.

"Karina," Karina said, getting straight to the point. Not much harm now. At least, no more than what they might already have to deal with.

"Maxwell."

Lex nodded. "Now that greetings are out of the way," he sat forward, "I have a question for you. Why didn't you leave an avenue for escape? You just met me. You should be incredibly cautious. What did you do when you came in here earlier?"

Maxwell blinked at the sudden question before his eyes darted to the closed door once more. Lex nodded. "Exactly, you cut off your only route for escape. What if I or whoever helped you was instead taking advantage of you? You wouldn't have time to open that door, nonetheless escape…" Lex waved as if it was no concern. Karina gulped. "Any questions?" he asked, somewhat sarcastically.

Karina and Maxwell exchanged a glance before Maxwell shook his head.

"If that's the case…" Lex yawned before he lay down on his side.

"Time for some sleep." He closed his eyes and, after a moment of stunned silence from both teens, started to snore softly.

"What?" Karina growled in frustration.

She wanted to smack the person in front of her. He wasn't making any sense. Calling them idiots, bringing them here, and just falling asleep. What the heck?

Maxwell didn't say a word, his thoughts obviously on something else. "Kari…it's pretty late, why don't we get some sleep as well? We have been moving all day, and both of us would probably like to rest up where it's warm and there is actually shelter," he said. "Plus, he's right, we were careless. What if you or I had gotten hurt? We don't know this place. We wouldn't know what to do and I highly doubt we want to go to the police."

Karina frowned before she sat back down next to Maxwell with a solemn sigh. "Whatever…" she mumbled as she dug into her backpack once more.

She pulled out the security blankets and handed them to Maxwell before trying to get comfortable in the tighter space.

The two stayed seated, finding that it was a bit too cramped to lie down, unless one of them wanted to lie next to Lex. Neither was very accepting of that idea. They sat in silence as the night dragged on. Eventually, their exhaustion took over and they fell into a deep and dreamless sleep.

Chapter Seven

Lex walked back into the room, regarding the two silently. He closed the door quietly and sat down. He scrutinized their relaxed expressions. They were obviously close to about the same age. Twins, maybe? He plopped the two bags on the ground, feeling hungry, but pushing the thought away.

He closed his eyes and leaned back, resting his head on the cool concrete wall. Who were these two? Where were they from? What were they doing here? Did he have a chance? A chance to keep that promise this time? Then again, to have such idiots follow him so easily was almost too convenient.

He heard a groan and opened his eyes to see Maxwell shuffling and blearily blinking his eyes open. The gaze fluttered around in confusion before resting on Lex. "I am surprised you two are still here."

"What time is it?" Maxwell muttered sleepily.

"Hm…probably around nine. You two must have been tired. I've already been out and back." He paused before he reached down. "Here."

He threw the two bags toward Maxwell and the slowly waking Karina. The two bags seemed to sag slightly from grease as they fumbled and caught them. They grimaced. Karina held the bag carefully between two fingers as she stared at it.

"Eat up, then I'll do some more explaining."

That seemed to get their attention. They opened the bags and pulled out paper-wrapped items. They stared at them in confusion before unwrapping them to reveal English muffin sandwiches. They raised an eyebrow before each took a wary bite. Both almost choked as the greasy food slipped down their throats before they scowled at the sandwiches.

"What is this?" Karina stated as she swayed the bag and food to and fro, eyeing it cautiously. Maxwell scrutinized his own, his stomach growling even as his nose crinkled up in slight distaste.

Lex spoke after some hesitation. "Egg muffin sandwiches, they're from a fast food joint right on Park Street, not that far from here, actually."

He shifted to get more comfortable on his bed. He pulled one leg up as he rested his arm on it. Maxwell and Karina looked at him before they started to eat the food. Their similar expressions made Lex's lips curl up in amusement.

Once both finished, he took the bags and crumpled them up. He threw them into a basket near his feet, originally hidden by his boots.

Karina reached into her backpack. She pulled out both water bottles. She passed one to Maxwell and downed what was left of hers. Maxwell did the same before he observed Lex quietly.

Lex sat in silence, surprised at the thoughtful look. He regarded Maxwell before he spoke. "I'll start simple. Were you born in the town across the river?"

"You mean the town with all the beautiful houses and the annoying welcoming committee?" Karina asked as she finally put down her water bottle. "The same one that both captured us and let us go?"

Lex mentally frowned. If they weren't from the city or from that area, then where? He shook his head before he continued, "That one, but from your response, I would say that's a no." He paused for a second in thought before he moved onto another topic. "Remember what I said last night in regard to wandering around alone?"

Karina slowly began to pack the backpacks back up. "Yeah…" Maxwell said, his voice slightly hesitant.

Lex regarded Karina, spotting her annoyed gaze. "What was your real purpose for walking around the downtown area?"

They looked at each other. Karina pushed herself to her feet. Maxwell stayed seated as he stared at Lex who threw on a blank expression. Karina slipped her backpack on her shoulder before she thrust the door open. Maxwell peered up at her as she walked out before he turned back to Lex.

"I'm sorry, but we already told you last night, we were lost…" He paused. "Thanks for the help, but we should get going." He stood up and patted himself down before he walked out the door after Karina.

Lex watched him leave before he stood up. He sighed before he pushed a hand through his hair. "Why am I helping these stubborn brats again? Oh yeah, because they remind me of him."

He groaned softly before he slipped out the door. With practiced ease, he followed after Maxwell and Karina. He watched as they talked to each other. They interested him, both seemed like they could be quite athletic, but their clothes and even mannerisms were different than what he himself grew up with. He couldn't really pinpoint who they could be.

They walked for a while and Lex wanted so desperately to yell at them for their stupidity. These kids are ridiculous. Though, why was he surprised? This always seems to happen.

After one more turn, he had enough.

"You two… are you trying to get yourselves killed?"

His voice caused them to jump and spin around. Karina squatted down slightly while Max gripped his backpack strap tightly. His legs were bent, ready to spring away if any problems arose.

Lex stepped out of the shadows as both their eyes widened in shock. "You're just getting deeper into the downtown. No one's going to help you around here."

Lex watched in frustrated bemusement as they stiffened before they peered at each other. Lex passed a hand through his hair. "I can't leave you two alone. Good thing I followed you or else you probably wouldn't be leaving here, except in a body bag or worse."

Both grimaced, possibly at the mental image. Maxwell moved out of his position. He stepped even with Karina as she slowly moved into a more casual pose. Her eyes stayed neutral, if slightly annoyed, as she looked into Lex's. "You could have. I don't see why you should have any reason to follow us, or even help us again."

Lex cast an eye over them before he spoke once more. "I can't leave two wandering kids, who have no idea what's going on, alone, plus…" He paused, gaining their attention before smiling softly. "You remind me of a friend who I made a promise to, but I think I told you that yesterday."

"Promise?" Maxwell inquired softly, confusion and thoughtfulness evident in his voice.

Lex paused in thought before he shook his head. "Don't worry about it. Anyway, I have another question for you, and I won't let you leave until you answer."

Both stiffened at the subtle threat, which was fine by him. It's better for them to be wary, that's just the way this and most places are. He leaned on one foot, eyes snapping around before he continued. "What is your reason for coming into Reinmark?"

Both glanced at each other in surprise before Maxwell murmured a quiet, "So that's what this place is called." Lex mentally raised an eyebrow at that, but stayed silent.

After a moment of silence, Maxwell spoke, his voice even as he gazed sidelong toward Karina. Karina slowly nodded her head in reluctance. "We're looking for our mother."

~ * ~

Maxwell bit his tongue. He really hadn't wanted to say that, but what's the point in hiding it? Not only that, but no matter what Karina thought, he didn't feel wary around Lex. Even though Lex berated them and spoke of the dangers, Maxwell didn't feel any need to raise his guard around him. He wasn't sure why, but he let it go.

He didn't realize that silence enveloped the road before he looked up to see conflicted emotions flashing across Lex's face. After a moment, his expression turned neutral. His posture tensed and hands once more were stuffed into his pockets. "So… why do you think she'll be here? Why are you even searching here? Where are you really from?"

"You said one question. We have no reason to respond," Karina snapped before she turned away, sadness and loss clouded her face before she schooled it into a cool expression.

Maxwell scrutinized Karina quietly before slowly shaking his head.

Maxwell's eyes flickered to Lex when Lex suddenly stiffened.

Karina faced Lex, arms crossed over her chest and head tilted to the side in misunderstanding. Lex let out a sigh as he relaxed and leaned onto his opposite leg. He brushed a hand through his hair. "You two… I'm starting to wonder if I should even bother."

"Why, Lex. How fortunate to see you so soon?"

Maxwell paused and cocked his head to the side as a man walked out of one of the buildings. It looked to be the same man from yesterday. He was slender with sharp eyes and an even sharper nose. His dirty blond hair was long and tied into a low ponytail and he wore tight black clothes that fit his frame perfectly.

Maxwell flicked his eyes toward Lex as Lex cursed and snorted softly under his breath. Maxwell gulped and sidled closer to Karina who was promising death through her eyes alone. Her lips were curled back in a quiet snarl.

"Antonio…didn't know you were around at this time. Figured you would be extorting money from someone," Lex said.

The man, named Antonio, just smiled evenly. "I do believe you misunderstand me. I was merely receiving what I was due."

"Stealing."

Antonio ignored the statement as he stepped forward, pressing close to Lex. He turned his nose up at Lex who was as tense as a coiled spring. Antonio's voice came out so softly Maxwell barely managed to hear it. "That is not your concern. I see you picked up some new ones. Now why don't you be a good little dog and stay away. Really, though, it's too bad they almost always end up coming to me in the end." Antonio smiled serenely before he scanned them up and down.

Karina shuddered while Maxwell glared at Antonio, feeling uncomfortable with the ever-present smile on Antonio's face.

"You know you can't protect them, so why do you always decide to take children like this in?"

"That's none of your business, Antonio," Lex stated coldly, his eyes were narrowed as his hands inched slowly out of his pockets.

Antonio shrugged before he took a step back, raising his voice. "I want to help you. You are looking for something, aren't you?"

That caught Maxwell's attention as Lex's eyes narrowed farther.

"What?" Karina asked quietly.

She looked toward Antonio who gestured to them. "What was it…your mother, right? I can help you find her."

Karina froze, her eyes widened in surprise as Maxwell mentally scowled. He wasn't sure if Karina heard the earlier conversation, considering she was behind him and a bit farther from the two, but something was definitely off. He didn't trust Antonio. Yet, he trusted Lex. He would have to sit on that later.

Lex scowled, about to open his mouth when Antonio continued. "You've probably seen Lex's…humble little abode. A little tight, isn't it?"

Karina slowly nodded as Lex growled in frustration. Maxwell just watched in silence.

Antonio let a smirk slip through as he continued. "He probably also got you those disgusting egg muffin happy meals, right?"

Karina slowly relaxed her expression, a mix of confusion and affirmation. Maxwell paused. His body relaxed visibly, except for his hands which were steadily tightening on his backpack straps. He knew he did that a lot. It gave him a sense of comfort because it was something real and the only thing he had left from home.

"I can get you the homemade stuff and a warm bed. I'll even be able to get you a room to yourselves, what do you say?" Antonio asked, extending a hand forward.

Karina blinked and touched her stomach.

Maxwell glowered before his eyes unintentionally slid to Lex. Their eyes met. Maxwell stared, stunned at the anger and worry. His expression was pained, yet Maxwell could not understand why that might be the case even when Lex turned away.

Why does he look…ashamed? Maxwell thought, trying to meet Lex's gaze again. He wanted to affirm that was what he saw. He continued to stare at Lex before he was snapped back into the present at Karina's voice.

"That sounds…" Karina began, hope flashed across her face.

Maxwell looked from Karina, who had a familiar gleam in her eyes, toward Antonio. Before Maxwell even realized what he was doing, he stepped forward. "No."

The word caused everyone to freeze. Karina, who was stunned, whipped around and stared at Max. Maxwell looked at Antonio with distaste. He didn't know why he didn't trust Antonio. He felt okay with Lex, which he really needed to analyze. It just seemed too easy, was it supposed to be that easy to find their ma, when they had trouble just speaking with their dad?

"Maxwell? What are you doing? What about Mom?"

Karina was fuming, her face distressed. He looked purposefully at Karina even as his own thoughts were still in turmoil. "And?"

Karina was taken aback, her expression turned from confusion to anger.

Maxwell felt all eyes on him and a part of him, a large part, wanted to run and hide. However, he needed to explain, to have Karina understand, even though he himself could not. "Kari, think about it," he began softly as he looked back into Karina's outraged eyes, so similar to his own. "Don't you think all of that is just a bit too good to be true? Lex has already helped us and taken care of us. He could have hurt us last night, yet he didn't. Yeah, so that egg muffin whatchimacallit was disgusting." Out of the corner of his eye, he saw Lex cringe while Antonio smirked. "He still got it for us. He even came after us to make sure we were all right. Sure, it might have been just because he was curious and didn't want this guy to have anything, but he still did it."

Karina paused. Her eyes softened as she thought about it.

"Lastly, we don't know him."

Maxwell gestured toward Antonio who had a subtle frown on his face. "Yes, he might be able to help, but for all we know, we'll join him, and never have a chance to see Ma again. Do you really want that? Do you really want to take the easy way out for once? That doesn't sound like you at all, Kari."

Maxwell let his hands fall to his side as he ended, mentally surprised at the rather long speech. *But it's the truth,* he thought before he scrutinized Antonio.

The final statement seemed to snap Karina back into reality. Her eyes widened before she looked down. Maxwell watched out of the corner of his eyes as she straightened up, facing Antonio. "Thanks, but no thanks. We'll find out about our mother by ourselves."

Maxwell's gaze moved toward Lex whose mouth was wide open in shock and disbelief. His expression was so bizarre on the previously stoic face, it caused Maxwell to laugh. He couldn't help it. The look was just downright ridiculous and he needed it.

Karina glanced over and chuckled as well.

"What?"

The exclamation caused the trio to stare at Antonio who was fuming. Obviously, he wasn't used to someone saying no.

"What are you saying? You would stick with him, ignoring everything I could and would have given you?"

Karina glowered. Her eyes dangerous as she moved back right next to Maxwell. "Sorry, but we're not that desperate." Karina stuck out her tongue as she grabbed onto Maxwell's arm.

"Inconceivable, what are you two? Rich brats always want everything handed to them," Antonio said with a narrowed and disgusted expression.

The two blinked before they looked at each other.

"We're not rich, are we?" Karina asked, a knowing smirk on her lips.

"Nope! As poor as can be." Maxwell shrugged.

Oh, this is going to be fun. He peered sidelong to Antonio, who stood there with a lost and disbelieving look on his face.

"Yep, just poor little ol' country folk with barely a cent on us." Karina sighed melodramatically as Maxwell chuckled.

"Sounds about right, and anyway, those mansions are way too big for my taste."

"Yeah, they were pretty, but you would get so lost."

They grinned then paused as a chuckle sounded from beside them. They stopped their conversation and peeked over to Lex who was holding back a laugh. His hand covered his mouth as his body shook.

"Wha…?" Antonio muttered as he slowly blinked.

"Let's get out of here," Lex whispered as he lightly grabbed their arms.

Antonio paused before he called out a loud, "Shit. Get back here!"

Maxwell and Karina looked at each other, then took off running. They leapt ahead straight past Lex. Maxwell, having finally gotten a decent night of sleep, joined Karina as she raced ahead. He looked back to see Lex blink in surprise before he also picked up speed.

They ran, right back the way they came, speeding right toward Lex's humble abode.

Chapter Eight

Once they reached the building, with Lex completely out of breath, Maxwell breathing somewhat unevenly and Karina barely breaking a sweat, they walked inside.

"Dang…" Lex gasped as he walked haphazardly up the stairs.

After the others were up, he grabbed the makeshift staircase and pulled it up. He laid it on one side, looking down through the hole. That would buy them a few minutes at least. He looked up. Those two were fast, where could they have learned that? They weren't from this city or any city, for that matter. Maybe one of the outlying suburbs? Probably not, there weren't that many around now and they seemed too healthy. "What are you two?"

"What I want to know is, what the heck was in those muffins?"

Lex's eyes shifted to find them holding their stomachs, pain flashed across their faces. He blinked before he mentally groaned at himself in annoyance. Of course, this happened more often than not. He moved away from the hole and up to Maxwell and Karina. He took off their backpacks against their will and hurried them to another doorway across from the guard booth. Karina dashed forward and opened the door before she closed it with a snap.

Lex shook his head. "You can go in, too. It's a multi-stall bathroom."

Maxwell just collapsed on his knees. He held his stomach tightly. Lex squatted beside him. "Sorry… Shoulda realized you weren't used to this food."

Lex grimaced and stood up. He walked back to the bags he dropped unceremoniously to the floor. He picked them up and, finding the water bottles, checked to see if there was anything left. To his dismay, there wasn't much.

He slipped them over his shoulders and walked into the booth. He dug around for a bit before he pushed some blankets and odds and ends into a backpack he was using as a pillow. Once done, he walked back out to find Karina standing where Maxwell was. She held her stomach uncomfortably as her face morphed into a disheartened scowl. A while later, Maxwell came out as well, a disgruntled and annoyed expression on his face.

"Come on, I'll get us somewhere where you can get cleaned up. It's not safe here and I have nothing to help you."

"It's fine," Max said hoarsely.

"Speak for yourself." Karina groaned out, leaning against Maxwell as her ponytail fell over her shoulder in random strands. They stumbled after Lex as he hurried toward a back fire escape that was rigged to cross to another building. Maxwell and Karina paused as Lex crossed over the wooden plank. He gestured for them to follow. After a moment, they did. They followed him through the building and slipped out onto a different street.

"Where are we going?" Maxwell asked.

Lex looked back. "You'll see soon enough, just wait."

Lex watched in amusement. They were learning. After that thought, he grimaced as he gazed forward once more. Of course, they would get an upset stomach, now of all times. Though if they weren't from the city, they wouldn't be used to the grease and processed food. *I'm not surprised this is happening, but I'm only used to that happening when someone's from THAT area. Their reactions indicate they are not, and don't know anything about it. You two, who are you?*

Lex glanced back occasionally as they walked. They moved slowly, but steadily away from the buildings.

They took one or two turns. They traversed empty roads and past brick apartment complexes. After a while, as the sun rose steadily into the sky, they reached a row of buildings with people milling about outside. Some buildings were a signature red brick while others were plaster or other construction. Spray paint decorated the side of some buildings and a painted picture of a healthy family stood near the end on the side of an abandoned warehouse.

Lex scanned left and right before he hefted the backpack and sack over his shoulder. He grimaced at the weight as he wondered just what was in them. Maxwell trembled while Karina murmured quietly under her breath as they walked down the lane.

After they passed a few houses, Lex stopped. He watched as, unprepared for the stop, Maxwell and Karina stumbled and almost tripped over each other before they finally came to a halt. Lex turned toward the doorway and knocked politely on the simple black painted door.

He didn't have to wait long. For only a moment later, Agatha darted out and practically slammed him to the ground. Good thing he tensed in preparation. "Uncle Lex," Agatha squealed as she hugged him around the waist as much as her little arms could.

Lex felt fondness for the little girl as he examined her. A blue bow he gave her for her birthday tied up one of the two pigtails in her brunette hair. She wore a blue dress which emphasized her eyes. She seemed healthier with rosy cheeks except she had a new wound on her arm and her skin was a bit flakey.

Lex put one arm around Agatha as Martha stepped out of the open doorway as well. Her messy brunette locks were frazzled like usual and she was wearing a newer, though obviously used green dress. Her left eye was slightly swollen and her limp was a little worse, but even as she went to berate her daughter, she had a small smile on her face that wasn't as strained as it was last time he was here. "Agatha."

The little girl blinked before she shyly pulled away and bent her head forward. "Sorry, Mommy."

Martha sighed before she looked up at Lex. "It's been a while. What brings you to this part of town?"

Lex gestured toward Maxwell and Karina. Both leaned heavily against each other. "We need a place to stay for a while. At least these two do."

Martha leaned slightly to see over Lex's shoulder while Agatha bent around his leg.

"What's wrong with them?" Agatha asked innocently. Martha had a wary look on her face.

"That one's my fault. I just gave them the wrong food and their stomachs got upset. I really have to stop getting those egg muffins from Park Street," Lex said.

Martha sighed. "Poor dears," she said.

Agatha pulled away from Lex's leg and walked forward. She peered up, and tilted her head to the side. "Are you friends of Uncle Lex?"

The two teens paused. Maxwell looked to Karina before he pushed away. He regarded Agatha for a moment before he responded, "I guess..."

Karina subtly nodded as she also pushed away from Maxwell, just to shiver and wrap her arms even tighter around her stomach.

"Your stomach okay?" Agatha asked as she reached a small hand up to pat her on the stomach. Karina shook her head, obviously deciding that responding might be a bad idea.

"Mommy, can they come in? They're not feeling well."

Martha let out an exasperated breath, but moved away from the doorframe. "Well, since my daughter is fine with them, come on in."

"Thank you," Lex said as he walked through the doorway. He paused.

"Come on, come on," Agatha said to the duo as she grabbed both free hands and pulled them forward. Once inside, Martha looked at them and pointed upstairs.

"There is a bathroom on the right, up the stairs. Take your time. You can use the shower if you wish. I will make something to eat. You're probably going to be hungry after eating that junk."

Lex snorted, but didn't say a word as he slipped onto a couch in the living room, followed by Agatha. He'd found he'd actually grown to like the fast food as of late. It did take some getting used to though.

Maxwell and Karina nodded gratefully, grabbed their bags from Lex and practically bolted up the stairs. Martha's gaze followed their departure before she walked into the kitchen. Lex watched her through the doorway as she flipped through the fridge. Once she was satisfied, she leaned out the doorway toward Lex. "Lex, dear, what would you like?"

"I'm fine, I already ate."

The young woman looked him up and down before she dug back into the fridge. "All right, I'll make a nice lunch so you can actually get some meat on those bones."

Lex went to open his mouth in protest before Martha stood up and sent him a glare. He shook his head in slight annoyance before he saw Agatha waiting patiently on the couch. "Hey… Uncle Lex?"

"Hm?"

Agatha fidgeted slightly before she peered up the staircase. "What'd they do?"

Lex blinked. "They had a run-in with a bad guy, that's all."

"Is it that scary Antonio?" Agatha whispered as she fiddled with her fingers.

Lex chuckled quietly before returning to normal. "Yeah."

Agatha gulped before she looked back down. "Does that mean they angered him? Will he come after us again?"

"You don't have to worry about that. I have a plan."

Agatha regarded him with wide eyes. She puffed out her cheeks before she nodded slowly. "Okay, just be careful please?"

Lex's lips curved into a subtle grin.

"Of course, you're not going anywhere until you eat. I bet you used the last of your money for the week to take care of those kids," Martha interrupted.

"No. why would you think that?" Lex said as he glanced at her.

She leaned out the doorway, scoffed and gave Lex a pointed look. "You do that every time you take in a child. You practically give up everything for them. It's too bad most don't really realize and decide to go over to that greedy bast…"

She stopped, glanced at her daughter before she turned back to Lex once more. "You know who I'm talking about." She moved back inside to cook.

The sun glowed high in the sky as Lex watched out the front window, the sunlight dancing in its red and gold hues over the street.

A short while later, footsteps sounded on the stairwell. Karina jumped down the last few steps. Her wet hair fell in her face, down from its ponytail. She wore short tan shorts, a blue halter top, as well as gloves and knee-high socks. “Thanks,” she said, seeming much better now that she was cleaned up.

Martha nodded as she looked her over. Lex frowned slightly. “No wonder…”

Karina peered at him with a raised eyebrow and he waved it off. She huffed and sat down. “Max should be down soon…eventually.”

Lex peered toward the stairwell.

As she said, a while later, Maxwell came down, dressed as before just with his sweatshirt wrapped around his waist. He walked down the stairs and bowed his head slightly to Martha. “Thank you for letting us use the bathroom and shower. I just wanted to say that, just in case Karina forgot.”

“Maxwell.”

Lex looked at them for a little longer before a movement caught his attention. Martha held a hand to her mouth, holding back a small chuckle. “Come on, dears, the food’s ready.”

Both teens glanced toward the table as Agatha grabbed their hands once more. They walked forward and took a seat. Agatha beamed before she hopped into her own seat. Martha bent her head and clasped her hands together in prayer. Maxwell and Karina froze before lost looks flickered over their faces. Lex noted as the duo forced on neutral expressions before they bent their heads and clasped their hands as well.

“We thank you for this meal that you provide us, Lord, and for the company and companionship of those around us. We appreciate everything you have done for us even in this time of need and I pray that you will continue to provide and nurture everyone here. I ask that you hold us in the palm of your hand and save us from those who may hurt us. In God’s name, we pray. Amen.” Varying volumes of ‘Amen’ were heard around the table.

Karina and Maxwell glanced at each other before they looked down toward the food.

It is not my business. They can take care of their own problems, hopefully. Lex noted Martha's expression, the worry she exuded for someone she just met. He wondered why she could accept someone so easily. Even if he did ask her to take care of them, she was already worried for them.

Agatha glanced at the duo and reached a hand onto Karina's. Karina jumped before she eyed Agatha. "Why so sad?" Agatha asked.

Karina paused before she tightened her hand slightly. She seemed hesitant to speak, as if unsure what to say. Maxwell let a quiet breath slip through his lips as he put a hand to his face. He let it drop. "It was…we were supposed to eat dinner with Ma the other day…she always made sure we prayed before the meal." He stopped.

Lex noticed Karina grimace, but ignored it, keeping his attention on Maxwell.

"Ma? What happened to your mommy?"

Maxwell paused and looked at the group. After a few minutes of thought, he finally responded with a quiet, "She went missing."

Martha's eyes widened as her hands covered her mouth in shock. *Ah, right. I almost forgot,* Lex thought. He chuckled weakly as the conversation continued.

"Missing?"

"That's enough, sweetie," Martha said.

Karina's expression was determined, her eyes sharp. Maxwell was quiet, but his own expression was resolute and firm.

"Well, why don't you get something to eat? I made a fresh salad. That should be able to help a little," Martha said.

Karina and Maxwell nodded. Karina reached toward the bowl and took a bite before pausing. Confusion showed before she looked up. "You said this is fresh, right?"

Martha nodded. Karina sent Maxwell a questioning look. Maxwell pulled up his bowl. He took a bite and stopped. "Strange…"

"I thought so. It's the same as the BLT from yesterday."

Lex scrutinized the duo. What were these two talking about? He took a bite of salad. While it was a bit old, it was considerably fresh by most standards.

Karina waved her hand, as if to dispel their confusion. "Sorry.

Must have just been the bite, it's fine. Thank you."

She continued eating and it was only the slight twitch of her fingers that showed her opinion on the fresh greens. Maxwell was a little better, but even he had a subtle confused frown on his face.

Martha gazed at them uncertainly while Agatha looked between them like it was a match.

Lex took another bite. He paused as he stared down at the food. He felt a little sick already. The food wasn't settling well. Not only that, but what they said about their mother. He might be able to help, but if he put it off till tomorrow... He put the fork down and stood up, to everyone's surprise. "Thank you for the food, but I'm not hungry anymore. Why don't you let someone else have it?"

He went to leave when he felt Martha's glare. She always was like a mother to him in such situations. At least, he thought that's what being a mother should be like. He didn't want to bother her and she still had to take care of the two kids. He paused and sighed. "I will come back, don't worry."

"Can't you finish that meal at least? I know…"

Lex looked over his shoulder. "I have something I need to take care of while I can."

He peered at the twins. Maxwell's mouth was full and Karina's hand was suspended in the air, a fork with food on it paused halfway between. Both seemed confused at his sudden change. Not that he was surprised, it was rather sudden, but he felt he needed to do it. They trusted him up to this point, so he would help them with everything he could. Plus, he was rather interested in these two. He walked purposefully out the door, leaving the warmth of a family behind.

"That boy, he just doesn't know when to slow down. Now eat up, he should be back in a little while."

Lex shook his head in bemusement as he closed the door and walked away.

Lex walked down the lane, unable to get his mind off of Maxwell and Karina. Their faces were sad, but determined, a rare thing to see in the past few years. He scrutinized the area before he dodged into the shadows. He slipped between buildings with practiced ease. After a while, he was once again even with his temporary home. Around the place were men. Antonio must have called for them. Their expressions were bored and their arms were crossed. He examined them quietly before he moved away. Lex took a few turns, reaching the area where he noticed his charges. The factory was on his right and the beggars, druggies and kidnappers were on his left.

He stared at them before he walked away. He shimmied past some more buildings until he reached where he had been only a few hours earlier. He gazed at the glass and brick building before he leaned back against the brick wall, hidden well within the shadows. He waited patiently, watching the glass doors as time ticked slowly by.

~ * ~

Maxwell patted his stomach in contentment. "Thank you for the food, Mrs…" Maxwell paused and glanced at the older woman with slight confusion.

Martha chuckled as she picked up his plate. "Call me Martha. I don't think I ever caught your names. What are they?"

"My name's Maxwell and this is Karina," he stated as he gestured toward Karina, who just wiped her mouth with a napkin.

"Those are nice names," Martha spoke as she put the plates down near the kitchen sink. Agatha helped her as she carried her own and Lex's to the kitchen.

"Thank you." Maxwell paused, unsure how to continue. After some thought he spoke. "I have a question though…"

Martha glanced over. Her head tilted to one side as she waited for him to continue.

"Why were you so willing to take us in? Also, why is Lex called uncle…? Is he really…?"

Martha chuckled before turning back to the sink. "No, he's not really Agatha's uncle, she just grew up calling him that. He's been here for about a year and a half and he's already been a great help to this community…" she said softly. "A year and a half ago, Antonio was getting out of hand. He would send thugs to barge into people's houses and take anything of value, even if they didn't owe him. Sometimes he would take the children, and later have the residents ransom them back…" She stopped and gripped the plate she was washing tightly. "Lex was like a miracle. Antonio was on one of his sprees. They were just coming to our street and were almost about to take Agatha when Lex comes walking down the road with a backpack on one shoulder, smoking a cigarette."

He smokes? Maxwell blinked as he thought back to the times he had seen Lex. He couldn't remember any signs of him smoking or even burn marks that might have shown he smoked in the past.

Martha chuckled at his confused face. "He only does that occasionally. He lucked out and is one of the few who doesn't get addicted to nicotine. To think, that would be the thing he lucks out on. Anyway, like I said, he came and the next thing I know, Antonio's men are running with their tails between their legs and Agatha is safe."

She paused. It was in that moment that Maxwell recognized a sort of fondness, her eyes softening at the memory. "I thanked him once. He only nodded and walked away. A few months later, Antonio's attacks stopped all together. It turned out he seemed to be focusing on Lex. We're not sure why. However, all the neighborhoods are grateful to him and so are willing to help him if he were to ever go against Antonio," she finished as she squinted out the window. "That's also part of the reason why I am willing to let you stay here. If Lex trusts you, then I have no reason not to."

Maxwell looked down in thought before he murmured a quiet, but sincere, "Thanks. I—we appreciate it. Still, why would she be taken?" Maxwell peered toward Agatha.

"Ransom, really. That's what usually happens around here." Martha looked toward Agatha as well.

"Why did he want us? We don't have any money on us, or anybody…" Maxwell trailed off as Martha's expression darkened.

"I think you should talk with Lex about that."

Maxwell and Karina peered at each other warily before Maxwell slowly nodded.

"He seems so stoic, though. I never would have thought." Karina interjected as she placed her arms on the table, leaning forward a little.

Martha looked between them and chuckled. She sat down with Agatha on her right. "Anyway, enough about that, how about a game?"

Maxwell and Karina grinned. "I—we would like that."

~ * ~

Lex shifted slightly before he stilled. He watched the door, tempted to just turn around and leave. His debate ended when the door was thrust open.

"What? You can't find those stupid brats? Are you looking everywhere? They couldn't have gotten that far." Antonio stopped in front of the doorway, a cell phone sat next to his ear. It was an older model, the traditional pre-paid flip phone Lex saw around the city and in most stores. "Search wherever you can. Got it? I want those kids found and brought here now!" Antonio slammed the phone shut. "Completely useless," he mumbled as he tightened his fist on the phone. He paused before his eyes flickered to Lex's spot. "That's daring to come back here so soon," he said coldly.

Lex's response was to step out of the shadows. He pushed a hand through his hair as he drew close to Antonio.

"I see you still do that. I'm surprised you haven't pulled out all your hair yet," Antonio observed, eyes narrowed even more so in annoyance

Lex scoffed in amusement. "I don't think I need to worry about that, of all things." He paused in thought as he dropped his hand to the side, leaning on one foot. "By the way? Those kids? I wouldn't bother, I already got them somewhere out of your jurisdiction. Plus, those kids aren't worth much at all. I don't see why you would need to put all this effort into finding two kids… That is, unless you're close." He paused as he noticed Antonio's grip on his phone tighten, he almost thought he heard a crack.

"That's none of your business."

"Really? If I recall, the other day, you came to me. How about a deal?"

Antonio paused before he released his grip slightly. "What deal?"

"It's simple. I know you have some connections, and I could get you the rest of what you need for your younger si…"

"Fine," Antonio cut Lex off. "What are you looking for?"

"I need to find a woman."

Antonio raised an arched eyebrow before he snorted. "That's rare. So, what's she like?"

Lex stared Antonio strictly in the eyes. "A missing mother."

Antonio paused; his face neutral as his eyes flashed through a set of emotions. "I'll see what I can do. Give me as much information on her as you can, along with the money you promised. In turn, I'll try to find something. However…"

At that, he stopped and turned away from Lex. "This is the last time I'll let you hang that over me. I won't let you use her again. It's my business, and unless you're giving me the goods, then stay out of it." He walked away, back into the apartment as Lex watched.

Lex let out a long-resigned breath and looked down before he muttered a soft, "I know that, Antonio. Believe me. I never meant to…"

~ * ~

Agatha screeched in laughter as Karina tickled her. Maxwell sat on the couch as he talked with Martha, feeling his stomach trying to settle and deal with the food. He hoped he would get used to it soon. Having a stomachache every time he ate did not help his appetite.

"So, what are you planning to do?" Martha asked.

Maxwell's eyes flitted to the duo rolling around on the floor before he responded. "We don't know. We want to look for Ma, but we don't even know where to start. All we've been doing is running for the past few days. We haven't had time to fully sit down, relax and think about it," he said as he faced Martha.

Martha nodded as she looked toward the ceiling. "Well, can you tell me about your mother? What's her name, what's she like? I want to hear a little about her, as a fellow mother as well."

Maxwell scrutinized her before he looked down. "Her name

was…" Maxwell cringed, "is Veronica Elifer. She's strong and, from most people's opinion, quite beautiful. Everyone in our town loved her and she would often take care of them during her free time. She was the only doctor and scientist in the town. So, she was always busy. She would sometimes talk about it. She mentioned that she worked with Enthrope… or something like that."

Martha jerked slightly before leaning forward once more. If Maxwell hadn't been watching her, he would have missed it entirely. Strange, did she know something about Mom's company? He shrugged it off. The reaction was probably just his imagination. "She would often leave for trips and stuff because of that, only to come back with little stories about things like the sea and adventures she went on. We would always demand she tell us about them…" Maxwell paused, unsure how to continue.

Suddenly, he jerked upward with a jolt before grabbing his backpack which he dropped on the floor after having used the bathroom earlier. Maxwell practically ripped open the backpack. He rummaged inside before his fingers touched slightly warmed glass. He pulled the thing out to look over it, glad that it hadn't been ruined in the storms. Thanking Karina for remembering the plastic bags that protected his more sensitive items, he handed it over to Martha. "I almost forgot I grabbed this. Here's a picture," he said as Martha took the picture carefully.

Karina stood up. She brought Agatha with her to look at the photo as well.

"Beautiful," Agatha chirruped as she peeked at the picture.

Martha scanned Maxwell's and Karina's faces before she went back to observing the picture. She sat in silence, then said, "She looks and sounds like a wonderful mother. I really hope you can find her soon. By the way, is this your father? Where is he?"

Maxwell stared at the picture, "He's gone." He shook his head, pulling himself from his thoughts. He noted Martha's expression and continued, "I, we hope so too." He gingerly took the picture back. Martha nodded and Maxwell was glad she let it go.

Maxwell shifted his gaze upward as Martha spoke. "Do you mind if I keep it for a little while? I'll give it back to you in the morning, all right?"

Maxwell looked into Martha's eyes warily. "Why? I could be wrong, but you wouldn't need it…and well…" He trailed off as he pursed his lips.

"I just want to see it for a while," Martha said gently. "If anything, we can use this as a clue to find your mother. Don't worry. I will make sure you get it back."

Maxwell bit his lip in thought before he peered toward Karina who, after a short pause, slowly nodded. "All right, but…"

"I know you're worried, it's understandable. I'll make sure nothing happens to it, all right?" she said warmly as she gestured for the picture.

Maxwell hesitated before he relinquished his hold on the picture once more.

Martha took it carefully before her eyes flickered to the window. "Well, it looks like it's dark out. Why don't you get some rest?"

"I guess," Maxwell muttered politely.

"Great. Having someone around in the morning would be nice. Agatha can be quite a handful sometimes, so it would be good to have other younger ones around."

Karina nodded. Martha chuckled. "Now if only I could get that boy to actually join us for a night instead of staying in that run-down building, he calls home."

"Boy? Do you mean Lex?" Karina asked as she picked up Agatha.

Agatha lay on her side, curled up with a thumb in her mouth against Karina's chest.

Martha walked forward and took Agatha from her before answering, "Exactly. I always call him boy, because that is what he still is. He might seem uptight and old-fashioned and even a little domineering."

A little? Maxwell thought, remembering the lectures.

Martha just continued, amusement on her face. "He is actually quite young. I think he said he was nineteen last time I brought it up."

Both teens froze as their jaws dropped in surprise. "What?"

Martha blinked before she lightly chuckled. "Yep, ignoring all the stuff on top, he's only a normal nineteen-year-old boy."

Karina massaged her temples as Maxwell put a hand to his face.

"I thought he was at least twenty-six," Karina said.

Martha laughed heartily before she quieted down. "I think that's enough surprises for tonight. Why don't you two get to bed? You can have the second room on the right, all right?"

"Uh… Thank you," Maxwell said as Karina nodded gratefully toward Martha.

Martha walked upstairs. She passed the first room, and gestured to the one on the right.

"Go on in. I have to put Agatha to bed. Make yourselves at home."

They opened the door as Martha went on her way. "I call the bed," Karina shouted before she ran and plopped onto the twin-sized bed on one side of the room. Maxwell groaned before he stepped into the room and dumped his backpack on the floor. Karina, after she sat back up, did the same.

Maxwell took a look around the room. It wasn't a bad room, just a little small and old. There was one bed, a cushioned and rather comfy-looking chair and a side table.

Maxwell grudgingly sat in the chair as Karina kicked her hiking boots off. She placed them next to the bed before she let her legs swing back and forth over the edge. She gripped the sheets tightly as her eyes flickered to Maxwell.

"So, why did you tell her so much about Mom?" Karina asked lowly as her legs stopped swinging.

Maxwell regarded her thoughtfully. "I don't know. I just wanted to talk about Ma for a bit."

Karina looked to the side and watched as the sun disappeared over the horizon of the city. "Mom said…"

"I know, but we don't know where we are. What are we supposed to do? We can't avoid trusting someone. What would have happened if we hadn't trusted Lex? Or…" Maxwell paused before he shifted in the seat, sitting up.

He saw Karina watching the dipping sun, her raven locks curved around her face making her eyes look even sadder. "For now, we'll just take our time. True, we shouldn't trust everyone. At the same time, if we trust no one, then we'll never find Ma. I don't think that's what she wanted to say in the note anyway."

Maxwell watched as Karina remained lost in thought. He looked out the window, not really seeing it. His mind drifted to dinner, more specifically the prayer. It wasn't that it was similar or different than what he was used to. It was more that it was said with the same fervor and emotion as their ma would say it. He couldn't quite point at one specific thing or another that drew him to that conclusion but it felt right. There was something behind the words that he couldn't understand.

His thoughts were interrupted when the door opened and Martha walked in. Behind her was a fold-up bed. "Sorry, we only have the one room available. Hope you don't mind," she asked.

"That's fine," Karina chirruped as Maxwell helped Martha unfold the cot and place it on the opposite side of the room. She set it up, whispered a quiet goodnight and left.

Maxwell flopped onto the bed, deciding to think of something else. He heard the springs groan at the sudden weight. "I missed having a bed. I would have loved having my own room, but I'm definitely not going to complain. It's really comfortable."

Karina nodded before she lay down. "I don't really care one way or the other." She yawned before she snuggled into the pillow. "I love nature and sleeping outdoors, don't get me wrong, but having an actual pillow feels great."

Maxwell couldn't argue with that logic, chuckling softly as he stared up at the ceiling. Moonlight glimmered on the white painted surface as wood creaked from movement in the hallway. He let his head snuggle into the pillow, relishing in the softness. His sore muscles were practically melting at the opportunity to lay down and on something that wasn't hard. His eyes drooped slightly before they closed into a deep sleep.

Chapter Nine

Lex hesitated before he knocked on the door. He waited, debating whether he really wanted to go in or not. The door swung open, ending the thought.

"You made it back." Lex glimpsed Martha's kind eyes before he nodded. "Well then, come on in. The kids are asleep. I let them have the guest room, so you'll have to take the couch. Hope you don't mind." She led him inside.

He just shook his head. "Thank you for the hospitality. Though I really…"

"None of that, it's late and I've told you more than once that you could stay with me. I just never expected you to bring two more along. They're such sweet kids though."

Lex sighed as he stepped through the doorway, just to stop. His hand flashed to his head as he stumbled forward. He wavered for a second before he collapsed onto the couch with a thud and groan.

He vaguely saw Martha jump before she grimaced. "It's bad tonight, isn't it?"

After a little while, Lex finally managed to nod. He let his body rest while he closed his eyes. "I managed to hold it at bay for a while, but…"

He felt terrible. He pushed it away before he slowly shifted to a more comfortable position on the couch, getting a sad understanding look from Martha. "And you? Are you having any…"

"It hasn't been too bad lately," Martha insisted.

Lex nodded before he slowly pushed himself back up. He groaned as he raked a hand shakily through his hair. "I just wish…" He stopped and sighed before he pulled his hand down and faced Martha. "Those kids shouldn't be in danger anymore, as long as they don't act stupid and leave this area," he said, changing the subject. "Though then again, they're probably going to do just that anyway, looking for their mother."

"I would too if I was in their shoes."

Lex regarded Martha as she sat herself down across from him. "I managed to ask them about their mom, along with obtaining a picture." Martha pushed the picture frame over to Lex as she continued, "She sounded like she really cared about them."

Lex eyed her gingerly before he took a peek at the picture. After another moment, he turned to face her. "What did you find out? Can you tell me what they told you?"

Martha sighed and reached forward. "I can tell you this once, but it would be best if you just talk with them from now on. I can tell you're interested in them and..." She paused before she forcibly looked Lex right in the eye. "It looks like you have finally decided what you want to do since the last time you were here."

Lex froze. He stared at Martha as she pulled away. "There are some leftovers from dinner in the fridge, you can heat that up and I'll get the blankets," she finished as she headed quietly upstairs.

"I don't know what she means..." Lex muttered in quiet annoyance.

His lips twitched downward before he got up and went to the fridge. After heating up and eating dinner, he meandered back into the living room. The pillows and blankets were all laid out for him.

On the opposite side, knitting a scarf, was Martha. "All done? Well, I guess I should tell you a little, but afterward, promise you'll get some sleep before you do anything reckless again."

"Fine, I promise," he responded evenly. He peered at Martha as she put down the knitting equipment.

"They didn't tell me much, but..."

~ * ~

The next morning, Karina woke to the smell of food and the soft sound of music slipping up the stairs and under the door. Her eyelashes fluttered open as her eyes adjusted to the morning light streaming through the window. She could blearily see Maxwell sitting up. His bangs drooped into his tired eyes. Karina curled tighter into the blanket, her eyes opening and closing as she forced herself awake. Maxwell yawned before he swung his legs out of bed. The bangs he just flipped out of the way fell into his face once more.

"Maxwell, would you just go back to sleep? You're being annoying," Karina murmured as she hugged the pillow.

Through half-lidded eyes, she saw Maxwell give her a half-hearted glare before he stood up. "Now you know how I feel almost every morning," he managed to mutter as he stretched. Karina sighed.

After she noticed he wasn't going back to sleep, she got out of bed herself.

"No, it's normal for me to be up first. Having my brother up before me is just weird," she managed to say around a yawn as she slid onto the floor.

Maxwell huffed, but ignored it as the smell of cooking intensified. He peered toward the doorway before he looked down at himself. He shrugged before he hurried out the door and down the stairs to the delicious smell.

After she cleaned up and put her hair back up in its traditional ponytail, she walked downstairs.

Maxwell was already sitting at the table, waiting for the food.

"Good morning, Karina," Martha said as Karina looked around, taking note of both the four places set on the table and the couch with pillows and sheets strewn everywhere.

"Good morning." Karina scooted forward and took the last empty seat next to Maxwell. Martha and Agatha were already sitting across from her, having just finished setting out the food when she came down.

In the background, a voice spoke about the weather, saying how it was supposed to be another beautiful day out.

Karina peeked at Maxwell, who seemed to be a bit more awake than a few minutes ago. She saw a radio playing on the kitchen counter.

"Did someone else stay here?" Maxwell asked as he finally

seemed to take note of the messed-up couch.

Maxwell can be a bit unobservant in the morning, Karina thought.

"Yes, Lex was here earlier, he already went out for the day."

"Oh…" Karina muttered before she looked at the food. Martha chuckled while Agatha cocked her head to the side.

"You tired?" Agatha asked, eyes flickering in confusion.

Both nodded with differing levels of enthusiasm.

"Did you sleep okay?" Martha asked.

"Yeah…fine," Maxwell muttered as he let out another yawn. "Sorry, been a while since we have had a full sleep like that, that's probably why we're not waking up as fast as usual," Maxwell said, cordially.

"I have to agree with Max. It's just been hectic lately and that was the first time we really got a chance to rest somewhere comfortable."

Martha nodded before she gestured once more to the food. On the table was a simple meal of toast with jam and a side of scrambled eggs to share. Karina paused and, steeling herself, dug in. She had to admit, she was grateful to have something she recognized after the disastrous breakfast from the day before and the rather disappointing salad from last night. They slowly began to wake up as the sun rose over the horizon, casting a beautiful red glow into the room from the kitchen window.

After they were done eating, they were wide awake.

"Once again, thanks for the food and the night's sleep, but we really should get to finding Ma," Maxwell said with a bow of his head.

Martha shook her head. Maxwell blinked in confusion while Karina leaned back, her eyes narrowed slightly as she waited for Martha to speak. "I need your help. Can you wait to leave until after?"

"Please?"

Karina twisted to see Agatha. She was looking at both with wide pleading eyes as her hands clasped in front of her chest.

Karina stared at the girl before she let out a long breath and spoke. "Since you let us stay here, I guess I don't mind."

Maxwell watched as Agatha cheered in delight. After a moment, he turned back to Martha. "I guess it's decided, we'll help and, I guess, stay here."

Martha nodded in thanks before she got up. "I have to go to work so you can watch Agatha. Please also make sure to clean up Lex's mess as well if you get the chance," she said as she scrutinized the pile of blankets thrown haphazardly over the couch.

Maxwell nodded before he frowned. "What about the picture? You said you would give it back this morning."

Karina jerked her head up as Martha hesitated. "Lex has it, he is…he will return it to you later, but I really have to go. I'm already going to be late. But, thank you for helping. Oh, and for lunch, there is stuff in the fridge for making sandwiches."

With that, she grabbed a black purse and ran out the door. They watched her leave, Karina feeling a bit miffed, before they turned to Agatha.

"Mommy usually takes me with her because she has trouble finding someone to stay with me, but I don't really like it there. It's no fun."

"Where is there?" Maxwell asked as he crouched next to Agatha.

He seemed fine with staying, probably since it was Lex and he seemed to be helping them a lot. Karina pursed her lips. Hopefully, her brother was making the right choice. Oh, she trusted him, but at the same time, she didn't trust anyone who might want to hurt him. With the way things were, she had no idea who that might be. Maybe it was just paranoia, but she cared deeply and did not want to see him hurt just because he trusted the wrong person.

Like I almost did, she thought a bit morbidly.

"A big place," Agatha said. Karina drew herself back into the conversation as Agatha spread her hands wide to either side of her.

"Oh, well then, while she's gone, what do you want to do?" Karina asked, focusing on a lighter topic as Maxwell shrugged.

"How about house?"

Maxwell moved away slowly, probably remembering when they played that as children. Karina withheld a grimace. "Are you sure you don't want to play something else?"

Agatha shook her head quickly before she pouted.

"How about hide and seek?" Maxwell asked carefully.

"Or even just…" Karina trailed off as she peered at Maxwell for advice.

"I want to play house. Mommy plays it with me all the time."

"Hey, Agatha, how about a game of tag?"

Agatha stopped and looked down sadly. "I can't. Mommy doesn't want me to…"

They regarded each other, before Maxwell kneeled down next to Agatha. Karina sat on the floor and crossed her legs while Agatha sat between them. Agatha twiddled her fingers as she peeked up at them. "Why won't your mom let you play tag?"

"She doesn't want anything to happen to the house and I can't go outside, she doesn't allow me to…" Karina raised an eyebrow while Maxwell frowned.

"Hey, Agatha are there any other games you know?" Maxwell asked as he looked Agatha in the eye, changing the subject in the process.

Agatha paused before she frowned. She put a hand to her chin, as if debating. "Um… I guess we could try hide and seek," she mumbled.

"Okay, we stay inside, we can hide anywhere in the house, but that's it, okay?" Maxwell asked before he received a nod from the beaming little girl.

~ * ~

When Lex finally came back, later in the evening, Maxwell was seated on the couch while Agatha was running around, calling out Karina's name.

Maxwell peered up from his place on the couch. He sat up. "What were you doing?" Max asked carefully as he peeked over toward the young girl who was in the kitchen, checking the cupboards.

"Looking for information about your mother."

Maxwell snapped his head around. He sat up straighter as hope seared through his veins. "Really? And?"

Lex shrugged before he sat on the couch opposite of Maxwell. "The person I asked said it would take some time to find out anything. We'll have to wait and see before we can get anywhere. Hope you don't mind waiting."

Maxwell slumped downward. "No, that's fine. Thanks for looking." He paused as a thought slipped into his mind. "By the way, do you happen to have the picture?"

"Picture? Oh, yes, here." Lex dug into his backpack, draped carelessly over his shoulder.

Maxwell took the picture. His eyes narrowed as he pulled it to his chest. "Martha told me you had it, but why? Just to get some information?"

"That's about it. No one else touched it."

Maxwell looked at Lex before he slowly relaxed. His fingers loosened on the frame as he placed it into his lap. He felt Lex's eyes on him before Lex looked away. Maxwell raised his head as he stared at the wood paneling of the wall in silence. Lex peered back at him. "So, you mind telling me where you're from and what exactly happened to make you leave?"

Maxwell looked at him, then toward the still searching girl. He chuckled at the failed attempts, knowing for a fact where his twin was. The clattering of kitchenware and the sound of small running footsteps were the only things heard within the home. "We're from a town in the middle of the forest near here, at least I think so. We walked for a long time. Either way, it was called Claremore. The place is rather small with only about three thousand people."

Lex's eyes widened for a second before he leaned forward, his posture screaming his interest.

Maxwell just let himself speak. He was kind of glad he could talk to someone besides his sister, even if he only knew Lex for a day or so. "A few days ago, we went out to explore in the forest. It began to look like it was going to rain, so we came back. The streets were completely empty, not a soul in sight. When we got home, we found the house trashed and a letter from our mother saying to not look for her, run and don't trust, she never got to finish that sentence, so…" He paused and thought back to the moment before he continued. "We decided to pack up and leave. It was a good thing too because while we were downstairs, we noticed some policemen in black..." He paused once more. His gaze shifted to the side as the memory flooded his mind. He pushed it away forcefully. "They were the same ones who took Dad from us."

"Wait." Maxwell stopped to look at Lex who stared at him with confusion. "You said your mother was missing, and now you're telling me something happened to your father? What is going on?"

"We...don't know," Maxwell stated truthfully, as he tilted his head back enough to see Agatha with a disgruntled look on her face. "We just know that our father left with these policemen in black four years ago and never came back." Maxwell watched as Agatha ran up the stairs, calling Karina's name. He let his head fall back to see Lex lean away from him as he massaged his temples.

"Well, this is getting weird," Lex said quietly before he brought his voice back up to say, "Continue."

Maxwell nodded before he spoke. "As I just said, four years ago, our father was taken by them and never returned. So, not wanting to deal with them, we ran. For the next few days, we traveled through the forest, stopping once to get through this old metal fence before continuing. Once we got here, we ended up in that rich town across the river. They called us city dwellers and dropped us off here. Not knowing what to do, we wandered around until we met you," He stopped before he looked at Lex.

"I thought my parental situation was a nightmare," Lex mumbled.

Maxwell frowned in confusion. "By the way, Lex, what was Antonio talking about? I heard he used to kidnap the children around here for ransom, but what would he have done if we decided to go with him? We don't exactly have someone to ransom us out."

Fleeting disgust shone on Lex's face before he schooled it and spoke, voice level. "Not the best thing to talk about here, but..." He peered past Maxwell's shoulder for a moment, as if clearing his thoughts before he continued, "Now, this is conjecture, but Antonio's slipped a few times. As you well know, he's been a hassle around here with money and theft."

Maxwell nodded.

"I've...already taken in three others before you. All of them decided to go with Antonio. From there, he would treat them well enough at first before one day, they just disappeared. One time, I happened to be around." Lex hesitated, expression dark. "In search for money, Antonio took the children and, because they were still clean, sold them to the black market."

Black market? Maxwell thought worriedly.

Lex sighed, probably noting his expression. "He sold them into slavery."

Maxwell suddenly felt sick. A hand went to his mouth as he shivered. He remembered the horror stories. Black servitude before the Civil War. The cruelty in foreign countries. People seen as nothing more than objects. He read about them, but always thought they were something of the past. How could something so horrific be happening now so close to home? "We were so close to…" His breath shuddered at the thought. He and his sister almost ended up…

His mind flew a mile a minute. "But why? What does clean have to do with it? Why would they even want us?"

He saw Lex wince. He looked away, obviously thinking of something before turning back to Maxwell. "I'll explain later. Your sister might want to learn as well, so why don't we leave this till another time?"

Maxwell hesitated. Why couldn't he learn now? Maybe he didn't want to know.

Agatha streaked past and pounced on Maxwell. Maxwell fell over with a yelp. He barely managed to keep himself from falling off the couch as one hand grabbed the couch back. His other fingers tightened around the picture frame as his heart raced.

"I found her. I finally found Kari!"

Maxwell grimaced and tried to straighten himself as Karina walked in. She peered over the couch at Maxwell's uncoordinated position and chuckled, only to stop. She leaned forward as Maxwell righted himself. "Max?" she asked, voice apprehensive.

She must have noticed. Stupid twin recognition. He really didn't want to worry her.

Maxwell scowled at his sister before he looked down at Agatha. "That's great, you know, Lex is here. Why don't you play with him for a while?"

Lex frowned at Maxwell as Agatha turned her big eyes on Lex.

"Uncle Lex. You're back!"

Agatha beamed before she went over and hugged him. Lex's expression crinkled into one of consternation as he hugged Agatha awkwardly.

"I'm starting to see how he might be nineteen," Karina murmured as she leaned over the couch. "Now, Maxwell, what's wrong?"

Maxwell jumped, having just finally gotten back into a sitting position. He looked back at the two. "Sorta," he replied as Agatha pulled on Lex's arm. He hesitated. "I…Lex was just telling me what would have happened if we went with Antonio."

Karina leaned forward, laying her head on her crossed arms. "And?"

Maxwell hesitated for a split second before he spoke. "He said that if we went with Antonio…"

He peered at Lex and Agatha. Agatha was obviously distracting Lex, pulling him around. Maxwell shuddered as he continued. "We would have been sold into slavery."

Color drained from Karina's face. "Are you sure?"

"I…" Maxwell paused. Was he sure? Why would Lex lie about that? If anything, he would say something that wasn't as bad, and Martha did say Agatha was almost taken as well. Was it so hard to believe something like being sold was possible? "Yeah."

Karina gulped and her hands tightened into fists. "That just means we have to be more careful. Don't we?"

Maxwell nodded as he noticed Lex sigh. Lex looked like he wanted desperately to say no to Agatha before he finally conceded, much to Agatha's delight. The twins chuckled as the little girl told Lex to cover his eyes and start counting.

"Hm…want to annoy him? I've been waiting for some time to get back at him for the idiot comments." Karina smirked devilishly as she brought her head up and leaned precariously over the back of the couch.

Maxwell chuckled as he slowly stood up during the beginning count. "Music to my ears," he said.

They looked at Agatha, who was already running to hide. Maxwell felt a grin slide over his face, worried thoughts pushed away as he darted away with Karina at his heels.

Hopefully, his sister could push the fear away as well.

Chapter Ten

It was a couple hours later when the door opened to reveal a tired Martha. Maxwell tilted his head up from his sprawled position on the now cleaned-up couch. Karina was seated on the other end, arms draping over the side in a marvelous display of boredom. Agatha was on the floor and Lex was sitting in a chair, hat tipped down as if in sleep. "Looks like you had fun," she said as she closed the door. Lex snorted while Agatha giggled.

Martha walked forward. She dropped her purse on the table before she headed into the kitchen. "So, you guys are probably hungry. Why don't I make something and then we'll all just relax?"

Maxwell shrugged, uncaring and too tired and lazy to move.

She nodded before she started making something to eat. "Anything in particular you might like?"

Maxwell finally decided to pull himself up. He walked into the kitchen and peeked into the fridge. He pointed at an orange. "Can I have that? I wanted it earlier, but I wasn't sure if you would let me."

Martha blinked before she looked at where he pointed. "Sure, but don't you want more?"

"Not at the moment, not really. I'm just in the mood for that, if you don't mind," Max said.

Martha laughed. "It's rare to see a young boy like you liking something so healthy. Here you go, I originally bought it for Agatha, but it turns out she was allergic, so…" She reached in and pulled out the orange before she handed it to Maxwell.

Maxwell took it gratefully as Karina leaned in. One look at the orange was all it took for her to groan. "Ugh, not again. You know, he is freaking addicted to those things…"

"What, oranges?" Lex asked evenly as he subtly glowered at them, having joined everyone in the kitchen. He was probably still annoyed that they managed to evade him for quite some time while playing hide and seek. It was definitely fun to mess with him.

Karina rolled her eyes with a huff of agreement while Maxwell was already peeling off the hard outer skin to get to the juicy and delicate innards.

Lex blinked slowly before he shook his head. "I don't think I'll be able to understand you two," he muttered as Karina saluted proudly.

"I guess we're doing our duty well." She paused. "Would you mind making something spicy? Like curry or even just a side of jalapenos," she asked. Her eyes twinkled in hope at the prospect of the hot food.

Lex just sighed.

~ * ~

A few days later, Martha asked them a serious question. "I have to ask, do you two have anything besides what you are wearing?"

Maxwell looked up from layering jam on his toast. He hadn't really thought about it. "Er, not really. I mean, we grabbed a change of clothes and things, but we don't have much money and we didn't have time to grab much."

Martha sat down with Agatha yawning sleepily beside her. Lex was there as well, reading through an article. He looked over the page with a moment of curiosity before he brought it back up, once again reading. "If that is the case, I have a day free, what do you think of going shopping for some clothes and other things? That includes you, Lex."

Lex just huffed, but didn't comment.

Maxwell sat in thought as Karina leaned back in her chair, hand to her chin. "Sure," Maxwell said.

Karina agreed.

"Good, let me get some things organized, finish breakfast, then we will go out," Martha said. Maxwell nodded and continued to lather his toast before taking a bite.

Once done, the group from Lex, who did not look amused, to Agatha, who was jumping up and down in excitement—or trying to anyway, she kept stumbling occasionally—were on their way. Martha pulled on a coat and stepped out the door, followed by the rest. It had gotten chilly and a breeze was moving down the street. Maxwell huddled in his sweatshirt while Karina mumbled something about wishing she had worn her warmer set of clothes. Considering she was in her shorts, he wasn't too surprised.

They walked through the streets, passing pedestrians and vendors. On the way, they stepped into an area neither Karina nor Maxwell had visited before. It was an older street, filled with vendors set up similar to home. Maxwell noticed fruits and vegetables lined up on the stalls and people walking back and forth through the crowded street.

"Right, was there any food you wanted to get, since we were coming this way?" Martha asked. Maxwell looked around at the different stalls. An odd smell filled the air, and it took a moment for Maxwell to recognize it.

Rot.

He stepped up to one of the vendors and peered at the apples on sale. He spotted older ones and grimaced as he noticed some flies sitting in a corner. Was this normal? He peered to Karina who was standing in front of a corn shop. She seemed perturbed by what was on display. He walked over as stepped away from the stall. "The vegetables and fruit here…"

"So, you noticed too," Maxwell finished.

He looked over in time to see Martha examining some lettuce, carrots and leeks before buying them, Agatha by her side. Lex held a bag of grapes, munching them quietly off to one side.

"Of course." Karina gave him an exasperated look as she walked away from the seller. Maxwell followed. "I've noticed since we first arrived, with that BLT. I thought it was just the way it was prepared. It's not. This produce, it's old, spoiled. It's worrying. What's been happening around here?"

Maxwell shook his head, unable to answer her. What seemed

worse to him was the fact, to everyone else, the food here was fine. Maybe he was just spoiled, living in a community that was self-sufficient, but still. Something wasn't right. Maybe it was what was used to grow it? He wasn't sure. Hopefully, he was just being paranoid. Maybe it was just in this city. Not all cities were alike, after all, at least according to Ma. Though now that he thought about it, why did Ma not say anything? Maybe she didn't know?

No, she must have known. Though…she never left home after Father disappeared so, maybe this happened recently?

He was pulled from his thoughts when he bumped smack into Karina. He yelped and rubbed his nose as she glared back at him. "Jeez, pay attention next time." Maxwell rolled his eyes and stepped around her to see Martha finishing up. She thanked the seller, then turned to the twins. "Did you want anything?" They shook their heads and she subtly frowned.

Not wanting to upset their caretaker, Maxwell quickly looked around. Spotting another food stand, this one without as many flies, he pointed. To his relief, there were some oranges there that she let him buy. She seemed happier after and that was fine for Maxwell. Karina merely looked at him, her eyes saying her thanks.

After some time, they arrived at another street, holding a large and wide building. Martha stepped into the doorway, followed by the others. It was a mall. People milled about, walking in and out of doorways that led to different shops. Many were closed with shutters, but others were open with mannequins sitting in the windows, decked in clothes of all types. They moved through the mall, commenting on the styles and designs. Lex stayed silent, almost huddling into his vest, his bag of grapes already gone. Maxwell recalled there hadn't been many in the bag, so he wasn't too surprised.

He looked around the place, noting that a few seemed to be special stores. Maxwell wanted to cringe at some of the styles. Karina was beside him, looking like she wasn't too thrilled either.

He didn't like the idea of a one-piece suit or frilly shirts made for women and, if he was reading correctly, men as well. He laughed at the thought. He couldn't imagine his sister or himself wearing half, if any, of the stuff in those special stores. They finally found a store that wasn't so over-the-top and was cheap enough for all of them. After walking through the aisles of clothes, they each grabbed a few and tried them on.

Lex disappeared for a while.

Maxwell laughed at some of the outfits as the girls tried them on for fun. Karina tried on one of the one-pieces, giving a pose before bending over, hands on her stomach, laughing at how she looked. Maxwell tried on a couple suits, grabbing some sunglasses and walking out with a confident gait, getting laughter from Karina and chuckles from Martha. After a while, they found clothes they wanted. Karina bought a pair of cotton pajamas that were a thicker fabric with little snowflakes on them, courtesy of Agatha, as well as a sweater and socks. Maxwell got some cotton pajamas that were light blue except for some flame patterns, some socks and a pair of sweatpants. Agatha got a new hair tie. As they exited the store, bags in hand and chattering loudly, they met with Lex. He held a single bag, hanging delicately between his fingers.

"Are you all done?"

"Uncle Lex. Yep. It was fun!" Agatha nodded as she held up a hair tie. "See? Momma got me this."

Lex squatted down and looked at the hair tie. "It's nice, I'm glad. Take good care of it."

Agatha nodded, pulling the hair tie close. It was quite pretty. It held a fake blue flower attached to a silver-like pendant. Lex stood and looked toward Maxwell and Karina. "Looks like you're all set."

Maxwell nodded. He was ready to head back. Shopping was just tiring.

~ * ~

The days continued, one turning into the next before they even had time to realize. Karina woke up to the smell of breakfast and the radio softly playing a country tune. They ate before Martha headed to work. Lex always left early, saying he was finding out if there was any information about their mother. The duo asked if they could help, but every time, they were shot down and instead were told to take care of

Agatha. Grudgingly, they did, wanting desperately to search for their mother, but feeling indebted to both Lex and Martha who were taking care of them. Occasionally, Karina went out to ask around, promising not to go far. Maxwell decided to stick with Agatha, knowing uncomfortably that he would probably get lost. When Lex got home, both were usually crashed on the couch or in the kitchen. Every time, he carried a newspaper and he read through it before either sleeping or playing with them a little.

As the days progressed, they got more accustomed to the new lifestyle. Occasionally they managed to get Agatha outside to play tag and other games, convincing Martha they would take care of her. It was hard, though. Agatha seemed to need breaks quite often. It was worrying, but they had no idea why she was so tired all the time. They stayed in the neighborhood. News traveled fast about them staying with Lex and many people said hello whenever they were outside. It was an interesting turn of events for both of them, but it vaguely reminded them of home, even in the weird environment.

It was peaceful and both teens felt good, being able to relax after suddenly being ripped from their home. Relax in a sense that, while they weren't fearing for their lives as much, anxiety still gripped them with worry whenever they thought about their parents or what could happen to them if they weren't careful.

It was a little over two weeks later that life began to move once more.

Chapter Eleven

Maxwell yawned as he stretched his arms toward the ceiling. He blinked out the morning sun before he swung his legs over the side of the bed. He stood up and threw on his sweatshirt. He noticed Karina's bed was already empty, which didn't surprise him. He stepped downstairs to reach the main room as Martha finished setting the table. She said a pleasant good morning before she sat down herself.

Maxwell joined her. Agatha sat across from them. She bounced up and down in her seat with a wide grin on her face all through breakfast prayer. It was obvious she couldn't hold whatever she wanted to say in and, as soon as the prayer was done, spoke quickly. "Mommy said we can go to the park. She said that she would bring us there before going to work. Can you come? Please, please, please?" she asked as she looked at them pleadingly.

"I don't see how we can say no," Karina said, as she walked into the room. Maxwell jumped. He turned to her as she sat down next to Agatha, wondering where she came from. "All right."

Maxwell glared at his sister who gave him a sheepish look. He sighed. His sister took such a liking to Agatha, who probably reminded her of a little sister she never got. It was nice to see Karina being a bit more relaxed. She was reckless, but when it came to him, she was incredibly cautious. It was a wonder how she worked sometimes.

"Thank you," Martha said, her posture seemed sad as Maxwell examined her expression. "I just haven't had the time or energy to take her out, and since she's been getting weaker…" She paused. "She hasn't had a chance to really go to the park for more than a few minutes so… Please take care of her."

Maxwell exchanged looks with his sister. Weaker? So, she was sick, but with what? What's going on? Did this have to do with Lex's comment? He pushed the thought from his mind.

"We would love to," Maxwell and Karina said in unison.

"I've been missing trees and greenery for a while," Karina stated, obviously all too happy to see something that reminded her of home.

"Um, I have a question," Maxwell asked. "What do you mean by getting weaker? And… I've been meaning to ask, but does this have anything to do with the masks?"

Martha peered at them quietly, obviously debating on something. "I guess you can say that. Unfortunately, we can't get any masks so…" She shook her head. "It's not something to think about, she's sick, but you probably already realized. Still, I want you two to enjoy yourself today. If it makes you feel better, there's nothing we can do at the moment, we just have to wait it out."

Maxwell frowned as Martha's eyes seemed to dim. It was gone as quickly as it appeared, making him second guess whether he even saw it or not. Maybe it was just his imagination, but he noticed that Martha was limping lately and seeming much more tired. If that was the case, then they both must have been sick. It made sense, but what were they sick with? Was it something genetic or was there something else? Would it affect them? He exchanged looks with Karina who just shook her head. Yeah, he could think of this later, they weren't sick, so it was possible it wasn't too bad. *Or it is and you're just fooling yourself*, he thought. He pushed that thought away. Martha or Lex would tell them if it was really something terrible. "All right, I hope she feels better…" he trailed off, not sure what exactly to say. Plus, it still didn't really answer his questions. He also didn't really want to bother her. She helped them a lot already.

Martha just nodded before she stood. "Well then, why don't we finish up? We should get going soon."

Once everyone finished, they left. Martha led them through the streets with ease, heading first to the shopping district before taking a sharp right toward a part of town neither teen was in before. This area was a lot more serene than other places within the crowded city. In front of them was an open gate. Agatha's eyes widened as she gripped her mother's and Karina's hands tightly.

Martha let go. "You know the way home, right? You should be fairly safe as long as you take the same route home."

Karina nodded as Agatha quickly grabbed Maxwell's hand. Martha bent down in front of her daughter and ruffled her hair. "Have fun, sweetie, okay?"

"Okay. See you, Mommy."

Martha walked down the road. They watched her leave before they headed into the park.

Almost instantly, both teens noticed the difference. They breathed in. Maxwell let his expression drop to one of disappointment when, instead of the rich scent of earth and the soft flavor of fresh air, all they got was the smell of pollution with hints and teases of what they remembered. Weak beams of sunlight shone down on the trio and slithered through the trees as a small breeze tried to push away the lazy air.

Karina sighed before she brought Agatha forward. The little girl was gazing at the trees and quaint greenery with awe.

"It's so nice," she whispered as she watched a bird chirp in one of the trees before flying away into the sun.

"Yeah…" Maxwell said sadly before he joined his sister.

They continued on through the park, occasionally letting Agatha go to chase butterflies or the animals that scampered around.

They watched her in silence as they tried to soak in the wildlife. They noticed other kids playing in the trees and near a small pond a few yards away from where they stood. Maxwell blinked, and did a double take of the pond. Near the edge was a girl a little older than them. She had long brunette hair which fell in waves and she was wearing a sun hat over her head. One of the girl's hands was placidly swirling through the water. A peaceful countenance adorned her pale face. Maxwell gulped, feeling a light blush on his cheeks. She was really pretty.

He felt Karina's eyes and looked over just in time to see the cat-like grin. She nudged Maxwell and gave him a sidewise look. "You like her."

"No way…" Maxwell interrupted, mentally wondering how the heck Karina always seemed to do stuff like that. He looked up just in time to see Agatha hurry back to them.

She skipped along happily with a small flower in her hand. "Brother Max. Sister Kari, what are you doing?" she asked.

Karina suppressed a chuckle as Maxwell scrutinized the flower. Perfect. A distraction. He bent down to get a better look at it. When Agatha noticed what he was looking at, she extended it forward, holding the delicate stem proudly. "Isn't it pretty?" she stated.

Maxwell carefully took it. "Man, I didn't expect to see one of these in autumn…" He paused, and mumbled quietly to himself, "I think this was called narcissus pseudo narcissus?"

"Why don't you just use the regular name, daffodil?" Karina stated as she also squatted down. She rolled her eyes as Maxwell scowled.

Geez, he was just trying to think of something from home, that's all.

"I was going to…" he responded as he handed the yellow trumpet-like flower back to Agatha. "Take good care of it," he said. "It's symbolic of spring, so…"

"It often has the meaning of new life, or to toot your own horn as well."

Karina and Maxwell jumped and peered up to find the girl from earlier next to them. She looked closely at the flower.

"I thought that was what it was." She looked at Maxwell, who couldn't suppress the blush as warm brown eyes gazed at him. "I didn't think anyone else would know that name or know anything about what it means," she said before she looked once more at the flower and Agatha who was looking at her curiously. "Hello," she said. She squatted down in front of her, her hands on her knees.

Agatha blinked, then muttered a shy, "hello" in return.

She nodded warmly before she stood back up. She held one thin hand to her hat to keep it on as she turned to Maxwell. "Sorry to intrude, but I overheard you talking and I was just really happy to meet someone else who had some knowledge about flowers," she said as she bowed slightly.

Maxwell gulped. The girl was really pretty. The sun hat meshed well with her long brunette locks and chocolate brown eyes. Her skin was pale as snow and she was thin with nice curves.

"My name's Roxanne. What are yours?" she asked as she looked at them with wide eyes that seemed to be full of childish delight, even though she looked about three or four years older than both of them.

"Uh… Um…" Maxwell began, stuttering slightly while Karina rolled her eyes.

"Sorry about him, my name's Karina, the one blushing and stammering like an idiot is my brother Maxwell, and this is Agatha," she said teasingly as she put both hands on Agatha's shoulders.

Agatha held the flower tight to her chest while Maxwell growled lowly in annoyance.

"Oh, I have a brother too. He's older than me though," Roxanne said, her tone turning soft. "He's really sweet, but he has been busy lately, what with…" The girl stopped. "What other flowers do you know about? Where did you learn about them?" Her questions came one after another, surprising Maxwell and startling Agatha.

Roxanne seemed to realize what she was doing and stopped sheepishly. "Sorry, when I get excited, I find myself talking a lot more."

"It's fine," Maxwell finally managed to say, earning an appreciative grin from Roxanne.

"Why are you so interested in flowers?" Karina asked as she bemusedly looked between her and Maxwell.

Maxwell wasn't sure, but he could see her shifting closer to him, her posture a little tenser.

Roxanne's attention drifted toward the pond. "Because I always wanted to see them," she said as she observed them before she looked at the daffodil held carefully within Agatha's hands. "For as long as I can remember, I never had a chance to see them blooming. That's all in the past now, thanks to my brother. I'm able to see them myself instead of just reading about them in books," Roxanne said. "This was my first time ever coming to this park. My brother actually brought me. He needed to go somewhere and it took him forever to actually leave." She sighed. "It was nice to meet you two, as well as you, little Agatha." Roxanne spoke gently. "It's getting late, and my brother's probably really worried. I promised him I would meet him near the park entrance." Roxanne bowed slightly before she walked purposefully out of the park toward an older boy. Neither teen got a good look at him, except for a flash of dirty blond hair tied in a low ponytail and a worried look crossing rather sharp features.

"Roxanne…" Maxwell exhaled as the girl walked away, smiling sweetly.

"You're drooling. Oh, and Max?"

Max blinked and peered over toward Karina who looked at him with an exasperated look. "She's out of your league."

Maxwell glared, but decided to ignore the comment turning to check on Agatha instead. "Hey, why don't we head out? It is getting rather late," he said.

He got a nod from Agatha as she loosened her grip slightly on the flower's stem.

Right on cue, their stomachs started to growl. Agatha giggled at the sound while Maxwell pursed his lips to hide a blush. Karina laughed as she took a hold of the little girl's hand. They walked out of the park, Maxwell mumbling quietly behind her the whole way.

~ * ~

Lex walked slowly down the lane as he stared up at the afternoon sun. The late beams of sunlight glimmered weakly off buildings as cool air chilled heated skin. His hands were in his pockets as he scrutinized the surroundings with a mixture of emotions. He could see masks everywhere, along with the signs of sickness. A young man walked by, hiding a slight limp while an older woman had a coughing fit, only to panic and make it worse. The air was rather quiet, considering the nature of a city and the light breeze was sluggish.

Lex slid to a stop as familiar voices flitted to his ears. He scrutinized the street to see if he could find them.

"Who were those kids? I couldn't tell who they were," a male voice asked.

Lex's head turned in the direction of the voice as another voice, this time a girl's, responded, "Just some knowledgeable kids, they were really sweet. I kind of wish I could have talked to them longer."

"I would have let you if you asked, you know that."

"I know, wait…"

At that moment, Lex's eyes met chocolate brown.

"Lex."

Lex looked in suppressed shock toward the young woman standing before him, a mirroring expression on her own face. Next to her was an annoyed older brother.

"Roxanne, Antonio, I didn't expect to see you here," Lex said.

He quickly hid the surprise behind a neutral air as a hand raked through his bangs. He couldn't wait to get them cut. If only he actually had the money. He scoffed at the thought, pushing it away.

"Same," Antonio said evenly as he glared at Lex.

"Brother, stop it. You know he was the one who helped us. Can't you just get along?" Roxanne pleaded as she tugged at Antonio's arm.

Antonio scrutinized his sister before he let out a long groan. "Fine," he groused, getting a beaming grin from Roxanne and an amused eyebrow from Lex, who quickly hid it.

"I see you're doing better, I'm glad you're out of hospice," Lex said as he looked toward Roxanne.

"Yeah, thanks to you and your uncle."

Antonio scoffed. "Yeah, I guess we actually should thank you. For once, the government did something useful. Who knew your uncle was needed by them due to his business?"

Lex winced. "Neither he nor I like to think about that," Lex stated.

He noticed Roxanne's eyes linger on him. He ignored it.

He could well see the glare Antonio was sporting as he began to speak. "I'm just glad she didn't end up in one of those overcrowded hospitals where that damn new sickness is spreading around. There are enough problems already with her old one. Oh, and about that information."

Lex studied Antonio who had a mixture of emotions on his face before settling to one of slight confusion. "I finally got something. Who knew it was going to be such a hassle?" He shook his head before he threw a slip of paper at Lex. "That's the approximate address. My contacts were rather quiet for once, so I don't know how accurate the information is, and…" He paused before he glanced at Roxanne, only to look away. "Thanks."

Lex let a genuine smile cross his face. "Of course, I'm just glad it turned out well. If it wasn't for that chance encounter…"

"Yes, we get it." Antonio cut in sharply, getting a chastising, "Brother," from Roxanne.

Lex chuckled softly before he stuffed the note in his pocket. "I guess I have to say thank you as well. Those two are way too determined and naïve for their own good."

"I'm not arguing," Antonio said with a hint of amusement. "Dumb enough to get lost, yet surprisingly not as gullible as they appear."

Lex pursed his lips. "You should know about that."

Antonio's expression grew grave and he narrowed his eyes. "You know why I do it. I don't regret it and I won't."

"So, Lex, where are you heading? Do you want to join us for lunch?" Roxanne asked, her cheeks tinting a light pink in the process, yet her eyes showing her annoyance and intentional disruption.

Lex looked at her, then at her slowly angering, dangerous older brother. "If I want to keep my life, I think I'll have to decline. Your brother would probably try to fillet me alive."

"I know how to," Antonio whispered menacingly, quiet enough so that only Lex could hear.

Roxanne rolled her eyes in annoyance and pulled at her brother's arm. "Fine. Maybe one of these days, my brother will manage to actually cool off enough to let me go somewhere for more than a couple minutes."

"Not any time soon," he said firmly.

He got a small dirty look from Roxanne and a quirked smirk from Lex.

"Watch it, buster, I might have been in hospice for the past few years, but that doesn't mean I lost the ability to defend myself," she said sternly as she slapped the back of Antonio's head.

Lex had to hold back a laugh at the ridiculous sight of the 'Demon of Reinmark,' as many citizens liked to call him, getting swatted in the back of the head by a thin sickly girl almost six years his junior. It was definitely a sight one didn't see every day.

Roxanne faced Lex as Antonio rubbed the back of his head. "I guess we should get going. It was great seeing you. If you're leaving, promise me I'll get to see you again. Okay?" Roxanne tilted her head up slightly so that she was looking directly into Lex's eyes.

Lex paused and slowly nodded. "Sure."

"Then it's a promise. Don't you dare die before then," she demanded as she regarded Lex sternly.

"I can't really control that, but I'll try. Take care of yourself and your brother," Lex responded with a nonchalant gesture.

Death was inevitable in this day and age. It was really only a matter of time anyway.

Antonio growled, but stayed silent.

"I will. I know better than anyone how stubborn he is, I'll make sure he keeps his head on straight."

Lex tilted his head toward the sky. "Looks like I should be heading back."

He walked forward and stepped around the duo as both walked past.

"Don't you dare lose those kids, or else you'll regret it."

Lex glanced back as both continued walking forward. Roxanne was gazing around in glee while Antonio stared ahead. In the glass reflecting from the buildings, Lex could see his face set in an impassive expression, as if he had never spoken.

Lex watched them leave before he exhaled and responded with an exasperated, but sincere, "I know…"

~ * ~

Maxwell and Karina gazed around as they walked slowly down the street. Agatha joined in and watched as the sun's beams gleamed off of windows and large buildings. Agatha still held the daffodil tightly in one hand while holding onto Karina's with the other. Maxwell was following slightly behind as they headed for the shopping district. Maxwell watched as Agatha browsed around, taking everything in. Her eyes were wide with a childish innocence.

They continued down the lane as a light breeze ruffled hair and clothes alike. The sun shone as clouds darted through the sky at their own speeds. Pedestrians walked around and occasionally gave the trio odd fleeting looks, which the three ignored.

After a few turns, something caught Maxwell's eye. He froze in surprise. Maxwell noticed his sister's scrutiny, but ignored it as his eyes widened. "Kari…" His voice wavered as he noticed Karina turn to where he was looking. He could see her grip unconsciously tighten around Agatha's hand as her eyes narrowed to slits.

In front of them, looking around, was a police officer, all in black.

Both teens recognized the medallion on his chest, an eagle with words curved where the body would be. He wore a cap and he had a baton clasped to his hip.

"Come on," Karina whispered. Maxwell shook his head to snap out of his stupor, before he followed after his sister who turned left down the nearest alley. He scooped Agatha up in his arms as he took off after her.

"Brother Max, what are you doing?" Agatha asked as she held onto his neck as he ran. The petals of the daffodil tickled the back of his neck as Agatha gripped it tightly.

"We'll explain later," Maxwell said firmly as he tried to stay even with his sister.

They swerved around another corner. They raced down the street before they ran straight to the doorway of Martha's home and slammed it shut.

They panted, breathing heavily as Maxwell collapsed to the floor. Karina hurried up to him and took Agatha from his arms. Agatha observed them worriedly.

"Brother Max, Sister Kari?" she asked as she looked into the worried and slightly panicked face of his sister. "Are you okay?"

"Fine, sorry, why don't we get something to eat," Maxwell said after he finally got his breath back. He stood up and walked over toward the kitchen with Agatha right behind.

"What were they doing here?" Maxwell muttered out loud, as he began to rummage through the fridge to grab something to make.

The fridge was sparse and the cold air sent a chill down his spine. The sunlight wavered through the room, sometimes hidden by clouds moving swiftly through the sky. He peered up in time to see Karina shake her head. Her lips shifted downward in worry as she slid into the wooden kitchen chair. Maxwell heard a creak and groan from the chair.

"What I want to know is why they were in the city? Because of Mom? Then why haven't we heard anything?" Karina frowned as she crossed her arms over the table before her and leaned her head against them.

Maxwell lightly bit his lip before he sighed. "I haven't a clue. That's why we'll have to find Ma. She might know something since she did keep in contact with Dad through letters, at least, for a while."

Karina pressed her cheek into her arms. He saw her clench her fists tightly before she forced herself to relax. She stopped as Agatha lightly touched her leg. She peered down to see Agatha looking up at her, her blue eyes wide with worry.

"Sister Kari?" Karina lifted herself up enough to allow Agatha to crawl onto her lap.

"Sorry, Agatha, we were just surprised, that's all."

Maxwell stayed silent as he watched the two girls sit there. He pulled out some food he managed to find, right as the door opened.

All three glanced over to see Lex walking in through the doorway.

Lex looked between the three residents before he placed himself onto the chair right near where Karina and Agatha were sitting. There was a moment of silence before the older teen looked back up. His gray eyes met their waiting ones before a small smirk shifted onto his face.

"I think I found your mother."

Maxwell shot up from behind the fridge door. "You found Ma?" Maxwell inquired as he extracted himself from the fridge completely. He let the white door swing shut on slightly rusted hinges. Karina just stared, wide-eyed and anxious.

Lex sat up and raked a hand through his hair before he regarded them. "I said, I think. The person I was getting information from heard some rumors about a woman by that name and looks to being moved to New London city. That's about a hundred miles from here if you were to go south down the river."

Maxwell sighed in relief, and then paused in thought. "So how are we supposed to get there? We don't have a car and there's no way we can walk it. It would take days and by that point, Ma might already be gone," Maxwell murmured, feeling a hint of frustration.

"That's if the information is true. For all we know, it could be somebody else, a false lead."

"We?" Karina asked as her arms wrapped around Agatha.

Lex nodded before he leaned back against his seat. "You two don't know a thing about the world outside your home and the little you have seen of this city, correct?"

Maxwell nodded stiffly while Agatha regarded them with confusion.

Lex continued. "So, since I already seem to have involved myself with you two, I might as well continue. Also…" he paused as he looked at both of them with a critical eye, receiving a tilt of a head from Maxwell. "My conscience would never let me rest, nor would my friend, for that matter." He pursed his lips as his eyes flickered to the window.

"Friend?" Agatha asked.

Lex winced. "Don't worry about it. Anyway, we got the information, so we can set out at any time."

"Sooner rather than later," Maxwell said as he leaned against the counter. "I want to find Ma quickly and learn what's going on."

Karina nodded, as Agatha jumped from her lap to the floor.

Agatha regarded them, her eyes sad. "You're leaving?"

Maxwell looked away while Karina squatted down and pulled Agatha into a hug. "Yeah… Our mom's probably waiting, plus…" She stopped and pulled away.

"Those people, the ones you ran from, they are looking for you, aren't they?"

"Probably," Maxwell said in a hushed voice.

He could feel Lex's narrowed gaze, but ignored it to pay attention to Agatha.

"Who are you talking about?" Lex asked carefully as he walked to one of the chairs in the dining room.

Maxwell tilted his head up and watched as Lex leaned against the chair and crossed his arms over his chest. The chair creaked, but didn't move.

Karina glanced at him uncertainly. Maxwell stayed silent, debating. After some time, he said, "Remember I told you about when we left our home? Regarding the police? Both Karina and I saw them while we were coming back from the park. They didn't seem to recognize or see us though."

Lex stayed silent. He stared out the window with a small frown. He held a hand to his head, then let the same hand push through the dark locks. "You two just love to make things more difficult. I was going to have us go by train, but that might be out of the question, considering how well those are guarded. I'll talk to my uncle. He might be able to do something."

"You have an uncle so close by?" Karina blinked as surprise flitted across her face.

Lex lowered his eyelids into a deadpan look. "Yes, he was estranged from my parents a long time ago. I've been working with him in order to obtain some money and, other things. He's a business man and is always in the business district. A workaholic if I ever saw one," he said with a shake of his head.

"We would like to meet him as well. Can we come?"

Lex eyed them. He then looked toward Agatha who was giving him puppy dog eyes, also wanting to join. He sighed and raked a hand through his hair once more. "Fine, but don't blame me if something happens."

Maxwell mentally chuckled at the scene as he responded with a subtly amused, "We won't."

~ * ~

It didn't take long for everyone to decide a plan of action. Lex would organize everything and, the day before they were to leave, Maxwell, Karina and Agatha would get to meet his uncle. After, Maxwell, Karina and Lex would go their separate way from Martha and Agatha as they moved on to the next city. Martha was a little wary about letting Agatha go so far without her seeing the place first, but after Lex mentioned all three would be going, she was fine with it, glad her daughter would have a chance to see something new. She was pretty quiet in regards to their moving on to the next city. However, the encouraging expressions were enough to get the idea she was fine with them going. Once satisfied with the decision, Max and Karina went upstairs.

Maxwell fell back on the comfortable cot. His hood billowed up around his head as he spread his arms out on either side of him. He stared at the ceiling, his expression showcasing his swirling thoughts. "Do you think we'll really be able to finally see Ma?" he asked.

Karina chuckled softly. "I hope so. We can't know until we get there though, right?" She sat on the bed, swinging her legs back and forth. "If she's really there, then I can't wait either. I'm actually looking forward to doing some more exploring. This city is pretty cool, but I want to see more, I want to go beyond here."

She felt that familiar sense of adventure she always got when something new was occurring. She jumped out of bed, landing evenly on both feet. Oh, she was afraid, but that didn't stop her from wanting to see new things and experiences.

She walked toward the window, thoughts in turmoil as she stared at the setting sun slipping between the buildings. "Plus, I want to know what's going on, not just with Mom. Why did we not know about this place? Why do we keep getting such weird looks? What is with this city? And… What are they doing here?" She turned toward Maxwell who pursed his lips in contemplation.

"I want to know that too," Maxwell said as he slowly sat up.

He peered toward the setting sun before he stood. He walked over to the chair, laden with clothes, and grabbed a pair of pajamas. "Lex said he was meeting his uncle. I wonder if we'll really get a chance to meet him as well. I would like to thank him," Maxwell murmured as he headed toward the doorway.

Karina watched Maxwell before she looked back to the window. “Thank him for what? For helping Lex? Why? I know I should trust him. He’s done so much for us already, but…”

She reached a hand up, massaging between her eyes. Deciding not to think about it, she grabbed her own set of clothes. “I wonder how we’re going to get there though. Will his uncle really be able to help us?” she whispered under her breath as she changed. She slipped under the sheets and lay there for a while before she let herself slowly nod off into sleep.

Chapter Twelve

Karina groaned quietly and blinked. Her eyes were blurry at the edges. The room was dark, with the moon shining brightly through the curtains. She sighed and tried to go back to sleep, but now that she opened her eyes, she couldn't seem to get those tendrils of sleepiness she once had.

She let out another soft groan and slowly pushed herself up into a sitting position. The sheets pooled around her, slightly dropping off the side of the bed. She looked across the room to see Maxwell. He was sleeping quietly, curled up in the blankets and wrapping his arms around the pillow. She chuckled and pulled herself out of bed, the hem of her pajama pants just brushing the floor. She treaded softly over the boards and toward the doorway. Maybe a glass of water would help. She opened the door, wincing as it creaked, before slipping out and closing it once more.

She walked toward the bathroom, yawning, only to pause as her eyes were pulled to a soft light flickering at the bottom of the stairwell, along with the quiet hum of voices. Drink pushed to the back of her mind and curiosity taking its place, she meandered down stairs, stopping as the sound of Lex's and Martha's voices wafted up to her.

"…going?"

"Ah, you don't have to worry."

She heard a chuckle before Martha spoke. "You know I'm going to worry. You've become like a son to me in your time here, the least you could do is make sure to take care of yourself."

Lex stayed silent and Karina could hear footsteps before a shadow moved past the light and toward the door. "You know what a promise that is, but I will see what I can do. Now, if you can excuse me?"

Karina watched as the door opened to illuminate Lex. He looked tired, his dark hair fell around his face, casting it partially in shadow, but he seemed confident, assured. He nodded toward Martha before he stepped outside and closed the door.

There was a quiet huff before a long sigh and a shuffling of chairs.

Karina was about to move back upstairs when she heard the sound of movement once more. She stepped back just as Martha peered up the stairwell, her face visible in the dim lighting.

"Karina… You couldn't sleep, could you? I'm sorry if I woke you, why don't you come downstairs."

Karina tentatively walked the rest of the way down and into the kitchen, where there was a candle flickering softly in a holder. A book sat next to it, wide open. Karina stared at it, surprised to see that it was a Bible, and it was opened to the New Testament.

Martha gestured for her to take a seat before she walked to the fridge. After a few minutes of bustling around the kitchen, she came back with a warmed glass of milk. She set it down and took a seat next to the book.

Karina picked up the warm glass and gingerly took a sip. It actually wasn't too bad.

"Are you okay?"

Karina looked up to see Martha's face. She wore a questioning expression and her hands sat on the table, draped over each other. Karina looked down at the glass of milk, watching the white swirl gently as she rocked her hands back and forth. "Yeah. I don't know what to think. I feel like we haven't done a thing. Lex did all the work for us. What I don't understand is why? Why would he do so much for us? Go so far? It doesn't make sense. Not only that, but he's willing to go with us, even though he's lived here for, what? Over a year? I want to know why…" and can I really trust him? Karina decided not to say the last part as she continued to stare before taking a sip. She wasn't even sure why she was telling Martha. She hadn't even told her brother. Yet, Martha had been very kind to them and so had Lex. So why was it she could trust Martha, but had so much trouble trusting Lex? What made him so different?

She heard a quiet exhalation of breath before she felt a hand on her own. She looked up to see Martha give her a gentle look. "That is something I do not know. All I know is what he's done. He's been trying to atone for something. I don't know what, and I don't intend to pry. Just know that he's doing this because he wants to. He's a good man, which is very hard to find nowadays…" She trailed off. Karina stayed silent as Martha looked away, her hand gripping Karina's tightly.

Karina stared and paused as realization flitted through her mind. Martha, she looked so young, but so lonely. She thought of Agatha and felt her gut clench. "Martha… may I ask you something?"

"Hm?"

Karina's voice got caught in her throat as she caught Martha's gaze. After a moment she pushed on. "May I ask, what happened to Agatha's father?"

Martha stared at the flickering lights of the candle before she responded, "It's fine. It was a long time ago." Martha gazed out the window. "He was…he was fighting for his beliefs when he passed. Agatha was barely two at the time, so she can't remember." Martha shook her head. "That's in the past. Right now, I'm looking more toward the future. You two, you two are so strong."

Karina cocked her head in confusion, and Martha chuckled. "It's not often that two people as young as yourselves go out to search for a loved one. I really do admire you."

Karina felt a blush squirm onto her cheeks and she promptly pushed it back down. "Thank you. It means a lot to hear that."

Martha nodded before she stood. Karina watched as Martha rummaged around for a bit. "I know you aren't leaving for a while, but I wanted to give this to you before I forget." She reached into a drawer, letting out a soft 'ah-hah' before she pulled out what looked like an envelope. She handed it to Karina who took it, puzzled. She opened it and peered inside, only to jerk back in surprise.

"What? I can't. Why are you giving us so much?"

Martha chuckled at her reaction as Karina tentatively leaned forward once more and pulled out a wad of bills. The green sat delicately in her hand. She looked at them. They were all twenties. She tilted her head up to stare at Martha. "No way, I can't accep…"

"Think of it as payment," Martha stated as she sat back down. "Payment for taking care of Agatha for me all this time and to help take care of your brother as well as Lex. Goodness knows that boy gets into all sorts of trouble."

Karina closed her mouth, not knowing what to say. She wanted to argue, to hand it back, but Martha looked so insistent that she finally crumpled. "Thank you," she said softly as she carefully folded the bills and put them back into the envelope before pulling it closed.

Martha nodded and after they sat in silence with Karina sipping at her milk and thinking of what sat in her hands while Martha quietly read the book. The pages rustled as she flipped and the candle flickered and sputtered. Karina finished the milk, once more feeling sleepy. She let out a yawn, drawing Martha's attention.

"Why don't you head up to bed? You have a long week ahead of you."

Karina nodded before she stood. She walked toward the staircase before she stopped. Martha had her hands crossed in front of her face and she was leaning into her hands, her forehead supported by the bridge. In the flickering light, she looked so tired and lonely. Karina stayed silent. Martha looked toward Karina before she gently gestured with her head toward the stairwell.

Karina pursed her lips before she slowly walked up the stairs and back to her room. She settled into bed, clutching the envelope to her chest. She paused and looked over to her brother. He was curled on the bed, the sheets haphazard, as if thrown on last minute. She chuckled softly. "I see I wasn't the only one who couldn't sleep," she whispered, letting the words drift off as she yawned and slowly slid her eyes shut once more.

~ * ~

Open-mouthed and wide-eyed expressions decorated Karina's and Agatha's faces as they tilted their heads back and stared at the glass and steel monolith before them. Maxwell knew he definitely wore the same expression. Lex's uncle actually worked here? A set of steps led up to a set of sliding glass doors that were constantly opening and closing as men and women in fancy suits and ties ran in and out of the building, holding briefcases and, as they exited the building, throwing on the white masks the duo saw throughout the city.

"This is where your uncle works?" Maxwell asked incredulously, holding onto Agatha's hand as the little girl just let her wide blues eyes take in the scene. Lex nodded before he walked up the steps. He stumbled slightly on the last step, startling the trio. Maxwell went to comment, half-tempted to go up to the obviously disoriented boy, only for Lex to shake his head and walk through the doorway, unassisted.

"What was that?" Maxwell murmured, thoughts flickering back to the sickness Martha mentioned the other day. Agatha was surprisingly silent as she held their hands in a tight grip.

"I have no idea, but let's go, I don't want to be left out here," Karina said as she walked up the steps.

The inside was as grand as the outside with a pristine granite service counter. Potted plants twisted around the place to give it a nice splash of green and a black marble wall with water cascading over it in a thin stream finished the ensemble.

Maxwell, Karina and Agatha shivered. Agatha held the twins' arms closer to herself while Maxwell and Karina wrapped their free arms around their chests. The doors closed behind them as the frigid blast of air hit them.

"Cold," Maxwell gasped out while Lex just gave them an unsurprised look.

He turned forward and walked away. They rubbed their arms to get away from the chill. The air-conditioning must have been on high, though he also felt a bit of steam or moisture, maybe a spray? Maxwell wasn't sure, but decided to ignore it as they followed. Agatha shivered constantly as she held their hands in a death grip.

Lex walked to the counter and tapped a bell sitting right on top. The little chime rang through the room as a young woman with blonde hair tied up in a bun walked in from a door to the left of the desk.

"Oh, Lex, nice to see you again, didn't expect you back so early," the young woman stated as she moved behind the desk. "Seeing your uncle today?"

Lex nodded curtly.

"All right, I'll notify him that you're coming, he should be in his office at this time," she said before she gestured toward the right. "Oh, and who are these three?" she asked.

"Acquaintances," Lex said as the woman looked them over.

"Well, aren't they cute?"

Maxwell bristled for a second while Agatha beamed graciously.

"Thank you, miss," Agatha chirruped. She received a chuckle from the receptionist.

Karina sniggered while Maxwell felt a hint of annoyance.

"I'm not cute," Maxwell said under his breath.

He received a suppressed laugh from his sister as she overheard the exclamation. He glared, but stayed silent.

"Let's go," Lex stated as he hid his own smirk.

Maxwell huffed, but followed as the two girls walked forward. They peeked up ahead of where Lex was heading to see a set of doors with white lights flicking occasionally above them. On their right were the glass windows and on their left was what looked like a staircase.

They ran to catch up as Lex pushed one of the gold embossed buttons situated near the doors. There was a ding as a light flashed over the doorway, which opened to reveal a rather lavishly decorated interior. They stepped in along with Lex and gawked at the furnishings in awe.

They stumbled slightly as the elevator moved. "Whoa," Maxwell exclaimed as he scanned the area in wonder. "So cool. I've never been in one of these before. I've only ever read about them. It's really smooth."

Karina frowned, but didn't comment. Agatha's mouth was slightly ajar as she looked around, holding onto Maxwell's hand since Karina extracted hers as soon as they stepped into the elevator.

Lex just leaned against the wall with his eyes closed and his arms crossed lazily. A grimace flashed across his face as his hands twitched. After another minute, the elevator came to a stop and the doors opened to reveal a nice room.

Just like the first floor, it had a whole glass wall and potted plants decorating the sides. Unlike the downstairs, there were black leather couches, glass coffee tables and a used mahogany desk. Behind the desk was a man whose brown hair fell into his face as he furiously scribbled on a piece of paper before him. A pair of spectacles sat perched at the end of his nose.

Lex cleared his throat as he stepped out of the elevator. He pushed his hands deeper into his pockets as Maxwell, Karina and Agatha followed him in slight wonder.

The man continued to scribble and murmur under his breath as he unceasingly moved down the page. Lex sighed in exasperation as he raked a hand through his hair. "Uncle Hugh."

Hugh held up his free hand and quickly wrote down a few more things before he nodded and pushed the paper to one side. He peered up. "Well, if it isn't my favorite nephew. How are you?" Hugh said as he massaged his wrist.

"Fine," Lex murmured. He put a hand to his head for a second.

Hugh flashed a worried look toward Lex before he fully turned to them. Maxwell decided to ignore the exchange and observe Hugh instead.

Hugh had a large build with a kind and rounded face. Brown bangs curved around his face with the bulk of his hair gelled back elegantly. He was wearing a pinstriped suit and a bandage on his right cheek. Maxwell could just barely see the white of a mask, sitting in his breast pocket as he stood. Hugh pushed back a rather comfy-looking leather chair as he leaned forward. "It's nice to meet you. My name's Hugh Roberts. You two must be the ones my nephew was talking about the other day." Hugh walked around the desk, and headed to the couches. "Come on, take a seat."

The trio eyed each other before they walked over to one of the long black couches. Maxwell and Karina sat at the ends while Agatha wiggled up between them. Lex continued to stand.

"You must be little Agatha. I've heard about you as well. Looks like you're doing well," Hugh said.

He scrutinized Agatha who looked back at him nervously. After another moment, she nodded. "That's good," Hugh said, voice soft, before shifting his attention to Maxwell. "I heard you are in need of going to New London City. Is this true?"

Maxwell nodded. Hugh sighed and put a hand to the bridge of his nose and massaged it tiredly. He observed Lex before speaking, a hint of worry heard in his voice. "Recent reports indicate that it's gotten worse there since the last time you passed through. We're barely keeping it at bay here. I don't know what it's going to be like there…are you sure?"

Lex eyed his uncle. "I need to…for my friend."

Friend, who is this friend? What is worse? Maxwell stayed silent, annoyed at new questions that never received any answers.

Hugh winced. "There's no denying you when you bring him up." He paused. "Just be careful. You're all I have left."

He shook his head before he straightened into a firm posture. He faced the trio and looked them each in the eye with a practiced look.

"You two," he began, speaking with a more confident and authoritative air.

Maxwell moved his attention fully to Hugh as he continued, "I heard that you are having some problems with certain people. I happen to be sending a shipment of goods by truck to a place about a mile or two away from the city. It might take a bit longer, but it's much safer than going by train or bus, especially if people are looking for you," Hugh said. "I also normally don't allow this, but because my nephew is so determined to help you, I'll do what I can as well. The truck will be departing at one p.m. tomorrow. Make sure to be on time, no later, or it will leave without you."

"Wait…a truck? How is that going to work?" Karina asked, raising an eyebrow as she leaned back into the couch.

Hugh caught her eye before he responded, "You'll find out tomorrow."

Maxwell nodded as Karina puffed out her cheeks in annoyance. "Fine," she said under her breath.

He chuckled before he continued. "Take care of my nephew for me, will you? He can often get pretty reckless if he's determined about something." Hugh winked at them.

Maxwell grinned in return while Lex glared. Agatha looked

between them, then to Hugh who gave her a softer smile.

"Be careful. I don't have much influence in that city. I won't be able to help if something goes wrong."

Maxwell looked into Hugh's worried eyes. Lex sat up, but didn't say a word.

"Don't worry. We appreciate what you have done for us already. It's more than enough. Thank you," Maxwell said, drawing Hugh's attention.

He considered Maxwell for a moment. "You're welcome." He stood up and eyed his desk before he turned to the group. "Contact me if you need anything, Lex should know my number. You do still have that phone I gave you, correct?" Lex nodded. Hugh once more peered at his desk.

"Workaholic as ever," Lex stated, amusement ringing clear in his voice as Hugh grimaced.

"I just have a lot to do," Hugh said. He walked toward his seat once more.

"That's because you give yourself too much to do," Lex replied before he stepped to the elevator. "Take care of yourself, Uncle," he finished as the doors of the elevator opened with a ding.

"You too," Hugh said as they all walked into the elevator, which closed behind them with a clunk.

~ * ~

They traveled down in silence before reaching the ground floor. They walked out, right past the empty reception desk with a note near it saying, "out for lunch." They walked through the doorways into the warm noon sunlight. The sun gleamed brightly from the glass and steel buildings surrounding them as cars whizzed down the road. People meandered around. Masks sat on their faces as they moved in and out of buildings.

The group moved down the road and walked slowly as the sun's warmth seeped into them. Agatha began to swing her arms back and forth as Maxwell and Karina followed suit. Soft clouds floated through the clear city sky. A breeze whispered around the streets.

Lex led the way. He turned right and left as they moved through the seemingly endless roads of concrete. Karina browsed around, taking in the buildings and occasionally pointing out ones she found interesting or odd. Maxwell did the same. Agatha giggled in delight as she skipped between them.

"Want something to eat?" Lex asked as they turned down another street.

Karina eyed her brother before she nodded.

Agatha jumped in glee as she shouted a loud "Yep!"

A moment later, she stumbled and almost fell to the ground, if not for the twins' grasp. Maxwell and Karina yelped as they tightened their grip on the little girl. Agatha shivered as her eyelids blinked rapidly. After some time, she seemed to steady herself. A tired look crossed her face.

"You okay?" Karina asked as she squatted down next to her.

She knew the worry shown clear on her face. Agatha nodded as she rubbed her eyes with the hand Karina released.

"Yeah, just tripped," she mumbled before she grabbed Karina's hand once more.

This happened occasionally while they were playing. What was it that was causing it? It couldn't just be some sickness like Martha mentioned, could it? She felt Lex's gaze and discreetly peeked at him. His eyes closed as a small wince flashed over his features. A hand shot to his head before he quickly forced it back into his pocket. Karina narrowed her eyes before connecting with Maxwell, who wore a similar expression to her own.

After some convincing, the group was once again moving, with Agatha walking along happily. Her pace was a little less wild, but she still had a childish spring to her step. After a while of walking, they arrived at a restaurant in the shopping district. Karina's stomach growled in anticipation and hunger. She was glad she finally got accustomed to city food.

Agatha practically jumped up and down in place. Lex walked toward the doorway and opened it to the trio. Maxwell stepped forward with Karina and Agatha right behind.

They froze as a scream erupted from behind them.

It resonated around the street with its piercing wail. Karina whipped around as Agatha hid behind her leg. The pedestrians on the street reacted the same way. However, after the initial reaction, they did something that surprised Karina. Within seconds, a gap opened as people pushed and ran from the direction of the scream. Their hands were held to their masks tightly as panic flashed through their eyes. The road cleared almost instantly to reveal a woman who was backing away from another young woman.

Both had on masks.

The young woman was scratching at her throat, her nails tearing into the skin and her mask slipping from her mouth to the blood-stained neck. Her eyes were bulging as coughs racked her body.

"He…help…" the woman pleaded with a low gurgling sound as she walked forward toward the other woman, who backed away in fear.

Screams of panic filled the street as doors slammed shut and cars screeched to a halt. Karina was frozen. She had no idea how to respond or what to do. Even her brother looked to be in shock. Before they could even think of doing anything, a firm hand was placed on their shoulders. Karina glanced back as Maxwell continued to stare.

Lex was holding them tightly, an odd look in his eyes as he watched. "It's too late…" he said solemnly as the woman continued to beg. Blood began to drip from her mouth as wounds on her arms opened viciously.

Karina turned back with a sense of panic as she watched the stumbling, panicking and tearful woman. The woman dropped to the ground as her nails dug into her throat, leaving painful and ragged gashes. Her watery eyes caught both twins' gaze.

"Hel…p…" she whispered pleadingly, the words forming on her lips catching Karina's attention more than the sound, which was merely a gurgle.

Karina grabbed her brother's hand. Maxwell responded in kind, squeezing as if it was a lifeline. Karina watched as the woman rasped before collapsing sideways, lying still with her eyes wide open. The watery blue orbs, dull and lifeless.

Karina felt numb and, out of the corner of her eyes, she could see Maxwell stare in morbid shock as Agatha hid her face into her leg. The other woman had tears flowing down her cheeks as she collapsed onto her knees, still a bit away from the now-dead woman.

Lex pulled at them, causing them to stumble slightly in his grasp. Karina felt her mind wanting to shut down. Everything seemed faint except for the grip on her leg, the hand on her shoulder and the trembling hand in her grip. Sirens blared in the distance, crying out with their own deathly tune.

Chapter Thirteen

They arrived back at their temporary home.

Karina shivered while Maxwell just blinked slowly, as if trying to figure out what exactly happened. Lex closed the door with a sigh. He bent down and slowly extracted Agatha from Karina's leg. Tears ran down her face as she snuggled into Lex's embrace. Lex could understand. For such a young girl, something like that was terrifying. Actually, he observed the twins who seemed to still be trying to process what happened. That was something no one should have to see. He held Agatha close as he shuffled the twins to the couch. Once they were seated, hands still clasped and expressions ranging and flashing so quickly, he couldn't interpret them if he tried, he lightly placed Agatha on the other couch. With quick strides, he hurried into the kitchen and filled some glasses of water.

Lex came back and handed Maxwell and Karina the drinks.

"What was that?" Maxwell finally asked after he gratefully took the cup and took a sip. Lex closed his eyes and raked a hand through his hair while Agatha curled up next to him.

After a moment of silence, he spoke. "Have you ever heard of the word 'epidemic' before?"

They shook their heads.

Lex's lips twitched in bemusement before he continued. "An epidemic is a widespread and infectious disease. It is usually titled this way when the occurrence of a sickness, such as influenza or the measles, is spread throughout a wide area. About three years ago, the first cases of a new virus appeared within this country. It starts as a simple cold, which is kept at bay for a while with drugs like penicillin and over the counter items. After a while, it always manages to move to the next stage, which entails a high fever and random throbbing pains. After a while, that dulls before it moves to the third phase, a visible infection. You've seen it around probably everywhere. Common occurrences include pockmarks, swollen eyes and shallow cheeks, along with some of the open wounds and thin skin."

He stopped as contemplative looks crossed their faces. A moment later, Lex continued calmly. He wasn't keen on explaining this, but there was no point in hiding it. It's better to know what you're dealing with, after all. "That stage is the stage that can last from anywhere between a week to a year. Some never even move past that stage, though one or two have skipped that stage altogether. Throughout it, you have dizzy spells, infections and blood loss, as well as any numerous other problems..." Once more, he paused as they scrutinized Agatha and Lex.

Their eyes slowly widened in realization. As they continued to stay silent, he went on. "The worst is the fourth and final stage, which you saw today, unfortunately."

"What we saw earlier... Did she really die?" Maxwell half-asked with a tiny voice. He gripped his cup tightly, eyes not meeting Lex's.

Lex wasn't surprised. This was a lot to take in at once. He wondered how they would take it when they actually got to the worst part. Lex nodded. "The official name for the fourth stage is the death throes. Since the timeframes for the third stage are so sporadic, it is hard to tell when one will occur. It can change over with the twitch of a finger and can lead to widespread panic. No one knows if or when they might hit the fourth stage. In the fourth stage, your throat starts constricting as wounds reopen, the lungs slowly fill with fluid and bodily functions slowly begin to shut down. If you're lucky, you'll die quickly like that woman. However, there are some who last for hours within these death throes, practically trying to kill themselves the whole time."

Maxwell tightened his grip on the cup. His knuckles were stark white as his long bangs covered his eyes. Karina was eyeing the table, looking sick as her fingers trembled around the shaking cup. Lex watched quietly before he continued. "The government," at this, he felt his face screw up slightly in annoyance before he quickly smoothed it back into a neutral expression, "has called it an SS level phenomenon and has been searching for the last few years to find a cure. Or at least, that is what we are told," he said as he took a sip of water.

"If it's infectious, then why…?"

"Are there so many people still around and why aren't we doing anything? What can we do? Most people don't have the money to leave this place, those that do barely get as far as the next city before they're out of luck. Plus, there is no way to stop the epidemic, no cure has been found and only one or two things seem to stave it off for a little while. The hospitals are packed and only certain people are even getting a smidgen of attention. Even then, those treatments only work for so long, often shortening the third phase."

"Oh…"

Lex closed his eyes, and took a deep breath, calming himself. He opened his eyes to look directly at both distraught teens. "Most people have already hit the third stage. In hopes to stave off the final stage, many wear those white doctor's masks that you have seen throughout the city. That's also why they ran away from the woman earlier. Since no one knows what would trigger the final stage, there's always a panic when something like that happens. Only a few have managed to avoid the epidemic all together." At this, he once more felt his face contort into one of shame and disgust. He quickly pushed the thoughts away. "They are usually too separated from the people to actually obtain the sickness."

He stopped. Maxwell's face was thoughtful. Karina frowned as she dipped her head toward her drink.

"I didn't think, this wasn't anything like home, we didn't know…" Maxwell murmured under his breath.

Lex sighed and leaned forward enough so he didn't disturb Agatha. "You said you lived in the forest, correct?"

They nodded.

"I, and many in this city, have heard about those communities," Lex stated. "They are said to be completely separated from the world. Some say it was a forgotten people, others say that they are under government protection. No one really knows. However, no one has ever come through before and people who go in don't leave."

They glanced at each other as shock and recognition flashed through their eyes.

"The fence…" Maxwell said slowly.

Lex sat in silence. "You two aren't lying then. You truly are from those hidden communities." He paused before he leaned back once more. "Weird." He shook his head. "Unfortunately, that is all I know about those communities and about the epidemic," he said.

Maxwell shifted back and tilted his head toward the ceiling as Karina leaned forward.

"So that's why…" Maxwell mumbled quietly.

Anger flashed across Karina's face as she took over. "That's why no one was willing to help that woman, because they were afraid."

Lex watched as she growled in anger. She slammed the cup onto the table, practically snapping the cup in half. Lex was glad he found some plastic cups instead of the normal glass ones.

"That would explain so much," Maxwell said, as he looked down.

Karina looked at her brother before she nodded. "For instance, why we were thrown in a stupid jail truck and practically shipped away from our forest. The suspicious looks we kept receiving while walking through this city and…"

"What you meant by clean the other day," Maxwell interjected as he turned his head toward Lex, eyes narrowed. "It also fits with what Martha said. How there was nothing we could do and we just have to wait. You're all just waiting to die."

Lex pursed his lips. The kid was too perceptive.

Maxwell's hands shook. "Why didn't you tell us this earlier? Why didn't we know? What the heck is going on?" Maxwell finally demanded.

A determined look crossed his own face as he stared Lex in the eye. His posture was rigid as he waited.

Lex blinked as Maxwell and Karina continued to stare at him. Karina was practically in his face, anger evident on her features. Maxwell, meanwhile, just sat in a type of stoic silence even though his face held confusion and a want to know more. Lex felt surprised. "That's what you're commenting on?" he asked quietly, only to get an annoyed scowl from them.

"What else are we supposed to say?" Maxwell responded.

He placed his cup down, which was as crumbled as Karina's. He put his elbow on the armrest as he laid his chin in his hand. Karina followed suit a moment later. She moved backward as she waited impatiently for his response.

Lex shifted slightly before he replied, "Most people would freak out if they just saw someone die and, right after, learned the cause of death was an infectious disease that no one has a cure for. Yet you two are more upset about the fact that no one was willing to help, or that no one actually told you."

Lex shook his head in bewilderment. Even though their emotions seemed to be as plain as day on both of their faces, Lex couldn't find a trace of fear. He raised an eyebrow as he spoke. "Why is it that neither of you seem to be afraid at the prospect of getting infected? You've been living within an infectious household and everything. Wouldn't you want to flee as soon as you found out?"

Lex stopped, fear clear on their faces. Ah, so they were still in shock. They probably hadn't thought of that yet. Almost as soon as the emotions appeared, their expressions turned neutral. He wasn't sure whether to feel annoyed or amused at how in unison their reactions were. They were both trying to hide their fear from the other, why wasn't he surprised?

"Why?" Maxwell asked after a few minutes, only the slight tremor of his voice indicated that he wasn't quite as calm as before.

Maxwell's gaze flickered to Agatha who held onto Lex quietly. His annoyance seemed to dissipate as he continued, a little softer. "If we're infected, then we're infected. You said the third stage can last for a long time." Maxwell stopped before he turned back to Lex. "If that's the case, then we should have time. Time to find Ma and maybe, in doing so, find a cure. You're waiting anyway, so, I guess we can do the same."

Lex regarded Maxwell before his eyes flickered to Karina who's own were closed. She opened them to reveal determined sky-blue eyes, their crystal gaze unwavering, just like Maxwell's. After a moment, he let a soft chuckle slip through. "You two are interesting. I'm starting to understand what Martha meant…" He sat up and pulled Agatha along. "All right, to answer earlier questions, I didn't tell you because I already thought, one, you knew, or two, you were already infected. It is very rare to find someone who has no knowledge of the epidemic at all. So, most people just infer that you already know. Many are scared to even talk about it, so they use roundabout ways to explain it, for instance, my uncle." That seemed to catch their attention as he continued. "My uncle stated that things were worse in New London City, correct?" They nodded. "In some cities, the epidemic is more pronounced and causes bigger problems, both economically and physically. This city is pretty lucky at this point, but others are not so much. Some cities are completely quarantined while others are on the verge of it. New London is one of the latter cities and my uncle was simply warning about that fact."

Maxwell stayed silent while Karina frowned. "Our mother is supposedly in this city. Why?"

Lex looked at her. "I don't know. My informant could only find bits and pieces. His contacts are being awfully tight-lipped regarding things lately."

Maxwell put a hand to his chin. "Since that's the only clue we have to finding our mother and we don't know a thing about finding a cure…" Maxwell trailed off.

"We'll just have to go and check it out," Karina finished for him.

Lex let a hand push through his hair, partially as a calming mechanism and partially out of habit. "You two are going to be the death of me," he muttered before he peered toward Agatha.

She shifted slightly before she slowly pulled away. "Is it over?" she asked softly as she looked up to Lex, who nodded.

"You don't have to worry, we're done."

Agatha nodded weakly before she peeked at both teens. Maxwell's and Karina's eyes saddened as they took another look at her. Agatha walked up to them as Karina opened her arms and picked Agatha up into her lap. Agatha hugged her as Karina cradled the little girl, holding her tightly. Lex could see the sleep dragging at her eyes.

"Let me bring her to her room."

"Can I?"

Lex looked at Karina before he nodded. Karina gently stood and walked upstairs. He stared after her, feeling Maxwell's gaze on him. A hand shot to his head as a wave of nausea hit.

"Is that one of those dizzy spells you were talking about?" Maxwell asked.

Lex dropped his hand and peered at Maxwell before he looked away. "You don't have to worry about it. It'll go away."

Maxwell stayed silent. He closed his eyes, breathed in and slowly let out a long breath. Lex gazed at Maxwell, noting with a touch of sadness that he seemed so much older than a boy his age should be. Lex pushed those thoughts away quickly as Maxwell said, "Since it's our last day here, when Karina comes back down…why don't we play a game?"

It was around dinner when Martha returned home to see the tired children. Lex was certain the twins were probably still in shock since their mischievous nature seemed to have dulled a bit during the games, even when Karina rejoined them. He couldn't blame them.

"Glad to see you're back, I take it everything went well?" Martha asked as she draped her coat on the stand next to the now closed door.

"Mostly…" Maxwell said. He looked closely at her before he shook his head. "We'll be heading out tomorrow."

"I better make you two a good dinner before you go."

"That would be appreciated."

Martha paused and eyed Lex, the slightest of frowns on her face.

Lex subtly nodded and Martha let out a soft, barely noticeable sigh as she went into the kitchen. Lex leaned back against the couch once more.

Karina sat down with a sleeping Agatha on her lap, hugging her waist. Even after the earlier nap, when Agatha tried to join them for games, she kept falling to sleep.

They sat quietly as Martha cooked. "So, how was your visit?" Martha asked to interrupt the uncomfortable silence.

"Fine," Lex said as he regarded Martha. "We're leaving at one p.m. tomorrow."

Martha nodded, before she scrutinized the twins. "You two are awfully quiet. What happened?"

They jumped. Maxwell blinked before a small fake grin crossed his face. "It's nothing, we got to see Lex's uncle. He was pretty nice, actually."

Lex could see that Martha wasn't convinced, but she let it go. "All right, as long as none of you are hurt. That's what matters."

Martha turned the stove on before she paused. She peered back at the group before she let out a long breath. "I usually don't like to do this especially so late at night, but why don't I turn on some music," she said as she walked to the radio and flipped it on.

Soft music began to float through the speakers as she walked back to the oven. She watched it quietly, moving between places until she was done. She pulled the baked mac and cheese out of the oven and set it carefully on the table before she sat down.

They joined her, Agatha yawning as Karina gently woke her. She wiped her eyes tiredly as she held on to Karina's shirt. They sat down, eating in silence. Every so often, one of them would give a fleeting look up, only to return their eyes to their food. For some reason, this both amused and annoyed Lex. The radio continued to play as the sun lowered in the sky.

About halfway through dinner, the music died down and a voice took over. "Hello, everybody. It's seven o'clock so you know what that means. That's right. Time for the daily news special. Today, we have just recently learned that famous pop star, Rose Thornfield, will be touring around the country for the next few months and again next year. Her concerts have already been quite famous and even now, tickets are selling out quite fast. Get them while you can! Next up in recent news is a volleyball tournament, hosted by your very own Green Liberties. Let's see who will win this year's championship." There was a pause and shuffling before the voice continued. "This just in… President Brian Obin has officially proposed a new Medicare proposition regarding the SS level Phenomenon. The bill dictates that…"

Martha's eyes flashed as she slammed her hands on the table before she briskly got up and smashed the radio off. An annoyed and uncharacteristically violent emotion careened across her face as she glared at the radio. "Those damn hypocrites! This is why I hate having the stupid radio on at night. Those biased bastards. It's just disgusting to watch this once-great country fall to ruin just because of those stupid privileged folk."

Karina and Maxwell started and turned in unison to squint at the oddly furious women. Martha's hand shook as she glared at the radio like it was the most offensive thing in the world. Surprise crossed their faces at the usually peaceful woman's outburst as spoons and forks lay suspended in midair.

Lex couldn't agree more with her statement, or their surprise. With a quiet calmness, he gazed at Martha. He took another bite of his own food with a feeling of subtle disinterest. Agatha didn't even react.

"It is a disgrace," Lex agreed and took another bite. "They're more focused on the privileged than on finding a cure." Lex stopped and glanced quietly to the side, annoyance slipping onto his face against his will.

Martha paused from her rant, looking at both surprised and slightly frightened twins. Her expression softened as she walked back to the table and sat down. "Sorry about that. It's just that, I always get overly annoyed about that. How they can talk about such stupid things. I just can't stand how messed up things are…" Martha sighed before she looked pointedly at both teens. "Go on, eat up. This is your last night, right? So, enjoy it."

They looked at each other before they slowly went back to eating, probably surprised to find that the suspended food hadn't fallen off during the incident.

Lex watched in silence as the meal slowly came to a close, tension and confusion foremost in the air. He took another bite, relishing in the warm food as his eyes closed. He didn't want to head back in that direction, toward New London City. He never wanted to, not after that. But he promised and now he felt he needed to. He opened his eyes as he stared at Maxwell and Karina. They were both deep in thought, occasionally exchanging looks before returning their focus to their plates.

Tonight would be the deciding factor. He knew they said they would keep going, but now that the adrenaline had worn off, along with a lot of the numb shock, would they make the same decision.

Chapter Fourteen

Once done, they left and went upstairs. Karina walked to the bed and sat down. Maxwell took a seat across from her after closing the door with a soft click. Karina looked out the window. Without a word, Maxwell fell onto his back, feeling the soft cotton of the sheets and hearing the springs squeal. His mind was working overtime, but it wasn't going anywhere, just running around and around in circles.

"Kari…" Maxwell trailed off as he continued to stare at the ceiling. It was only when he felt Karina's eyes on him that he continued. "Did—was that woman really…" He stopped, mentally scoffing even as his mind replayed the scene from a few hours ago. "I don't even know why I'm asking. It's obvious what happened, but I just… I can't believe everything that's going on. It's not making any sense for some reason." He stopped once more before he let out a long, tired sigh.

He faced his sister, feeling overwhelmingly weary for some reason. "I want to find Ma, but now we have to worry about a sickness with no cure and I even told Lex that we would find it. It's so stupid. How could we find it when the government itself can't even do that? Not only that, but why do those policemen want us? What are we getting ourselves into?"

Karina peered into his eyes before she looked away. She leaned back and let her hands support her weight. "I don't know…" She paused. "I've been saying that a lot lately, haven't I?"

Maxwell curled inward, pulling the sheets up, as if partly hoping they would protect him from the knowledge they gained. Karina looked at him. He turned on his side to face the wall. The painted plaster stared back at him, a pale white in the moonlight which was slowly starting to swim through the window. "I don't know why, but I got so angered about not being told anything. Now, I'm not sure I wanted to know." Maxwell closed his eyes. He didn't want to see his sister. Not right now. He felt overwhelmed.

"You know, I was pretty angry myself about not being told and disbelieving this epidemic could be happening, but if it is…" She stopped, her voice an odd croak that made Maxwell want to both wince and punch something, even though that would usually be Karina's job. "It's weird. I feel like today was almost surreal. I know more about what's going on, but I also seem to have more questions."

Maxwell heard a thump and guessed she let herself fall onto the bed. "I just wish Mom was here or even…" Her voice was a little hoarse. It held a slight tremor that he wasn't even sure he heard before. A tone he never wanted to hear from his sister that worried him greatly. "Max… I'm scared…"

Maxwell's eyes shot open. *Sis…* he thought as he stared at the wall. He heard his sister's voice tremble and could almost feel the anxiety rolling off her.

"So much is changing. I always wanted to go on an adventure. To leave Claremore. I never expected this."

He heard her shuffling around, probably trying to get comfortable. Yet still, he didn't want to turn around, because he knew that if both of them broke down, it would be over. "That woman… even as she died..." Karina choked slightly before she continued. "She was pleading with us and we couldn't do a thing. What if one of us ends up in the same situation? I know you said if we're already infected, then we're infected, but…" She stopped once more as she sniffled softly, so soft, Maxwell wasn't even sure he heard.

Maxwell bit his lower lip, suppressing the fear and worry and everything else. "I don't want to lose anyone else…"

Maxwell gripped the sheets tightly as he closed his eyes. After a moment of thought and hearing soft gasps, he slowly sat up to face Karina. After steeling himself and letting his wheeling thoughts settle, he opened his eyes.

Teary blue eyes gazed back at him with such worry he almost felt like crumbling to pieces. His sister was the only one left who was still with him. What if what she said was true? What if he lost her, just like he had lost Ma and Pa? He couldn't think of that, not now. No, right now, his sister needed the comfort. Before he could even stop himself, he stood and walked to Karina's bed. Karina shuffled over, sitting up. He sat down. He felt arms curl around him as Karina pulled him close. He didn't realize he was trembling until she pulled his head down to her shoulder, brushing a hand through his hair like their ma used to. Her other arm clung to him desperately, as her head rested against his. Maxwell leaned into the embrace, his eyes closing as he tried to relax. "I don't want to lose anyone either," he murmured just as quietly. "I don't know what else we can do."

Karina stayed silent, before she let out a long shivering breath. Maxwell didn't realize until he felt the sudden shift of clothing that he wrapped his arms around her as well. The hand continued to slip through his hair, a relaxing gesture instead of an annoying one.

He would admit it. He was scared. Scared for his sister, scared for his mother and father and, even though he knew it was selfish, he was scared for himself. He didn't want to die. Not like the way he saw today. He wanted to live with his family and go home. He missed Claremore with the safety and security it gave. He missed going to school and being carefree with his sister. Suddenly, the tension of the day washed over him, and tiredness warred with worried thoughts.

What were they going to do? What had they gotten themselves into?

~ * ~

Karina groggily opened her eyes, surprised to find she fell asleep. She slowly tried to sit up, only to pause when she felt a soft breath ghost over her shoulder. Karina leaned her head down just slightly to see Maxwell. He was curled up next to her, deep in sleep. They must have fallen asleep that way. She couldn't remember. Karina knew she was glad her brother walked over to join her. She was worried when he continued to stare at the wall. It was easy to tell how hard he was trembling, probably thinking he was hiding the emotions. Karina admitted to being somewhat grateful he tried to be strong. She brushed her hand through his hair, feeling the knots and tangles. He let out a soft snort before the breaths evened out again and felt herself softly chuckle. Any other time and she would be fine with kicking him out of bed, but right now, Karina was grateful for the warmth. Letting herself relax, it was easy to faintly hear the soft thumping of her twin's heart, calm and steady in sleep. It was kind of relaxing, knowing her brother was still there, alive and, for the moment, well.

Her gaze drifted to the window, watching the sun slowly rise over the horizon. They were leaving today. Usually, she would be so excited about going somewhere new. Now, instead, Karina was scared. There was so much against them. So much she couldn't fight off. How could someone like her, who knew nothing, protect her brother from the epidemic? The police? Even just people like Antonio? What about the black market? Damned if you do, damned if you don't, at least that's what Maxwell would say. If they're clean, they could be sold; if they're sick, they could suddenly die.

Karina held her brother close and shivered. She didn't want to think about it, couldn't think about. Her prerogative hadn't changed. The promise she made to herself about protecting him hadn't changed. But how could she protect him from things she couldn't even protect herself from? The weight of the world felt heavy as her attention drifted away from the sunrise to skim over her brother. He looked thinner and a little paler, though that could be the light.

"Come on, Max, it's time to wake up."

"'M…"

Karina huffed quietly in annoyance as she felt the arms around her waist squeeze tighter for a moment before the grip loosened. There was a soft exhalation of breath before the arms moved away. "Sorry, Kari," was his surprisingly quiet response.

Her expression softened. Karina felt him pull away as she sat up. A light flush shone on her brother's cheeks. "I-I didn't mean to fall asleep. I just…"

Karina ruffled his hair, getting an exclamation of surprise from

Maxwell. She chuckled at his annoyed expression. It turned into one of amusement as he laughed. It was such a stupid thing to be laughing about, but it still felt good.

Letting her chuckles subside, she swung her legs out of bed. Maxwell moved to the other bed, sitting down with a thump as the springs groaned and squeaked. Both watched as the sun rose over the sky. Karina felt calmer. A good night's sleep did wonders and, even though she had no idea what might happen, her promise still remained. Her abilities were limited. Karina knew she could only do so much, but that didn't mean giving up. Her job was to protect her little brother, that's all it was.

"I guess we should head downstairs." Maxwell continued to stare out the window, a content expression on his face. Green eyes turned to her, filled with determination.

She nodded and stood, patting her clothes down. "Well then, let's go."

After they quickly cleaned themselves up, they walked downstairs to find a full table. Martha was taking care of Agatha while Lex leaned back. He had a cup of coffee in hand and was reading a newspaper. Not the strangest thing Karina saw, but still a little unusual.

"You coming, slowpoke?"

Karina pulled away from her thoughts to see Maxwell already took a seat. She rolled her eyes and stuck out her tongue playfully. "Coming, my darling little brother." She made sure to add as much sarcasm as necessary as she took a seat beside Maxwell. She almost laughed at Maxwell's pout, though she knew for a fact he would call it a frown or something.

"I should have expected that. I really should have," he muttered under his breath. Her gaze flitted toward the other three. Agatha had her head cocked to one side while Lex watched, amusement clear on his face, as well as something like confirmation. Martha looked surprised.

"Did you sleep well?" Martha asked after a moment.

"Fine," Maxwell said with a wave of his hand. They grabbed some toast and buttered it, Maxwell adding some jam as well.

Lex narrowed his eyes slightly, but stayed silent.

"By the way, I know this is weird to ask, considering how long you've stayed with us and that you're leaving today, but how are you two related? You just said little brother, but…" Martha stopped.

Maxwell swallowed as Karina put down her fork.

"We're twins," they said before digging back into their food.

Karina hadn't even realized how hungry she was. They hadn't really eaten much the day before.

Martha blinked slowly. "I didn't realize, no wonder you two have such a close bond. It's been a long time since I've seen twins. What with what's going on recently and the privileged policy of separation…" Martha glared at the radio. Her expression relaxed. "Just knowing that, I want to root for you two even more."

"Thanks," Karina said quietly before she took another bite of food.

She jumped as a loud clatter tore her gaze away from the couch. She looked over to see Lex swaying in his seat. He looked pale and one trembling hand held his head. Karina gulped as she gripped her brother's hand tightly, noting him tense as she pushed back in her chair ever so slightly.

She sighed in relief when Lex stabilized, only letting go after Maxwell relaxed. Lex slowly breathed out and dropped his hand.

Martha's eyes saddened as she looked Lex over. Karina felt the worry from yesterday pierce through her as her eyes gravitated to Maxwell's. His own were just as apprehensive.

Agatha tilted her head slightly as she quietly asked, "Are you all right, Uncle Lex?"

Lex weakly nodded. "Of course. I'm fine. Don't worry."

Martha gave him a pointed look, which he readily ignored. "Martha, I have to thank you for your hospitality. I know how hard it is to take care of so many…"

Martha relaxed her expression before she responded. "Lex, it was an honor to have you three over, you've been great with Agatha, and it's nice to see so much life in this house. I appreciate you playing with Agatha and taking care of her, she doesn't have any other children to play with, especially with…" Martha stopped.

"No, thank you, you took us in, even though we were strangers."

Maxwell said politely. "Both of us are grateful to you for taking care of us and letting us stay here. Thank you."

Karina nodded. Martha chuckled. "I wish you two the best of luck. I hope that God will be with you."

"Thank you."

They finished eating, the atmosphere seemingly clear, compared to the tension from the day before. Lex left after breakfast, saying something about making sure everything was all set. Martha went to leave a little after, with Agatha at her heels.

"Looks like you're ready to go." Martha looked them over, Agatha's hand in her own. "Please be careful and…come back whenever you need some shelter. We'll always be willing to help."

"Thank you," Karina said. She squatted down in front of Agatha who seemed sad.

"How long will you be gone? Will you come back?" Agatha asked as she looked into Karina's eyes.

Karina nodded she reached a hand forward, then hesitated before she gently pulled Agatha into a hug. "Don't worry, I promise we'll return, and this time, we'll bring Mom." Karina ruffled Agatha's hair.

Agatha nodded into her embrace, hugging her arms around Karina's waist. "Pinky swear?" Agatha asked as she gingerly pulled away.

Karina let a small chuckle escape before she extended her pinky forward. Agatha extended her own to grip it for a second before she let go. Agatha beamed up at Karina before she gave her another hug.

Karina gently patted the girl's head and stood up. "We'll return."

"I guess my sister said it all already so…" Maxwell spoke weakly.

"Stay safe."

"You too. See you."

Karina chuckled as Martha led Agatha out the door. Martha paused before she looked back at the twins. "Thank you for staying. The door is locked, so once you're ready to go, you can. I wish you luck and take care of yourselves."

"See you, brother Max, sister Kari." Agatha waved as the two walked out the door. Maxwell and Karina waved until the door swung shut.

"I'm going to miss them," Karina said as she slowly dropped her hand to her side. Maxwell nodded.

"Yeah…"

They spent the day relaxing before they made a lunch of sandwiches and, for Maxwell at least, orange juice. Once done, they went to their room, the noon sun shining brightly through the window. Maxwell grabbed his backpack, which was pushed under his bed. He peeked into it, before he threw it on the cot. Karina grabbed her own and plopped herself down next to it. "I wonder what New London City is like."

Maxwell glanced up from rummaging in his backpack. "We won't know until we get there," he said.

"Oh yeah, did you put the picture away?" she asked as she peered up from her searching.

"Of course, I did it while we played hide and seek that first time. I made sure it was more protected later when I got the chance," he replied.

Karina nodded, only to pause as her fingers brushed over the coolness of leather. Her eyebrows furrowed inward as she wrapped her fingers around the item. She slowly pulled it out.

"Is that..."

Karina peered up in time to notice Maxwell's surprised expression. His eyes stayed on the little book in her hands.

"Yeah, Mom's Bible. I forgot I packed it." Karina glanced at the book and took note of the worn bookmarks and post-it-notes on random pages.

Karina started to flip through the pages at a leisurely pace. After a moment, she stopped at one of the pages that was highlighted in a bright yellow.

Her eyes slowly shifted over some of the words before she stopped at a random sentence. "So, we do not lose heart." Karina began to read it out loud for Maxwell.

He listened in silence as he continued to pack.

"Though our outer self is wasting away, our inner self is being renewed day by day. For this light momentary affliction is preparing for us an eternal weight of glory beyond all comparison, as we look not to the things that are seen, but to the things that are unseen. For the things that are seen are transient, but the things that are unseen are eternal. 2 Corinthians 4:16 through 18," she finished, her voice softer. She stared at the passage, not sure what to feel.

"You ready to go?" Maxwell asked, interrupting the weighty silence.

Karina slowly nodded before she gingerly closed the book. She slipped it into her sack before she quickly put the rest of the stuff away. She gripped the strap and let it swing over her shoulder and land on her back with a thump. "Ready," she said as her brother looked away. He seemed conflicted.

They headed toward the stairs, walking down them slowly. They looked around the house, pausing at the bottom when they noticed Lex in the doorway.

"Ready to go?"

Karina grasped Maxwell's wrist as Lex walked out the door. "Let's get going."

Maxwell, for once, let Karina pull him along. They walked out the door, letting it swing shut with a soft click. The red-bricked home shimmered in the sunlight as they moved down the street. Karina tried not to think about leaving behind the comfortable home they were now used to. Instead she focused on the thrill of something new and the chance, she hoped, to once more be with their mother.

~ * ~

The trio walked through the town, through winding, vaguely familiar roads. Maxwell and Karina scanned the area, gingerly taking note of what they missed before, the subtler symptoms of the epidemic. Maxwell frowned worriedly as they regarded each other.

"I don't think you're infected yet."

Maxwell saw Lex peer over his shoulder before he looked forward once more.

"If you were, you would have shown some signs of at least the first stage, a cold. It doesn't look like you have anything like that," he said.

"Maybe you're right," Maxwell said. "Then again, I've never been sick. I wouldn't know if the symptoms were to appear, what they would be like."

Karina nodded, a thoughtful look on her face.

Lex narrowed his eyes before he slowed down slightly to walk even with them. "You've never been sick?" he asked.

"Never…even when there was a cold going around our school. Most of our friends caught it, but we managed to avoid it. It was pretty recently too, now that I think about it," Karina said as she frowned in thought.

Lex looked at them in silence. "We're almost there. You should recognize the place," he said as he took the next corner.

"Oh yeah. I recognize it," Maxwell said, feeling his eye twitch as a deadpan expression crossed Karina's face.

Karina rolled her eyes as she looked up toward the puffing and very familiar factory. "The main place we saw when we first arrived. Of course, we're not going to forget any time soon," she said as they slipped past the enclosing fence into the factory proper.

They walked down a gravel road toward one side of the giant building. They curved around the red brick wall to see a tractor trailer in front of them. The white forty-eight-footer gleamed against the smog and dirt of the factory. Its two back doors were being shut by a couple of workers. Karina and Maxwell scrutinized the truck before they turned toward the big cab in the front.

Maxwell looked at Lex. "Is your uncle going to be here?"

Lex scoffed. "No. He's a workaholic, he wouldn't take his time to come here."

"So, are you the ones I'm supposed to help transport?"

Maxwell and Karina jumped. To their right was a man with a short scruffy beard and mustache. He wore a white shirt, gray trousers and a pair of suspenders. The man's eyes twinkled with mirth and a hint of fatigue as he walked up to them.

"Ah, Lex, long time no see, how have you been?" the man asked as he extended a welcoming hand out toward Lex.

Lex took it and smirked. "Not bad, didn't expect you to be taking care of us," he stated as he dropped his hand to the side, before he eyed the truck. "Though, thinking about it, you're probably one of the few willing to travel around here, what with everything that's been going on."

The man let go as well, before he pulled off his hat. "Well, I'm definitely not going to lose any more hair over it," he replied.

Lex rolled his eyes while Maxwell blinked. The other man was bald on the top of his head with scruffs of black curly locks around the crown. The man put the baseball cap back on. "Sorry, I should introduce myself. My name is Garrett. It's nice to meet you." Karina and Maxwell nodded as they accepted the hand shake. "Well, come on, we should be heading out soon. I have a schedule to keep," he said as he gestured toward the cab.

Maxwell gazed up at it in awe while Lex walked up to the red cab. He swung the door open with ease and pulled himself in.

"If you two don't mind, could you head to the back? Technically, I'm not supposed to be driving with passengers, no matter what situation they're in," Garrett said as he gestured to where Lex disappeared to. Maxwell nodded as Karina shrugged. Karina swung herself up and jumped in with ease, closely followed by her brother.

The inside was comfortable, with two leather seats in the front and a red curtain dividing the front and the back.

Karina moved to the back as Maxwell eyed the area in curiosity. Right behind the curtain was basically a small bedroom. There were closets and open cabinets with meshing on the sides. A fridge sat in one corner and a long couch sat in the back, facing toward the front. Closed windows sat on either side of the couch, blocked off by leather blinds.

"Well, get yourselves comfortable, it's going to be a long ride," Garrett said as he pulled himself into the truck. He tugged the curtains closed and after a few minutes of arranging himself, the truck roared into life. It rumbled underneath them. Maxwell jumped while Karina found herself stiffening in surprise.

Lex leaned back on the couch. He grabbed a pillow and put it up by his head before he rested against the side of the cab. Maxwell sat in the middle and peered out between the slit in the curtains as Karina inclined back and played with the fabric of the windows blinds.

They set off. The first part of the trip was slow as they traveled through traffic and city pedestrians. They could hear the honking of annoyed passengers along with a chuckle from Garrett every so often. "The city is a great place since everyone likes to tell you you're number one," Garrett said. Maxwell and Karina stared in confusion while Lex let a chuckle escape.

"What's he mean?" Maxwell finally asked in curiosity.

"I learned pretty quickly that it's his term for someone who sticks up their middle finger at someone."

Maxwell blinked before it clicked and he chuckled as well.

"Oh brother." Karina rolled her eyes as a smirk danced on her lips.

Other than that, the ride was silent until they finally left the city. Right at the outskirts, Garrett hissed for them to hide as he drew to a stop. Maxwell and Karina exchanged looks as the sound of rummaging and voices talking back and forth reached their ears. Maxwell and Karina hurried toward the curtain, pulling themselves in the shadows between curtain and cabinet. Maxwell heard the truck door open and even Lex was up and alert. His body was tense and ready to spring forward if necessary. Though, to a casual viewer, he still looked to be asleep. Maxwell held his breath as the curtain shifted a bit. "I see, so that's your brother-in-law, well, it doesn't seem like anyone else is here." The voice was masculine and bored, pulling away so that the curtain could drop back in place. "Looks like you're all clear, go on ahead."

Once the door closed and they were moving, Lex settled back down. Maxwell peered side long at Lex and gulped, hands clenching into tight fists for a moment before he forced himself to relax. *It's fine. Lex was just tired. It's been hectic lately. He wasn't going to die. Right?* Maxwell watched for a few minutes. He walked back to his seat and sighed. It would be fine. He just needed to keep thinking that way. He peered ahead, trying to push the worry to the back of his mind.

Once out of the confines of the buildings, the drive was smooth and the curtain was lifted slightly. "You two can take a peek for a moment, if you want," Garrett said. Maxwell hurried forward into the front seat which left Karina to stand in the middle as she held onto both seats.

Lex was asleep once more.

All around them were fields of green and yellow. They could see trees in the distance as puffy clouds floated in the azure sky. There was almost no traffic as they trundled down the long stretch of road.

Maxwell noted Garrett's furrowed brow. "What happened?"

Garrett gave him a fleeting look before shifting gears to pick up a bit of speed. "Security. It seems like they were checking traffic coming in and going out of the city." Garrett's expression morphed into a slight frown as he continued, "If they're already putting that much effort into finding someone, or more specifically, you two, you're going to have to be careful."

Maxwell nodded.

"We will," Maxwell responded as he leaned back to continue examining their surroundings. He paused in his surveillance and, peering around Karina, asked, "By the way, what do you transport?"

Garret chuckled as he shifted gears. "Ah, odds and ends such as machinery, just different equipment that is needed to repair factories and such. For instance, I have an AC1025 which…"

"Ah, what is that?" Maxwell jerked and glared at Karina who smirked. Obviously, she purposely changed the subject. Garrett peered over and shrugged. The radio came on, the talking muddled and full of static over the air waves. Garrett turned up the dial, attention back on the radio.

"Sorry little brother, wasn't in the mood to listen to the nitty-gritty of some machine."

"It was an air compressor," Maxwell responded with a sigh.

Whatever, it didn't matter anyway. He just thought it would be kind of interesting to listen to. He gazed outside and watched the grass sway softly in the breeze as they moved by.

After a while, the meadow curved inward until trees and houses surrounded them. Wires and poles hung on either side, cutting through the trees. The road dipped and curved subtly every so often. Part of the way through, Karina managed to squeeze next to Maxwell to get a better view. Maxwell glared and shifted over some more before he looked back out at the surroundings.

The day was absolutely beautiful and it was fascinating, seeing everything from so high up. It was about two hours later when Garrett asked them to move back into the room portion of the cab. They did so grudgingly. They sat down as Garrett turned down another few roads. After a few turns, through the break in the curtains, they could see a large building with a fence around it.

"Well, this is your stop," Garrett stated as he came to a halt on the side of the road, right before the plant. "You're not far from the city. Just go a mile south and you should be there."

"Thank you," Maxwell said as Karina woke up Lex.

Lex jerked awake, eye darting around before he settled down. He shook his head and got to his feet.

Karina raised an eyebrow. Maxwell frowned, thoughts going back to earlier opinions before he promptly pushed them away. Lex wasn't going to die. He couldn't.

Why he couldn't die? Maxwell was unable to answer, but he kept insisting it, as if a reminder and hope. He nodded toward the driver before he opened the door. He jumped out, followed momentarily by Karina.

Maxwell let Karina pass as he turned back to the truck to see Lex hadn't gotten out yet. He heard Garrett speak and paused.

"Your uncle told me to give this to you and to warn you."

Maxwell peered into the vehicle as Lex took the package Garrett handed over. It looked rather thin. Lex gently pulled it apart and stopped. It was a dagger, sharp and new. He looked at it closely before he took note of the sheath. He slipped the knife into the sheath. "It's becoming a lawless zone in there. Stay on the main streets if you want to keep your life."

Lex peered up at Garrett's serious expression before he nodded and strapped the knife to his waist, under his vest.

"Oh, and he also stated that if you needed help, there was a doctor friend of his still in town, you should remember him."

"I see. Tell him thank you when you see him," Lex replied as he got out of the truck. Maxwell scrambled away, joining his sister.

"Tell him yourself," Garrett called before the door closed behind him.

Maxwell followed Lex's gaze as the truck continued down the lane, hearing a soft, "I will."

Maxwell stared at Lex a little longer before he took in the surroundings. He stretched as he smelled the open air. While it wasn't as clean as his hometown, it was still a relief from all the smog and pollution of the city. He shifted his backpack so it sat more comfortably on his back. Karina was in the same boat, shifting her sack around even as she enjoyed the cool evening air.

"We'll grab dinner at the food stand over there, then find a place to stay tonight. I know someone who can help us in this regard. Once we have a solid base to work from, then we'll look for your mother."

Lex hefted his own fairly small backpack. He eyed them before he took the road that continued on into the city. Next to where they were dropped off was a hot dog stand. A few men and women were gathered around it, either picking up their goods or ordering. Maxwell could smell the hot dogs from here, grateful that he was now a bit more used to the food from the cities.

"Let's go."

Maxwell grinned while Karina rolled her eyes. They walked over. Lex dug into his pocket for money. After ordering their dogs, they grabbed one of the benches set up nearby to eat.

Maxwell munched happily on his meal while Karina scrutinized the house and tree-lined road.

"So, who is this person that can help?" Maxwell asked as he swallowed and looked toward Lex.

Lex finished his bite, his expression somewhat amused. "A doctor friend of mine and my uncle's. He should be in the city proper. Hopefully, he's in the same place as I remember him. Now, let's get going, we have some traveling to do and it's late already." He stood and dusted himself off. With a flick of his wrist, he threw the wrapper into the trash and started to walk. Karina huffed, but followed suit anyway.

In the distance, they could see another city similar to Reinmark when it came to large buildings. However, the city itself seemed to sprawl outward more than the other seemingly confined place that they were just in.

They continued for a while as traffic slowly began to build around them. Cars moved down the roads as people began to roam the streets. Sounds and smells they got used to in Reinmark reappeared with a vengeance. Karina grimaced while Maxwell tightened his grip on his backpack. Lex peered around casually, as if he didn't have a care in the world.

The city was noisy with people chattering loudly and music playing on radios. Cars honked as people swore back at them. Lex seemed calm as they turned down one of the many store-lined streets. Maxwell and Karina were surprised. This place was distinctly different from the last. Buildings were older and more historical, and people were more diverse. Men and women in varying states of wellness and wealth were traveling over the streets, sometimes bumping into them, other times completely managing to avoid the trio. The only things that were the same were the masks and the tension in the air.

"This place seems different," Maxwell muttered as he gazed around the area.

"It's a lot different. Shouldn't it be, I don't know, darker?" Karina said as she scrutinized the different pedestrians.

Lex drew even with them. "It's definitely changed since the last time I was here. Don't be distracted."

Maxwell turned to Lex, who was looking around warily. "What's so different?"

"Just be careful," Lex said as they walked around another corner.

Maxwell tilted his head before he perused the area in curiosity. He winced and internally cringed as he noticed the wary and sometimes hostile glares. He noticed Karina move even closer to him, but he ignored it. His eyes gazed over the crowd, noting the edgy air around the city.

"Even though it seems so different, it's kind of tense," Maxwell said quietly.

He noticed Lex's surprised look before looking over toward a nearby street. He stopped as a mix of emotions welled up and his eyes slowly widened. "They're here?" he said worriedly. He noticed Lex and Karina stare back at him in confusion. He subtly shifted behind Lex as he gestured toward the street corner.

Lex and Karina tilted their heads up and gazed down the road. People gave movements and noises of discontent as all three froze. Maxwell winced as Karina gripped his arm tightly. "Those…" Karina trailed off as her eyes sharpened.

Ahead, and just turning the corner, was a large group of men in black uniforms with sparkling medallions. The group separated and started to move down the street, moving along at a fast pace as lights began to flash in the distance.

"Come on, let's go," Lex said under his breath.

Maxwell nodded and followed him with Karina at his side, grip still tight on his arm. They hurried into a nearby alley, hidden in the shadows of two larger buildings. The afternoon sun drifted down lazily and illuminated the darker road. Shouts could be heard in the distance as cars zoomed past the alley. Lex traversed down the darker road, before he turned another corner, to find a street symmetrical to the one they came from.

Lex let a hand rake through his long bangs as they continued down the street, a bit more cautiously. Smoke clouded the air and the prickling scent of burning wafted to their noses. Lex frowned and let out a drawn-out, agitated breath.

"Dammit…"

Maxwell looked back to see Karina mutter under her breath, "What are they doing here? Shouldn't they be in the other city? Are they really that spread out?"

Lex stayed silent as Maxwell took a step forward, not quite sure what to say. Karina gave a fake smile. "If they're here, then Mom must be as well, right?"

Maxwell stared at Karina, reminded of last night. "You're probably right."

Karina looked away and slowly nodded, joining Maxwell as they continued down the street. Maxwell bumped his shoulder lightly into

Karina's, who just gave him an amused look in return. There it was. His sister was back to normal now.

"Either way, if they're the ones after you, we should get moving."

Karina stayed silent, though she did grip Maxwell's wrist once more. Maxwell mentally winced, but didn't comment on the tight grip.

Lex scrutinized the red-bricked and car-lined street. Pedestrians were fewer and traffic seemed more haphazard. Maxwell gazed into the sky, noting hints of murky smoke and sounds that didn't seem quite right. "Lex, where are we going? You seem to know a lot of different ways around these cities," Maxwell asked in confused curiosity.

"Experience. I've been in these cities before and many have the same general patterns to them," he said simply.

Maxwell heard Karina huff, only to hesitate as Lex slowed to a stop. His eyes narrowed as his hand extended next to him to stop them. An odd expression crossed his face, almost one of pained annoyance. Maxwell wasn't sure as he caught Lex's look.

"This way won't work," he said as he quickly scanned the area.

Maxwell tried to listen. What was it that Lex caught that they hadn't?

"Wait…is that?" Maxwell swiveled his head toward Karina who furrowed her brow, one hand to her ear.

"What?"

He saw something flash, and looked over Karina's shoulder. They really did not have good luck, did they?

Chapter Fifteen

Behind them was another group of men with the same uniforms. The afternoon rays glimmered off their badges as the sun began to sink, a cop car coming up quickly behind them, its siren off.

He heard a soft growl of annoyance and it took him a moment to realize it came from Lex. "Keep up with me, or you're dead," he said as he grabbed Maxwell's and Karina's wrists. Maxwell nodded. Karina's was pale as her gaze snapped between where they were going and behind them.

"He's got to be kidding," Karina said, barely loud enough for Maxwell to catch.

What was it that his sister and Lex could hear? He put his free hand to his ear as they moved down a side street that seemed to curve to the right at the end. There were no alleys, the houses being mushed against each other and crumbling. The air felt almost stifling and, were those screams? Fear slipped up his spine. Lex pulled them along as they darted forward toward the sounds and sharply acidic smells.

They turned the corner and Maxwell almost stumbled to a stop. It was mass chaos. Down the dilapidated street were a group of men and women. They seemed to be fighting. Blades flashed as gunshots cracked. Farther down the street, a building was on fire as people whooped and hollered, throwing things into the flames. Houses burned as smoke curled into the sky. Pedestrians, if that was what they were, wielded torches, wood implements, chairs, whatever they could get their grasp on.

A riot, Maxwell realized with a sense of downright horror. They ran right into a riot, by running from the police. There was a whoosh of air before Karina suddenly cried out. Maxwell regarded his sister quickly as Lex pulled them sharply down the road. Maxwell let him lead as he saw Karina stumble before she regained her footing. A grimace sat on her face as something dripped down her arm. Something Maxwell couldn't quite identify as she held her arm close to her chest.

"Kari? Are you all right?"

"Peachy," was her curt response.

Maxwell hesitated before he nodded and looked ahead. Lex let out a noise of something like relief. "Come on," he said sharply, yet soft enough to stay under the screams of the rioters.

Wood littered the ground in smoldering heaps as people huddled in the shadows, scared of the mayhem. A little before the main focal point of the chaos was an alley which Lex seemed to be heading toward.

"Riot. The owner must have done something to anger someone," Lex whispered quickly as he eyed the alley and group, affirming Maxwell's suspicion, but doing nothing to assuage it. "That's probably what the police you saw earlier were here for… damn."

Something didn't sit right with him. Was this normal? Were riots and such something that occurred normally? Was it because of the epidemic? Many people in the crowd looked incredibly sick.

Lex didn't stop, even as the chaos grew. People ran into them, trying to run from the source, while others, who were too drowned in the mob mentality, continued destruction along the street. Sirens blared and cries echoed up and down the road.

Something cracked, the noise louder than Maxwell thought possible. A gunshot? Maxwell felt Lex stumble. His eyes snapped toward Lex as he maneuvered them into the shadow of the alley before letting go. Karina fumbled and used her now-free hand to grab her arm. Pain adorned her face as Maxwell realized with a hint of shock that it was blood slipping steadily down her arm and staining her shirt.

He heard a groan, followed by movement. He looked toward Lex. One arm wrapped tightly around his stomach as he gestured them forward. "We're not safe," was all he said, the voice cracking slightly at the end. "We have to move." He pulled one hand away from the wall and moved unsteadily down the street.

Maxwell's head swiveled back and forth in heightened worry,

looking from his sister and Lex to behind them, even as they continued down the alley. He could hear screams and he could see some people run by the entrance. The shadows become lengthier as night drew closer. He hated this time of year sometimes. Days were incredibly short and this wasn't an exception. He happened to look ahead in time to see as Lex started to pitch forward. He quickly grabbed Lex around his waist, stopping him from slamming face first into the ground. He clenched his teeth at the almost dead weight as Karina moved next to him, trying to help.

What am I going to do? Maxwell thought. *They're both injured.*

They took another alley, seemingly parallel with the main road. He gazed back. It seemed that there was no one following, yet he could still see the smoke from the fire, and hear cries, screams. Now, on top of all that, sirens blared through the air, discordant and screeching.

He shook his head and shifted. He draped one of Lex's arms over his shoulder as he put a hand around his waist, feeling the warm liquid slip past his fingers. Karina led the way even as her grip seemed to tighten more and more on the wound to her upper arm till her knuckles were white. They moved down the alley as quickly as they could, reaching another back alley. Maxwell gritted his teeth as Lex's weight seemed to get heavier and heavier. His breathing was shallow.

"Damn, the doctor, we're so close," Lex managed to whisper in pain, his free hand still holding his stomach.

Maxwell looked at Lex, then heard hollers. His head twisted back, seeing shadows play on the wall behind them from the alley. Figures seemed to be moving toward them and whether they were hostile or not, he didn't want to find out.

Maxwell's eyes flitted around the darkened road before he spotted a dilapidated entranceway. He gazed back and darted toward it. He pushed viciously against the door, which slammed open to allow him to stumble in. Dust billowed up as hinges screeched from lack of use. Maxwell coughed as he slid past the door, hoping that it wasn't actually someone's home he was barging into. He did not need that on his conscience.

The room seemed more like a storage place. It was dusty and dark with the vague hint of a stairwell next to one side. Barrels and boxes were thrown haphazardly around the room, giving it a dingy quality. Maxwell slid farther into the room as he pulled on Lex's limp frame. Maxwell curved around one of the boxes and slid to the floor with a sigh, pulling Lex down with him.

"Not good, there's a trail," Karina said.

Maxwell looked at her. "I'll lead them away. If they're police, they might come for us, and there's no way to defend ourselves in here." Maxwell looked at his sister and noted her tense posture even as her arms dropped to her sides.

She's not, Maxwell thought as his eyes widened. He opened his mouth to shout, only to feel a shaky hand cover his lips.

"She's distracting…" Lex said.

Maxwell wanted to yell to her to stop, feeling anxiety as Karina looked at him. Yet, no words came out as she moved around the boxes and bolted out the door. The door swung closed as footsteps resounded outside.

"Someone's there. They're getting away," a bellow came from outside as more pounding footsteps ran by, and metal clattered as sirens blared.

Maxwell stayed silent. His eyes were frozen on the closed door as the hand continued to sit over his lips. He could feel wetness slip down his chin as the hand fell away. Maxwell froze as he put a hand on his chin and wiped. He stared in horror as the liquid sat on his fingers, staining them a crimson red as some slid down pale skin.

He slowly followed the trail before his eyes slid to Lex. His hands were covering his side as he gasped for breath. Maxwell's mind ground to a halt before it clicked into hyper speed. Panicked thoughts swam through his head as he skimmed back and forth between the door and Lex. He gulped worriedly as the blood continued to slip past his shaking fingers.

"I'm fine…" Lex said as he grimaced.

Maxwell pursed his lips tightly before getting a sharp look from Lex.

"Just make sure we're safe. I'll be fine."

Maxwell frowned, but decided to do as he was told. He didn't exactly know how to take care of what could possibly be a bullet wound. He pushed against the box at his back. His eyes slid closed as he listened. He heard more footsteps and whipped his head toward the doorway, heart pounding. His breath caught, before the footsteps passed and he breathed once more.

His thoughts raced as he stared at the doorway. *Please, Kari, don't do anything else stupid,* he thought as he clenched his fist. Through the cracked windows he could vaguely see the sun's rays casting long hazardous shadows outside, splaying everything in reds and golds. He softly growled in frustration. Chilled air slid through cracks in the building as wood creaked. Trash and cement littered the floor with a thick layer of dust that was slowly falling back into place around the building. Lex groaned quietly as he leaned awkwardly against the wall. Maxwell winced.

He pulled himself up and, making sure Lex was comfortable, he slid close to the doorway and peeked out into the alleyway. Shadows danced on the walls as the night lights flickered unceremoniously. Crimson spotted the paved road, almost black.

He perused the street before he pulled back inside. He moved back behind the boxes and next to Lex. Lex's eyes were scrunched tight as sweat trickled down his brow. His back arched against the box. His hands were held shakily to his side as he tried to draw in breath.

Maxwell's eyes widened before he quickly took the hands away, scanning over the wounded area. Panic surged through his system once more. It was worse than he thought. He thought it was just a graze, considering how Lex was talking somewhat all right earlier, but with the amount of blood, it certainly didn't look like it. Now he just felt out of his league. What was he supposed to do? He helped his ma occasionally take care of Karina when she got too reckless, but this wasn't a minor scrape or twisted ankle.

"I'm…fine…" Maxwell's gaze shot to Lex as his eyes flickered open. They seemed slightly dulled with pain as he spoke in a trembling and quiet voice.

"Sure, you look like you're going to keel over," Maxwell growled semi-sarcastically as he grabbed the vest. He ignored the implications of the statement the first time, too worried about Karina and where they were, but he was not in the mood to ignore it this time. A part of him wondered why he was still fine, why he wasn't injured at all. That part was pushed aside as he looked over his hurt comrade.

"It should be fine now, just go. The doctor isn't far, just around the corner…"

"You talk like that and I'll have Kari slap you when she gets back."

Maxwell couldn't believe this was happening. It all happened so fast. He wasn't ready for this. He paused. No, he had to think positively. "Just hold on, we'll get some help. I'm not going to just leave you here to die, idiot," Maxwell said firmly.

His mind was shouting at him to do something, but he didn't want to just leave Lex here, and he was worried about Karina. Yes, the doctor was around the corner, but he wouldn't know specifically where and running out there without knowledge would be completely stupid. He quickly shifted Lex so he was lying on the floor.

Lex grunted in pain as eyelids flickered closed. He grinned and coughed. "I thought idiot was my word," he said.

Maxwell huffed as he pulled his sweatshirt off and stuffed it under Lex's head before he grabbed the damaged vest. "I think I'm allowed to say it if you're being stupid about taking care of yourself," he responded as he quickly unzipped the vest and pulled it away. A shiver ran up his spine, and he felt his teeth chatter. It had gotten cold quickly and his scattered thoughts weren't really helping in that matter.

"Though, I think you might want to stay quiet for a while," he murmured as he peeked at the shirt underneath. The wound was low, and blood slid out at an alarming rate. He grabbed the shirt and pulled it up to get a better look at the wound. He knew it probably wasn't the best idea to expose it to open air, especially since the place was so downtrodden, but he highly doubted that was the main problem at the moment.

The wound was deep. He grabbed a part of the shirt that was still clean and ripped it. After some struggling, he managed to get enough. He wiped away what blood he could. If he guessed right, then a bullet was probably still lodged somewhere. He grimaced and put his hand against the wound firmly to try to slow the flow as he felt the skin.

Crud, this is beyond me, Kari, he thought as he shivered once more from the frigid chill. Red glimmered dangerously in the dusty light. He pressed harder as Lex's breathing started to become more labored.

"Come on, Lex," he muttered as he pushed down.

Kari, where are you? Please be safe...and hurry.

~ * ~

Karina hugged the wall as sweat dripped down her brow. Black, soaked-with-sweat hair fell out of her normally neat hair tie, falling around her shoulders in a heap and sticking to her forehead and neck. She gazed out of the shadows of the alley, her back pushing against the wall behind a spilled over dumpster. She watched dazedly as the police ran by.

Lights flashed as shouts echoed around the area. *Please...please be safe*, she thought tiredly as she watched for a few more minutes. Slowly, the panic started to die as those who hadn't been taken yet were rounded up. Black-clothed men paraded up and down the street, raking the area for any escapees. She pushed herself farther back.

It hurts...it hurts, she thought as she shivered in the cold air, feeling weak. She slid down the side, tucking her legs in close as she continued to watch. After a few more people passed and it quieted down, she stood. She gazed left and right before she moved out of her hiding place, a small side street snuggled closely between two large buildings. Her feet stumbled over trash and other things she didn't want to think about as she started to make her way back the way she came.

She tried to shake herself out of her daze. *I have to get my brother. He's waiting*. She swayed before she took a few more steps forward. Her vision swam as the buildings shifted around her. She saw something. Was that a figure rushing toward her? Who's that? White? Doctor? What is a doctor doing out here? She closed her eyes. It was one second. At least, she thought it was a second.

She felt off center, off kilter, whatever the phrase was. Her eyes opened to see the ground a lot closer than it had been and she could feel something around her waist. *Arms? What? Why was the ground so close?*

"You'll be all right. I'll get you to a hospital, just hold on."

Hospital? No, then what about…?

"Come on, you're going into shock, I'll take you."

No. I can't…I can't leave Max. He's by himself… by himself with Lex who's also injured.

"What are you doing, stop struggling, you're losing too much blood."

Struggling? I'm just getting to Maxwell, I have to. I don't care. I need to get to my little brother. I can't lose him, not him as well. She shrugged the person away and stumbled.

"Please…" her voice wavered as she spoke, but she forced it out as she faced the doctor. "Please help them."

She saw him hesitate. Why wasn't he moving? Didn't she ask for help? Maybe?

She grabbed an arm, her sight slanted. She pulled at the arm, tugging and leading. She needed to hurry. She couldn't wait. She tugged once more before she took off. Her feet carried her around the buildings as a shout echoed from behind her, one that sounded muffled, as if through a funnel. Her sight was narrowed, her thoughts sporadic at best, all focused on her brother when coherent. She didn't care. She needed to know he was all right, that she was able to lead them away. That no one hurt her brother.

Max, please be safe.

Chapter Sixteen

Max glanced up and around the pillar as something sounded near the doorway. He went to speak, only to freeze as his mouth snapped shut. He jolted behind the box. Instead of Karina, he saw a man standing in the doorway, casting a small shadow into the room. Maxwell scrunched down more as he put a hand carefully over Lex's mouth. Maxwell's breath caught in his throat as he continued to press down on the wound, hoping against hope that the man wouldn't see them.

He could hear shuffling from the entrance and then a voice spoke up. "What are you doing? We already cleaned this area of rioters."

"I thought I saw movement."

"You always say that, come on, let's go."

"Right."

Maxwell sat there in silence as he heard the footsteps fade, before he slumped down and closed his eyes. After a moment of recollection, he peered toward Lex and pulled his hand away. He was quiet even as sweat dripped from his brow. Lex grimaced, before he started to cough viciously. Maxwell looked toward the exit as the coughing subsided. He heard sounds from outside once more and then the running of footsteps. He faced the door in time to see Karina come in. Her face was ashen and she seemed to be staggering. Dazed eyes gazed around worriedly.

"Max," she called in desperation.

"Here!" he called back, earning a sharp twist of a head from his sister and a relieved smile when she noticed him. She seemed to sway as her eyes flickered. Just as she was about to collapse, another man ran in, panting heavily. He grabbed Karina as she dropped to the ground.

"Karina?"

The man looked up.

Maxwell eyed the man, feeling lost, worried, confused, panicked, he wasn't actually sure anymore. Lex coughed again weakly.

"More? Is this…?" The man paused before he grabbed something out of his pocket and twisted it around Karina's upper arm, probably to ebb the bleeding.

After that was done, he carefully placed her on the floor and raced over to Maxwell. The man took one look and Max could have sworn his eyes almost popped out of their sockets for a second. Then again, he only half paid attention as his eyes snapped between Lex and Karina, not having a clue on where to go.

"Lex." The man quickly rushed forward until he was even with Lex. He knelt down and immediately went to checking the wound. Max was forced to pull his arm away as the man busily went over Lex's condition before he groaned in frustration.

"Damn, this isn't good, I don't have my equipment, and there is no way we can move him anymore, plus I can't call the ambulance like I was originally going to for the girl. Argh!" He growled once more until he glanced toward Maxwell. "You seem to be the only one uninjured, help me get him up, we're going to have to carry him, I don't like it, but there's nothing else we can do and we don't have the time."

Maxwell looked between Lex and Karina, hesitating.

"Come on. You can come back for her later, but we have to get him there now."

Maxwell opened and shut his mouth.

The doctor growled and squatted down. "Fine. At least help me get him up, I'll take it from there. You get the girl and follow me."

Maxwell nodded and reached forward, helping the doctor hoist Lex onto his shoulder, his legs dangling down and blood staining the doctor's clothes. The doctor stood with Lex draped over his shoulder like a filled sack. He walked forward as Maxwell moved to his sister. Maybe he could carry his sister the same way? It was worth a shot.

He knelt down to look at Karina. She was out cold. Maxwell shivered as the chilled air invaded everything in the area. The sun continued to creep closer and closer to the horizon. He needed to hurry.

He couldn't lose track of the doctor now. He put her over his shoulder, holding her legs tightly. Now that he thought of it, this must be the fireman's carry he'd read about.

He didn't think he would have to use it.

He went to stand and stumbled under the weight, just in time to see the doctor move out the door. He staggered after him, trembling. Karina was heavy, way too heavy. He hoped it wasn't far.

To Maxwell's immense relief, they really didn't have to go far. After turning the corner, they just went straight for a short time before they reached a clean-looking white building. They slipped inside to find a pristine little waiting room. Plants sat in the corner, along with a few sets of plush armchairs. The area was quiet, the sounds of the riot all but gone. The doctor raced into a back room. Maxwell went after him, struggling under Karina's weight. He managed to get into the room to find Lex already laid out on an examination table. It looked almost like a trolley. Lex seemed even worse, if it was possible, than before.

The doctor was busy in the room, collecting supplies and tubes. He looked up and then gestured his head toward the second table. "Boy, my staff just went home, so you're going to have to help."

Maxwell nodded as the man quickly washed his hands and slipped gloves and a mask on. "Damn, of all times to let them go, it had to be right before a riot, damn this epidemic," the man said as he gathered tools and placed them on a rolling trolley. "It's going to be touch and go for this brat, but either way, you have to focus on the girl. She pushed herself too hard."

Maxwell placed his sister onto the examination table, and almost sighed in relief. His arms ached and his shoulder was screaming at him. He looked her over, hoping she was all right. He heard movement and looked over to see the doctor begin to carefully dig into the wound with a set of instruments Maxwell couldn't name. Shock slipped through his mind as he stared in horror.

"Clean up that girl's arm and start bandaging it. Don't forget to elevate her feet," the doctor stated as he continued to work.

Maxwell nodded before he focused on Karina. He looked around before he pulled the pillow from under her head. *Sorry,* he thought as he placed it under her legs so they were up. Once satisfied, he washed the wound with the water bowl sitting on the trolley. He heard a clink and looked over to see a blood-splattered bullet on the metal tray. Cringing, he grabbed some ointment and wiped Karina's wound off, trying to focus on something else. He applied the ointment before he grabbed a set of bandages he spotted nearby.

He lifted Karina's arm and placed one end of the bandage above the wound, leaving some available, before he had the rest circle down over it. He covered it and finished it off by tying a quick knot and pulling it tightly. She was still pale. He went to grab his sweatshirt, only to realize he left it back in the abandoned building. He mentally swore before he cast an eye over the room. His eyes caught on to what the doctor was doing and he stared, transfixed. Quick hands slid a needle in and out of the wound and skin, before it was pulled together and clipped shut. The doctor wiped his brow and walked up to what looked like a fridge and opened it. He stared and cursed.

"Boy, what blood type are you?" he asked as he turned toward Maxwell.

"What?" Maxwell asked, taking a step back and bumping into Karina's bed.

The doctor sighed. "Sorry, I have Lex on plasma at the moment, but he lost a lot of blood and you happen to be the only one around who's healthy. My blood wouldn't work. I'm not the right one."

Oh, Maxwell thought as he peered toward Lex. "I'm not sure..."

The doctor grimaced before he walked out the door into another room. After a few minutes, he returned with a syringe. "All right then, I hate to do this, but at the moment, I don't have much choice. Let's hope you have a blood type we can use."

Maxwell hesitated before he closed his eyes and extended his arm. The doctor took it carefully and after a quick examination, slid the syringe in. Max winced, but held still as the doctor carefully pulled it out and covered the wound. Maxwell slowly opened his eyes and pulled his arm down. The doctor was gone, probably checking. He felt so lost and confused, his gaze shifted between Karina and Lex, he shuffled so that he was between them and gently laid a hand on each bed. He wasn't sure what else he could do.

"Looks like you're a type O. That's good. I'll need a pint." Maxwell turned toward the voice as the doctor once more entered, a relieved expression on his face.

Maxwell nodded and the doctor gestured for Maxwell to follow him into another room where there was a table set up. This one looked like a regular examination table, one that couldn't be moved. The doctor gestured for him to lay down and he did. He quickly looked away, holding out his other arm. He stared at the wall as the doctor worked. It was a bland room with gray walls and a painting hanging off to one side. Tools were sitting in closed, windowed cabinets.

Maxwell stayed silent, only to shift his eyes when the doctor pulled away. The blood slid into the bag suspended above.

"You were lucky, neither wound was fatal."

Maxwell regarded the man silently as he leaned heavily against the counter.

"While the bullet did stop, it only hit muscle and skin. He lucked out that it didn't chip or smash into bone." He let out a world-weary sigh.

Now that he wasn't as rushed, Maxwell took in the doctor's appearance. He was a dark-haired man with brownish skin and light brown eyes covered in thin-wired spectacles. He was tall and lean but muscular. However, even he did not seem immune to the disease that was present everywhere.

"Now, can you tell me what you were doing? Did you get caught up in the riot or part of it?" the man asked in annoyance.

"We got caught up in it. We just arrived in town and were looking for you. At least, I think… Unfortunately, we got caught up in that thing. What was that about anyway?"

"Just too much anxiety. When things get rough and tempers rise, it's common to see people going out of control, and with the epidemic…" The doctor shrugged as Maxwell nodded. "By the way, the name's Girshwin, I know Lex's, but what are yours and the girl's?"

"Maxwell, and that was my sister, Karina," he said.

The doctor nodded and said nothing more.

The two sat in silence as the doctor watched the bag fill.

"That should do. If I take any more blood, you're going to be lying next to those two." He walked to Maxwell and slid the syringe out. Maxwell winced and turned to the man as he secured the end. He cleaned up Maxwell's arm as he spoke. "If everything goes well, they should be fine within a few days. Now why don't you get some juice? I have to do some things, but you can use whatever is within this clinic." The man pushed his glasses up with one hand while the other finished applying a bandage to Maxwell's arm. "There's a kitchen down the hall." He walked out.

Maxwell stood up, only to put a hand to his head in slight dizziness. "Oh…that's what he meant," he said quietly as he moved toward the door.

He slipped out into the hallway that led to the waiting room and, in the other direction, more rooms. He started down the hallway. The first room seemed to be a bathroom. The one after that was another pristine medical room. It was after that when he finally found a kitchen.

He stepped up to the fridge and, inside, found a bottle of orange juice. He pulled it out and opened it before downing half of it. He put it down and looked out the window set above the sink.

A half-moon shone brilliantly down through the small window. He tried to peer at the stars, but once again, they were blocked by the city's smoke and light. He heard knocking and walked down the hall to see a woman run in. "Doctor Girshwin. Doctor!" She looked around, panic-stricken.

The doctor walked through the front door, much to Maxwell's surprise, and spotted the woman who ran up to him. Maxwell saw them have a quiet conversation, not sure what they said. The doctor nodded before he turned to Maxwell. He threw a set of bags on the floor. "I put a chair into the room, go take a rest," he said before he went out the door, followed by the woman.

Maxwell squatted down and scooped up the bags, holding them close. Did he actually go back to get them? Maxwell thought as he stared at the three backpacks. He looked toward the doorway once more.

Maxwell walked into Karina's and Lex's room. He peered at the two sleeping quietly on the beds. Tubing hung around Lex as a quiet beeping filled the air. Maxwell could see a blood bag sitting over Lex, his own, probably. They already looked a bit better. Each had a blanket over them, which must have been thanks to the doctor. He yawned. He noticed a chair near the other end of the room. He walked over, placed the bags down and pulled it next to Karina's makeshift bed. Maxwell sat down and crossed his arms before laying his head against the bed. He could look for another bed to bring in, but he really just wanted to stay near his sister for now. Plus, the beds didn't look that comfortable at all. His thoughts were scrambled and a little sluggish.

He closed his eyes as his bangs drifted in front of his face. *Who were those guys? Why couldn't we take Lex to a hospital?*

Fatigue started to take control, both from the lack of sleep the night before and the running around and anxiety from the past hour or so.

He felt his eyelids flicker again as his head slumped forward. He closed his eyes to feel a comforting darkness before he forced them open. After another moment, he gave up and leaned his head into his hands and fell asleep right next to Karina's slowly rising and falling chest.

~ * ~

Maxwell blinked his eyes blearily as he slowly sat up. His back ached and his neck was stiff from sleeping at a weird angle. He saw his sister and Lex, still sleeping comfortably. Maxwell yawned and sat up to stretch. He felt something pop into place and winced before he tilted his head to the doorway. There was a light knock, then the doctor walked in, looking tired.

"Looks like they are recovering nicely. I managed to place a new order for blood last night, so it should be in by later today. I also cleaned up the girl a little, just to make sure she didn't get infected," the doctor said as he yawned.

He turned to Maxwell. "I know you probably want to stay here, but after giving blood like you did, you have to get some food in your stomach. You might also want to wash up. Here, I'll lead you to the bathroom. You have a set of spare clothes, correct?"

Maxwell nodded and stood. He blinked as he wavered before

stabilizing. "Whoa…" he said as he put a hand to the bed. Doctor Girshwin frowned before he stepped forward. Maxwell straightened. "I'm fine, it just surprised me, that's all."

He grabbed his bag and walked toward the doorway. He sent back a fleeting look before he slipped out. He followed after the doctor who walked past the kitchen. He gestured toward the bathroom then walked toward the kitchen.

Maxwell watched him go before he stepped inside. It was a small bathroom. A standing shower stood to one side, barely big enough to wash. A railing clung around it, and Maxwell suspected it was for patients who had trouble standing. He placed his clean clothes down and pulled off his shirt.

He stared at the blood and threw it to the floor, feeling slightly sick.

"How did I manage to avoid getting hurt?" he muttered as he stripped down, staring at the blood stains. He stepped into the shower, relishing in the warm water. It felt like forever since he'd been clean. He scrubbed till his skin felt almost raw, the water at his feet started out grimy and slowly started to disperse as it drained.

Once he finally felt clean, he stepped out and threw on his clothes. He already felt better. The little nap earlier helped and the shower woke him up as well. His stomach churned, growling quietly in hunger. He glared at it and stepped outside. His dirty clothes were wrapped tightly into a bundle, held under one arm.

He ignored the smell.

He stepped into the kitchen as Dr. Girshwin put down a plate filled with a large omelet. He looked up. "You clean up well. Let me take your clothes. I'll have one of my nurses clean them up when she comes in. They should be coming in shortly, I'll introduce you."

Maxwell nodded. He handed over the clothes, then slid into his seat.

He picked up his fork, then paused. "By the way, you met Lex previously, what happened last time he came through?"

Doctor Girshwin paused for a second before he got back to work. "He came in needing help, that's all I can say. You'd have to talk to Lex if you want to know more. I can tell you that it was a rather rude meeting, if I say so myself. Once he was recovered enough, he told me he came from a city east of here. By the way, where are you from?"

"We just came from Reinmark."

"I see, a nice trip, and yet he still manages to come knocking at my door, half-dead," Girshwin said. "Now eat, that should help you get some strength back."

Maxwell went to scoop up a bite. Before he got too far, he heard the front door open and footsteps walk down the hall. He looked over toward the doorway, just as a young boy ran in. He looked to be about ten with a darker complexion and cold hazel eyes. The boy looked at the doctor before his eyes moved to Maxwell, who just placed the food down.

The boy's eyes seemed to narrow dangerously as he looked Max over before he shot forward. Maxwell yelped as he tried to get out of the way. The chair slipped and fell back which caused his legs to tangle in the wood and his head to smack painfully against the floor. His hands shot to his head as he felt someone sit on his chest. He blearily opened an eye to see the boy was on top of him, a hand raised dangerously.

"Oliver. What are you doing?" a feminine voice shouted from the area near the doorway.

Oliver seemed to pause as Maxwell hissed painfully. A moment later, Oliver dropped his hand as he peered over his shoulder.

"But Mom… he's a Richie. Can't you tell? Don't you always tell me Richies are clean and…"

"That doesn't mean you should attack them!"

Maxwell slowly turned his head as he continued to massage the sore spot. Near the doorway was a young woman with a child in her arms. The little girl couldn't be more than three. Both had the same complexion as the young boy. The mother's face was stern.

"Oliver, will you get off one of my blood donors? He needs to eat."

All three sets of eyes shifted to Doctor Girshwin. His hands crossed leisurely in front of his chest, belaying the tense posture.

Oliver scoffed before he slowly climbed off Maxwell.

What the heck just happened? Maxwell thought as he pulled

himself up, along with the seat.

"Sorry about my son, I didn't expect him to do something like that," the mother said as she gazed over Maxwell worriedly.

Maxwell noted her eyes staying on his sweatshirt and face a little longer than necessary, they were filled with fear. "You're not going to take repercussions…right?"

"Don't worry, Jeanne, this boy won't be doing that, he has enough to deal with besides Oliver's snap-judgments."

Maxwell saw the woman slump, as if relieved. The doctor was still leaning against the kitchen table while Oliver glared at Maxwell from one side of the room. Jeanne was near the doorway.

"Boy, why don't you start eating? If you don't, you'll faint from lack of nutrients."

Maxwell slowly nodded as he focused back on the food. He knew the others were watching, but he was too distracted to care. He grimaced as a bitter taste touched his tongue before he quickly swallowed. He took in the food. He saw spinach and cheese oozing out of the crispy egg. He sighed in annoyance before he took another bite.

"So…he's a blood donor?"

Maxwell stopped and placed his fork down as Jeanne peered at him.

"We just had an emergency, and it turned out his blood was compatible." The doctor spoke as he stepped forward. "Now, Jeanne, why are you honoring me with your presence?"

"My daughter, she's been sick lately, I think it might be…"

The doctor walked up to the little girl in Jeanne's arms. Maxwell managed to take a closer look. The young child's skin looked pale and she was shivering. The doctor put a hand to the child's head before he opened her mouth. After a few more minutes, he pulled back and sighed in dismay.

"I'm sorry, it seems to be the case."

"What? My little sister's sick? That can't be right. Why not this Richie? Why my sister?" Oliver shook in anger.

"I'm sorry, Oliver, I'm a doctor, but for this, there is nothing I can do…"

"Everyone's the same. All you stupid medical people. None of you care for us at all!" he yelled before he ran past his mother and out the door.

Maxwell felt uncomfortable.

The doctor groaned. His expression was distant as he looked at the mother as she ran after her son.

"That boy," the doctor said.

Maxwell looked at his plate with only two bites taken out of it before facing the doctor. "What was he talking about?"

The doctor glanced toward Maxwell before he reached a hand to his face. "I guess it wasn't like that in Reinmark… Anyway, I'll try to explain. For a few years now, many of the people in the upper class have separated themselves from the middle and lower classes. They began to live in gated communities and started to create their own ecological system. As a result, the middle and lower classes were left out to dry, unable to find work. Many grew resentful and even more started to detest the hierarchical system all together. The economy seemed to be on a decline, years passed and after some work, the people began to recover. This country, which used to be powerful about fifty years ago, slipped into third world conditions for a while."

Maxwell narrowed his eyes. That was definitely not what he learned in history.

"That's weird, I learned history in school, and it said nothing about that."

Doctor Girshwin pulled his arm down and gave Maxwell a calculated look. "What were you taught?"

Maxwell frowned before he spoke. "We learned about world history, about the wars, such as World War I and the Eternal War Era… The Eternal War Era was the time between World War II and the Vietnam War, named that way due to the fact America was involved in every war between those times. It was after that ended the United States closed off its borders and turned internal, no longer involving itself with the rest of the world. Imports and exports stopped. Our history says, according to the quiz we just took before leaving, that the culture boomed once more and, because of that, my hometown wasn't needed. If I remember right, my hometown before then was being used as a way to live off the environment and survive even after the country was devastated, but since that wasn't necessary with the lack of involvement world-wide, it just became a place for people to go for peace and quiet."

Doctor Girshwin raised an eyebrow and seemed to contemplate what he said before he responded, "That doesn't sound like Reinmark. What do you mean your community?"

Maxwell hesitated. He had forgotten others might not know about his hometown. "It's an area near Reinmark."

The doctor narrowed his eyes, after a few moments his shoulders slumped. "Your history is right up to the closing of the borders, but that was when things fell apart. The government, which had been focused on other countries, turned inward and started layering restriction after restriction on the people. As time passed, the rich, still getting richer, deemed the lower and middle class were inferior and, as a result, they moved into those gated communities. With no import or export between countries and no jobs from upper class rich, the country spiraled down. Unemployment boomed and the government didn't do a thing about it, saying that they were helping as much as they could. They deliberated, fought, voted, but nothing ever occurred. Three years ago, this damn virus hit. The hospitals, many of which are government-owned, rejected the lower class, saying they were going to die anyway. Private businesses and hospitals helped for a while. Soon, however, they got their hands full with the abundant amount of people who were in need of care. They had to pick and choose. Those who had a purpose for society and could be used were saved. Those who couldn't were left to die."

"That is really different."

So why is it that in class, we learned something else? Why did they lie? He thought, vaguely recalling the quiz they took before this whole thing began. They got everything else right, but why did they lie about the fact that instead of America booming in private businesses, it crumpled? What did that do? What was the point?

Doctor Girshwin continued. "The government, in order to avoid the war, secured the borders so tightly no information is allowed to come and go unless expressly admitted by the officials."

Maxwell slumped back, letting out a breath as he watched the sun rise through the kitchen window. Smoke and fog polluted the sky as a cry was heard from nearby. “That’s just…that doesn’t seem right,” Maxwell said. *What is going on around here? This just keeps getting more confusing, what was our community for? Why did they lie? What happened to this country?*

“Why don’t you finish eating? I’ll check on the patients, after I have to find Jeanne and talk with her once more.”

“Oh. That’s right. They just bolted out the door.”

Doctor Girshwin nodded as Maxwell stumbled to his feet. “I can help…”

“No, you need to recover. My nurses should be in soon as well. Please watch out for them. Let them know I’ll be back soon,” Doctor Girshwin interjected firmly.

Maxwell looked at him before he sighed and nodded.

Doctor Girshwin pushed away from the kitchen counter and walked out the door. Maxwell finished eating, cleaned his plate and went to check on Karina and Lex. He slipped inside and dropped into a chair.

Maxwell sighed and his head slumped to the bed. He let his arms dangle.

Too much had been happening lately.

Why hadn’t anyone explained the odd history before then? Were these Richies those people who separated themselves from main society? Were they the people who were from his community? How did Oliver know he was a Richie? Just from being clean? Didn’t Lex say the other day that it was possible that his hometown was forged through government need? That riot, was it really as common as the doctor made it out to be?

He closed his eyes. They got into a new city and already their lives turned crazy once more. He sat up and, after a quick scan of the two patients, he walked out the door. He didn’t want to just sit in there any longer, his mind was buzzing and, now that he knew they would be all right, he wanted to move around, just a bit. After a little exploring, he found an old computer. He regarded the area before he sat down and booted it up. After a few minutes, he found he was into the system.

"What? It's not locked? That's odd," he muttered as he clicked on a button for Internet Explorer. "Good thing it's just like my home computer."

He waited as the system slowly came up. The first thing that appeared was a news website. Not much was on it of interest. It was all about tournaments, government bills, debates and other things that made no sense to Maxwell. He moved the mouse over to another tab that was open right next to the original. He clicked it.

The first thing that popped up was a map with different colors and pins all over it. He gazed at the map for a moment, taking in the location of a peninsula. It was a map of the United States. He quickly let his eyes flit over the map once more, surprised to find that the west coast looked like someone had taken a bite out of it. He looked over the colored areas. There seemed to be five different colors and, on one side, was a guide. He looked at the guide.

So, this is a site that shows the spread of the epidemic, he thought in surprise as he peered through the guide before he looked back at the screen. *All right, red means that it is in the quarantine stage, yellow means it's on the boundary, blue means that it's under control, but present, green means it's still unaffected and white means they don't have data.*

Red seemed to cover most of the middle and southern states. Yellow decorated the northern states and parts of the lower middle. Blue was spotted throughout the map at random points. He managed to zoom in and found Reinmark to be in one of the blue areas, which somehow surprised him, yet at the same time, didn't. However, his eyes shifted to right next to it, where he knew his hometown should have been. In a wide area that looked like forest, it was pure white. He looked down. There were one or two areas in white, thrown throughout the country, but theirs seemed to be the biggest block. He tried to look for the green. To his dismay, he only found it in the northern west coast and a part of the northeast close to the borders.

"This..." he muttered in shock. "What is going on?" He slammed his hand onto the table to stand. He stared at the screen. This was beyond him, there was no way he could imagine all those places on that map being so badly affected by something he just found out about.

"I have to focus, if not, we'll never find Ma. That's what I have to do. I have to find Ma, then we'll figure out what to do," he stated firmly before he swung around and slid out of the room down the hall.

There's too much to deal with. There is too much that is messed up. I can't do a thing about it. We just have to find Ma and hope... He slumped against the wall close to the room, his shoulder held him up as he stared at the off-white wallpaper.

"Are you okay?"

Maxwell slowly tilted his head to the side to see who he suspected was one of the nurses. She was dressed in white with her thin blonde hair pulled up into a bun. He hadn't heard her come in. He must have been more out of it than he thought.

"Ye...yeah," he said. "Dr. Girshwin said you were coming."

"Yes, I'm the head nurse, where is the doctor?"

"He went to check on Oliver and Jeanne. He said he would be back soon."

The nurse sighed. "All right." She looked him over. "By the way, who are you?"

Maxwell fidgeted under her hard gaze, noting the scar down her arm, probably also from the sickness. "I'm Maxwell, I arrived last night with Lex and my sister. Dr. Girshwin took care of us."

The nurse nodded and sighed. "Of course." She hesitated. "Let me know if something's wrong, okay? I need to get back to work, patients will be coming soon." She hurried past and into another part of the clinic.

Maxwell watched her go. He closed his eyes as he let himself slide to the ground.

He tilted his head back to look at the ceiling as daylight shimmered over the clean environment. *What am I supposed to be doing?*

After a few minutes, he forced himself to his feet and stumbled into the doorway. He walked to Karina's side and slumped into the seat, wishing he hadn't gotten out of it to begin with. He sighed as he laid his arms against the side and placed his head on them. He let out a breath just to jump as he felt something twitch against his arm.

He dropped his hand to his side as he looked at his sister. Karina was breathing evenly, her eyes closed. He almost shook his head, thinking his mind was getting to him when he saw her fingers twitch again. He quickly picked up Karina's hand in his own.

"Kari? Hey, Karina…" he spoke carefully as he gently squeezed the hand. Karina's eyes scrunched slightly before bleary blue opened slowly. Her eyelids flickered for a moment before she turned to face him. Maxwell smiled widely in relief.

"Hey, little brother," she spoke softly, almost hoarsely, but Maxwell didn't care.

He removed his hands and quickly wrapped his arms around Karina, surprising his twin.

"You idiot! You're not supposed to act like a decoy and bleed yourself to death." Maxwell growled half-heartedly as he gripped Karina's waist tightly. Before she could do anything, Maxwell pulled back. He glared at Karina. "Don't go getting hurt again, got it?"

Karina grinned cheekily and nodded before she spoke. "Was little bro worried for his big sis?"

"Kari!"

Karina chuckled softly before she leaned back with a tired sigh. "What about Lex? Is he okay?"

"He's stable, but I don't know anything besides that. It's been kind of hectic around here," Maxwell said.

She seemed to think about it for a second. "Oh, right, I got that doctor guy and…I went back to get you."

"Because of that, you went and collapsed on me. What were you thinking?" Maxwell snapped before he slumped against the bed next to his sister. "At least you're all right now," he muttered sleepily.

A weight he hadn't even realized he was carrying lifted off his shoulders, leaving him, while not exhausted, very close to it. He yawned.

He could feel a shaky hand slip through his hair and he sighed. He was just going to ignore it today. He would knock the hand away when he woke up…probably. His eyes closed and he slipped into sleep.

Chapter Seventeen

Karina noticed her brother sleeping, feeling relieved. Maxwell looked a little better, but still, he was thinner and while he was healthy, he looked tired. Karina winced as she used her uninjured hand to run through Maxwell's hair comfortingly.

She looked around, scrutinizing the different medical items before landing on Lex. His eyes were closed. He looked to be sleeping peacefully.

She noticed the small bandages attached to the inside of her brother's arm. A quick glance confirmed it. Her brother had gotten or was given a shot of some sort.

She shifted subtly as she tried to sit up without waking her brother. She gasped in pain as she hit her arm wrong. She gritted her teeth, but ignored it as she finally managed to sit up. Her free hand still slipped through his hair, which had gotten considerably longer in the past few weeks.

She scanned the room before finding her attention drifting toward Lex. Now that she was sitting up, she could see he was bandaged around his abdomen and he was breathing steadily. He was slightly pale, but not like she expected.

She yawned. It seems like she wasn't quite recovered yet. She blinked tiredly before she heard a sound. She glanced up to be met with brown eyes covered in glasses. "Who?"

"You're awake. You shouldn't be sitting up quite yet, you're still recovering," he said as he walked forward.

"Are you the doctor?"

He nodded and pushed his glasses up as he looked at the trio, the boys were gone in sleep, so she was the only one awake.

"My name is Doctor Girshwin. You three arrive, and everything seems to go to hell. Now tell me, what would you have done if I hadn't found you? I could have easily been a policeman or someone else that would have followed you for a completely different reason. That would have brought trouble on all of you and Lex would probably be dead," he said evenly.

Karina glared. "I would beat them to a pulp if they dared to hurt my brother."

Her hand shifted so that she hovered protectively over him as he shifted in his sleep. She paused before she looked down. "Still, thank you," she mumbled quietly.

She saw surprise flicker over his face before he schooled his features and asked, "Why is Lex with you? He told me when he left, he was going to his uncle's, and didn't want to head this direction ever again. What made him come back?"

"I don't know exactly what you're talking about. Anyway, that's Lex's business. All I know is that we are looking for someone, and last we heard, she was in this city," Karina replied.

The doctor nodded slowly before he looked to Lex. "He should be recovered in a few days. That boy has a tenacity you rarely see these days. Oh, that reminds me, you should thank your brother when he wakes up. He helped take care of both you and Lex. He also gave Lex the necessary blood needed until I could get replenished. I'm surprised he was still so awake after…" He eyed Maxwell with a critical air, as if he noticed that something wasn't right. "I must ask, what was the last thing you two ate?"

"And he calls me an idiot," Karina murmured as she tried to think of what they ate recently. "Hot dogs? I don't think either of us ate much and I know we only drank a little because I forgot to refill our water pouches…"

Doctor Girshwin looked at her. Karina's stomach growled softly before she coughed. The doctor walked out and returned to give her a glass of water and some soft food. "The fact you're still sitting up shows how stubborn you are, but if you want to recover, have this and lay back down. You'll be able to get out of bed tomorrow," he said calmly as Karina looked at him warily.

After a moment, she took the drink and guzzled it down to soothe her dry throat before munching on the food.

"Finally, he's getting some decent sleep. He needs it after all he has been through…" Doctor Girshwin trailed off.

"What do you mean?"

"While you've been out for the whole night and late into today, he's been awake and moving for most of the time," he said. "Needless to say, all three of you are tenacious brats. That's for sure."

"Doctor Girshwin?"

In the entrance of the doorway was a young boy. The boy gazed over the group in a mixture of surprise and, was that repulsion?

"What is the Richie still doing here?" the boy pointed at Maxwell, yelling harshly.

The doctor seemed to want to sigh once more, but refrained from it. "Girl, go back to sleep. I need to talk with this one for a while." He frowned as he walked toward the door and pushed the boy out while he closed it.

Karina could just barely hear him ask, "Oliver, you need to stop just walking into my patient's rooms. What are you doing here anyway?"

"Who was that little brat?" she murmured as the voices faded. "What did he mean by Richie? Why did he call Maxwell one?" She gazed at her sleeping brother. She lay back down, her hand moving soothingly through his hair. "Good night, little brother…"

~ * ~

The day passed quietly into the next. Lex was still asleep, but Karina was finally able to move around, seeming to have recovered. Maxwell recovered as well after being forced to eat and drink every so often at even intervals.

About three days later, Maxwell happened to be in the room, helping the doctor trade out the bandages on Lex, when Lex moaned. Max froze before he hurried next to Lex's head.

"Hey, Lex?" He spoke carefully as he worriedly hovered over him.

Lex's eyes flickered open to reveal hazy gray-green. Lex looked at Max. Maxwell noticed a flicker of a smile and sighed in relief. "Hey, how are you feeling?"

Lex huffed softly as the doctor carefully pulled off the oxygen mask. "I hurt like hell," he coughed out hoarsely.

Maxwell chuckled as the doctor walked to the other side.

"I'm not surprised. Hold on, let me check a few things," Doctor Girshwin said. After checking vitals and his stitches, he frowned. "How strange, you seem to be recovering a lot faster than I thought," he said as he pulled away. "It seems like you're accepting Maxwell's and the other's blood well, that's good."

"Doctor. Sorry, I seem to have a habit of bothering you."

"Brat, this place would be boring without people like you spicing it up, I'm just surprised you've lasted so long."

Lex huffed. "I can't believe you still call me that, it was one time. One time."

Dr. Girshwin laughed while Maxwell peered between them curiously. "You shouldn't have tried leaving when you were passing out every couple minutes, or…"

"Ugh, I get it." Lex yawned and seemed to struggle to stay awake.

"Hey, you okay?" Maxwell asked, his smirk fading into worry.

"He'll be fine, he just needs more sleep, now that he's awakened once, it should be, as some phrase it, smooth sailing from here on out," Doctor Girshwin said as Lex's eyes closed. Maxwell felt relieved as he pulled away.

"That's good to know, I'm glad I was able to help."

"Thanks to you, we actually had something to give him until I was able to get more." He yawned. "Well, now that he's all set, I have to head out again. Oh, that reminds me. Do you know who happened to use the computer?"

Maxwell paused before he nodded. "I did, I was bored the other day. I'm sorry I didn't tell you."

"It's okay. However, notify me next time you wish to use it.

Though, you're probably still going to forget anyway, so never mind."

Maxwell winced, only to relax as the doctor chuckled softly. "By the way, you seem awfully busy. What have you been doing?" Maxwell asked as he leaned forward.

"I'm one of the few physicians and doctors in the area, and a lot of people get injured or sick around these parts, especially with the escalating riots and…" he seemed to pause, then sigh, "…protests. It's my duty to help. There are quite a few doctors like myself throughout this country. Actually, my mother is helping in the area near where parts of California, Washington, and Oregon used to be."

"Oh, what happened?" Maxwell asked as he remembered seeing the bite out of the country. He looked at the doctor. "Protests?"

The doctor waved the comment away before he spoke. "It happened ten years ago. It was a natural disaster. An earthquake that obtained a ten on the Richter scale hit and resulted in the ground weakening enough to cause a couple miles of the state to slip into the ocean, while the rest were affected by tsunami like waves. Millions died." He looked at the wide-eyed Maxwell. "My mother ended up staying around there to help those in the aftermath. She's one of the best around that's not affiliated with the government. Actually, she abhors them." He chuckled before he glanced at the clock.

Maxwell could hear the rattling of tires. One of the nurses must be running through. "Hm, looks like I have to go, keep track of him for me, will you?" he asked as he headed out the door. Maxwell slowly nodded as he left.

Maxwell regarded Lex, who was breathing evenly. He seemed comfortable. He slipped out the door and walked down the hall that he memorized over the past few days.

The place they were staying in was a one-story building with multiple doors that led to different parts of the clinic. It was spectacularly clean. The doctor was constantly coming and going from the place, to the point where Maxwell barely saw him at all during the day. The nurses were just as busy, flitting around from place to place. They had only recently returned his clothes. The shirt was unsalvageable, but the pants still worked.

After the first night, the doctor gave him a room for long-term patients, or so he said. The beds weren't the most comfortable in the world, but they were still better than the chair he had used. Karina moved to that room a day or so later, once she was recovered enough to move.

Maxwell sighed and stretched as he walked into the room he once again shared with his sister.

I'm glad I've gotten used to this, or else we would be at each other's throats a lot more often, he thought with a sigh as he walked to the bed and fell into it. He stared at the wall for a while in thought, letting the minutes drag by before he sat up. *I wonder where she went. I haven't seen her today,* he thought as he pushed himself out of bed once more. The sweatshirt clung to his frame as he stuffed his hands into his pockets. *Hope she's okay.*

He walked back out and down the hallway, passing by a nurse with a young patient in tow. After a few minutes, he came upon his sister, who happened to be on the very computer he found the other day.

"Max…"

Maxwell stiffened at Karina's voice and warily walked over. "Yeah?"

"Did you…have you seen this?"

He paused and peeked over Karina's shoulder before he cringed. It was the same webpage he saw earlier, the very one detailing just how bad the country was. He didn't know why, but he really wanted to distract his sister, pull her away from what she was seeing. Usually, he would be happy to talk about this, try to figure it out. He had a strong urge to protect his sister, whom he was almost positive was not fully recovered from the ordeal they just went through. "You know… it's been a while since we've been out, why don't we go outside for a while, get some gear and a little recovery gift for Lex. Oh. That's right. Lex woke up."

Karina stayed silent before she turned to Maxwell with a roll of her eyes. "Little brother…" She paused, as if biting her tongue before she continued. "Anyway, when did he wake up?"

Maxwell almost stumbled, surprised that the usually bull-headed girl was giving in so easily. "About ten minutes ago."

"How is he?" she asked.

"He should be fine now," Maxwell responded, recovering from the momentary shock.

He felt a sense of worry as they continued on with the conversation. Obviously, his sister was still a little out of it.

"Well, that's good." She looked back at the computer before she pulled away.

"I think I want to check on him. Want to come?"

Maxwell stayed silent. *Kari,* he thought, *you're still not feeling well, are you?* He watched as she peeked back at the computer. *Maybe I was right,* he thought, *because I never would have been able to pull her away if she wasn't still weak.* He turned and headed toward the door.

They left the room and walked down the hall in silence. Maxwell watched his sister as she stared listlessly at the wall. The duo reached the doorway and slipped inside.

"He doesn't look awake," Karina deadpanned.

Lex's eyes were closed and his breath was even. The oxygen mask no longer sat on his face.

"He fell back to sleep while I was with him. The doctor said it was normal," Maxwell said as he walked next to the bed.

Karina joined him a moment later and gazed at Lex. "Is it just me or does he look less pale?"

Maxwell had to agree, Lex didn't look as sickly as he remembered. "Yeah, he does," Maxwell said as he leaned against the chair he used earlier.

"Huh…"

"I hope he recovers soon."

"I hope so as well," Karina said as she pulled up a seat. She heard a soft mumble. She jumped while Maxwell looked over.

Lex was awake.

Maxwell grabbed the chair. Karina leaned forward. Relief was clear on her face. "You're all right."

"Yeah," he said, trying to sit up. He gave up after some struggling and instead decided to just use the pillows. "What's been happening while I was out?"

"Well…" Maxwell spoke, relating to him all the events that

happened after Lex was hurt while he slipped in and out of lucidity over the past few days. Karina chimed in occasionally, but stayed surprisingly silent. Maxwell wondered if it was because of what she'd seen earlier. Lex didn't seem that surprised. If anything, he just looked sad.

After he was done, Lex sighed and replied, "Not surprised. Uncle did say tension was rising around here. I'm guessing you haven't had a chance to go look for your mother?"

Max shook his head.

"I see…" He stared at the ceiling. "Finding her might be harder than we thought, with tensions so high. There might even be outright sanctions soon and that could escalate things way too fast for any of us to handle." Lex paused and looked over to Maxwell, who looked at him, confused. "Sanctions are restrictions." Maxwell nodded so Lex continued. "If that's the case, your mother might not even be here. It's highly possible that my person obtained off information, considering how hard of a time he had getting any in the first place."

"But, why would the information be so hard to get? What's so important about our ma?" Maxwell stated in confusion as he crossed his arms over his chest. "She's just a simple doctor and scientist."

"I really don't know, but from the sounds of it, it's not just her. What about you two?"

Maxwell thought before he leaned back in his chair. "I've been wondering that for a while. If they just wanted Ma, then they wouldn't be after us. Are they using Ma as bait or something? Or…" he put a hand to his head tiredly. "I really don't know."

"For now, we don't have the information. We'll just have to wait and see. After I can get out of bed, which should be by tomorrow or the day after, I'll see if I can contact my informant. By now, he might have more information to give us."

"Really? Are you sure?" Karina asked skeptically.

A small grin crossed Lex's face. "Yeah. That man can sound like a devil, but give him a challenge and he'll do everything he can to complete it. If he can, he will find your mother and make sure you get her to safety."

"I see. I hope so," Maxwell replied.

Chapter Eighteen

The day passed into the next. The twins watched as Lex recovered. People came and went from the clinic. Lex began to spend more time awake than asleep.

It was about three or so days after that when Karina, who was now much better, brought up a small problem.

"We need to go out and grab some things, we're out of travel food and you need clothes." Maxwell peered up from his orange. He peeled another slice off and popped it into his mouth.

"Really?" He paused as he munched on his treat and then remembered his trashed shirt and lost sweatshirt, thankfully, he had a spare, but that didn't mean much with the weather quickly getting colder. "Never mind, but shouldn't someone stay here? Not only that, but are you sure you're feeling better?"

"Of course," Karina said as she waved at Maxwell from the fridge, her eyes glued inside the cold appliance.

"If you say so…"

Karina pushed away from the fridge and looked at Maxwell. "I can go out for what we need, essentials-wise, then, later, you can get a new set of clothes. Deal?"

Maxwell nodded. "Do we have the money for all that, considering we've been giving a lot of it to the doctor to help pay for staying here?"

Karina stayed silent before she closed the fridge. "Yeah."

Maxwell stopped chewing as he paid attention to Karina. A quick memory of Karina talking with Martha made him quietly exhale before he nodded.

Karina waved. "If you're worried, I'll be fine. The doctor said I should get some fresh air anyway."

"Yeah, not around the entire city though. Try to be careful, okay?"

"Of course, and I'm going to say the same exact thing to you when you head out as well," she said before she slipped out the door.

Maxwell stepped toward Lex's room, just as a nurse walked out. She looked over and, before he could ask, said, "He's fine. Why don't you head inside?"

Maxwell nodded and walked in, closing the door behind him. Grabbing a chair, he slid into it, then noticed Lex was staring back at him. Maxwell jumped in surprise feeling a bit sheepish. "Sorry, did I wake you?"

"No," Lex said before he let out a long breath. "So where is your sister?"

"She went out to gather some supplies. We decided to split up. How are you feeling?"

"Like I got run over by Garret's semi," he said as he tried to shift. He winced and stilled. "Note to self, don't get shot again."

"Shouldn't that be obvious?" Maxwell said under his breath. He took another look at Lex who was sitting up with the help of a bunch of pillows. "What are you doing up? Shouldn't you still be sleeping?"

"Oddly enough, I'm good. I think I got enough sleep over this past… Has it been a week?" He frowned. "Interesting. I do feel better though."

"Didn't you just say you felt bad?"

"I do, but I don't feel as mentally tired." He paused. "It's probably just my imagination."

They sat in silence. After a while, the silence started to weigh on Maxwell. He sighed and stood before he peered around.

"Why don't you go out for a while? I'll be fine."

Maxwell slowly nodded. He stepped out and walked down the hallway and into the kitchen. "Dr. Girshwin," Maxwell stated in surprise.

The doctor looked tired. His glasses slipped down his nose and his clothes were ragged. "Oh, boy, I didn't see you," the doctor said. "How are the patients?" The man pushed away from the counter and grabbed one of the kitchen chairs before he sat down.

"Fine, but you look like you're going to keel over. What happened?"

"A sanction. This city is going to be shut down. It's officially reached quarantine levels."

Maxwell froze as the doctor put his head in his hands. "I could be wrong, but I heard the government officials within the city finally decided, after the riot the other day, that things have gone too far. They're closing the borders and forbidding public gatherings. Their excuse is that they don't want the infection to spread. It's a bunch of bullshit." The doctor looked Maxwell square in the eye. "That means you have to leave. If you want to ever leave this city, you're going to have to do it now."

"Our mother. She could be in this city. We have to…"

"If she is, then she is probably…" He shook his head, as if dispersing a terrible thought. "You're lucky. Most people don't know yet, I just happened to overhear some feds talking. It might just be a false alarm, but better safe than sorry."

Maxwell stared down at the floor. "That map, is this city going to turn red as well?"

"Probably…"

Maxwell grimaced. There already was a lot of red. He didn't want to imagine seeing more.

~ * ~

Karina hummed quietly. Bags layered her arms, including new clothes for her brother. She found it for sale and it was just too good to pass up. She walked down the brightly lit street as the sun danced over the glass monoliths around her.

She regarded the area curiously, taking in the sights.

While the city itself was beautiful, the air had a tension and overbearing darkness to it. She could hear whispers and mutters and she wouldn't be surprised if a man just came out of an alleyway and started swinging a knife or something equally as dangerous.

That didn't make her feel any better.

She looked around warily as she continued to hum to calm herself. She really didn't like this city and it took all her willpower not to lash out at the tension. It didn't help that every so often, she would see one of the officers in black, who seemed to be going around like a patrol. Cars zipped by as sirens blared ominously. What is with this atmosphere*? It almost seems like the whole city is at the point of snapping in two,* she thought as she turned another corner.

She sighed in relief, glad to see a street she recognized. With speedy, but even, steps, she walked up to the doctor's office and opened the door. She stepped in and quickly swung it shut.

She pushed her body against it as her heart pounded in her chest. Her eyes stayed closed as she tried to calm down. She mentally berated herself. *You're getting paranoid,* she thought as she lightly smacked herself upside the head. *Calm down.*

She finally managed to get the emotions under control and walked forward into the clinic proper. She passed by the waiting room to see it empty. She heard voices from the kitchen. She moved toward the doorway.

"That map…is this city going to turn red as well?"

She frowned. Map? Ah… Her thoughts momentarily slid to a halt before continuing. Now that she thought about it, she hadn't really thought about the map since Maxwell distracted her. Actually, she mused, she let that go easily. When did her brother start doing that? Was she really that tired? She pulled herself out of her thoughts. She would think of that later, just like her sibling suggested. She didn't want to think of that map, not right now.

"Probably. Now come on, let's get something to eat. Your sister should be back any time now."

I think that's my cue. She mentally smirked as she swung the door open and walked in. "Hey, little brother, Doctor." She nodded to Doctor Girshwin. "I managed to get some stuff, how are you two?"

She noticed Maxwell's surprise. "Good. Kari, you okay? You seem a little pale."

Stupid twin recognition, she cursed. "I'm fine, so, here." She put the bags onto the table before she grabbed one and passed it to Max.

Maxwell took the bag with a raised eyebrow and dug into it. Plastic rippled as he reached down and pulled out what was inside.

He froze, his expression morphed to one of embarrassment. A moment later, the thing was out of his hand and he held a new bag.

“Why was I just holding girl underwear?” he murmured in slight shock as he blinked at the new bag, then sidelong at his sister who coughed.

“Uh, don’t worry about it. Your outfit should be in that one.”

Maxwell frowned. “It’s not an outfit. It’s clothes,” he said brusquely, yet cautiously put his hand inside anyway. He felt around warily this time before he slowly pulled out a box.

“There should be two boxes in there,” Karina said, ignoring the comment, her blush having disappeared. Maxwell grabbed the other out before he laid them side by side. He opened the first to reveal a short-sleeved gray jacket with a hoodie and a long-sleeved black undershirt. In the next was a pair of faded jeans. Both looked a little used, but extremely comfortable.

“Do you like it? I managed to see it at a thrift shop and I thought it would look cool.”

“Thanks,” Maxwell said as he pulled the clothes out and put them together.

“Why don’t you try it on?”

“Maybe later, for now.” He eyed Doctor Girshwin seriously. “How about Lex? He won’t be able to leave anytime soon, and we do have to find Ma.”

Karina pulled out a chair. She swung it around before she sat down and laid her chin onto her crossed hands. “What do you mean, leave? I thought we were staying here for a while longer? It’s been a week, but we have yet to have a chance to leave and find her.”

Maxwell peered at his sister sidelong before he leaned against his chair. “This place is going to become quarantined. If we don’t leave, we won’t be able to. Not only that, but it will be harder to look for Ma with all those black uniforms around.”

Karina winced as she thought about that. “Yeah, that atmosphere felt really tense when I went out earlier. It’s almost like an explosion waiting to happen."

"I was afraid of that."

They glanced over to see the doctor sigh. "Tension has been rising for a while. It's no surprise it feels like everything is about to snap. That's the other reason why you three should leave. Your mother might be here or she might not. If you stay, you won't have a chance to find out. This place is going to be locked down tight, and if someone is looking for you, they will find you. I told Lex the same thing last time he was here, though it wasn't nearly as bad then."

Maxwell watched the doctor as the man gazed at both teens.

"If you're still worried, then talk with Lex, see what he suggests."

"Why?"

"Hm? Maybe because he has a bit more experience than you two? Don't know." He shrugged before he pushed away from the table and walked toward the door. "If it makes you feel better, I will ask around to see if anything strange occurred recently. Either way, I have to get things situated before this place blows sky high. I'll be back soon," he said before he walked out the door.

They watched him go before Karina turned to her brother. "What do you think?"

Maxwell thought, leaning back in his chair. His hand shifted, not knowing where to go. "Don't know, let's just talk with Lex. He did say earlier that this might be the wrong place so…" he trailed off as he stood and walked out the door, closely followed by Karina.

They moved down the hall and slid into Lex's room. Karina was surprised to see Lex was trying to slip his legs over the side of the bed in order to stand.

"Lex," Maxwell yelped. He ran forward and caught him just as Lex stumbled and fell out of bed with a groan.

"That didn't work," he muttered as Maxwell groaned under the weight.

"Obviously," Maxwell grunted as Karina joined them and helped Lex sit back down onto the bed.

"And you call us idiots," Karina murmured as Lex sat down with his legs trailed over the side.

He regarded Karina with sharp and surprisingly clear gray-green eyes. "You two are still idiots, but that's beside the point." He winced as he stretched his legs out and touched his bandaged torso. "I need to get to my phone. I know for certain I should have gotten something…"

Maxwell peered at the backpacks lined against the side of the room.

Karina stood and walked over. After she perused through the bag, she dug out the phone and tossed it to Max, who handed it to Lex. He powered it up. He sighed in relief as he found there was still some power left on it. The phone rang and startled all three in the group.

Lex flipped the phone open and held it to his ear. A moment later, he moved it away as a voice yelled through it.

"What the hell, you son of a bitch! I've been trying to contact you for half a week."

Karina and Maxwell glanced at each other in confusion as Lex moved the phone back to his ear. His eye twitched in annoyance. "Sounds like you're doing well. I've been a bit bed-ridden as of late. Now, tell me, what made you act like a spaz?"

The voice seemed to calm down, to the point where neither teen could hear him. Lex stayed silent as he listened, only to respond in short statements and questions. "Really...? Are you sure this time...? Crap… Why...? Got it, thanks. And say hi to your sister for me."

There was a growl on the other side before a harsh comment. They could hear as the phone snapped shut.

"What was that?" Maxwell asked.

Lex closed the phone. "My informant. He was just telling me the person he had been getting information off of warned him about a trap, then a day later, he died from the sickness. My informant doesn't believe that to be the case and managed to dig a little deeper. He told me he was suddenly rather curious about you two," he said as he gazed at the phone in thought. "He suspects your mother isn't actually here."

"But..." Karina felt Maxwell's gaze on her, firmly ignoring it.

"I'm just saying what he said, and I have to admit, I trust him on this. He doesn't lie when it comes to information, unless the stuff he gets is false itself. He isn't sure, but he suspects we should head southwest from here, and soon."

Maxwell watched while Karina gritted her teeth and clenched her fist. "What if Mom's here? We just abandon her because of an opinion?" Karina growled in frustration as she unclenched her hands. Why did she feel so angry? The tension? She couldn't tell, but it was bothering her greatly, she knew that much.

Maxwell looked away as a thoughtful expression crossed his face.

"So, you want to stay here and get caught, along with your brother, for something that the rest of us suspect is false information?" Lex asked.

"Why not? This is your fault anyway. You brought us to this damn death trap just to say that she isn't here. What's the point then? You almost got us killed because of wrong information? How dare you even say anything!"

Lex scrunched back into the pillows, holding his hands up.

"Karina…" Maxwell tilted his head back up, expression neutral, if a little sad. "Please calm down. Don't you think something isn't right about this place? Ever since we've come here, we haven't heard a word about anything. There are rioters going around causing havoc, patrolmen running around just as frantically, and everyone we've talked to recently has told us this isn't the place. I feel like they're telling the truth. Why would Mom be here? Why would they bring her to a town that's about to become a war zone, from what I can tell? To get her killed? Why didn't they just do that instead of take her? It just doesn't seem right." Maxwell calmly looked at her. Yet Karina could still see the worry and confusion in his eyes.

"Little brother?" she spoke softly. "We can't just..."

"Karina!"

She shut her mouth for a moment, then growled. "No, Maxwell, you have to listen, if there is even a small chance Mom is here, then we should check it out. I'm not trying to say we should stay here forever. That would just be stupid. I'm saying we should hurry and TRY to find her, right now."

"Kari, you're not thinking straight. If you do that, all of us will just get injured. I want Ma back as much as you do, but we can't just charge forward without any information, and, at least here, there isn't any."

"No, you listen, little brother, if we leave now and it turns out Mom is here, we won't be able to come back to get her out. Even if we could get back in, we wouldn't have a chance to get back out a second time." She reached her hand forward and grabbed her brother's wrist. She tugged. "This place is getting shut down within the week we have to hurry and…"

"And if we stay, we'll be caught up in it. We will never even have the opportunity to LOOK elsewhere, don't you get it?" Maxwell snapped as he wrenched his hand out of her grip. He stood in front of his sister with a stark serious expression.

Karina slashed her arm sideways as she growled back, her expression just as serious. "No, I don't! Why should we just go according to what others say? We've lived with Mom for the past four years by ourselves. The one time we follow someone else and we almost get killed. Now come on. If we don't hurry, we could lose our chance to find her. We KNOW…"

"No, we don't, we don't know anything. Ever since we left home, we haven't known a THING about what is going on around us. If it wasn't for Lex helping because of a promise, we would have never had the CHANCE to know. Now you're saying we should go against the people who do? The people who actually live in this world of sickness we just found out about barely a week ago?" Maxwell's voice softened. Kari took a step back, feeling like she was slapped. "Kari, we can't get away with the same things we did at home. One wrong move and we're all screwed. You saw those rioters, the police and even just the animosity. Even though we know nothing, everyone judges us because of what THEY know. We can't escape that, at least, not with the knowledge we have now. I want to rescue Ma, there's no denying that, it's been the main thing on my mind since we found her missing, but we can't do that if we let our emotions run us. We can't find her, let alone help her if we…"

"No, we can't, but we also can't just run." Karina replied sharply, voice a bit softer. Yet, she felt frantic, why couldn't her brother understand? "Maxwell, can't you see that this might be our last chance?

The last time we can see this city and see if Mom is here or not? We don't have to be here long, but if we can just…"

She stopped as footsteps sounded in the hallway. She looked back to see the doctor emerge, his face haggard and expression tired. He leaned back against the wooden frame as one hand pushed up his glasses. "I could hear you guys arguing from down the street." He lowered his hand to look right at Maxwell and Karina before he tilted his head toward Lex. "Unfortunately, now isn't the time for arguments, you're leaving, right now."

"What?" Karina's eyes widened as the doctor pushed away from the doorway.

"I talked with Jeanne, you remember her, right? I was able to speak with her. She will help you get out of the city and take you to her sister's. Even if she isn't too fond of your class, she won't abandon children that need help. From there, you will be able to move on, but if you want to leave, go now."

Karina opened her mouth and then she closed it. She clenched her fists and looked away. She could feel Maxwell's heavy gaze on her. It was painful.

"Can we really trust her?" Maxwell asked.

Dr. Girshwin looked at Maxwell before he nodded. "She won't do anything. She'll bring you out of here safely and do not worry about this city. I'll take care of things here, and if I hear anything, I'll find some way to let you know. I wish you luck." He reached into the pocket of his smock. "And here." He pulled out a letter and handed it to the twins. "I meant to send this a while ago, but never got around to it. If you happen to pass through the city of Lynn on the west coast, can you give this to a woman named Regina Girshwin?"

Maxwell stepped forward and gently took the letter as Karina stared. Maxwell slipped it out of the doctor's hand and nodded. "Of course…" he hesitated.

The doctor smiled. "Now get out of here, brats, or I'll kick you out myself," he said as he pushed away from the doorway. "Jeanne will meet you down the street, good luck." He disappeared out the door once more.

An uncomfortable silence followed as Maxwell held onto the letter and stared at the door. After a moment, he grabbed everyone's bags and darted to the kitchen. The slam of the door jerked Karina out of her reverie.

"Idiot." Karina gazed back at Lex, who once more tried to push himself to his feet, this time with success. "Help your brother. It'll help you calm down. This city's tension is getting to you."

Karina looked away. "I know."

Maxwell hurried back over, backpacks in hand and sweatshirt on. "Here. Let's get Lex out of bed, al… oh… never mind…" Maxwell trailed off.

"Lex?"

"I'm fine, a little weak, but I'll be able to walk."

Maxwell scrunched his brow before he slowly nodded. He walked over and grabbed one arm to pull it over his shoulder. Lex seemed a bit surprised by this.

"You're standing for the first time in over a week, we'll help until you can get strength back."

Lex opened his mouth, only to get a look from Karina. "Idiot," he muttered softly as he leaned on Maxwell. After a little finagling, the two were able to walk at a decent pace. Karina took up the rear, backpacks in hand and her sack on her back as she followed after the two, hoping Maxwell was right. She wasn't sure if she could handle the situation otherwise…

Chapter Nineteen

They walked out into the sunlit street. Pedestrians passed like usual as cars honked, but the tension was so tangible, one could taste it. Maxwell walked forward, his thoughts in turmoil. He hadn't meant to argue with Kari like that. They almost never argued. Everything must have just gotten to them finally. He understood Kari's side, but at the same time, he trusted Lex. He mentally groaned, only to look up as Lex shifted. He noticed him looking over his shoulder and he followed the gaze back to see the clinic. Near the front was the doctor, his expression sober and tired. A weak smile crossed the doctor's face before he turned and walked back inside.

He heard Lex whisper something, but he wasn't quite sure what it was. He once more faced Lex. Lex just shook his head. Maxwell let it go, figuring Lex would tell them if it was important, and he figured he should allow Lex some privacy anyway.

They continued down the street in this fashion and occasionally got an odd or critical look from passersby.

It was Maxwell who saw her first. He felt a hint of worry before he called out. "Mrs. Jeanne? Is that you?"

Jeanne, dressed in a simple shirt and pants, peered over in relief. "Ah, it's good to see you're out of the hospital. Oliver's still rather upset about that, but…" Jeanne trailed off before she fully turned to the trio. "I heard from Dr. Girshwin. If he trusts you, then I'll help." She frowned as her fingers fidgeted. She pursed her lips before she gave them a steely gaze. "Follow me, I know the shortest route to get us out, hopefully, the patrols haven't really picked up yet."

Maxwell stumbled after her as she started at a clipped pace. "Um, what about Oliver and…"

"They're already out of the city, I couldn't let those two end up in this," she said as she continued to look forward.

"Lead the way and we'll follow as best as we can. If anything happens, just go to your children," Lex said quietly.

Jeanne looked at Lex before she started down the road.

Maxwell could feel Lex leaning heavily on his shoulder, grunting softly as he stumbled forward.

Pedestrians hurried around, just like any other day. Jeanne weaved through the groups of pedestrians, closely followed by the trio. There were one or two scares with a group of policemen and a police car, but with careful maneuvering, they managed to avoid them.

Maxwell and Karina stayed silent throughout the trip. Lex, however, made small talk with Jeanne, probably trying to distract himself from the pain. The quiet conversation rang over the group as they got closer to the edge of the city. A block or two away, Jeanne came to a stop.

"Wait."

Lex's eyes narrowed. "Well, that's lovely," he muttered under his breath before he pushed away from Maxwell, who quietly yelped. "How do you propose we pass?"

Jeanne looked back at the trio before she looked ahead. Maxwell eyed Lex who seemed to be shaking where he stood. "Timing. As soon as we get through, run."

Maxwell's gaze snapped toward Lex. Run? How is Lex going to run?

"Don't worry, I'm feeling rather strong," Lex said

Maxwell frowned. *Strong? He has a barely healed bullet wound to the gut and the epidemic…*

Maxwell's thoughts were disrupted when he noticed the group already on the move. He hurried to catch up to them. Lex was walking slowly, his hand drifting to his gut. He seemed to notice, his hand jerking back down.

They turned the corner to find the street crowded with pedestrians and police. The police were, obviously, on patrol, ready to close the city.

Lex and Jeanne grabbed one of the twin's hands and walked forward. Maxwell felt Lex squeeze his hand, his arm trembling.

It didn't take much to realize how much pain he probably was in.

He peered toward his twin, whose eyes flitted to his before she looked away, her shoulders hunched.

Maxwell kept his head down as they walked down the street. He glanced over when he heard a ruckus. It was another group who was intercepted by the police. He gulped, and silently urged Lex on even as he limped beside him. Somehow, it worked. How? Pure dumb luck was how Lex phrased it later once he wasn't groaning in pain.

The police, their focus on the first group, hadn't noticed Maxwell and the rest of them as they passed through.

After going past a group of squat suburban houses, they made it to a small, tree-lined area. Karina ran up to the nearest tree. Her fingers ghosted over the branches as the sunlight streamed through the leaves. "These seem better than the ones in the park, don't they?"

She looked at Maxwell.

Maxwell covered his eyes to shield them from the sun's rays, glad that they were out of the brunt of the city. "Yeah, maybe because they seem natural, the park felt like it was man-made."

Karina bobbed her head in agreement.

"Mom!"

Both twins glanced down to see Oliver and a little girl step through the trees. Oliver didn't even look at them as he hurried to his mother's arms.

Jeanne knelt down and took them in gently, relief evident on her face. "Good. You two are all right."

"Of course. What are…"

"Not now, Dr. Girshwin asked me to take them with us. Now let's go, we have to make the bus before it leaves." She took his hand and stood before she faced the trio. "Luckily, it's not far from here. We'll be able to get to the bus station if we follow the tree line. Once on, it's a straight shot to my sister's place. Now let's go."

The trio trudged after the happy family as they walked past the quiet little woods. Cars slowly moved down the paved streets as wind whispered through the front lawns.

After a few minutes, Maxwell saw a sleek bus pull in a little ahead of them, next to a sign with a batch of people in front, all of them jostling for position. Maxwell wondered if they also knew about the quarantine, which was why they were all fleeing toward the bus.

He hoped that they would be able to get a spot.

"That's our bus," he heard Jeanne say as the woman picked up her pace to draw even with the others that were ready to get on. Maxwell moved behind her and followed suit. To his relief, they managed to get one of the last spots on the bus. Karina was scrunched up beside him, sharing a seat. Lex sat next to them, eyes closed as his fingers fidgeted in his lap. Maxwell was grateful they didn't have to pay that much, considering how little money he had, as well as how little space. A couple people were standing, jumping on right before the doors closed.

People chatted softly as the tires churned constantly over the gravel road. Maxwell kept his hands in front of him, feeling squished between Lex and Karina. He decided not to complain though. At least he had a seat.

His sister stared bleakly out the window, both arms positioned next to the glass. Her chin rested on her hand as raven locks fluttered into her face.

"Kari?"

"Hm?"

Maxwell turned to his sister, brushing against Lex, who grunted. Maxwell sent him a quick apologetic look before focusing back on his twin. "Are you still upset? That's a bit ridiculous, don't you think?" She stayed silent as Maxwell scowled. "All right, so we argued, you don't have to get so sullen about it."

"I'm not…"

Maxwell blinked and mentally backpedaled. "You're…not?"

Karina sighed before she faced Maxwell. They were really close. "I'm just worried… worried about Mom, about this stupid disease and…" she trailed off. "It's nothing, I'm over the argument, I don't like to say this, but for once, you were right, it would have been stupid to stay any longer."

Maxwell cautiously reached forward to put a hand on her head. She stared at him with a raised eyebrow.

"What?" she asked, her lips thinning.

"I was checking if you had a fever," he said as he pulled away. Karina gave him a deadpan expression. Maxwell just shrugged before he leaned back in his seat and stared up at the ceiling. He followed the curve of the metal and plastic plates as the engine rumbled softly underneath.

I guess we're both worried about things. We've lucked out though. Things could have been a lot worse. Everyone we've meet has been nice and helpful, well, for the most part, but still. He noticed Lex as he shifted in probable discomfort, his face shadowed by his cap and hair.

I know he said he made a promise, and that's why he's helping, but why is Lex doing so much for us? We're strangers, it doesn't make sense. Maxwell let out a sigh and tilted his head back up to the ceiling once more. *I guess I'll find out eventually.*

Maxwell blearily blinked his eyes open as he felt someone lightly shake him. He was leaning heavily against his sister, his head on her shoulder. He sat up to rub his eyes. "Huh?"

"We're here, let's go."

Maxwell turned to his sister, who seemed to be curled into the window. He woke her before he stepped after Lex. Maxwell hopped onto the ground and looked around as Karina jumped off the bus. He saw the door close and the bus move away as he took in the suburban street. Houses looked worn with age and unkempt yards littered the dilapidated place. Jeanne stood to one side with Oliver next to her and her daughter in hand.

Late day sunlight shone over the houses as Jeanne once more led the way. Low buildings sat along the sides of the road, a little bedraggled.

"It's not far from here. We should be there soon."

Maxwell hefted his backpack. A chill wind blew through the place which caused a shiver to run up his spine. He grimaced and rubbed his hands to keep them warm as the fall chill settled on his bones.

After a few minutes of walking, the group stopped in front of a simple two-story house. Jeanne stepped forward and lightly knocked on the door as the group, bundled behind her in a tight clump, stood in silence.

Maxwell took the opportunity to look around again.

The area was a cluttered neighborhood with, to his surprise, trees and gardens as well as the stocky houses. On the horizon was a city and off to one side, where he could just see the ground start to incline, was a familiar golden gate. The gate glinted in the light just like the one from Reinmark.

Maxwell heard a soft snarl off to his left. Oliver glared venomously at the gates. Next to him was Lex, who also seemed to regard the gates with an odd, wary expression. His eyebrows were scrunched in consternation as his features remained impassive.

Maxwell jumped as the front door finally swung open to reveal a stumpy, yet kind-looking woman. The woman smiled at Jeanne before she looked toward the group. Her eyes shifted over everyone before they stopped on Lex's. Her eyes narrowed imperceptibly.

The woman focused back on Jeanne. "Sister, what a surprise, and you brought guests and is that little Oliver?" She grabbed the ten-year-old into a hug. The surprised boy yelped, then growled at the contact.

"Yes, we just came out of the city a way from here. We need a place to stay. Would you mind letting us stay for the night? We will leave in the morning," Jeanne said as she gestured toward Maxwell, Karina and Lex. Maxwell caught the woman's gaze. She fidgeted before she turned away.

"Well, of course, come on in."

Maxwell pursed his lips. He glanced toward Lex whose eyes were drooped from weariness. He had one hand on his gut and his posture was weak. Maxwell winced as he watched him walk through the door. Karina stepped forward to follow, before her eyes shifted to his. "Max?"

"Sorry, it's nothing," he responded before he walked inside, happy to get out of the cold evening air. Inside was a cozy living room. He could just see a kitchen past the room and the corner of a set of stairs just past that.

"My name is Lydia. You all look like you've had a long day, why don't you go upstairs and rest? Jeanne, you can have your normal room. You three can have the first two rooms on the left." Maxwell's gaze shifted to Lydia. Lex scrutinized her, as if unsure, before he yawned and turned toward the stairwell.

"Dinner should be ready in twenty minutes. It'll be a light meal since I didn't expect so many people, but I believe it should be enough."

Maxwell nodded as Karina headed toward the stairwell. "Thank you for the hospitality," Maxwell said to Lydia before he followed his sibling who was already halfway up the stairs.

He saw an odd expression cross her face before she turned away toward Jeanne. From the corner of his eye, he could see a man sitting in the kitchen. Maxwell stayed silent even as he moved up the stairwell.

The first room was a simple guest room with a queen-sized bed, a dresser and a bed-side table. Lex was already laid out, curled up on his side under the sheets, a grimace on his face. They exchanged looks before they quietly closed the door and moved onto the next room. The second held a twin-sized bed, much to their distaste.

"I wish we could stay in a hotel instead, but unfortunately, money is still an issue," Karina groused as she tapped her foot on the entranceway. A second later, she darted forward, and flipped onto the bed. She took up the whole middle while Maxwell stared in surprise.

"Wha…?"

"I love you, little brother, I really do. But I'm not sharing a bed with you," she said bluntly as she sat back up and pointed firmly toward him.

Maxwell grimaced at the idea, he was fine with it the other day, but he wasn't keen on sleeping with his sister in such a small bed. "Where do I sleep?" He scrutinized the room to see it was also plain. Though, the fact there were two guest rooms was surprising in and of itself. Maxwell paused in thought. He could stay with Lex, but as much as he trusted him, he wasn't too fond of sleeping with him. Plus, he still needed to recover. Maxwell sighed as he hefted his backpack onto his back while Karina put a finger to her lips in thought.

"We can ask if they have one of those moveable beds like Martha did, then we'll be all set. We'll ask after dinner," Karina said.

Maxwell shrugged. He couldn't think of anything better, plus the idea of food sounded great. He hadn't realized how hungry he was until dinner was mentioned.

Karina almost burst out laughing as his stomach growled and he blushed.

"Not funny," Maxwell said under his breath even as his cheeks became more flamed.

"Nope. Not funny. Not at all."

Maxwell ignored the heavily dripping sarcasm as he glared at Karina. He huffed, and walked back out to check on dinner, all the while Karina continued to laugh.

Dinner was a quiet affair. Lex continued to sleep, so the twins were left to talk with the family by themselves.

Jeanne took care of her youngest child while Oliver chewed grumpily on his sausage. Lydia was talking quietly with a balding man in his thirties who was only nodding while chowing down on his meal. From the looks of it, the two were husband and wife. Even then, they barely talked before moving back onto their dinner. The quietness was anything but peaceful, in Maxwell's opinion. He caught Oliver's glare and Lydia's confused, questioning gaze one too many times for his liking.

Maxwell was relieved when he could finally head back to their room. It was at the last minute while they were on the staircase that Maxwell remembered to ask for a cot. It turned out they didn't have a spare, much to his chagrin.

Night fell on them as they entered the bedroom once more. Food heavy in their stomachs and tension layered over their exhausted frames.

"Ugh, I'm so glad we're leaving soon, I don't think I could stand staying here. Martha was so nice to us. I miss her and Agatha." Karina fell onto the bed with a groan.

Maxwell only nodded as he sat himself down on the floor with his back against the wall. He stared out the window and toward the starry night before his gaze shifted to his sister. "Well, no one said finding Ma would be easy."

Karina sat up and nodded. She looked at him, then the wall, as if trying to figure something out. She grimaced. "If only we knew what's going on. Why take Mom? Why did they take Dad too?" She shifted on the bed. "Not only that, but, Maxwell, will you be all right sleeping on the floor like that?"

Maxwell shifted and withheld the quiet groan. He couldn't really think of anything else. Besides the bed, the room was barren and at least this way, he could lie down instead of trying to sleep in a chair. He wasn't fond of the idea of sleeping away from Lex or his sister, not in this house.

Karina watched before she groaned and placed a hand to her face. She looked at the bed, then shuffled over. "Come on, I doubt you'll get any sleep on the floor." Maxwell stared at the floor. The floor did not look comfortable at all. He looked around, still hoping to see a bed pop out of somewhere, but instead, all he saw was bare wood and raw, cold moonlight. He sighed and stepped forward. He sat at the edge of the bed, feeling the mattress bend under his weight. His sister shifted to one side. He looked at his clothes, then toward his sister. "Should we get changed?"

His sister nodded sharply and Maxwell promptly looked away. They got changed in silence, neither looking at the other. Once both were comfortable, they pulled the sheets up and lay down. It was warm under the sheets. Maxwell shifted as far away from his sister as possible, feeling the edge of the bed. Honestly, he didn't mind being in the same bed as his sister, but she had a habit of being clingy in sleep. There was once when they were younger that he'd woken to find himself in something like a headlock. It wasn't fun to get out of, and it didn't help that his sister hadn't wanted to wake up. Hopefully, if they started on opposite ends of the bed, he wouldn't be smothered.

The quilt sat over them, pulled to the limits. He felt his sister move, noting as the quilt moved and he shivered. "Kari, stop taking the quilt," he said as he grabbed the sheet and pulled back. His sister growled and wrenched it back. Maxwell frowned and looked over to see Karina's back to him. The whole middle of the bed was empty. Karina was curled up in the quilt, somehow managing to cocoon herself in the sheets. He shivered and rolled over. He grabbed the quilt and pulled back. Karina yelped as he pulled the quilt around him and snuggled into the warmth.

"Maxwell," Karina almost seemed to whine.

Maxwell sighed. This wasn't going to work, why did he think it would?

He looked at his sister, who seemed to realize the same thing. She groaned, “Fine.” She sat up along with Maxwell. They stared at the quilt, just big enough for the bed, and looked at each other.

“Well, brother, what do you think?”

Maxwell handed the quilt over. “Give me the sheet. That should be good enough.”

“You sure?” Karina asked as she took the quilt. Maxwell nodded. He grabbed the sheet and pulled it around himself as he lay back down. Karina looked at him, then at the quilt. She lay back down and threw the sheet over the both of them. Maxwell looked over as Karina lay on her side. Most of the quilt was on her, but parts of it trailed over him. It warmed his back and the sheet helped suppress some of the cold.

It would do.

He closed his eyes, curled into the bed and fell asleep.

Chapter Twenty

The next morning came a lot quicker than Maxwell expected, or wanted. He yawned blearily, feeling warm and cozy. He blinked his eyes open, then paused to find a body lying right next to him, arms and legs tangled around his. He slowly tilted his head up to see Karina, still fast asleep. Her face was inches away.

How the heck did they end up in this position? He thought as his brain caught up with him. His mouth and body, however, were way ahead of his thought process. He let out a loud yelp and pushed backward. His arms pin-wheeled, trying to recover his balance, as air met his back and the sheets slipped from underneath him. He hit the ground, groaning in pain as his sister cried out. A dull thud sounded on the other side, followed by a curse.

"Maxwell! What the heck?"

Maxwell messaged his head as he sat up, looking over the bed to see Karina pushing herself up as well, her legs having been tangled in the sheets that caused her to half fall off the bed. She pushed herself back into bed and glared at Maxwell as she massaged her head. Maxwell grinned sheepishly, what could he say?

"You were the one curled around me when I woke up, how did that even happen? We were at opposite ends of the bed."

Karina blanched before the glare deepened. "Don't blame me for that." Maxwell raised an eyebrow as Karina looked away, he almost laughed as he caught her embarrassed expression. "Anyway, why don't we get something to eat? You know. Food?"

This time, he did chuckle. He nodded and stood.

They padded downstairs, surprised to find that everyone else was already awake. Maxwell moved to the kitchen counter while Karina took a seat in the dining room on the other side of the stairwell and stared at the table, pushing away the barely lingering blush.

Paper rustled as Lex lowered the newspaper in his hands. He dug into his pocket and pulled out a cell phone before he slipped it away. Lex's gaze, full of life, peered up at them in amusement. Next to Maxwell at the counter was Lydia.

"All right, here's some food, we don't have much, so I hope you don't mind the meager meal," Lydia stated. Maxwell nodded and brought the food over with Lydia. On the other side of the table, having been out of sight because of the stairwell, was Oliver, Jeanne and the little three-year-old, being rocked gently.

"Sis, we were thinking of heading to New York. Do you think you have some money to spare?" All eyes shifted to Jeanne.

"You're heading out today, right? I'll get it," she said as she swished out of the room. It wasn't a moment later when she returned with a few bills that she handed to Jeanne.

Maxwell munched on his toast as he watched the exchange, his expression impassive.

"What about you three? Are you heading out?" Lydia asked curiously as her eyes slid over the trio. Karina shrugged while Lex lowered his paper enough to look at the woman. Maxwell just tilted his head in thought.

"We probably should leave as soon as possible, we don't want to be a burden to you," Lex said as he gently folded the paper and leaned forward. "We need to wait around here to get in contact with a friend. Would you advise a place to stay?"

Jeanne glanced over, then looked at her sister. "Why don't you let them stay the night? They won't be a bother."

"Of course," Lydia said after some thought, and with that, the decision was final.

Maxwell held one hand up to block off the noonday sun. Jeanne, Oliver and the little one stood out front as they said their good-byes. Lex was inside, eyes glued on yet another newspaper while Karina sat on the fence right next to where Oliver stood. Why Lex was reading so many newspapers, Maxwell had no idea.

Maxwell watched as his older sister spoke, only to get a glare or growl back from Oliver. Maxwell rolled his eyes at his sibling's antics. He walked forward past the two and stood next to Jeanne.

"Thank you. You helped us even though you didn't really know us." He stopped, not sure where he wanted to go with the statement before he mentally sighed.

"You might have looked like one, but you don't seem like the Richies," Jeanne stated uncertainly. "If Dr. Girshwin was okay with it, then I didn't see a reason to not bring you along. I had to come this way anyway to see my sister, right?" She finished as she turned to her sister. Lydia nodded. "I think we'll head out while it's still early. Take care of yourself, okay?"

Maxwell backed away. He said what he wanted to and now it just felt uncomfortable to stand next to the group as they said their family farewells.

He looked at his sister, who was staring at the golden gates that glimmered in the distance. Oliver finally walked away, moving beside his mother and glaring in their direction. Maxwell ignored it as he walked up to Karina and leaned against the rail of the fence.

"I wonder, what exactly are Richies? Are they just people who are overly wealthy or...?" Karina paused before she jumped down from her perch on the fence. "I'm kind of curious, want to take a closer look?"

Maxwell gazed sidelong at his sister. A wide cat-like grin sat on her face as she looked back just as intently. Maxwell pushed away from the fence. "Honestly…"

Karina muttered a quiet 'yes' as she practically elbowed the fence.

"You two." Both peered up toward Lydia who bore a complex expression. Jeanne and her entourage was already gone, having left while they were talking. "Why don't you come back inside? Even though I'm letting you stay doesn't mean you can just laze around. I need some things taken care of and cleaned." Maxwell nodded and mentally chuckled at Karina's face. He knew for a fact that his twin hated cleaning and her disgruntled expression as they walked back inside was anything but enthusiastic. He wasn't particularly fond of it either, now that he thought about it, but at least he could do it.

They walked into the dining room to see that, next to Lex at the table, was the balding, middle-aged man from dinner. A wispy mustache sat on his lips as brown eyes shifted up from his cup of coffee. "Ah, the two from yesterday, good to see you again, sorry I didn't introduce myself last time, the name's Marcus."

"Marcus, what took so long? You were supposed to be up hours ago."

"You know I can't force myself out of bed at such ungodly hours of the morning, it's unhealthy."

Lydia huffed. "Whatever, anyway, I need to talk to you…"

Lex pulled his head from out of the newspaper with a raised eyebrow before he shrugged and dipped back into the pages.

Marcus stood and walked away.

Karina glared as Maxwell raised an eyebrow. "What did you want us to do?"

Lydia shrugged. "Just make yourselves comfortable, this won't take long. I'll tell you after."

They did just that, getting comfortable at the table.

Lex frowned and peered sidelong at the kitchen doorway the husband and wife slipped through. He paused and reached into his pocket to pull out his phone. After a moment, he huffed, shrugged and looked back down. Karina leaned back in her chair and took another swig of water. Maxwell stood, grabbing his glass.

"Where are you going?"

"I want to get some orange juice. I saw some in there earlier."

Karina rolled her eyes, but didn't comment. Maxwell meandered toward the kitchen. The living room door was closed. Though he'd only seen it once, it was connected to the entranceway connected to the dining room, almost like a four-roomed box. Walking past the doorway, out of sight of the others, he paused. He could hear voices if he paid close attention.

"Lydia, you have to stop this, I don't know where your mind has been for the past day or so, but it's nothing good."

"What are you talking about, I already told you my opinion, and I think it's a damn good one."

"No, what you told me is ridiculous, even for you. Can't you see that's only going to end badly…"

"No. We need money and this is the best…"

"You're not listening. I'm telling you, this is a terrible idea."

There was a moment of silence before Lydia spoke once more, voice cold. "If you think it's so terrible, then just leave. I'll do it myself and prove that I am right."

"I'll leave, but I'm doing it for your own good. You better rethink your priorities and realize this decision won't help us, or anyone, except for putting him in the line of fire."

With that, footsteps raged on wood before fading into the distance. Distantly, Maxwell could hear a door open and close. Silence enveloped the area before the woman let out a choked breath. Maxwell backpedaled, hurrying back to the dining room. Sirens blared in his head. He went to open his mouth, when he heard the door open. He quickly took a seat.

Lydia walked back in through the doorway and paused. She glanced between Lex and Maxwell. Maxwell forced himself not to react as the conversation played in his mind.

She took a seat, giving off a tired sigh. Maxwell wanted so desperately to say something, but couldn't, so he shut his mouth. He waited, feeling agitated. Why? He wasn't completely sure. However, he knew the conversation was wrong in so many ways, plus Lydia had been looking at them strangely a lot in the past day. It bothered him greatly.

After a moment, she looked up. "Sorry about that. Anyway, if you wouldn't mind, I need you to do some stuff for me."

Karina groaned quietly while Lex lay down his paper, folding it carefully. Maxwell stiffened before forcing himself to relax. To his relief, it didn't look like she noticed, but he did see his sister look at him with a questioning expression before turning toward Lydia.

"I need someone to go pick up some groceries. Like I said, I didn't expect so many people to come here." She looked at Lex. "Would you mind?" Lex seemed to contemplate the suggestion for a moment.

Maxwell could almost see the indecision before he sighed and nodded. He stood, only to pause as she held up a hand. "Hold on." She walked into the other room, only to return a moment later with a pad of paper and pencil.

Maxwell tightened his jaw in agitation. He noticed the gleam in Lydia's gaze as an uncomfortable feeling in his stomach twisted. They were in danger.

He watched her quickly write, noting with trepidation as the list got longer and longer. "I also need you to pick up a few other things. I'll give you some money, as well as a little extra to get yourself some lunch." Lex took the paper and money hesitantly. He looked toward Maxwell and Karina. Maxwell wanted to tell him to wait, that he wanted to talk, but before he could even convey that, Lex nodded.

"All right," Lex said as he headed out the door.

The door closed and Lydia paused. "Oh no! I never told him where to go. Oh dear…" she muttered as she stared at the doorway. Maxwell looked toward the doorway as Lydia sighed. "Oh, I hope he finds them, it shouldn't be too hard, but still." She turned to the twins. "As for you two, would one of you mind helping make lunch?" She looked at Karina who shrugged and stood. Maxwell sat in silence as the two walked into the kitchen. He wanted to pull out his hair. First Lex, now his sister? When would he find a time to talk?

A moment later, Lydia reappeared with a broom and dustpan. "Make yourself useful and sweep the upstairs." She thrust the items into his hands before heading back into the kitchen. Broom in hand, he looked toward the doorway before he headed upstairs.

The late afternoon sun shone down as Lex returned, laden with bags. Maxwell looked up from where he was dusting the side table, sighing in relief. He was glad Lex was home now, so he could talk to someone. The entire afternoon, he tried to talk to Karina, only to end up having to do something else. Even when they were all sitting together for lunch, Lydia wouldn't leave them alone, so he was unable to say anything.

Maxwell stood as Lex called for help with the bags. He hurried over as Lydia and Karina entered the room. They unloaded the bags as

Maxwell looked for an opportunity to pull either Lex or Karina aside. He managed to pull Karina away at one point while Lex talked with Lydia.

"Max? What's up? You seem a little out of it today."

"I've been trying to speak with you. We need to get out of here."

"Why?"

"Because I overheard Lydia and Marcus talking earlier, I think they're up to something, you know as well as I do that this place doesn't feel right."

"I've been with Lydia all day. I think you're just looking at this wrong."

"I'm not sure. They were talking about money and someone being in the line of fire. Not only that, but Marcus has been gone all day…"

"What does that have to do with us? Couldn't it be anybody? Plus, maybe he works. You know. Like a normal job?"

Maxwell sighed in frustration. Why did his sister have to be so stubborn? "If it makes you feel better, we'll just keep an eye out, we're leaving soon anyway."

Maxwell didn't respond as Karina walked back into the kitchen. Maybe she was right, maybe he was just paranoid.

By the time dinner was ready, Maxwell was resigned to the fact he would just have to keep an eye out.

Dinner was a quiet affair yet again to Maxwell's disdain. He noted Marcus still wasn't back and wondered if his paranoia from earlier was justified. The restlessness dwindled as the food sat heavily in their stomachs. Karina let out a yawn as she patted her stomach in contentment. Maxwell let out his own yawn, feeling sleepy for some reason. He eyed the food warily as he sipped once more at the glass of orange juice Lydia gave him.

Lex came back from the kitchen with another refill of water from the tap, having decided to get his drink himself, so as not to bother Lydia. Lydia argued for a little while, but finally relented. Maxwell felt Lex's gaze as he asked, "You two all right?"

"I guess the day caught up with us." Maxwell let out a soft resigned breath. "Plus, we didn't get much sleep last night. Actually, I think I'm going to turn in," Maxwell stated as he got up from the table.

He was feeling a little woozy. Why was that? Karina gave him a look which he ignored.

"I think I'll go to bed too, thank you," Karina said before walking up to him. He felt Karina press against his side. "Max? You okay?"

"Fine," he replied softly, letting out another yawn. It was probably just his imagination. Maybe all this stuff happening so quickly was getting to him.

"Have a good night," Lydia said.

Maxwell looked back as Karina stepped past. He saw Karina stop out of the corner of his eyes.

"What about you, dear? Are you going to bed?"

He heard Lex respond, "I think I will, thank you for the food." Maxwell saw Lex follow them up, a frown on his face.

Maxwell let out another yawn as he finished moving up the stairwell. *Why am I so tired?* Maxwell peered down the hallway.

"Idiot, get some sleep."

Maxwell jumped before he looked over his shoulder to Lex. He paused, then slowly nodded before he walked to his room. What was the point of bothering Lex now? He was a bit too tired to think straight. Maybe in the morning? He spotted Lex going to his own room. He turned as Karina opened the door. "So, what do you think, a lot more comfortable, don't you think?"

Maxwell stared at the room and chuckled softly. The bed was crowded with pillows, all plopped in the middle to make a wall. Two sets of sheets lay on either side, creating the semblance of two separate beds, even though the space was barely enough to curl into. She probably did it while they were separated.

"Where did you get the pillows from?" he asked as he walked forward.

"I had to make some beds and so grabbed some then."

"Ah," he replied as he fell onto left side of the bed. "Yep, these are quite comfortable."

"Max, that was supposed to be my side."

"Really? Sorry," he replied with a playful tone as he cuddled into the warmth, his thoughts already drifting toward sleep.

"Geez..." Karina muttered as she took her own position. The two lay in silence as the moon glimmered through the window. Pale light shone over their faces as Maxwell closed his eyes.

He heard the sound of movement and quiet breaths signaling that Karina was going to sleep. Maybe he was just overly paranoid, because right at that moment, he felt comfortable and warm. He curled tighter into the warmth and slowly drifted off to sleep.

Chapter Twenty-one

Lex's eyes snapped open. He scrutinized the room as he slowly sat up. Sweat dripped from his brow as sodden dirty locks clung to his face. He frowned as his brow crinkled up in confusion. Light streamed in from the window. A cold breeze shifted through the floorboards as the quiet hum of electricity filled the room.

What woke me? he thought as he slowly got out of bed. His hand instantly reached toward his pocket as his fingers clasped over cool leather of his knife. His socked feet padded lightly to the doorway and slipped out to the hallway. The house was quiet. No sound besides soft snores and sniffles invaded the premises. He frowned as apprehension slid up his frame. Even with the peaceful house, something seemed off. No, not off. It just felt wrong.

He couldn't put his finger on it, and it bothered him. He regarded the stairwell with unease.

Voices.

He froze. Quiet whispers drifted up the stairwell as footsteps sounded softly. He couldn't make out what was being said, but he could tell there was someone else in the house.

His gaze flitted back to the twins' room before he turned to the stairwell. He moved down a few steps as the voices filtered through the air. He stayed quiet.

"…with these two. They were young, not sure how they're related, but they seem to trust him. At least, that's what Jeanne told me and what I've seen since they've arrived."

Lex gritted his teeth as another voice drifted up the stairwell that he recognized. The smooth voice was both mocking and sincere. "Hm? I see… I'll take care of them for you, here is your reward."

"Thank y…wait…hat are…HE…"

Lex's eyes narrowed dangerously as a startled cry was cut short and a thud sounded from below.

"Honestly, peasants are such a nuisance. They need to learn their place. Hm…well, let's go see how he's doing and who he deemed worthy to take care of."

Lex quietly cursed as he darted back upstairs. His gut throbbed and he winced as his hand shot to his stomach. His wound, still smarting, cried out at the sudden abuse he inflicted on it after so much rest. He entered the twins' room, closing the door behind him.

He only paused for a moment to take in the fact that both twins were on the bed, surrounded by pillows like it was some type of fortress.

Lex walked up to the two, curled around each other. He went to put a hand on both their mouths to wake them up so that they wouldn't scream, when the door swung open.

Instinct caused him to jerk forward in front of the twins, knife in hand. Silver flashed in the moonlight as he gazed evenly at the doorway.

He felt slightly sick as he stared at Caym.

"Why, Lex, I didn't know you were awake," Caym said.

His voice was suave. His hands were clasped behind his back. Lex stayed silent as his thoughts raced. Caym chuckled softly as he stepped forward, followed by two bulky men in suits. "That's so rude, you didn't even say hi to your older brother?"

"What are you doing here?" Lex responded stiffly.

His wound throbbed, but he ignored it.

Caym's grin had a predatory gleam to it, emphasizing his sharp gray eyes. Blond hair hung around a sculpted face. "I came to see you. Mother and Father have been worried. They couldn't stand the idea that you wanted to live with peasants. Really, I don't blame them…"

Caym let the words linger as he tilted his hand down to examine his fingernails. Lex shifted his stance so he was fully in front of the twins. Caym seemed to spot the sleeping teens.

"Why, Little Leo, I didn't know you were interested in that."

Lex hissed, "Don't call me that. And I'm not. Only you would think that."

Caym shrugged before he leaned against the doorway, arms crossed. "What? Can't an older brother fantasize? I mean, Mother has wanted you to settle down…"

"That's why I left…" Lex hesitated, examining Caym quietly. "You know that as well as I do," he finished coldly as he straightened his posture.

He felt his expression contort to one of disgust. He knew he had been gone for a while, but how could his brother have become, this. His knife hovered before Caym in a threatening manner.

Caym didn't bat an eye. "True, but that's beside the point." One finger gestured to the men on either side, who stepped forward. Lex frowned as he watched the duo out of the corner of his eyes, his attention on his older brother. Caym brought his arm up. It held an expensive gold watch clasped on his wrist. He sighed sullenly, as if he just found out that he missed the last ticket to a favorite concert. "Well, looks like we're out of time. Men?"

Lex cursed. He shot forward. His knife sliced through the first man as crimson splattered on the floor. With a twist of a wrist, the handle slammed down on the already injured man. He slumped to the ground, unmoving. Lex heard Caym whistle as a thump sounded behind him. Lex spun low and quickly tried to swipe at the second man's feet. The man jumped out of the way.

Lex leapt forward as the man dodged out of the way to avoid the sharp edge, only to give a sharp jab back. Lex got out of the way just in time as wind whistled past. He jumped back, weapon up even as a slow clap sounded from the doorway.

"You've improved, I'm not surprised. Though, you really shouldn't underestimate me. You know I don't leave things to chance."

Lex pursed his lips as his gaze sharpened warily. He heard glass shatter and a thump at the same time as his attacker darted forward once more. Lex jumped out of the way and, bringing his leg up, roundhouse kicked the second. The man slammed to the ground, groaning quietly.

"Now, little Leo, come quietly or we take these two along with yourself by force."

Lex glanced over his shoulder, only to freeze. Where the two twins lay was a third man. Glass shards sparkled on the black outfit as he put a gun against Karina's skin. Lex almost did a double take. Behind the third man was a shattered window. *No wonder,* Lex thought.

Still the twins continued to sleep, as if dead to the world. Lex frowned before he gritted his teeth. "A drug…"

Caym gestured toward the twins. "Now, little Leo, drop your knife and come quietly."

Lex growled softly. Where had he gone soft? He would have fought tooth and nail to get away. He never wanted to go back and would have done everything, even, to his distaste, break that promise. So why? His posture straightened as he turned to face Caym.

"Now, was that so hard?"

Lex stayed silent even as his knife fell out of his hands, his eyes staying peeled on the awake and alive occupants of the room. The second man got back up, holding his head. The first didn't, his brain caved in slightly from the hit on the head, blood pouring from his throat.

Caym's neutral expression shown with slight disapproval as he said, "Well, either way, we have to get going. No need to get the peasant sickness, now is there?" His gaze flickered to Lex. "It's good to see that you haven't gotten it, Leo." For a brief moment, a faint smile settled on his lips.

Lex wondered if he was just imagining it, both the smile and the words. Part of him hoped he wasn't…

Chapter Twenty-two

Lex was furious. No, that wasn't the word. He was more than furious. Livid sounded much better in his head. Yes, he was absolutely livid. More so now that he saw that brief, familiar smile. He glared forward even as he kept the rest of his expression as neutral as possible. Oh, the joy of poker faces.

"Oh, come now, Leo, we didn't hurt them. You know we couldn't have let them stay awake now, could we?"

Lex stayed silent. His eyes were shadowed by long raven bangs that pooled into his face. Lex forced himself to walk forward. Behind were the two drugged and unconscious teens. They passed the slumped-over and bloody form of Lydia, her eyes glassy. That was the only reason he was glad the duo was asleep. They didn't need to see that.

In front of him, through the open doorway, was a long and sleek black limo. Lex stepped in and sat near the back. The two men who carried the teens out placed them into the vehicle. Lex picked up both teens and moved them closer as his brother also stepped in. Lex's arms crossed over his chest as he stared with a deadpan, yet dangerous expression. "As per usual, Caym, you seem to have a habit of screwing with everybody."

Caym raised an eyebrow. "Well, that's one way to phrase it," he replied as he sat down and picked up a half-filled glass of wine. He took a sip. "You know, Mother and Father have been worried sick about you, like I said. We looked everywhere, even called that deranged uncle of ours, but no one could find you. Where were you, my little Leo?"

After some time and the soft rumbling of the engine, Caym let out a breath in what Lex translated as quiet annoyance. "Silent as ever.

So why are you with these two? I already gave you my first thought, which I wouldn't think is too far off considering what mother always says. Alas, that is wishful thinking."

The two in question shifted in their seat. Karina leaned her head against Lex's shoulder as Maxwell did the same on the other side.

"How fascinating."

"I suspect that there was money involved. Did you at least pay your end of the deal before killing her?" Lex finally spoke as he faced his brother.

Caym rolled his eyes. "The prodigal son speaks. Don't worry, she got what she deserved. A peasant will always be a peasant, the filth."

Lex gritted his teeth, but made no other movement. He thought he caught a bit of sadness in his brother's eyes before a grin appeared on his face once more. Had he really seen that?

"Now, once we get to the gates, the doctor will be checking on you three. You'll probably be fine, but you know the protocol. Oh wait, never mind."

Lex glared as Caym leaned on one hand and took another sip of wine. "You left before that. Hm…well, you'll just have to hope that they're clean or all that effort will be in vain. What a shame."

Lex shifted uncomfortably in his seat. The posh leather interior grated on his nerves as much as his brother did right now.

Caym's gaze meandered to the outside as he took another sip. His fingers tightened on the glass flute, seeming to contradict the next few words. "We're here, good timing."

Through the tinted windows Lex could see a set of high golden steel gates right in front of them. They sparkled even in the moonlight. The car pulled to a stop and, after a minute, the side door opened.

"Ah, Sir Caym, and if it isn't Master Leonard..."

"Lex," Lex said softly as he stared ahead before gazing sidelong at the doctor. "Doctor, you should know not to use that name."

The doctor gulped and stuttered out an apology.

"Well, get on with it, we don't have all day. Mom wants to see him, and we have to do something about these two peasants."

The doctor hurriedly nodded.

"Check them first, if they're sick, get them out of here and get rid of them."

Lex's eyes widened and snapped toward Caym as the doctor stepped in.

"What? It's common sense. If you are sick, you're going to die anyway. We're just putting them out of their misery before that happens. It's a rule they instated after your little departure."

"It wasn't that bad when I left," Lex said quietly as he eyed the doctor.

The man stepped around Lex. He squatted down in front of Karina. The doctor reached forward and lightly prodded her hairline before he opened her mouth and examined it. He pulled up Karina's shirt. He checked her stomach and back before he checked her legs. After a few more pokes and prods, he seemed to breathe in relief. "Clean."

"Well, well," Caym muttered as the doctor pushed Karina back into position before doing the same thing to Maxwell. After a few minutes of carefully checking him over, he nodded once more.

"Also, clean."

Caym raised an eyebrow as Lex closed his eyes in silent relief.

How did they manage to avoid it? he thought as he slowly opened his eyes to a half-lidded position. *At least I might be able to get out. They won't want me back with the sickness, so I'll be able to get away, but that won't do any good now, will it?* He closed his eyes and sighed in defeat. This wasn't going to end well.

The doctor had him lie down and quickly checked his vitals before he started to poke and prod. Lex gritted his teeth painfully as the doctor poked dangerously close to his healing wound. After a few moments, the doctor pulled back.

"Other than a gash on the girl's arm from some sort of projectile and a bullet wound to Sir Leon…Lex's gut that is still in the healing stages, they're all clean."

Lex's eyes snapped open. Thoughts whirled through his head at a mile a minute. *Clean? I haven't been clean in more than a year. How?*

"Well, no surprise, we do have a better bloodline than the peasants, but to find two peasants who are also clean, now that is surprising."

Lex schooled his features. *I'm cured? When? How? That's impossible, there is no cure.* It took all his willpower not to glance at the two twins. Conversations and interactions came back to him as the car roared back into life and trundled forward once more. Could it be? No, that's impossible…

"Leo, are you that worried about seeing family again?"

"No, I'm just tired. You did wake us up rather abruptly in the middle of the night, unless you didn't notice," Lex said as he sent his brother an unamused expression.

Caym shrugged. "I'll give you that. Though, I'm not sure how you can sleep on those things they call beds."

"I can do it rather well, thank you. I think cotton is actually more comfortable than those idiotic silk sheets you always seem to love."

Caym paused in his sip of wine before he lightly put it down once more. "I see," he said. They sat in silence for a while before Caym turned to the window. "Ah, home sweet home, time for the prodigal son's return, wouldn't you say, dear brother?"

Lex watched as a set of intricately delicate gold gates slid open to reveal a long hedge-adorned paved driveway. It led all the way up to a large circle entranceway with an equally large fountain, spewing water. It was lit beautifully in the night. Water cascaded down to create a constant sound as they pulled down the long driveway.

Past the fountain was what would have been a beautiful three-story mansion that seemed to gleam a pearly white in the moonlit night, if it wasn't for the fact that Lex wanted desperately to run in the opposite direction of it. The limo drove forward and curved around the fountain to pull to a stop in front of a set of steps that led up to mahogany wooden doors.

Caym gestured forward. "After you. Though, I forgot to mention, Father isn't here at the moment. He was called away an hour before we got the call, so he'll greet you in a few days, but you don't mind that now, do you?" He slipped out the door.

Lex gazed at the twins. Maxwell finally settled down and Karina was in a peaceful slumber next to her brother.

"I'm sorry…" he muttered softly as disgust filtered into his voice. "I promised, I promised that I…but…I'm sorry, Allen…" He peered after his brother, sadness foremost in his mind. "And I'm sorry…Caym…"

Lex stepped through the doors. He held onto Karina tightly as one of the males that attacked them carried Maxwell. Before he could take more than a step, he heard the sound of a gasp before dainty footsteps sang on the ceramic floor. A moment later, he took a step back.

"Mother," Caym stated firmly.

Lex's mother stopped, just a bit in front of Lex, her arms wide. She pursed her lips and dropped her arms to her side. She smiled up to him widely. "Leonard. My poor sweet Leo. Are you okay? You aren't hurt, are you? Those disgusting peasants didn't harm you, did they?"

Lex grimaced as he shifted enough to get Karina out of the way. He saw teary blue eyes stare back at him worriedly. After a moment, she froze and glanced down into his arms, then to the guard behind him who still had a grip on Maxwell.

"Who?" She looked between Lex and the duo. "WHAT ARE FILTHY PEASANTS DOING IN MY HOUSE?"

Caym sighed and stepped forward. He whispered into mother's ear, too soft for Lex to hear. His mother hesitated then nodded. Caym backed away, he spared them a glance before leaving.

Lex regarded him for only a moment before he turned back to his mother. She pulled away, hands behind her back, picture of grace once more. "Sorry, first reaction. I haven't seen you in years and you come back with a young girl in your arms, even if she is just a filthy peasant. I will never understand that about you, son."

"Mother, you really don't have to overreact like that all the time." His arms shook and he shifted to rebalance Karina's weight. "May I…we go to bed?"

His mother closed her eyes and seemed to debate for a moment. When she opened them, Lex felt he was caught in a predatory gaze. Maybe that was just his paranoia about being back, but he still felt on edge. "Of course, but we're going to talk later. Now get some sleep. I'll see you in the morning. Make sure you all take a bath, will you? I'll have the doctor and butler in to sterilize everything, and I'll get your clothes."

Lex winced before he nodded. “All right. Good night, Mother,” he stated firmly before he started to walk forward. He heard footsteps behind him and mentally sighed with relief. After a while of walking and his arms and gut hurting like crazy from Karina’s weight, they finally arrived. He pushed open the door and walked into his room.

It was an over-the-top lavish room with two separate areas, divided by a small set of stairs and a railing. The four-poster bed was in the higher area with annoying silk curtains and large double-wide windows that opened to a balcony blocked by trees.

The lower level had a bunch of couches, a TV and anything else one might want, things used for playing alone for hours on end. On one side were two doorways, one led to the bathroom, one to a closet. On the other was a single doorway which didn’t look to have been used in a while. *The servant’s quarters, if I remember right,* he thought with forlorn exasperation. He walked forward and lightly went to place Karina on one of the couches when a voice interrupted him.

“My lord.”

Lex cringed, yet sat up to see the open doorway. Machael stood in the doorway. He was in a traditional butler’s outfit with coattails and all. “Machael, it’s been a while.”

“My lord, I was informed you had some servants with you.”

Servants? He paused before he peered at the duo, then slowly nodded. “Of course, they’re my personal helpers, so please give them the utmost respect.” He spoke carefully.

“Indeed. Yet, even so, they are in need of sterilization, as are you, my lord.”

Lex closed his eyes, then nodded. “Of course,” he said as he walked over.

The butler bowed deeply, then walked into the bathroom. It was different than he remembered.

The room was wide open, with a bath and marble sink. Those were standard, however, there was something new, a separate shower area that looked distinctly like a chamber. He glared at it.

“My lord, if you will, please?”

“What of these two? Do you know when the sedative will wear

off?" Lex asked.

The butler paused. "I believe it will be soon, my lord."

"Please, just Lex." Lex sighed.

"My lord, you remember I can't call you that."

"It was worth a shot. Now can I shower in peace?" Machael paused as Lex walked up to the one holding Maxwell. Through the doorway to his room he could see Karina on the couch. *I hoped the man would just put Maxwell next to his sister, but I guess that didn't happen.* "Set him down." The man nodded.

Instead of walking back into the main room like Lex thought he would do the man put him on the ground and walked out. Lex frowned as he squatted down next to Maxwell.

"Of course. The sterilizing shower is quite simple. Please put all the clothes into these bags, and we will bring fresh ones. After that, just stay in the area for three minutes, then you're all set. We will be back within the hour for any last-minute things."

Lex noted the relief and uncertainty in Machael's eyes as he said, "Thanks, you can go."

Machael hesitated. "It's good to see you back, my lord." With that, he left.

Lex waited to hear the door click before he spoke. "What am I going to do now?" He scanned the area. He sighed at the lack of exits. He did that a lot lately.

After a moment, and making sure Maxwell was all right, he grabbed a couple sets of towels. With towels over one arm, he squatted down once more and tried to wake Maxwell. He was unsurprised that the kid didn't respond. He frowned and grabbed some water. He splashed it onto Maxwell.

Maxwell spluttered and shot up. "Cold," he yelped before his green eyes raced around in fear. Maxwell silently scanned the room in obvious confusion. "Where?"

"My house."

"Yours?" Maxwell paused, his posture tensing. "This, is a huge bathroom."

"It's the smallest in the house, which is what I asked for. It's too over the top for my taste," Lex replied, feeling a hint of distaste at the incredibly expensive and lavish equipment.

Wide eyes snapped to him in shock, before they morphed into a wary look. "Once more, where are we?"

Lex mentally smirked in amusement, the kid's as sharp as usual. "We're inside the gated community. This is my…home, as you might call it," he replied as he noted Maxwell's expression.

Emotions flashed across his face, too fast to name. Maxwell scrambled to his feet. "Wait, where's…"

"She's in the other room," Lex interrupted.

Maxwell peered through the doorway and sighed with relief. He slumped as he put a hand to his head. His legs shook as he used the wall for support. "What? What did they…?"

Lex pursed his lips. He wasn't quite sure how to respond. He knew they were drugged, but how, when or why he wasn't? He hadn't a clue. The only thing he could think of was the fact that he grabbed his own drink and only picked at dinner. "You two were drugged, from my guess…" He cut himself off, rethinking what he was going to say before continuing. "My brother might have had a hand in selling a drug to someone to do this. It would be just like him to sell even as someone is seeking a reward…" he let the end trail away as Maxwell sat in silence, thinking over what he said. "He's a genius when it comes to drugs and money."

"Lovely," Maxwell murmured under his breath.

"You must still be a little tired. Why don't you rest up?" Lex stood.

"I'm fine," Maxwell murmured as he pulled his hand down. Water dripped from his bangs as he looked straight at Lex. "I didn't know you had a brother." He seemed to debate for a moment. "Why didn't you tell us?"

"It never came up," Lex replied.

Maxwell frowned as he pushed away from the wall. "So, are you one of the Richies? The people Oliver mentioned?" he asked quietly. Thoughts churned behind forest green eyes.

Lex nodded. "Yes. You can put it that way. Though, it's not

something I want." Lex blinked.

It happened again, just like when the twins first met Antonio. Maxwell's eyes had the steadiest gaze he ever saw, as if the young teen could look into him through and through. They always did say the eyes were the windows to one's soul.

"I see." Maxwell stopped and examined the room once more. "Considering we were, did you say drugged?"

Lex nodded and Maxwell winced. "Considering that, I guess I can kind of see why you wouldn't want to be here." He hesitated and nodded, as if coming to a conclusion. "That's how you knew about the groceries while we…wait, what happened to Lydia? Was she the one who…?"

"She did…" Lex hesitated. Should he tell him what exactly happened to her? He was taking it surprisingly well, though he was obviously freaked out, if the trembling was any indication. "Don't worry about it."

Maxwell frowned. Lex thought he heard him mutter, "Of course I'll worry, what with this screwed-up situation." Before he continued at a louder tone, "That's also why Doctor Girswin mentioned you never wanted to come back this way. If that's the case, why were you willing to join us?"

"I…" Lex paused.

He didn't have a solid answer to that, he could use his normal reason, but it just didn't seem right. Maxwell narrowed his eyes, taking a step back, as if tensing to run even though he had nowhere to go. "I honestly don't know what to tell you. I originally was helping because of a promise. Now I'm not so sure."

Maxwell relaxed slightly and nodded.

"Come on, let's wake your sister."

They walked into the main room. Maxwell peered around warily. He seemed uncomfortable, almost agitated. Lex wasn't surprised. He himself felt like he was hanging over a precipice. He hated the feeling.

Maxwell hurried to Karina's side and squatted down next to his sister. He reached forward, lightly slapping her cheek. "Come on, Karina, wake up."

Lex heard a quiet moan. Karina curled inward. "Maxwell, I'm

tired, shut up."

"Kari, come on," Maxwell said, his voice shaking.

Karina must have noticed the uncertainty because her eyes opened. She stared blearily at her brother for all of a minute before she shot up and looked around wildly.

"Where? How? What the heck happened?"

"Looks like you're up," Maxwell said weakly.

"Maxwell? Where are we?"

"Lex's home."

Karina's gaze snapped toward Lex, who suddenly felt awkward, just standing next to the bathroom. He raked a hand through his hair to calm his nerves.

"But…" Karina's gaze shifted between Lex and Maxwell before finally landing on her twin. "How the heck did we get here? Why?"

"We were drugged. It must have happened sometime last night," Maxwell responded as he stood. Karina tilted her head up to see him. "I don't know anything more than that." He turned to Lex. "I was hoping, once we were both awake, you would explain it."

Lex grimaced. "Ah, well…" Lex had to admit, he was incredibly surprised Maxwell was still listening to him, considering the situation. "I guess you can blame my brother for that, like I told you earlier. He found out we were staying there. He's the one who dragged me back and, for some reason, decided to bring you two along. Don't ask me why, I haven't seen him for years and even then, I don't understand the way he thinks."

"Brother?" Karina asked quietly.

"Yeah, supposedly Lex has a brother. He sounds interesting," Maxwell said.

Karina pursed her lips.

"Come on." Maxwell extended a hand and helped Karina stand. She stood, holding onto Maxwell as her legs shook.

Lex peered toward the doorway before stepping back to stand next to the twins. Karina pulled away, checking her brother who only seemed to half-heartedly complain. Lex walked toward the doorway and felt the handle. It was locked.

He sighed and walked toward the bathroom. “Come on, we need to get cleaned up, or else the butler might do it himself. It’s happened before.”

“Butler? He has a freaking butler?” Karina said as she finally pulled away from Maxwell.

Maxwell just shrugged.

“Karina, do you want to go first or last?”

“What do you mean?” Karina asked.

Lex sighed, quickly bringing her up to speed. Maxwell just listened quietly. After Lex was done, he repeated the question.

Karina paused before she said, “I’ll wait.”

Lex nodded, as Maxwell’s gaze flitted between them. “Um…how does the sterilize thing work?”

“Oh…” Lex walked into the bathroom. Maxwell hesitantly followed, peering through the doorway. Lex explained.

After a moment, Maxwell nodded. “All right, you go first. I’ll let Karina know how it works.”

“All right,” Lex said as Maxwell hurried back to his sister’s side.

Chapter Twenty-three

Maxwell peered at the doorway. He could hear a soft sound of running water and the vaguest hiss of steam, probably from the sanitizer.

He stepped up to his sister who was curled on the couch. Her knees were pulled up to her chest and her arms were wrapped tightly around her legs, as if trying to squeeze the life out of them. She looked up as Maxwell took a seat next to her. She dropped her hands and let one leg trail to the floor. They didn't say anything.

Maxwell withheld a yawn. He hated this feeling, being tired and scared at the same time. Why were they drugged? Obviously, Lex was dragged home, so why did they need the two of them? Maybe Lex was… Maxwell stopped that train of thought. While he was terrified, a part of him could see that Lex seemed just as worried as them. He seemed almost frightened, in a way. It was the first time seeing such an emotion from their normally stoic companion. He wouldn't have dragged them along.

He pulled himself from his thoughts as the door opened. Lex stepped out, rubbing his hair dry. Karina took one look at Lex, muttered a quiet, "Never mind, I'll go next instead," and ran into the bathroom.

Maxwell blinked and stared before he closed his eyes and rubbed them. "I'm too tired for this…"

Lex let out an uncharacteristic snort before he dug into his closet and pulled out some clothes. He quickly pulled them on before he let the towels drop.

"Well, they're a bit snug, but they still fit, hopefully Machael will…"

There was a knock on the door before it swung open to reveal the butler. The male, probably Machael, Maxwell assumed, bowed before he handed the items over. Maxwell went to take them, only for Machael to shake his head.

"You have yet to be cleaned," he said before he left.

"Rude," Maxwell said as Lex separated the clothes. Maxwell stared at the doorway. Maybe, no, he couldn't leave, Karina was still in the bathroom.

"These should work," Lex muttered as he shifted through the clothes, separating them out accordingly.

Maxwell looked at the clothing before he turned toward the bathroom door. This unsettling feeling made him feel sick. He wanted to just go back to sleep. Maybe when he awoke, he would be back in Lydia's place, or even better, back home. He hoped he was just dreaming. Being drugged and dragged to this place seemed as surreal as any dream he had recently.

It was a while later when Karina was done, and a bit longer before Maxwell finished as well. The sanitizer felt weird on his skin, the spray almost itchy in a way. He was all too happy to get out once the three minutes were up. He got changed and headed out. He saw his sister, facing away from him, squatting down behind the couch. He took a seat on the couch, arms laid over the back to see what she was doing.

He saw her grumbling before she tilted her head back to see him. Her expression morphed to horror and anger. She snapped up, standing in front with hands on her hips. Maxwell tried to backpedal, also trying not to fall off the couch. Lex just leaned against the wall.

"What is it, Maxwell? It's funny, isn't it? A dress? Who can sleep in a dress?" Karina growled as she pulled at the long frilly outfit that adorned her frame. The sleeves went to her wrists and the outfit flowed all the way down to her ankles. Lace rimmed the edges.

"It's a nightgown. I would give you my clothes, but it seems they took many of mine," Lex said.

Maxwell stared at the light pink outfit, trying and failing to hide behind the couch cushions. It seemed like she finally snapped from the stress. Still, he spoke before he could stop himself. "I have never seen you in a dress, let alone a nightgown." She sent him a glare and he recoiled. "I'm just saying. I mean…" He pulled at his own clothes uncomfortably. They were a set of silk pajama-like pants with a button-up long sleeve blue shirt. "These clothes are so high end. It's almost uncomfortable. That's all I'm saying." He frowned as he pulled at it once more.

Lex shrugged. His own clothes were similar to Maxwell's. "It's all we have at the moment. You'll get another change of clothes in the morning."

"If they stick me in a dress, I'm going to murder someone," Karina said as she glared daggers at the flowing item.

Maxwell shivered. "Okay. You hate dresses. Good to know."

"Hate is such a strong word. Loathe is much better," Karina said with a deadpan expression, her voice layered in sarcasm. Maxwell chuckled nervously.

The room, besides the trio, was quiet. Moonlight filtered in from the tall windows as Karina paced back and forth over the rug. Her bare feet padded softly on the wool carpet. Lex walked forward and leaned against the rail between the upper and lower floors, a bemused expression on his face.

"Kari, glaring at the clothes isn't going to help. They're all we have at the moment."

"You think I don't know that?" Karina snapped before she slumped next to Maxwell. "Still, where are our backpacks? Why did they bring us here? It seems pointless if all they wanted was Lex."

Maxwell agreed. It still didn't make sense. Though, then again, did anything make sense anymore?

"Either way, we can't do anything else for the night, and tomorrow is going to be a long day. So, we might as well try to get some sleep," Lex said as he pushed away from the rail. "I'll see if I can answer any other questions you might have tomorrow. I have a feeling you'll probably have a lot more..."

Maxwell sighed, feeling annoyed. Of course, they'd have more questions, when didn't they? Honestly, couldn't he and his sister catch a break?

"I guess," Karina said after a few moments of silence.

Maxwell peered at Karina, who seemed distracted. He turned to

Lex, "So where are we sleeping?"

"I would have you sleep in here, but…" He peered up to one corner of the room.

Maxwell and Karina looked up to see a video camera sitting in the corner. "I think quite a few people might throw a fit about that. So, you'll have to use the servant's quarters. Luckily, there are some right through that doorway. And, before you ask, I'll talk to you about it tomorrow. You need to get some rest. The drugs probably aren't completely out of your system."

Karina continued to stare at the video camera. Her eye twitched in annoyance before she stomped toward the doorway Lex was pointing to.

Maxwell watched her, then Lex. Lex's expression was tired. He noticed Maxwell looking and gestured once more to the doorway. "Go on. There should be two beds in there. You can both sleep comfortably tonight."

Maxwell pursed his lips, nodded and walked through the doorway. Karina was already laid out on one of the beds. He closed the door and walked over to the other. He sat down and paused as he felt himself slip over the silk sheets. They felt cold to the touch and caused a shiver to run up his spine. He hesitated before he lay down, grateful at least for the soft pillow. The silk felt weird against his skin. Soft, yet cold, a weird mix that he wasn't sure he liked.

"Maxwell."

Maxwell hummed to indicate he was listening. He heard Karina huff before she seemed to hesitate. He heard shuffling, then she continued.

"What do you think. These beds are, well, the mattress is comfortable, very comfortable but…"

Maxwell nodded in understanding, his head sinking into the pillows as he struggled to stay awake. "Why don't we just sleep. We'll think about it in the morning, all right?"

Karina nodded, her eyes fluttering closed. "All right, sleep well."

Maxwell, after a few moments, finally let himself succumb to sleep's beckoning call.

~*~

Karina's eye twitched as she stared down at the outfit that sat innocently on the table. Lex was in the bathroom and Maxwell, to her relief, was still asleep in the other room. She glared until she thought the fabric would burn, but nothing, nada, zip. She knew it wouldn't, but she could always hope. It was such a small thing, but everything else was so confusing, it was just easier to focus on the horrid thing before her.

The bathroom door swung open as light footsteps sounded from the ceramic flooring. Karina looked at Lex. He was dressed in a nice pair of jeans and black long-sleeved polo. His lanky raven locks were cleaned up and curved around his face nicely instead of the way they usually sagged into it. He still had on a cap, like usual.

Lex frowned as he brought up an arm to feel out the cuff of one sleeve, tugging slightly. One hand raked through his hair as he pursed his lips. "It'll do…" He stepped forward and took a seat on the opposite couch before catching Karina's eyes. "Idiot, what are you doing just standing there, staring into space."

Karina swiveled her head to look back at her own clothing. She could tell Lex followed. She heard a light chuckle. "Ah, about that. The butler assumed you were my servants and I didn't feel the need to correct him."

Karina's eye twitched again, she was going to have to fix that soon, she really shouldn't be twitching that often, but whatever, with what was being said, she couldn't blame herself. "Really? You couldn't think of ANYTHING better?" Karina said under her breath as she grabbed up the outfit and marched to the bathroom. "Where are my shorts when I need them?"

She heard Lex chuckle once more before she slammed the door. A long breath slipped past her lips. "Well, either pajamas or this."

She quickly threw on the clothes and stumbled at some of the ties before she managed to get everything situated. She threw her hair up, then looked in the mirror.

Karina took in the maid outfit. The black and white material and lace fit around her slim frame nicely and showcased her blue eyes. Long white socks surged up her legs, just like her black ones used to and a pair of white gloves covered her hands. Black flats sat on her feet. She brought her foot up and flexed it. "How the heck do they even have the right size?" she asked, feeling self-conscious and a bit irked. She made sure to focus on those emotions instead of the roiling panic she'd been feeling since she woke last night.

She pulled at the material before she swung around. She had a few words to say to Lex. The door shut as she stomped up to Lex, who watched with a wary expression, along with a raised eyebrow.

"K-Karina?"

Karina froze. Her eyes widened as she caught Maxwell's gaze. They stared at each other.

She heard a snort before Maxwell pulled back. One hand covered his mouth, trying to hold in a snicker. Karina narrowed her eyes as Maxwell grabbed his stomach. He bent forward, trying desperately not to laugh. His other hand held the doorway that led to their sleeping quarters. He wiped one eye while he managed to gasp out. "I don't think I've ever seen you in something like that. It's too funny, even more so since you hate housework."

Karina felt a blush of frustrated embarrassment slide onto her face. She heard a soft chuckle and her eyes snapped to gray green. Lex's face smoothed out only to show the corner of his lips twitch upward in a slight smile.

"Both of you…" she growled before she snapped at Maxwell. "Maxwell Elifer, stop laughing right now, or by god!" Karina watched as his mouth slammed shut and his eyes widened.

He chuckled nervously. "Glad to see you're up. I'll just go use the bathroom now."

Karina watched as he scampered to the bathroom, holding his clothes. She could use a good laugh right now, too. Maybe laughing would help, it seemed to help her brother relax a little after all.

"Hell hath no fury like a woman scorned." Karina heard Lex mutter under his breath.

Karina ignored it as she walked to one of the couches and sat down, mindful of her outfit.

"So where are our clothes? What about all the stuff we had?"

"Well, from what I could tell, most of our bags are still back at the house we were taken from. The clothes on us, they were probably burned as soon as we looked away."

Karina's head snapped to Lex's direction. "Wha…"

"It makes sense. They don't want the disease here, so even though you two are clean, doesn't mean that it's not on clothes or something. That's why we had to take the special shower yesterday as well."

Karina closed her mouth in thought before she sighed tiredly. "Ah…" she muttered softly. The two sat in silence as the sound of rustling fabric and quiet cursing filtered from the bathroom. The door swung open. Maxwell stepped out. He looked incredibly uncomfortable with a light embarrassed blush on his face.

That's what you get for laughing at me because of this stupid thing, she thought before she actually looked at the clothing. Maxwell wore a long-sleeved button-up white collared shirt, a plain waistcoat, and striped trousers. Black shoes adorned his feet as his hand tried, and failed, to fasten on a pure black tie.

Karina stared before her hand crept up to her mouth. A chuckle slipped through as her brother started to get more frustrated with the obstinate tie. After a moment, she couldn't help it. She burst out laughing as Maxwell's flush grew.

"Karina!"

"Sorry," she said unapologetically, that short bit of laughter helping her feel a little better, almost like some of the emotions were finally able to be released. She heard Lex give a small chuckle as well before footsteps sounded behind her. Lex walked forward to have a better look at Maxwell's tie. After a quick fix and a little finagling, it was set properly. Maxwell fingered the collar and pulled at it, frustrated.

"That should do it. Why they gave you such attire, well, that's Mother and brother for you. Come on, I bet you're hungry. We'll talk afterward, and maybe find a way to get you out of here before my father comes back."

"Your father?" Maxwell asked as he dropped his hands to his

side.

Lex peered back in silence. "Simply put, it would be a hassle for you two to get out of here if he's around." He looked at both teens with an even expression. "Are you coming?"

Karina paused as she stared at the man in front of her. She didn't trust him. Not after finding out the whole fact that they had been lied to. Yet she trusted her brother's judgment. She frowned, conflicted. *Brother, what are you thinking? Why do you still trust him even after we've obviously been lied to? I know he helped us, but…*

She stopped as Maxwell's eyes flitted to her own. "I'm pretty hungry, so why don't we save this till later?" he asked.

Lex sighed in relief, before he nodded. Karina narrowed her eyes, but stayed silent.

Just what are you thinking?

Lex led the way as they walked out the door. Karina and Maxwell peered back and forth in a mix of awe and disbelief.

"Wow. This place is big," Maxwell said as he stared at the pearly architecture and majestic artwork. Vases adorned the rug-lined hallway and sparkled in the sunlight that beamed through wide windows on one side of the lavish walkway.

Karina frowned. "It's ridiculous that people like Martha are barely living off daily wages while these people…"

"Kari…" Maxwell trailed off.

Karina gritted her teeth. She could feel her brother's eyes on her, but it still aggravated her. Of the little she saw of the place, she could only remember what it was like in the city. The mention of how none of them could get help or even a decent job because of the rich peeved her. People like this and Lex who had more than they ever needed. It made her gut clench and her stomach twist painfully as tears stung her eyes.

It was a disgrace. She couldn't stand it, especially since she knew she wanted more, craving the comfortable bed she slept in and the deep bath with multiple shampoos and such.

Karina was pulled out of her thoughts as a hand settled on her shoulder, grateful to feel her brother's welcoming presence. "Come on. Let's get something to eat."

Karina paused and slowly nodded before her gaze drifted to Lex. Lex stopped. His black hair hung in his face to shadow his eyes.

"It's this way," he stated, his voice neutral, yet slightly coarse. Karina looked at the hunched figure before she followed after Maxwell. Her eyes flitted once more to her brother before she looked back at Lex.

"You know, he doesn't want to be here either," Maxwell whispered as he continued to stare ahead toward Lex's back. "That's why I think it's okay. He'll still help us. Plus, at the moment, we have no one else really to trust."

Karina tilted her head down and to the side. *Stupid twin recognition,* she thought before she slowly nodded. She heard her brother sigh before footsteps came to a halt. She glanced up to see Lex. He stood in front of a double doorway.

"For now, just stay silent, no matter what." Lex looked at Karina before he continued, "They may say some rude or rather uncouth things to you, or about those you have been with. Just try to ignore it and listen to me. After that, I'll answer any questions you may have to the best of my abilities. I'll try to get you out of here. All right?"

Maxwell nodded. Karina felt Lex's gaze move to her and she followed suit. Lex turned and opened the door.

Karina would have just stopped and stared if it wasn't for Lex's cough to get their attention.

The room was a well-lit dining room with large glass windows that let in tons of light that created an airy feel. There were a few servants flitting in and out of the side doors. A light brown table, decked with delicacies and all sorts of food Karina couldn't even begin to name, sat in the middle of the room, surrounded by quite a few chairs. On one end of the table was a woman with delicate features and a man who looked a lot like Lex, just older and with a constant smirk on his face.

"Leonard, dear, it's good to see you up and dressed in proper attire! Oh, your choices clean up quite nicely, no wonder. You always did have a good eye when it came to servants and things."

Karina withheld a growl as she noticed Lex wince. A moment later, she thought over what was said and discreetly gave Lex a sidelong look, Maxwell seemingly doing the same if his subtly raised eyebrow

was any indication. Leonard? What the heck? Lex's name is Leonard?
"Hello, Mother, Caym… It's good to see you again," Lex said, shooting the twins a quick look that seemed to say 'later'.

"Now, now, why don't you sit down and we can talk. I heard from Caym here that you seemed to be taking care of those two. I can't seem to fathom why," the mother said, as she waved her hand dismissively.

Lex pursed his lips and slowly sat down. Karina stood to one side of Lex. Maxwell stood on the other side, face impassive.

"Ah, how nice. With you home and having lost a few maids, it would be nice to have more servants around the house. Wouldn't you say, Caym?"

Karina watched warily as Caym examined them. His hands covered his lips as he leaned his elbows against the table. "Indeed, I can see your point, but it will be up to Father. We'll keep them here under watch until Father returns, then we'll decide."

Lex interjected evenly, "If it is all right with you, I would like they remain under my watch at all times. They do not know the lifestyle of our class. I have not gotten a chance to teach them, so they may do something qualified as rude or scandalous without knowing. I will take care of them till then so that nothing ill may occur. Will that suffice?"

Karina stared at Lex with feelings of incredulity. Scandalous? Ill? When the heck did Lex start talking in such an odd manner? She didn't even realize she held her breath until she saw the mother nod. "Of course. They are your things after all, right, Caym?"

"Right," Caym replied.

Karina could have sworn that a flash of anger appeared on his face, but it was gone as soon as it appeared.

"Now, Lex, why don't you sit down and tell me what happened? It's been years since you disappeared. I was worried I would never see you again. With this filthy peasant sickness going around, I worried greatly."

Lex smiled congenially.

Karina carefully bit her tongue so as not to say anything, or do anything, for that matter.

"Ah, you know. Simple things. I went to figure out the business ventures and opportunities." He quickly raised his hand to halt his mother's objection before he placed it back down and continued, "Before you can say I could easily do that from home, Caym has already taken over most of the business-oriented side of the family and already obtained a wife and kids, though last I heard they weren't around much at all."

Lex sent Caym a look and Karina could see a hint of pain wash over Caym's features, only to once more solidify into his normal smirk. "I did not want to just marry into another family to continue the bloodline and live off the money. I doubt you would want to lose money, now would you?"

The mother paused as Caym continued to watch behind his raised hands.

Karina felt herself fidget in uncomfortable silence as Lex continued. "It was an opportunity, something new and exciting to get those paychecks up and running once more. Unfortunately, I happened to have gotten lost and had no way of contacting home," he finished with a wave of his hand. Karina mentally raised an eyebrow.

Well, he is a decent liar, I'll give him that, she thought. On his face was an expression she never saw before and hoped to never see again. It was a fake smile, obviously worked on and practiced over the years for such an occasion. It held no hint of warmth.

"Ah, of course. But, don't worry, you're home now. Now you can settle down with a nice wife and have kids, just like I wanted. Maybe even take these two." The mother clapped her hands in glee.

What is with these people? Karina thought as the woman looked at her and her brother. After a moment, the woman grinned and spread one arm out over the table.

"Well, why don't we get some food, it's getting pretty late after all," the woman stated.

Lex stood, pushing the chair back. "I'm sorry. I am going to have to excuse myself, since my servants do not know the lay of this land. I will have to show them where they can obtain their meals unless you want them joining us."

From the horrified look on the mother's face, Karina could guess that was a no.

"What are you talking about? Those servants are the last of your priorities, now sit back down and eat like you're supposed to."

"Mother. That is not your concern. I will do as I please and take care of them first. If necessary, I will come back," Lex stated sharply before he walked out the door.

Karina and Maxwell scrambled after him, wanting to get as far away from that room as possible. She was suddenly grateful to have Lex around, even if he was the one who got them involved with this situation in the first place.

They walked to a separate dining room nowhere near as luxurious as the one they were just in. It was filled with appliances and a long wooden table with cushioned chairs. Lex told them to sit down before walking to one side where there were some stoves and a few people standing in front of them. Karina watched warily as he talked with the workers before turning away and walking back over to them. "Don't worry, I'll be back shortly. These guys will take care of you." With that, he left once more.

Karina stared after him, silently wondering if he was heading back to that dining hall with all the elaborate food. Part of her was very glad she wasn't following. She looked up as a young man a little older than herself stepped forward cautiously. "Sir Lex asked us to take care of you. Is there anything you might like?"

"It's all right, we'll leave it up to you, thank you for taking care of us," Maxwell stated as Karina shrugged, nodding. The boy stepped away once more. Karina peered at her twin as he shifted in his seat, obviously uncomfortable under the curious gazes of the other servants.

Another servant came up, this time an older woman. She sat across from them, her expression stern, but her eyes soft and knowing. "It seems like you're new here. I know it's probably hard to get a hang of everything, but it really isn't too bad," she said.

Karina decided not to react, but she was curious, "Where are you from?"

"Around here. Our family was brought in as servants before the gates closed, thus we kept it up."

Oh, so that's how it is, Karina thought as she looked at the other servants. The boy from before returned, carrying two plates of eggs with toast. He placed them down. Karina looked at him and said, "Thank you."

The servant nodded before he hurried away.

"That was another of our new servants, poor boy. He grew up as one of the upper class, but when his family gained too many children, he was given away. It's how it works. Money is everything. If you have money, you're good, if you don't? Well…"

Karina mentally frowned. So, there were people like that even within the community. She dug into the food which would have probably been delicious, but she could barely taste it as her stomach curled in discomfort and her fingers twitched in restless anxiety.

As she was finishing her last bite alongside her twin, Lex returned, ushering them out. They followed after him and returned to his room.

Chapter Twenty-four

Karina watched as the tension seemed to ease out of all of them when the door closed with a snap. “That was quite a lie regarding your reasons for not going home,” Karina muttered as she walked over to the couch.

She sat on the couch and crossed one leg over the other. “And what is this about Leonard? That name doesn’t fit.”

Maxwell sat next to her as he worked to loosen the tie and buttoned collar. Maxwell looked toward Karina before turning to Lex. Lex stared at the door, then faced them, letting out a tired sigh in the process. “It wasn’t really a lie, at least not fully. A good lie is always a lie with some truth to it anyway.”

She took note of her brother’s curious and narrowed gaze as Lex walked over to the couch and plopped down on it. “While it is true I did not want to marry into another family just to be a stay-at-home dad, it wasn’t true about the business venture. As for the name? Well, that is my real name, unfortunately. I hate it. As you said, it doesn’t really suit me.”

“So, where did the name Lex come from?” Maxwell asked.

Lex hesitated. “It started off as just a cruel nickname. After it just kind of stuck, but I don’t think that’s what you want to talk about, is it?”

Maxwell and Karina exchanged looks before Maxwell shook his head.

Lex brushed a hand through his hair and slumped into his seat. Karina stared. In that one moment, the one in front of her looked ten years younger and older at the same time. Weariness and vulnerability clashed with resignation. It was an odd sight. Karina glanced down.

After another moment of silence, Lex opened his eyes and spoke.

"It was five years ago…" Lex tilted his head away from them, a far away and pained look in his eyes. He stared out the windows on one side of the room as sunlight streamed through the thin curtains. "I was tired of being cooped up in the house. Books and games can only get you so far and while there were always people that came and went with the constant parties and banquets, there was never anyone who I could talk to, one on one, besides my brother." He paused. "My brother was the only one who saw me as something other than a thing, a prize or trophy. I wish I knew what made him change…"

Karina and Maxwell exchanged looks as Karina wondered about the man, Caym. He was strange, she couldn't put her finger on it.

"I didn't like it. So, one day, with my brother's help, I decided to go outside. I wanted to see what else was there, besides these four walls, and I wanted to escape Mother's eye. She seemed determined to have me marry even though I was barely a teen…" Lex trailed off.

Karina glanced down once more. Her hands clenched into the fabric of her dress.

"I managed to make my way into the city, much the same way you did. At first, I had no idea where I was, or what to do. My clothes made me stand out quickly so I decided to buy something at the nearest shop. It was the first time buying something for myself, it was quite the experience, and I can still remember the clerk's face at my horrid choice." Lex chuckled softly. "I decided to keep my clothes in a bag and continued through the city until I came to a back area. I found some kids my own age, they were kicking around a ball, shouting and laughing. It was shocking. I hadn't realized how fake everything felt until I saw those smiles. Have you ever experienced being in a crowd, yet feeling like everywhere you looked, all you saw were masks and mannequins?" Lex paused once more, this time to look at both twins.

Karina shook her head. Lex smiled thinly. "In that back area, I just remember one of the kids kicked the ball in my direction. I managed to dodge out of the way, but in doing so, I caught the kid's attention." He paused as his face took on a nostalgic, yet sad expression.

Karina listened in silence, half-curious and half-confused.

"One of them asked if I could grab the ball for them. It took a moment, but I managed to get myself out of the ingrained disgust at the idea. I remember I grabbed the ball and tried to throw it, and accidentally hit the guy who asked for it. There was this silence, a tense one, before suddenly, the boy burst out laughing. I remember I stared as he sat up and rubbed his cheek. 'Man, you throw like a baby.'"

Karina chuckled as Maxwell smiled.

"Of course, I wasn't too happy with the comment and ended up chasing after him. It became a game and after a while, we became friends. It was the oddest friendship too. I would sneak back into the house, only to sneak back outside every so often to see him. Whenever questions about me, like where I came from, or who my parents were came up, I would dodge them. One day, two years later, I happened to not be feeling well, but I went out anyway. I let slip that I was from the rich area..."

"I remember I ended up fainting from a fever. Even though he knew I was part of the rich, he still took me to his home. It was a while later, and no matter how much I insisted about going home, he always told me to stay put until the fever broke. Finally, it did." Lex's eyes shadowed as he pursed his lips. "I remember asking him why he helped me. His response was so simple. 'It's because you're a human, just like me. Blood or class doesn't matter. It's what one strives for that counts.'"

Karina watched in surprise. She never saw such a soft and sincere smile on his face before. It was the first time she saw such a genuine one, now that she thought about it.

Karina and Maxwell exchanged a look and Maxwell slowly nodded, his lips upturned. Lex noticed, but continued. "I returned home later and found the house in a panic, much like the one from today. When they saw that my clothes were dirty and ripped, they managed to find out I went into the city. They berated me and told me how disgustingly vile the people in the city were. To stay away at all cost. 'They're beneath us, you shouldn't associate with people like that, unless you want to make them your servants'." Lex's gaze grew hard as his eyes moved back toward the twins.

"I never felt so disgusted, with both myself and my family. The next day, I left once more and took what I could with me. I went to his house and asked if I could move in. I said I would help work and pay. He disagreed at first, but finally let me in. We grew close, much closer than before. Eventually, however, I had to go back. I went back home a few months later when the guards got too close for comfort. They questioned me and berated me, they kept an even closer eye on me this time, and I couldn't find an opportunity to escape. Time passed until I happened to overhear my parents speaking…" Lex clenched his fists and gritted his teeth as anger flashed over his face.

"They mentioned about how the epidemic had begun, they discussed about how unsurprised they were that it began in the lower class. They spoke of it like it was a passing thing, a momentary blip on their radar. For a few moments, it was on mine too, until they mentioned that the first few cases were in the city right nearby. I don't know how, maybe desperation, but I managed to find a way to leave and quickly hurried to the city. When I arrived, I could sense the panic and fear in the people. I ignored it all and went straight to my friend's house…" he trailed off.

Karina felt Maxwell's worry, and even she felt a bit anxious.

"My friend was one of the first cases. When I arrived, he was already in the third stage, just having gotten out of the second. He was bed-ridden and could barely lift his hand. I never saw him so weak." Lex slowly breathed in and out, as if trying to collect himself. "He was crying, cursing his fate. He told me he always wished he could come with me, into the rich area just once, to have a touch of wealth and grandeur. To be able to eat till he was full. I tried to tell him he still could, it wasn't too late, but he knew, he could tell he wouldn't last. He made me promise to him that no matter what, I would befriend people like him. 'Take care of other poor bastards like myself,' he said. 'I guess… it was a good thing you threw like a baby all those years ago. I would have probably died thinking all Richies were stuck-up bastards without souls. Prove that you aren't one of them, that you can have something without turning into a monster…'"

Lex's face straightened into an impassive expression, as if to hide behind a mask. "He told me to leave right after that. I didn't want to, but he insisted. It was an hour later when the death throes hit. I can still remember the screams to this day. It was the last straw. With that, I decided to leave. I didn't want to return home, not to this place that couldn't care a rat's ass about my friend, or anyone besides themselves, for that matter."

His expression darkened as he growled softly. "I hopped on the first bus out of town and left. I left everything I owned, but the bus ticket to his family so they could at least bury him properly. Since then, I've wandered until I arrived in Reinmark and met my uncle. I always heard he was deranged, but I took that with a grain of salt and was glad. He helped me avoid detection and raised money to pay for things in the area. After that, I tried to keep my friend's promise and while I might have failed most of the time, this time, with you two, I'll try to fulfill my promise to him."

Karina stared. Her expression softened. Maxwell whispered a soft, "What was his name?"

Lex hesitantly responded, "Allen."

Maxwell tilted his head as Karina leaned forward to peer at Lex. She stayed silent as her brother asked, "You told your whole story, why?"

He responded with a quiet, "I don't know. I guess, I needed to tell someone eventually and now that you also know what I am, I felt it was probably better to tell you the truth instead of holding back." He finished as he peered out the window. The sun gleamed high in the sky as puffy white clouds slid over the horizon and wind sang softly in nearby trees.

"I see," she muttered before she leaned back.

"It's never a good thing to hold back," Maxwell said thoughtfully before he looked at Lex with a complex expression. "Still, we're just two random people you met on the street. What does that have to do with the promise? Wouldn't someone else be better? Why are you trying so hard?"

Lex turned to Maxwell. Shock flitted on his face as Karina's head snapped toward her sibling. "Max…"

Maxwell stared back sternly. His expression older than his fourteen years.

Lex seemed to ponder the question, "I guess, a small part of it is interest, but mainly, I think, it's to atone."

Karina felt confusion well up, and it seemed that Lex noticed. He sighed and leaned back in his seat to stare at the ceiling in silence. After a moment, he continued. "I couldn't save my friend, or any of the children I tried to help after the fact. Everyone around me died, disappeared or…" he seemed to pause, peering toward the doorway before shaking his head. "One day, I met these two idiots wandering alone in the most dangerous part of town. Who would be so idiotic to travel in a city late at night by themselves in an area known as a thug hangout? It piqued my interest. Of course, then said idiots decided to join me instead of following Antonio. Why did this look familiar?" At this, he tilted his head down, a bemused expression on his face.

Karina blushed and glared while Maxwell appeared more than a little sheepish.

"Well, I decided I would try one more time. Maybe I would be able to do something I couldn't before." He shrugged, his expression odd. "Since then, it's been one thing after another. It wasn't till now that I realized, I actually felt alive for the first time in a long time and honestly, I guess you guys remind me of Allen, both of you are quite idealistic, after all." He finished, a quiet chuckle to his voice, as if he knew something they didn't.

"Oh…"

"Huh…"

"Well, enough about me. We need to find a way to get you two out of here before Father comes home. We really need to…" Lex trailed off. His eyes narrowed. "Dad can't meet you two," Lex said with quiet finality, barely above a whisper.

He stood and walked around the room for a moment.

"Huh?"

"Don't worry about it," Lex stated as he noticed their confused expressions. "For now, think of something that can get you out of here."

Karina closed her mouth as Maxwell raised an eyebrow. The twins looked at each other, only to jump as a phone rang loudly in the silence. Lex shifted his gaze toward the bed and walked over. He looked back at the camera, then knelt down and reached under the bed.

"Had to hide it, I couldn't risk them destroying it," he stated when he noticed their inquisitive eyes. He flicked the still ringing phone open, glancing at the camera as he moved to one side.

He put it to his ear as Karina watched, Maxwell beside her on the couch. "Hm?" His voice was soft, as if trying to avoid speaking above a whisper. "I see. All right, we'll check it out. Though it's rather interesting to see you trying so hard to help. Curiosity? Ah, makes sense since you're not used to having a challenge, are you?" Lex stopped as the voice on the other side growled back. Lex continued, his expression somber. "Though we're in a bit of a tight spot right now. Yeah, yeah. Thank you for the information. We'll get on it when we can..." There was another pause and a smile flitted on Lex's face before it disappeared. "Oh, hello, Roxanne… I see you're keeping your brother in line." There was a muffled exclamation of indignation. "All right then, I'm glad to hear the treatment worked. I'll leave him to you," he stated. With that, he flipped the phone closed and faced the two teens, a sparkle in his eyes. He barely sent the camera a glance before he beckoned them to the balcony. Karina and Maxwell looked at each other before they stood and followed.

"I have our next destination."

"Really?" Karina stated in unison with her brother as they stepped into the cool morning air. The tree branches swayed as gardeners moved about. Lex leaned against the rail, arms crossed and eyes on the horizon. While she could tell her brother was excited, she felt wary. Lex said the same thing for New London City and look how that ended.

Lex nodded as he slid the phone into his pocket, once more on vibrate. He must have been trying to avoid the camera. "We're heading to Collern City, a two day's train trip away from here."

"Collern?"

"It's a city west of here, in Indiana," Lex stated as he stood and walked over to the closet.

"Indiana?" Karina spluttered in surprise while Maxwell widened his eyes.

"Isn't that far from here? I mean…" Maxwell stopped as Lex walked back into the main room. He rummaged around for a moment, before pulling out two pairs of jeans and shirts. They were big and baggy. He sent Maxwell and Karina a look before placing them back into the closet. He rummaged some more, before pulling out and stepping back toward the balcony.

He must be worried. Karina thought as she looked at the camera, watching its solid red light.

"It's not that far, considering. We'll take a train. It should be fine, they won't think of checking trains around here. Once you get out of here, I'll meet you at Liberty station. Those will be your clothes when we need them. For now…"

"Hm?" Karina questioned.

Lex let a smirk slip onto his face that sent a shiver down her spine. "I have an idea."

Chapter Twenty-five

Maxwell was admittedly annoyed. He frowned as he continued to polish the vase before him. He really was getting tired of this. He was still in the stuffy servant clothing. It was itchy and stiff, the worst combination. He finished polishing the vase and sighed in relief, glad to be done. He looked out the window to see Karina in the garden, helping with the roses. Another woman stood beside her, patting down the soil while Karina watered. She looked tired and her hair, usually in a ponytail, was in a tight bun. He turned and walked down the hallway.

This was their third day as servants. It was strenuous, but the other servants were very helpful and encouraging. They warned them to stay away from the mother and Caym, which Maxwell was all too happy to do. He turned a corner and frowned. He was lost again.

"This place is a freaking maze. You would think after staying here for three days, I would know where to go. Nope, not at all," he muttered as he spun to go back the way he came, only to backpedal, withholding a yelp. Behind him was Caym. Caym raised an eyebrow in amusement.

"Well, well, if it isn't one of Lex's servants," he stated before he moved past and down the hall. Maxwell shifted away as Caym paused. He looked over his shoulder. "I don't get why my brother is so attached to you two. What's so important about you two? He seems very protective…" He scrutinized Maxwell before he resumed walking down the hallway, out of sight.

Maxwell stayed silent. Caym honestly creeped him out. It was almost like Caym was looking at him like he was a chess piece or something. He overheard from the servants that Caym had a love of games, so maybe the idea wasn't too far-fetched, but still. He walked back in the opposite direction of Caym.

He was given a new assignment today and had no idea where it was. He moved from room to room, opening and closing the doors as he went. Finally, he came across what he thought was the room. The desk and floor were messy with papers. He remembered that his supervisor, the older woman from the other day, warned him, on high penalty, not to touch the papers, no matter what.

He let out a sigh as he began to dust the furniture, trying to avoid the papers. Books lined mahogany shelves. One window was open to let in the afternoon light as a breeze flittered through the room. He moved behind the desk, grateful for the open window. The clothing was hot and he really was tempted to take off the outer layer, then remembered he was told not to, also under penalty. He groaned, only to pause as something caught his eye.

The papers didn't have any specific order, or so it seemed. He looked them over, then shook his head. What was he doing? He was not supposed to touch them. He went to turn away, only to stop when a familiar name appeared on one of the pages.

He froze. His eyes widened as he darted over and picked up the paper.

October 5th, 20XX

It was discovered that patient 864-O543, also known as Felix Elifer, does indeed have gene HX5, an anti-byproduct of experimentation ten years prior. Said gene seems not to be fully functional, however. Further research is needed.

October 9th, 20XX

Research has concluded that gene HX5 has been degraded through too much exposure. Subsequent experiments have revealed a decline in protein production and a weakening in cell membranes. It is possible we will need to obtain another experimental unit, since it seems that the patient has shown symptoms of…

The sound of a door opening shocked Maxwell out of his reading. He jumped as the papers slipped out of his hands and fluttered to the floor. He looked over his shoulder to find the door still closed.

It must have been another in the hallway.

He was curious, he wanted to know. What happened? What happened to his father? Was there still a chance he might still be out there? Just like Mother? Maybe he just couldn't send out letters anymore. He could still be alive.

Maxwell looked down at the papers uneasily as sunlight filtered through the window and sparkled on the dust motes. He gulped. He would have just left, but then he saw another paper, another name.

Subject 526-0O34, Veronica Elifer, recently transported to Collern City, will remain as experiment 527 of HX5 continues. Meanwhile, acquisition of offspring…

He heard the door handle rattle and he dropped the paper, hurriedly returning to cleaning, away from the desk.

The door opened to reveal the older woman from earlier. "I see you found the room, just wanted to make sure you were all right."

"Fine." Maxwell dropped his hands to his side, with the duster. "I'm almost done, will we be able to have dinner soon?"

"That's the other reason why I came to see you. Sir Lex asked me to tell you and Karina to join him for dinner."

Maxwell had to withhold the grin as he nodded. "Thank you, I will be done soon."

"All right then." She smiled and left.

Maxwell let out a sigh and, after some time passed, hurried out of the room. He would have taken the papers, but in his rush and want to leave, he pushed the thought of grabbing them to the side until he was out the door. It seemed like the plan was about to begin after all.

He returned the duster to its place and walked back to Lex's room at a forced leisurely pace, trying not to draw attention to himself even with a feeling of anticipation running through his veins. He met Karina on the way. From the sparkle in his twin's eyes, he could tell she was just as excited as he was. They slipped into Lex's room to find he was nowhere in sight, but the jeans and shirts he pulled out the other day were lying on the couches, hidden from the camera. Karina changed in the bathroom, while Maxwell used the upper level of the bedroom, somewhat out of sight of the doorway.

He sighed as he dropped the servant's clothes on the floor with relish. He could finally understand why some of his classmates always made it a ritual to burn school books once classes where finished. If they were just as frustrated as he was, he would have done the same. He moved to the couch. Karina wasn't that far behind. Her hair was redone up in her signature ponytail and the sweat washed off with water. They sat next to each other as Lex arrived, followed by Machael.

Machael bowed, handing the tray to Lex before leaving, closing the door behind him. Lex placed the food on the table, pulling off the cover. It was just some sandwiches, but Maxwell was hungry and so happily dug into them. They ate heartily, finishing the meal in peace. Still, Maxwell couldn't suppress the grin that crossed his face.

"Max? What's that for?"

"I found out where Ma is!" Lex's gaze flickered to the camera and Maxwell stopped.

"Why don't we talk outside," Lex said. "It's nice out."

Maxwell nodded, following after Lex as he walked toward the balcony. Karina followed hesitantly. Once outside Maxwell continued, a little more subdued. "It's just like Lex said. She's in Collern City," Maxwell said with an excited wave of his hand. He felt like smiling, yet at the same time, was absolutely petrified that, even with all the information pointing toward the location, it would still be wrong.

Karina's eyes widened.

"Where did you find that information?" Lex asked cautiously, his eyes narrowed as he leaned forward, hands crossed over the rail.

"I was cleaning one of the rooms, the desk was a mess, with all these papers strewn everywhere. It was one of the papers." Maxwell paused and then dropped his hands to his side. "They also said things about experimentation and…" He spared his sister a glance as he continued, "information about Dad."

Karina jerked as if zapped and whipped around so fast, Maxwell would have been surprised if she hadn't gotten whiplash. "What did it say?"

Maxwell tried to remember, dearly wishing he grabbed the papers. "They were recently dated, not too long ago at all… They were talking about genes and mentioning how something had been degraded too much. I don't know exactly, but it might mean he's still alive."

Karina sat next to him, jaw working, as if unsure whether to speak or not.

"That may be the case, but we don't have the time to talk of it now. From the sounds of it, all you know is speculation. It's best to focus on your mother, since we know both that she's alive, and where she is," Lex pointed out.

Right, Maxwell thought as Karina closed her jaw and slowly nodded.

Lex sighed and pushed away from the railing. "So, are you ready?"

"More than," Karina said, Maxwell nodded, pushing away the thoughts regarding his father. He leaned back and looked at Lex.

Before him was the boy they'd known for a while now, yet he looked different. His eyes were alight with interest, shining in the sunlight. He looked healthy, and almost energetic.

"Well, we should get moving. I don't want to stay here any longer than I need to," Lex said. Maxwell exchanged looks with his sister and nodded. Lex stepped toward the doorway then turned to the twins. "Good luck."

Lex paused and Maxwell could see the hesitance in his eyes. "See you in a few days," Maxwell said, conveying more certainty then he felt.

Even so, Lex still got the hint, eyes alighting in relief. "All right. Be careful. If I'm not there…"

"We'll go," Karina stated softly.

Lex stayed silent, before he nodded.

Maxwell watched as Lex stepped out of the balcony, past the camera and out of the room. He exchanged glances with his sister before following. He peered through the slim gap Lex left in the doorway. Lex spoke. He held a bored tone as his posture seemed to change to a haughty look. "I wish to speak with my mother and brother. Can one of you notify them?"

Maxwell leaned forward to examine the two guards, standing on either side of Lex. That was one of the problems. Ever since Lex returned, he had a guard on him, and, in turn, on them. It was annoying.

"We are…"

"You were to watch me, is that wrong?"

"No…"

"Good, now get moving."

Maxwell narrowed his eyes. Lex had an odd look in his eyes as he surveyed the two guards. The buff men were silent, though one was a bit more flustered. After a few more minutes of conversation, he walked away. The flustered guard hurried after him, quietly followed by the second, stoic guard.

Maxwell peered toward the balcony where Karina still stood. Karina looked at Maxwell and mouthed a quiet, "See you soon."

Maxwell watched, feeling a hint of envy as Karina jumped over the rail and gripped the tree outside the window. She hung for a second, then swung until she was able to reach a more supportive branch. She grabbed it, moved toward the base and started to crawl down like a monkey. Maxwell hurried over to the balcony and tilted his head down to watch her progress.

She moved down the tree and jumped to the ground gracefully. She looked up and grinned before she raced off.

Maxwell walked back into the room, trying hard not to stare at the camera. It was already suspicious enough to be the only one in the room, now that Lex left, so he needed to hurry. He stared around, nodded and headed toward the doorway. He looked out through the partially open door before he slipped through. Maxwell hurried down the hallway, his thoughts on his sister. Was she all right? Would she be able to meet up? Would this work?

He ran down the hallway. His clothes were on the bigger side, but a lot more comfortable compared to the butler uniform which he wouldn't have been able to run in. He shook himself out of his thoughts as he slowed and looked around the next corner.

It had been Lex's idea. Since it would have been incredibly

difficult to move in a group, he decided that it would be better to go separately. Karina suggested the tree and, even though Lex was wary, he told her how to move about the garden. That left Maxwell with one route, through the house itself, which was what led them to their respective jobs, figuring out how to get around the place either in the garden, or in the maze of a house itself.

He slipped around the corner and ran down the hall. He heard a clatter to one side and slid to a halt as he pushed against the wall. He held his breath as the silence continued. After some time passed, he peeked around the corner before him and sighed. He passed it and continued down the hall and toward a stairwell. He hurried down.

The house was quiet with the coming of evening. From experience, he knew most servants ate during this time before they prepared for their night shift. Plus, the mother desired silence at least once per day since she was a god-fearing woman. He never had been able to figure that one out.

Maxwell raced down the hallway at top speed. He turned corner after corner before he slid into a room filled with boots and other assorted objects, the servant's mudroom. He scanned the area before he walked slowly up to the doorway. He jumped as a click sounded through the room. It was the only sound that marred the silence. He surveyed once more before he darted out the door.

~ * ~

Lex peered behind him, eyeing the two guards warily as he moved down the path. He turned back ahead toward the long hallway. With this, while it would be harder for him to leave, it would get the kids out.

He needed to stick around anyway. He needed to know. *Well actually,* he thought, *I need to confirm just what my father used to do.* Even though he didn't want to stay, he knew at this point, he had to. He told them he would meet them in a few days, but would it be enough?

Did he really want to see his father again?

He walked through the doors of the kitchen and peered around the room. To his relief, there was no one there.

“Sir, didn’t you say you were…”

Lex looked at the guard with a cold gaze. “I decided I was hungry, is there something wrong with that?”

The guard snapped his mouth shut. Lex headed toward the pantry. He stepped inside and peered at the wall of goods. He closed the door just enough to hide his hands from view and then reached into his pocket. He grasped the small lighter he snagged the other day from his father’s room. He stepped to one side, as if peering at the choices of health bars, as he flicked on the lighter. The flame sparkled. He placed it close to one of the items and watched as smoke curled up from the box. He snapped the lighter shut, grabbed a bar and hurried out of the room. He was promptly followed by the two guards as they moved toward his mother’s wing. He quickly ate the bar and stuffed the wrapper into his pocket.

It was only a few minutes later when a shrill screech pierced through the air. The guards jumped as Lex mentally sighed in relief. He looked out one of the windows as the signs of panic and the sounds of running footsteps rang through the once silent halls.

I hope they got out in time, he thought before he continued on his way.

Chapter Twenty-six

Caym watched the scene in silence as a slender hand pulled away from one of the many buttons before him. His eyes flitted over the screens as they hummed and glowed brightly in the dark room. He leaned back and crossed his arms over his chest as if to watch a regular movie.

"Interesting move, little brother. Interesting," Caym stated softly as he pulled his hands away from his body and leaned forward. The thin fingers shifted over the keys as the cameras changed, new angles popped up while some remained and others disappeared. He watched silently as he perused through the different cameras.

Brother… He really missed him. Obviously, the feeling wasn't mutual though. He stood and shut off the cameras before he slipped out the door. He walked calmly down the hallways as staff and family ran around in hysterics. He could smell something and was almost positive that it was something burning. He chuckled softly.

Sprinklers sparked and shrill sirens began to ring throughout the house.

He turned a corner to see Lex. Lex's eyes widened for a fraction of a second until they suddenly grew cold. The two walked past each other, like the calm amongst the storm.

"This seems like an interesting game. Let's see how long you can play, little brother."

Caym watched, amused, as his brother jerked at the words. Lex barely gave him a look before he continued on his way, his posture rigid. Caym stepped out of the house and into the backyard. He heard cries as he walked past guards and other officials into the tree-lined garden proper. It was getting dark and the sapphire sky was transforming into a rainbow of colors. A soft breeze played through the trees as he stopped and leaned against one of the many maple trees, his gaze on a small thicket seen through the underbrush. The two teens, dressed the same, stood side by side. Relief was obvious as the girl grabbed the boy in a hug.

"How sweet." He chuckled softly. "If only little brother could act like that sometimes. He's so uptight," Caym said as the two pulled away and began to walk through the trees.

He remained still for a moment and then followed at an easy pace. He knew where they were going. He was just curious what would happen. Would they actually arrive in time? Was the diversion not enough? He still couldn't figure out why Lex was so attached to them, but he would ask his brother that later.

The two shifted through the trees so easily, he was almost impressed. He smiled as they stopped. The girl pointed something out.

It looks like they won. Let's see how my brother does from now on. Caym paused as his chuckles subsided. He turned and, without even a look back, walked away.

~ * ~

Lex was mentally panicking. He knew he shouldn't, but after seeing Caym, and how calm he was, he was worried. Would the twins be all right? Would they escape? He pulled himself from his thoughts as he took another corner, this time being led by the guards as the sounds of the sirens screamed louder. They stepped outside and Lex looked back to see the smoke lightly curl into the sky. He could already hear the sound of water, and knew it would be taken care of soon, if it hadn't been already. He heard a radio crackle. One of the guards brought it to his ear to listen. Lex wished he knew who they were, but his parents must have gotten new ones after he left.

He hoped the old ones were still all right.

"Are you sure?" the guard on the radio said, eyeing Lex.

Lex just looked back at him, face neutral. Had they figured it out already? He shouldn't have been that surprised. In many ways, it was a dumb move, but that's all it was supposed to be. He saw the guard's features harden before a hand gripped his upper arm. He winced. "You're coming with me."

Lex didn't shrug him off, what was the point? Though he did wish the guard would loosen his grip a little. "So, where to?" he asked, with a quirked lip.

The guard glared. "Sir Lex, this behavior is unacceptable. Your father told us, if you were ever to return, to make sure nothing like this happened. We're bringing you to your room. Your parents will decide what to do from there."

Lex narrowed his eyes. He was grateful his father wasn't home then. At this, he wrenched his arm out of the grip and stood tall. He stepped forward. The guards didn't try to grab him again. The stepped to either side of him and walked down the hallway. Lex could see the servants returning. He walked past one hallway just as his mother stepped back inside. She looked at him, emotions clouding her face. A moment later, her face grew impassive. "Take him back to his room, I will call my husband." With that, she walked away.

Lex stiffened. He was afraid of that. A part of him wanted to run, but that wasn't going to work. So, he just accepted it.

They continued down the hallway, back to where they started. One guard stepped in, followed by Lex and the other. The first walked to the balcony and closed it. They both backed away and stepped back outside, closing the door. Lex looked over his shoulder before he stepped to the couch and sat.

His thoughts wandered all over the place, to the twins, to his own escape, to meeting his father. Around and around, his thoughts went. He closed his eyes and placed his head in his hands. He opened his eyes to stare at the woolen rug, seeing through his fingers, like staring through a cage. At least tomorrow, he could find out whether the twins escaped or not. Really, that was the only torture to staying here now.

Not knowing what was happening outside.

He sighed. The other torture was wondering if he would be able to meet up with the twins or not. In many ways, he highly doubted he would. He hoped, above all else, that the twins were safe, because he knew for a fact he was not. Not with Father or Caym around. Not with being stuck here. He shivered as his thoughts plagued him.

He fell onto his side, letting the cushions dig into him. Mother was calling Father, that meant his chance of seeing Father was even sooner than he planned. He wasn't sure if he was grateful or scared.

He closed his eyes once more and, even as his thoughts whirled, finally managed to fall into the depths of sleep.

~ * ~

Maxwell shrugged off the dirt as he slipped under the rotten part of the chain link fence. A leaf was stuck in his hair and his clothes were mussed from trying to squeeze through. Karina was in the same state.

"This reminds me of when we first left home. It feels like so long ago, doesn't it?"

Maxwell paused and shifted toward his sister before he nodded. He turned his head back toward the house before he hurried forward. He felt his sister's eyes before she grew even with him. The two moved quickly and, not too much after, reached the golden gates. Maxwell stared up at them with a frown before he heard his sister exclaim, noticing another small break in the gate. It was old and rusted and if someone wasn't being very meticulous, it wouldn't even have been noticed. Maxwell sighed in relief as they slipped through. They were finally out of there.

Maxwell patted himself down as he peered sidelong at Karina. "We should go grab our stuff."

Karina nodded and moved ahead, her grand sense of direction leading them back toward the house they were taken from. They moved quietly down the roads until they started to get closer to streets they recognized. The further they moved from the gated community, the more messed-up the homes were. Twisted trees danced in the breeze as the sun sank.

"There," Karina called as she pointed down the walkway. Maxwell looked up from the sidewalk, tired after the long day. A few houses down was the one they stayed at before. Karina peered around as

Maxwell moved to a stop next to her.

"Kari?"

"Wait here. I'll sneak in and grab our bags." Maxwell went to argue, but his sister was already gone.

She moved through the garden and toward the back out of sight. Maxwell pursed his lips and moved off to one side in annoyance.

Why did she always do that?

He waited in silence, watching the house warily. He remembered what Lex said, about what happened after they were taken. He mentally shivered. He was glad he was unconscious during that. Seeing one brutal death was enough for him.

He spotted curtains moving and stiffened. He shrunk into the shadows as a figure peered out into the street.

After a moment, the curtains pulled away and the door opened to reveal the man from the other day. He looked a lot worse for wear. His face was haggard and his clothes disheveled. He scanned the street, as if nervous and slowly stepped out. He looked around, jumping at every little sound before scurrying off down the road.

Maxwell watched and waited. He wasn't sure whether to feel sympathy or not. The man hadn't helped them, but he also argued against what was happening, only to lose his wife after. This world was doing a number on him, that's for sure. He closed his eyes and just listened as the wind blew softly through the trees and birds chirruped in the distance. He heard shuffling and looked up to see Karina peek her head out the door. She raced out, backpacks in hand. She threw two to him and quickly slipped on her own. He threw his on as they moved down the street.

"Karina, would you stop doing that?"

"We needed our bags, so I just grabbed them and left. Luckily, the only one there had the same idea. Still, the house was a wreck. It looked like a storm blew through."

I wouldn't be surprised, Maxwell thought, how would he react if he lost everything? He didn't want to imagine it.

"Did you at least check to see what was in the bags?"

She froze, as if she just realized. Maxwell had to run to catch up as she darted toward a distant tree line. They moved into the shadows of the trees and sat at the base of a stunted oak. Karina grabbed her bag and almost ripped it open. Her hand riffled through the items almost feverishly. Stuff slid out of the bag and slammed to the ground from books to rope to things Maxwell didn't even know she had in there.

There was a plop and Karina's hand froze. Her gaze slid to the object as Maxwell stared down in shock.

It was his mother's Bible.

Chapter Twenty-seven

He gingerly picked it up. The pages crackled and smooth leather clung to his fingers. Something off-white stuck out between the pages, its edges sharp. He let the book fall open in his hands.

Pages fluttered before they split open. A page, crinkled and worn from use, appeared. It was stained with dry wetness.

Maxwell grabbed the envelope that fell onto the ground.

The dirt-stained envelope opened to reveal two pieces of paper. He frowned before he reached in and pulled one out, curiosity getting the better of him.

As Maxwell opened the letter, his eyes fell on the curly script, the same script that was on the note at home.

"Mom…" Karina breathed.

Maxwell glanced at it before he grabbed the second letter and opened it.

He stared at the first word as his hand trembled in shock. Wide eyes stared at the curled script as Karina grasped his arm tightly, her eyes also on the letter.

"It's…a letter from Dad…" he whispered before he looked at the first letter.

"What were they doing in Mom's Bible?" Karina asked as she took Dad's letter.

Maxwell shook his head and looked down at his mother's handwriting.

"I want to know what she wrote. I wonder if she knew something was going to happen," he said softly.

Karina and Maxwell looked at each other before Karina slowly nodded. Maxwell breathed in and with steady eyes and a trembling hand, began to read the words. They flowed off his tongue and both swore they could almost hear their mother's voice as Maxwell continued on softly.

My dear children,

If you are reading this, then I have no doubt something has happened to me, and I pray you are safe. I thought I would have at least a little time, but if you are reading this, I guess I didn't. I know this might sound odd, but I want to say I'm sorry. We're both sorry. We did not mean for you two to end up in this messed-up situation of a world. We wanted you to be happy and live a healthy, normal life, but that could not happen. We tried. Your father and I really wanted things to work, but it seems that it was too good to be true. Karina, Maxwell, neither of us blamed you for what happened all those years ago. Your father knew that when they came, one of you would have been taken if he didn't comply at once. He gave himself up willingly to protect you and never regretted the decision. I put in his letter so you can read it. Hopefully, everything will be clear.

Now, let me tell you the truth. You two are special. A real gift to this world and it all started about eighteen years ago. Before you were even thought of, the city of Claremore was created by the upper echelons of the government. It was a secret that only the top-level personnel knew about. It was to be an experimental site. People volunteered or were convinced to go within the place. Restrictions were harsh and at first, many civilians had a hard time acclimating to the new environment. As a result, I was sent in, along with other doctors and scientists to monitor the people and watch their growth. During that time, I met your father. He was a charming man and extremely polite. Every time I came in to test him or check on him like a doctor would, he would smile and make small talk like it was nothing. We fell in love.

After a while, the project was forgotten and the doctors and scientists left to return home. Data that was analyzed and collected was sent in to the Bureau of Health and stored away. I stayed and a few years later, we had you two. We were so happy and blessed to have such wonderful children. But time caught up with us.

An epidemic the likes of which we never saw before began to

show signs of appearing. The information that was stored away was pulled out and it revealed that within the community, immunity to many sicknesses cropped up. To be sure, they asked me to send data on each individual. At the time, I had no idea what they were doing, so I foolishly agreed. I took samples of all the people who were around when the experiment first occurred and sent it in. A few days later, they came. They knew who you were because of my carelessness. Your father, who was the initial test subject, gave himself up, as you remember, by telling them that they knew he had it. Your father, however, did not have a full immunity. They experimented, and did everything to find a way to obtain the immunity.

I'm sorry. I didn't mean for this to happen. None of this. I just wanted a family, a place to call home, but life isn't that fair, is it?

I love you two, and I pray that you are both all right and please, take care of each other. You're all I have left.

Dearly, your mother.

Maxwell stared at the letter as his hands shook. Tears gathered in his eyes as he held it close. Karina trembled as her bangs curled into her face to cast it in shadow. The evening light shone through the tree leaves that swayed above them. Off in the distance, a car rumbled down the lane and a dog barked into the wind.

"What…what does Dad have to say?" Maxwell finally asked. Karina handed the letter over without a word. Her hands clenched into fists.

Maxwell took the letter and carefully opened it.

My dear Veronica,

I'm sorry, but this will be my last letter to you. I can't hold out much longer. The epidemic is spreading fast and they're getting desperate. I've seen more officials lately. There's talk that they might try our children soon. I hoped that I would be enough, but it seems I was wrong. Please, take care of them for me. They are this country's last hope.

It may be hard, I know that. It's painful to know this is all I can do for you. If this is the last time I can send a letter, I had to warn you and the children. No matter what, don't let them get them. Their only thoughts aren't on the country. They are on their own selfish considerations and power. I don't want our children to get mixed up in this. This country's government is ruined, but I can't stop it, so please, just protect them.

Karina, Maxwell, my dear children, if you are reading this, know that I love you. You've probably realized by now. You may or may not know that an epidemic is destroying the very heart of this nation. People die and suffer almost every day and it's only getting worse. I had immunity, but it wasn't a full one.

You two have the full immunity. In your blood, you hold the cure that can save this nation's people. It's up to you what you decide to do with it.

As a father, this is the hardest thing I'm going to have to ask for. Please help this country. You two are the cure. If the government gets a hand on you, like me, then only those they deem worthy will survive.

If you're reading this and have left Claremore, you've probably already seen it. There are just too many people. Their goal if they obtain you two is a complete and utter genocide. Anyone that doesn't fit the bill, those too weak, old, frail or sick will perish without a second thought. I wish I was lying, that this wasn't the truth, but it is. I've managed to get this letter to you safely, so that they don't know what I wrote, or that I wrote it, but this will be the last time. I pray that, for the sake of the country, you two stay safe. You are our hope and don't forget, even if you don't believe everything I've written here. Please believe your mother and I truly do love you and wish this never had to happen.

Take care, my precious family,
Your father and husband, Felix

Maxwell stopped, his voice grew hoarse as he finished and stared at the letter in morbid shock. "Genocide… Cure… Wha…?" he managed to stutter out weakly as the letter slipped out of his hands. Maxwell stared at it in confusion. "Kari… what?"

"I…" Karina trembled as her voice cracked. "I don't…" They

stared at the letters in silence. Maxwell's thoughts ran rampant through his brain.

"We're…"

"The cure…"

"Why?"

"What are we?"

"Why didn't Mom tell us?"

"Why us?"

"How is it even possible?"

"If Father only had half immunity…"

"Why do we have full?"

Maxwell clamped his mouth shut as he clenched his fist. He tilted his head down and noticed the Bible was still open, words slid past his eyes, unseen. They finally stopped at one sentence. His lips mouthed the words, even as his brain ignored them.

A moment later, he blinked and his eyes snapped to the beginning of the sentence. "Therefore, put on the full armor of God, so that when the day of evil comes, you may be able to stand your ground, and after you have done everything, to stand." Maxwell paused and muttered a soft. "Stand…"

He glanced up and looked over to his sister who looked back at him, confusion and distress evident on her face.

"To stand…" he paused. "That's it! Karina, don't you see? We need to stand. Ma and Pa are depending on us. So maybe we are the only ones who can save these people. If that's the case, then we should at least try. If this is right, then Ma will still be alive, maybe even Dad, like in those reports I found." Maxwell stopped, thoughts flickering to the reports.

Now that he thought about it, they made so much more sense now. The experiments, talk about genes, proteins and such, they were talking about the cure. He pulled from his thoughts. "If they need us, they will use her to lure us out. Not only that, but we know where she is."

Uncertainty flitted on Karina's face.

"Hey, at least we now know why everyone is after us. We're not going to sit around and become experiments for someone else's goals.

We won't be able to save Ma if we do that, right?" Maxwell said.

Karina paused before she slowly nodded. Comprehension and a bit of hope shone on her face. "Wait, does that mean…?"

"Yeah, not only that, but…" Maxwell stopped as realization dawned on him. "I-I think Lex is cured. That's why Lex is so much better, he doesn't have the epidemic anymore." He glanced toward Karina. "I think it was my blood! Remember? I had to give him blood after the riot?"

"Right and after that, the doctor mentioned how he was recovering faster than usual. Lex even mentioned himself that he felt better than he had in ages…"

Maxwell gazed out over the street before he looked at his sister firmly. "Well, then. I guess we know what we need to do."

"Get Mom in Collern City."

"Spread the cure to the people."

"We know where to start, the station Lex mentioned."

"We even have a destination for who can help with the spread of the cure, after we get Ma."

Maxwell grinned as he grabbed his bag and pulled out another letter from the front pocket. He waved the white envelope in front of him. "Dr. Girshwin's mother."

Karina chuckled before she grabbed up the letters and carefully put them back into the Bible. She gathered the items into her bag and threw it on her back. She stood in front of Maxwell, hands on her hips. "Well then?"

Maxwell glanced up as the sun's light gleamed brightly over the horizon in beautiful golds and oranges. He clenched his fist in determination. He grabbed his own bag and stuffed the letter back inside. He looked at his sister, smiled widely and stood.

"Liberty Station, here we come!"

About the Author

Julie Boglisch is a twice-published twenty-seven-year-old who thoroughly enjoys a good book, a good cup of tea and a good video game to play in her spare time. A graduate of Gordon College, she double majored in Communication Arts and Music. Working the odd job to maintain her livelihood, she knows a lot about rolling with the punches and is not afraid of stepping forward into the unknown.

Also by the Author
at
Rogue Phoenix Press

Demon's Song

Alex always wished to see the Overlands, a place of sunshine and freedom. However, as a slave in the far corners of the Underlands, it was all but a dream. That is, until he's framed for murder and is forced to flee during a demon attack.

Searching for the answers to why he was framed and seeking a chance at the fleeting freedom he's always dreamed about, he journeys to the capital, meeting friend and foe along the way. But the Underlands are both beautiful and dangerous. Having a demon hunter on his tail and a witch whose sole desire is to become the high Seer around him, he's in for quite the journey.

Chapter One

Alex stared out over the crystal-clear water. Thin streams cascaded from the rocks to one side, falling into the pool that shone with the light from the moss. The rock felt scratchy against his bare feet and his hands were bruised from scrabbling up the steep slope that led to this little cave, but it was worth it. He breathed in the smell of the water and knelt down, delicately dipping one hand. He pulled his hand up, watching the water flow between his fingers.

Water such as this was such a rare thing to find in the Underlands, so pure and untainted. Of course, the rivers were clean, but this, this gentle sparkle and warm glow was just something else. He turned his head up to the ceiling where the moss glowed softly. He wondered if there was water like this in the Overlands? That mythical place of sunlight… Would he have a chance to go there someday? No…he knew. With every fiber of his being, he knew it was impossible. After all, he couldn't leave these lands…

Even so, he reached his hand up, touching the cool moss as his thoughts wavered. He wanted to see it, to see what it was like above the stone. Sunlight, blue skies, meadows…

Alex's hand dropped to his side as he toed the cold water with one foot. He loved the feel of the water on his skin, how it just flowed over in gentle waves, just like he imagined an ocean would. It helped calm his thoughts.

He sighed. For some reason today, it only made him feel a bit depressed. He shook his head before turning away from the spring. He glanced out the cave entrance and quietly cursed. The day stones were starting to wane. He needed to get home soon or his mother would have his hide. He peered down the steep slope, trying to find a safe path down. After all, this was only his third or fourth time here. He never used the same path so he didn't know the best way down. The cave was high up, hidden by the curve of the ceiling. He could clearly see one of the day stones, its brilliant yellow white light, beaming down, even as it slowly faded into the blue of the night stone right next to it. If he reached up, he could touch the top of the ceiling. That didn't mean much though, considering the ceiling curved downward, dipping starkly toward his spot.

It made sense. It was near the edge of the Underlands, after all, buried deep underground beneath the stone and earth. He shook his head and focused on finding a path safely down. To his relief, he managed to find the path he used to get up this time and scurried down, just barely avoiding sharp rocks. His skin was already scratched from the climb up and was only made worse as he barreled down the hill. In the distance, he could see his home, the owner of which was the Grand Duke of Liliay. Past that, he could see a road, which stretched to a town in the distance. Off to the other side was a river, the only indication of it being water, being the thin blue band seen against the stark gray.

The slope eased up until he was once more on flat land. He raced ahead, dodging through the tall rocky outgrowths that resembled a forest, something that existed on either side of the house, blocking it from intruders on all sides except from the town.

At least, that was what his mother called the rocky outgrowths, but she was told that by her mother so who knows?

He took a sharp corner around one particularly big outcropping and came upon a large, but squat home, being only about two stories. The dirt path stood on his right, weaving out of sight. He could almost see the set of gates, blocking the way in. He turned toward the home, hurrying up to the delicate entranceway. It held a front porch with wood double doors and wide windows, set with weak light stones. He could see Riviera working on the house, repairing parts of it that had rotted away and replacing what he couldn't fix with stone. He was standing on a stone ladder, the duel sides stopping it from pushing into the rotting wood. Alex slowed down, wincing as the pain from his sore feet was made known to him now that he was stopped.

"Yo, Alex. Good to see you back!" Riviera called down, as he continued hammering the board into place, his signifying wrist chain jangling with a steady clacking sound. It was thick and looked heavy.

"Watch what you're doing," Alex called up right as Riviera yelped, barely avoiding smashing the hammer into his hand.

He grinned sheepishly. "Well, yes… Anyway, better get inside. It's late."

"I know." Alex waved him off as he stepped up to the doorway, ignoring the white flowers decorating either side of the entrance, the only other form of life and the only flower that somehow managed to survive in the Underlands. He pushed the door open as slow as possible, peering around the doorframe.

The inside was quiet, barely a light on in the house. He opened the door more and almost cried out as the Grand Duke of Liliay stepped from the shadow of the doorway with a 'boo.'

"Duke..."

The Duke frowned and Alex quickly adjusted his wording. "Grandpa!"

Alex placed a hand on his chest to catch his breath as the Grand Du…Grandpa gave a hearty laugh with great booming chuckles. He was fit for his age, but the wrinkles and liver spots were quite visible on his skin. Wispy white hair was partially slicked back and a wide smile with surprising white teeth shone as brightly as the pale skin of an Underlander. His signifier, a delicately made earring shaped in the form of a pair of wings, swung gently from his right ear as he turned and flicked on the lights. It was pretty, the signifier his grandfather had. It was carved of the finest metals, completely unlike the clunky signifier of a slave like Riviera and himself. After all, the duke's signifier was part of the upper class, a sign he was of a higher caliber then those bound by wrist or sometimes neck chains made of cold harsh metal. He looked down at his wrists. He heard his grandfather step down the hallway and turned his head up.

Alex watched as the stones heated up like the rising of the day stones, slow yet sure, until they were glowing with a soft ruby color.

"Lad, that's what you get for worrying an old man and your poor mother. Don't you know what time it is?" he asked, quieting his chuckles into a knowing look as he turned to face Alex. Alex gave a sheepish grin as he shrugged, toeing the rug.

Grandpa sighed and shook his head before gesturing. "Well come on, son, come inside. Your mother's making dinner as we speak."

Alex groaned.

"Oh, don't be like that! You know she tries her best. Plus, if you got home before all the day stones died for the day, you would have had a chance to make something yourself," Grandpa chided, his tone lighthearted. Alex sighed, mentally agreeing with the assessment. It was partially his fault for staying out so late. "Now hurry on into the kitchen, I will see you two when dinner's ready."

Alex nodded as Grandpa walked off. Alex watched him go. The foyer was now lit bright enough to showcase the splendid items of porcelain and jewels. A picture frame sat over a mantelpiece, front and center.

He recalled his mom and, vaguely, his dad both eyeing it oddly when he was growing up. He personally didn't mind the picture. It showed a knight holding the head of a grotesque creature in the sign of victory, sword gleaming in what Alex could only deduce was sunlight. Green could be seen as far as the eye could see in the picture and Alex always wondered if that was mostly what the Overlands consisted of, sunlight and green. What an amazing sight it must be…

He shook himself from his thoughts, trying to convince himself, as usual, that there was no way he would be able to go there, no matter how much he dreamed of it. He hurried to the left toward one of the two hallways. Traversing the long halls, he finally arrived in a room where the distinctive smell of burning came from. He winced before he opened the door and stepped inside.

Close to the stove was his mother, running around in a frenzy. Her frazzled expression was only amplified when smoke billowed out of the stove when she opened it.

Alex shook his head as his mother gave a quiet whine. He grabbed the nearby extinguisher and liberally spread the gunk that came out of it onto the fire. Slowly, it died and he stopped, letting the last of it dribble to the floor as he sent his mom an exasperated look.

"Oh, hey, honey…" she said somewhat sheepishly, though confusion still sat on her face. "I could have sworn I set it right this time. Four hours and fifty minutes at one hundred and twenty-five degrees."

"Mom, did you check to see which was time and which was temperature?" Alex deadpanned.

His mother looked at him like he had multiple heads before she picked up a surprisingly unscathed box and looked at it. She pointed and said, "Yeah. It says right… here…"

She stopped before glancing guiltily at Alex. Alex resisted sighing as he gave his mother another deadpan expression. "Let me guess, you were supposed to set it at four hundred and fifty degrees for one hour and twenty five minutes."

"Well, that's all in the past. I made some sandwiches earlier, and I only nicked myself a few times this time."

"Why…Mother…are you in the kitchen again?"

"Because Agatha called in sick and you know how my lor…" She stopped before shaking her head and continuing, "Callen likes to make sure his people are okay. She's on bed rest until she feels better and the others have other priorities."

Alex shook his head, wondering about that. The others would have come running to stop his mother from entering the kitchen. Alex stepped over to the cold storage. An ice stone sat in the corner, cooling the small cubby considerably. He looked around at the shelves before spotting the plate of sandwiches. He grabbed one after pulling off the paper wrapping and stepped out. He bit into it.

Damn. How was it she was so bad at the directions, but could make something taste so good?

"Hey, Alex, honey?"

"Hm?" He asked around a mouthful of sandwich.

He swallowed as he turned to his mother, who was already cleaning up the place.

Her black hair fell in sheets around her thin shoulders. The green dress she wore almost every day showed a petite figure. She had long fingers and wide brown eyes that seemed to look at everything with a type of naivete.

He knew his mother was nowhere near naive though, even as she turned, exposing the scar on her neck and the thin chains around her wrists. He shivered as he remembered one story she told him about her childhood, when she talked about it.

It happened long ago, before Alex was even born. Supposedly, she was seen as a rare specimen. Alex didn't ask why. Mother never explained, but that made it so she was often feared. In this particular instance, she'd just gotten through a…beating, she phrased it.

Alex had a sinking suspicion she meant something else, but didn't interrupt as she continued to explain. It was around that time she met Father, they fell in love at first sight, but…fate was cruel. Father was promptly sold, punished for grabbing her affection and she was secluded, unable to even leave her room.

Thankfully, after that, the duke, who managed to buy Father not long after that initial exchange, found her and bought her off her original owner.

Still, all the things she left out…it sent chills up his spine. After, she insisted he knew how lucky they were to end up working here, under the Grand Duke. Alex glanced toward her wrists, watching the chains shift against her skin, scars crisscrossing thinly across her flesh, just like it did around her neck.

In comparison, his skin was practically unblemished. He knew, from the conversations with the others, he was qualified as a slave, property of the duke. All he could recall was the duke caring for him like a parent would.

He pulled himself from his thoughts as his mother huffed and put her hands on her hips. “You weren’t listening to me again, were you?”

“That depends,” Alex replied, looking toward the stove.

His mother let out a long sigh and dropped her hands. “Alex…” She shook her head and looked him in the eye. “I heard that the Martinets are coming through soon, so please stay in the house, okay? You don’t wear your signifying wrist chains anymore.”

Alex glanced at his wrist, vaguely remembering the cold bite of the chains. He couldn’t remember when they came off, but he knew he was still very young. It was only thanks to the Duke he got them off, and his mother. For some reason his mother fought with a vicious tenacity to have him no longer wear them, even though he was given them by the Martinets of the time.

Once the Martinets left, the duke conceded very quickly, supposedly having wanted to do that anyway. Still, it meant he had to avoid Martinets like the plague.

Why did his mother insist on his being removed again? Part of him didn’t mind, considering how harsh, clunky and overbearing they were. Still, he vaguely wondered where they were now.

His thoughts were quickly returned to the present when his mother continued, “Both the duke and you could end up in trouble. So, don’t make it hard on him. The Capitol is already giving him a hard time for not trading in his old slaves for new ones. We don’t want to make it worse.”

Alex hesitated. He was one of the only ones that worked for the duke that didn’t have the signifiers. For some reason, everyone else was so used to it, they felt weird without them. Alex couldn’t fathom why.

Still, she took his silence as acceptance, relief clear in her voice as she thanked him. “Now get to bed, it’s late.”

“Yeah, yeah.” Alex waved, muttering under his breath as he walked toward the doorway.

"And sorry about not having dinner ready for you. I need to bring what I can to the others."

Alex nodded, knowing how busy his mother was. Even with her botched cooking, she did have to feed the duke and the other slaves. He also knew the duke planned to meet them at dinner, but Alex doubted there would be enough food if he went, so he stuck with the sandwich. His mother sent him a kiss, which he promptly looked away from, before calling another good night. Alex let the door swing shut and climbed up the stairs, chewing on the last of his sandwich.

He would have to watch out for those Martinets. From the stories he heard from the older slaves, it wasn't pretty to be caught by them. In all honesty, he would be seen as free bait, considering he no longer held a chain tag.

Maybe he should stay in the house the next few days…

He shook his head and stepped into his bedroom. It wasn't big by any stretch of the imagination, but it was cozy. A bed was set off against a small window with a stand next to it made of stone. On top of the stone side table was a simple, yet elegantly designed light stone. He wasn't sure what the history was behind the stone, since he never was able to go into school or anything. From what he'd gathered from the books in his grandfather's library, they were leftovers from the age of the demons, a race very similar to humans, long since thought to be extinct.

Alex gently touched the light stone, feeling it pulse slightly under his fingers. To him, they felt almost alive in a way that was different from the normal everyday stone that surrounded him and everyone else in the Underlands. He closed his eyes, feeling the slight pulsing of the light stone. He wondered what it was like above. What did a sky look like? The sea? He wasn't even sure he could even imagine, what with being confined to the manor his whole life.

He knew he was luckier than many people. He couldn't deny the fact. Even so, it felt like he was just there, another person to live his life and die.

He didn't want that.

He opened his eyes and pulled his hand away from the light stone and turned to his bed. He fell onto it and curled into himself. It was a pipe dream, he knew. There was no escaping the Underlands, even more so for those seen as slaves.

Yes, he didn't have the mark, or the chains like he once did, but that didn't make a difference down here. Unless you were known, unless you were part of a family, an elite, then you were nothing more than a piece of property. His hand slammed into the bed, feeling the mattress give under his hit. After all, a signifier, the only indication of where you lay, was created upon birth. The only signifier he ever had were chains with no meaning, something his mother threw away for him years ago, almost to the point where he couldn't even remember what they were. Yet he couldn't get a new set, even if he wanted to, after all, the census had him qualified as a slave, even now.

Why was he even thinking this? These thoughts never got him anywhere and only ever made him more upset.

Still, even though he knew how hopeless it was, he couldn't seem to give up, he would see the Overlands, just once. He let out a sigh and uncurled his fists. He would think on this tomorrow. He needed to get some sleep tonight, especially if the Martinets were coming. He'd need all the rest he could get.

www.ingramcontent.com/pod-product-compliance
Lightning Source LLC
Chambersburg PA
CBHW072345020726
47506CB00004B/1016
9781624205149